~ Penury City ~

Volume 1

Light of Gabriel

by thomas e

Wounded Crow Publishing

Wounded Crow Publishing
Rochester, New York 14626
info@woundedcrowpublishing.com

Second Edition 2021

ISBN-10: 1-955383-00-6
ISBN-13: 978-1-955383-00-4

~ Penury City ~

Volume 1

Light of Gabriel

by thomas e

Edited by
Michelle Buckman

Cover art by
Hazel Grace Camero

Special thanks to
Debby, Guinevere, Barbara

Dedicated to Saint Anthony,
who finds the way to that which was thought lost.

Penury City ~ Light of Gabriel

Prologue

~ Paul ~

The first time I saw the old man in this insufferable city, he was sitting atop the same rickety wooden stool with three uneven legs on which he is perched today. The stool bobbles from side to side and front to back on the broken, grayish concrete sidewalk in a way that seems to delight the eccentric fellow. The tiny throne, or his cathedra as he so fondly refers to it, was carried here by me, his assistant. From street corner to street corner, neighborhood to neighborhood, this three-legged relic has been brought in for this kind and warmhearted gent to speak to the people in the city's streets. Near the bottom of the legs, where the sidewalk punched its time, marks of scuff wore thin the wooden spindles. However, for reasons that seem to defy the laws of physics, the legs did not splinter or crack and held firm through the tides of time.

I remember the first time I met him, as though it were yesterday. I had not been in town for very long nor had I been impressed in the slightest regard to anything I had seen. The city definitely had not lived up to its famous and illustrious legacy, but then again, how many things really do live up to our dream's expectations? I had been expecting a golden city filled with riches and people dressed in fine linens. I expected to see families walking together through beautiful parks filled with luscious greenery on a summer's afternoon. However, what I saw was a place with impoverished-looking people, broken down buildings, swirls of dust and dirt, and barely a blade of grass. In all, the place was a total disappointment. However, this was before I understood the meaning of it all, before I met my wonderful guide, who had the task of taking me throughout the city to explain its meaning and teach me The Way. How patient that wonderful woman was with me. Even through all of my arrogance and complaints, she stayed with me. It was her strong faith that saved me. All of this happened even before I met our speaker, il mio Papa, and it was before I met the.... But then, there I go again, getting far too ahead of myself. A storyteller I am not; I am more of a man of academia, of facts and science. The old gent is really the passionate storyteller.

I will say that never in all of my life had I lived in a place as poor or wretched as this undernourished hole in the Earth. It is a city that was and still is so impoverished that it does not even have a local government or governor or mayor. This somewhat fascinating city of hovels seems to just get by on its own without the need for such oversight. And yet, in spite of all its poverty and strain on the community, the people who scamper about this forgotten parcel of dirt are not in the least saddened by their fate. In fact quite the contrary, they almost seem unaware of anything beyond the black gates that lead to the outside world. They want nothing but to live day to day in their city. They barter each day for work with which to receive that day's needs for themselves and their families. They are the residents of broken concrete and mortar dust, and find their entertainment and comfort in the lessons from what the locals call the Doctore, or the teacher. These lost city folks live a simplistic life, but it is an honest one. The surrounding area is full of ancient stone from buildings that should have long ago turned to dust; and some of them have done just that, becoming part of an easterly wind that has since carried them off to become grout for some new structure.

The layout of this land is divided into seven distinct subdivisions or cantons. This particular canton is called Scientia, which means knowledge. This is why the Doctore and I are here, to teach these residents about The Way. Il mio Papa would say that it is a great honor and responsibility to teach and before I utter one word to anyone I must not only know this knowledge myself, but live it daily. The other six cantons have unique names as well; however I will wait until we come to those places before revealing their names. Everything, Papa says, happens in proper order and in due time.

It's a good job being the Doctore's assistant. I follow him from place to place taking care of him and learning from him. He is a terrific teacher and mentor. Had he been my professor at the university I would have graduated in half the time and with a great deal more knowledge. His teachings instruct from within using incredibly thought provoking exercises that drive a person to meditate on who they are and why they exist. Anyway, he really doesn't require much help and mostly insists upon doing everything himself even at his age. Another benefit of being his assistant is that I get to see my old friends, the ones who took the journey to the city with me. In fact, today we are setting up just outside the shop of a couple of people who I had the pleasure of getting to know on that excursion—Domingo and Sevita.

Their shop, called Dom's, is here, behind me, just outside the alleyway near the corner of Faith Street and Francis Avenue, and at a meager fifteen feet wide, it struggles to look bigger than its girth, like a small boy reaching with all his might to touch the next height mark on the inside of a doorjamb. Taking into account the small backroom, its length was a scant twenty-five feet. What it lacks in available space it more than makes up for in hospitality and meticulously grown produce.

When I had walked up to the storefront, I noticed only one large glass window, which displayed the bargains of the day. A single wooden red door, opened invitingly to its fullest extent, welcomed me as I walked past the hand-painted "open" sign hanging from a crooked, rusty iron nail. I wanted to talk about the supplies I would need today with Domingo, a sturdy young man from the northern country. Domingo, who spends his days stocking and restocking shelves, seemed temporarily distracted by his wife Sevita's comforting smile.

I met them along The Way as they made the journey with us into the city. For the most part, they were inseparable, which still appears to be the case. Domingo fell completely into her brown eyes, which are even more prominent now, the way she keeps her thick strands of blonde hair pulled up in a bun held in place with a metal clip. She prepares her enticing appled dough treats for the city's children, who tend to eat them so quickly she often cannot keep up with the demand. The other products in the store seem to leave just as quickly as the treats. When I told Domingo I was setting up the storyteller outside his shop, he was delighted. Not only did it mean that there would be more business for the store, but he too enjoyed listening to the insightful teachings of the old gent.

Now, standing just a few feet from the store, I see he has moved to the open door, and is leaning against it, awaiting the beginning of the tale, as are we all.

Sevita's voice rises from within. "I'm coming!" And there she is in the doorway, pulling the apron over her head and pulling at the strands of her hair that have fallen out of the clip, quickly pinning them in place before settling against the doorframe beside her husband.

"You made extra treats for them, didn't you?" he asks with a grin as he put his arm around her waist.

"Just a few."

"I'm sure the kids will appreciate it. Look at them; they're really excited right now, and he hasn't even started yet."

The days when the teacher is in town are always special for those who come to enjoy his narratives. No one ever knows when he might show to tell his stories, but when he does arrive, he is seen as a giant in the community. He stands patiently with his thinning white hair curling gently at the sides of his head in a somewhat disheveled fashion watching the people of the city with his forgiving eyes that are surrounded by bushy, white eyebrows. With a friendly "hello" or a hearty handshake, he looks fondly on his flock. He has a very kind and understanding face, but at the same time it is a face that wears a serious expression full of concern and worry that the years have scored across it. At full height, when he is able to stand upright, the elderly gent measures only five-foot-seven inches. But leaning as he is against the corner of the store with his cathedra in place, he appears much shorter and yet full of wisdom despite his diminished size.

People begin to pour in all around him, filling up the alleyway and the street just in front of Dom's market. Pushing, pulling, or dragging various sitting arrangements, they all come with their boxes, crates, cardboard, blankets, or whatever they can find to make themselves comfortable. They sit on the sidewalk in their tattered clothing or put together makeshift benches from planks of wood found in dumpsters from the back alley. The women hold tightly to their children as they sit by open windows in the buildings along Faith Street to listen. Somehow, the entire town became aware of his presence and mystically show for his street-side sermons. His podium is the morning dew, his spotlight the sun, and his microphone the gentle breeze that carries his voice to the people standing across Francis Avenue. The last of the night's chill is driven from the air by the day's light; thus the silent grips completed their tasks, once again setting up perfectly the "Grand Hall".

What an absolutely peculiar gent he is with his tattered Jesuit garms all wrinkled with holes and rips throughout. One might think he has slept every night in the home of moths. Wearing a pair of what looked to be homemade sandals; his feet are colored with dirt and dust. The sandals have very thin leather soles in which enters and exits a leather strip as it encircles his foot. He ties his humble dirty-white robe across his rounded belly with a knotted rope that has an arrangement of clusters in a somewhat predictable pattern. The configuration has ten smaller knots in between larger knots, except at the one end there is just three smaller knots between two larger knots. I once thought it to be some sort of time keeper to remind him of the history he so elegantly spoke of during his stories. Some have said his commentary is the embellishment of a story that at some point was of historical importance. It is of no matter; that Jesuit with his magnificently smooth and calming voice really knows how to capture an audience. Even now, his melodic arrangements of poetic verse still captivate me….

~ Doctore ~

"My dear Domusi (people of my house), this legendary account is not for the weak of heart. Oh no, the message it brings is not watered down to make it palatable for the masses. It was inked to stand as record and handed down through generations of believers, its certainty gives to mankind what truth is said to offer—a momentary pause allowing one to think and to feel. Man's intellect aspires to discover those ancient building blocks once used to create the universe and all things in it. The cosmic carpenter's tools were left behind in the seas and in the sands of the Earth. The Divine builder entrusted this creative power to Man to discover over time and to wield them with honor and purity of heart. However, distrustful of Man's predisposition for weakness and his thirst for power, He shredded those blueprints and tools into minute pieces then scattered them unequally throughout the universe so no one nation would find them and know their secrets. As an equalizer for the mind's thirst for discovery and its lust for power, the Creator took a small piece of His own entity, and with it, constructed Man a heart to ensure balance. Its constant rhythmic beat keeps Man in tune to nature's gifts; a pulsing metronome reminding him of the need for charity, integrity, honor, and love, driving its song through the veins of existence with the sounds of an effervescent brook. The balladic message is that mind and heart must be kept at equilibrium, else they consume one another in an epic battle over ownership of the soul.

Mankind's perpetual dual between his head and heart is like two princes ruling over a small plot of land each seeking to inherit the empire. If the younger, the Prince of Intellect, defeats his older brother, the Prince of Sentiment, the northern prince will consume the body and drive out its very soul. Eventually this triumphant new king will wither through self-pride and arrogance into a pile of dust. However, if the southern prince is victorious over majestic discernment, this conquering but naïve royal will be led down darkened alleyways in pursuit of romantic whims without regard for truth. This lustful king, having gotten lost in murky passages, will be consumed by the very desires that led him there. If only the two princes would share equally in ownership of the kingdom, it could flourish with discovery and great cities might be built where magnificent art would don the subjects' happiness, chefs might prepare exotic dishes that whet the appetite of the most finicky palate, and architects would design and construct cities unequalled in all the land.

Only, Man has had trouble in the past keeping his balance; often stumbling over his arrogance and pride as he struggled to share equally with his brother. One such instance of this dire effect of a throne not shared is twenty-first-century Earth, which became home to despair where there would be no consensus on a faith-based belief. Words of the ancient cosmic truth were abandoned altogether in favor of a secularist approach to the moral scheme. All evidence of God and His word, His teachings, the relics of saints, and the truth were removed or destroyed from public life. This new structure led to relativism where there was no right or wrong. Existing was only what is and what was desired. The spread of this selfish mediocrity darkened more than the home from which it started. It became an epidemic cancer, grown from spores in the American capital, infecting all that came into contact with it. There was no passion, no care, no love or hate, no harm or foul, no good or evil, and all was dependent upon instant gratification. The once great kingdom of the Northern Continent that grew from European persecution of its subjects had forgotten its core faith. How wicked they had become in their ways, all in such a miniscule turn of the celestial clock. How tiny must have been their memories, for had they been but the size of a mustard seed, they could have remembered the story of their ancestors.

O malicious pendulum, your western liberal swipe to recklessness was often followed too quickly by an eastern conservative rave of callousness. How is it you never knew enough to stay at center's home, but instead grow weary from lack of stimulation and frantically swing about in search of drama? Why after completing your sway from the passionate and creative few of the eighteenth and nineteenth centuries did you not come home to rest? No, instead the anxious keeper began its shift backwards producing the weakened and desolate society of the twenty-first century. The history of their ancestors and the magnificent word that once gave men meaning and courage to seek out the path to their purposeful end had long been trampled underfoot, buried deep into the archaeological record. Most had forgotten all about the old ways. However, what has been forgotten, history begins to repeat, and the mistakes of Man come to know their place once again. Often becoming restless themselves; the gaffes of arrogance awaken to play their part in the nightmare, forging their participants a fearful and deadly recollection."

~ Paul ~

And so the wise Doctore is off to a magnificent start while his audience settles in for the morning's tale. As for me, I'm leaning against a broken street light eating half of a cantaloupe purchased from the fruit stand. From time to time, I find myself searching the crowds for my adored guide. This would have been just the kind of story that would have engaged her soul.

I am Paul by the way; Paul of Chicago. But that is neither here nor there. There will be plenty of time for introductions later, as there is still so very much to tell.

~ Penury City ~

Light of Gabriel

Volume I

Part 1: The Great Myth

Chapter 1

The Shekel

~ Paul ~

I suppose I need to back this story up a little bit in order to give a better understanding of the amazing events that transpired. The world has become quite a decadent place over the past several decades, and America was no exception in taking part in this immoral behavior. For some reason unknown to me, there was a small group of people who were chosen to be led away from all this decadence and into a very different kind of world. We were all invited, or maybe simply driven, on this journey. It was and quite frankly still is a very fascinating kind of excursion that never in my life would I have imagined that I could be a willing participant. However, here I am telling the tale of how I and a group of people, who I now call my friends, came to know The Way. These individuals were scattered all across the country and the world. I will attempt to introduce them as the Doctore and I walk the cantons. It is at these moments that I hear Papa's words echo in my head, "Paolo", mostly Papa calls me Paolo, which is "Paul" in Italian. "Paolo, people believe they are all individuals and disconnected from one another, but the truth is that we are all joined together in one unified entity provided by the love of the One. What one person does has an effect, good or bad, on all the others." So, with the help of my esteemed mentor and master, Papa, I will try to explain this fascinating story.

Here in the canton of Scientia (knowledge), strong, gray clouds gather from the south and begin to take over the sun. They were neither dark storm clouds nor white billowy clouds, but instead, a lackluster neutral type of cloud that brings neither good nor bad, but indifference. It is their sole intent to simply cover up something of purpose or beauty. As the shadows begin to move over the city streets, the Doctore shifts about on his small stool and readies himself for the next section of his somewhat unprepared sermon. While the city dwellers at first feel relief from the sun's heat, there is something uneasy and contradictory to their well-being with this blotting out of the light.

Listen closely, as this is the part of the story where the white-robed gent launches into the dark accounts of history where all are reminded of the forces of evil. The children's eyes will become large white saucers with dried raisins centered in the middle, while their parents feel the cold chill of fear go up their spines. My dear friends in poverty, the curse of Man never comes

3

through the front door with trumpets sounding its arrival, but instead it sneaks through the small cracks of a foundation like a poisonous gas that slowly chokes off our breath in the night whilst we sleep. We must never be caught asleep if we wish to live.

As our teacher leans forward on his cathedra with his arms resting across his legs and his fingers interlocked, the stool wobbles toward the right front leg. Scanning his audience with a fiery gaze, he begins his opening monologue before the clouds send out their gusts trying to steal away his words.

~ Doctore ~

Turning through the yellowed and torn pages of historical Man, it appears that we are bound to a certain course, a plotted trail worn by the footsteps of kings old and new, in which they guided their armies in pursuit of extraordinary claims. Their ambitious passions and determination led them to plant their kingdoms' flag on conquered land, to expand their territories. With a quick dissatisfied look back to their homelands in the east, the King turns his troops and marches opposite his shadow, dragging it over a torn and bloodied Earth. The new territories to gain will be treacherous as they happen to be on the soil of their brother.

The decision to take this treacherous path, one destined to bloodied battles, is neither here nor there, for far be it from this scroll to solve an age-old riddle that has been contemplated by thinkers more capable to ponder it than any philosophers of this time. Though most have forgotten it, there is an ancient curse that was set upon Man, brought about when the Creator sent us the One King, a truly remarkable king unlike any others who had come before or since, who had taken the path least traveled to teach us what the Creator intended for civilization. This king had been a great teacher and a healer of both body and spirit. Many crowds traveled great distances to hear him speak or to have him heal them of their afflictions. He was loved and adored by many who had come to know him. He provided more leadership than any previous warrior, more wisdom than any mystic, more loyalty than any friend, more honor than any father, and more nurturing than any mother; his gifts were his love of all humanity and his willingness to suffer and die for it. This man, this king of all kings, was betrayed for thirty pieces of silver by a weak-spirited man who had been his pupil, his follower, and his brother. The One was imprisoned, humiliated, tortured, and put to a slow and agonizing death. Though, he had the power to save himself from all the misery, he chose to instead endure the pain and sorrow for his final testament to truth. And with his last breath, he still pronounced his love for humanity and offered his forgiveness for their cruelty.

4

The thirty silver Shekel coins that had been used to pay for the betrayal of the One were marked for destruction. All of these treacherous coins were destroyed; all except one. This one silver coin, stained with the blood of the ultimate gift, survived, but remains cursed forever. Throughout time, anyone who had been so unfortunate as to have it in their possession was filled with its evil wickedness and treachery. All who were near to it suffered great pain and sorrow. Its effects consumed the bearer's mind and heart until they were filled with a darkness and madness never to be overcome. All of their light was extinguished and fear took hold of them.

It started with the initial traitor, who hung himself. The second holder of the coin was Rome's emperor Caligula, who ruled from 37 AD to 41 AD, not long after the ultimate betrayal and the death of the One. Caligula was a vile and wretched creature who slowly tortured many men, women, and children just for his sheer amusement. Forcing parents to witness their children's executions, feeding prisoners to lions and bears, and senseless murder were only a few examples of the testament to his cruelty and insanity. He had declared himself a living god and had ordered the building of a bridge between his palace and the temple so he could converse with the deity. After he was killed in a revolt by the officers of the guard led by Cassius, the Shekel coin disappeared for thirteen years. But then, in the year 54 AD, Rome's fifth emperor, Nero, found the evil coin and was mesmerized by its trickery. He brought the entire Roman Empire to ruin and burned its cities. He murdered thousands of people including his own family. These treacherous tortures and killings included beheadings, stabbings, burning and boiling people to death, crucifixions, and impaling prisoners. Nero was responsible for the death of Peter and Paul, two of the greatest followers of the One. Paul was beheaded and Peter was crucified upside down. The silver Shekel burned its evil and treachery deep into Nero's mind and heart, turning them black. Eventually, he too, committed suicide, ending his reign of horror and terror against the Roman Empire.

Once more, the silver Shekel coin was laid to rest and the world had peace. For four-hundred years the trader's mark lay dormant in some dusty pouch or jeweled box until a creature from the Hunnic Empire, which stretched from the Ural River to Germany, found it and became its next victim. Attila the Hun, a ruthless, bloodthirsty barbarian, sought to destroy the Roman Empire. His terroristic rule from 434 AD until 453 AD was so feared by Man that he was thought to be a punishment from the Heavens and was nicknamed Attila, the Scourge of God. He tortured and killed anyone who got in his way; whether they were his enemies or his own people, he showed them no mercy. Hundreds of thousands were killed in some of the most hideous and tortuous acts known to Man. People were torn limb from limb. Some say he ate the flesh of his enemies. Eventually, those who bring death find death themselves. Attila died in 453 AD, leaving the Shekel to find its next prisoner.

It wasn't until the year 1206 AD that the cursed piece of silver made its way nearly seven thousand miles to the Mongolian Empire where it fell into the hands of Genghis Khan. Near the age of thirteen, he killed his older half-brother for control and power of the family and clan. This sovereignty-starved madman conquered lands from the Caspian Sea to the Sea of Japan. His destruction of countless numbers of cities showed his ruthless and bloodthirsty nature for power and greed. His cruel massacres eliminated hundreds of thousands of people. It is said that his marauding armies tortured men, women, and children. Women were raped in front of their families, and in the Iranian Plateau he murdered three-quarters of the population; ten to fifteen million people fell at the hands of this merciless savage. The Shekel marked his soul for death, and he became death. Wherever he drove his barbaric armies, destruction and death followed until 1227 AD, when he died. The curse of the traitor fell to sleep once more.

The plagued Shekel fell through cracks in the Earth and began its two hundred year journey back west towards its place of origin. Slowly, but methodically it migrated out of the Asian soil, past the Caspian Sea, past the Black Sea, and stopped before reaching the Romanian mountains of Moldoveanu, where it took residence in the hands of Vlad Dracula in 1448 AD. Here he became one of the foulest creatures to have walked the Earth. His methods of torture included impaling his victims slowly while he ate and drank, watching their misery with pleasure. This kind of torture, which went on for hours or even days, was perhaps the most gruesome in all of history. There was no one who was exempt from this torture; men, women, children, rich or poor, he showed no distinction and no mercy for their plight. The evil and vicious Dracula killed eighty- to one-hundred-thousand people as the Shekel consumed his mind of all its discernment of what is good and evil. His treachery ended with his own head being cut off by his enemies, which designated the end of another bearer of the traitor's mark. As such, it was recorded into the historical archives.

The despised Shekel found its way through the weakened hearts and minds of Man. Hand to hand, city to city, country to country, it knew well the path to take that led to the most corruptible of men. This time, it took a path north to the Belgium state where its king, Leopold II, was planning to control the territory of the Congo. Coincidentally, Leopold took his throne in 1865 AD, the same year the mighty American king, Abraham Lincoln, fell to an assassin. It is unknown whether the coin had any part in that tragedy. Nevertheless, it did find its way into the hands of Leopold, and he began his maniacal plot to brutally enslave the people of the African Congo. It seems somewhat more catastrophic that just as Lincoln freed the American slaves, Leopold was forcing the Congolese into slavery. And so it began; the diabolical Shekel took hold of Leopold, sending his regime of terror into the African villages. His men tortured, maimed, and killed millions of the Congolese people. At first, it was ivory that was plundered from the country for Leopold's treasure chest, but then later it became rubber that was tapped from the trees of the jungle and used to finance Leopold's lavish lifestyle. Leopold spewed lies and deceit to the world as he claimed he was helping to civilize the Congolese people. His forced slave labor filled the pockets of the elite while many Congolese suffered at the hands of his vicious armies. If the Congolese people did not bring enough rubber; their arms, legs, noses, ears, feet, or heads were cut off. Ten million people, nearly half the population of the Congo, were killed by the senseless acts of Leopold's men for nothing more than the profiteering of a rubber plant.

In 1922 AD, the coin reached Stalin in the Soviet Union and began its treacherous mind games. Stalin, in his efforts to force an atheistic and communistic ideology upon society, suffocated the entire country with his merciless tyrannical control. He sent people to slave labor camps where they were made to work, often to their death. People were tortured and killed if they didn't measure out at least four times their normal output. Stalin signed the death warrants of tens of thousands of people. Ten million people died needlessly in a famine. Hundreds of thousands of people from other countries were brutally tortured, raped, and killed. More than one and one-half million German women were raped by the men of the Soviet Union. Thousands were killed by mustard gas bombs. Stalin was the cause of nearly sixty million deaths, however even in all of that evil, the coin's thirst for power found a way to influence three other madmen a short distance away.

In just a few short years after Stalin begun his reign of terror, Adolf Hitler was made the Chancellor of Germany in the year 1933 AD. This immoral, foul, and cursed man decided to make the Jewish people his enemy. He performed experiments on over three hundred thousand people to test which methods worked best to kill a human being. Every Jewish person in Germany was sent to concentration camps where they worked until their number came up for torture and eventually death. People were killed by gas chambers, crematories, firing squads, lethal injections, poison, disease, and medical experiments. More than ninety percent of Poland's Jewish population was eliminated. Millions of children died. Hitler was directly responsible for the death of more than eleven million people and indirectly responsible for starting a war where more than fifty million people perished. After Hitler took his own life in 1945 AD, the evil Shekel found his replacement in Mao Tse Tung while still possessing Stalin.

Mao Tse Tung was the dictator of China from 1943 AD to 1976 AD. He was responsible for the greatest genocide and famine ever recorded in history. Millions of Chinese were killed by starvation, execution, or suicide. Tens of millions of Chinese were sent to labor camps. Under Tse Tung, children were turned against their parents, brother against brother, and friend against friend through fear and intimidation. Any criticism of his regime whispered in private could lead to public humiliation, torture, and death. The famine killed nearly forty-five million people, and millions more died from disease. More than seven hundred thousand were in such fear of Tse Tung that they committed suicide. Millions of children were killed, people were tortured through amputation, beatings, whippings, burnings, and other gruesome methods. In total, Mao Tse Tung killed seventy million people.

Lastly, in Japan, Emperor Hirohito, reigning from 1926 AD to 1989 AD, was building his own army to inflict heinous crimes on the Asian people. Ordering all Chinese prisoners to be killed, hundreds of thousands were slain. Over two hundred thousand women were raped. Ten million Chinese were forced into slavery where they were beaten and tortured. The Chinese were shot, stabbed, burned, boiled, impaled, and buried alive. The Japanese disemboweled, decapitated, and dismembered many men. Four million people in Indonesia died from famine. Over twenty million Chinese and ten million Asians were killed by the Japanese and millions more during World War II. Hirohito's standing command of "Kill all, burn all, loot all" left very little of the Asian territories or their people.

There was a short period of time when the evil curse fell silent and the world tried to heal from the horrific slaughter of the treacherous four. Although, just because there is silence does not mean there is peacefulness. As long as the traitor's mark lived, there could never be peace for mankind. A malicious plan was being devised that plotted to change the entire course of humanity. The vicious Shekel knew its power was limited to corrupting only a few weak men at one time. And those men would ultimately be met by more powerful men of substance and integrity that would put an end to the coin's plans. So the Shekel took a different approach to its treachery. If it could not reduce humanity to its immoral ways through brute force, then it would take an alternate path to secure their fate.

First, it had to ensure a method to reduce the population in the places where that population was loyal to the Creator. Second, it had to lure younger generations away from the religious traditions that were faithful to the One King and therefore would interfere with the Shekel's campaigns. And lastly, it had to play on the arrogance of Man convincing him there was no need to bow to a higher power, but instead use his own intellect and skill to create his own world. The cursed piece of silver enlisted a group of men in unique and powerful positions to start its maniacal strategy. It began in the year 1970 AD where the Supreme Court in America was hearing a monumental case having to do with the legalization of destroying unwanted pregnancies. It took three years for the decision to finally be handed down, but had it taken one hundred times that amount many lives could have been saved. In 1973 AD, the Supreme Court opened the door to a deluge of murder to the unborn child. Over fifty-seven million unborn children had been destroyed in America alone by 2014 AD. Over one billion, two-hundred million were destroyed worldwide by that time. This shocking figure outweighs the sum of all the vicious killings the Shekel encouraged since the time of the traitor.

As the first phase of the Shekel was set into action, it began its implementation of the second phase. In 1971 AD, continuing with its control of the Supreme Court, it set forth its second attack in a decision where it eliminated the religious activities in children's schools. If there were no teachings of the Creator and the Creator's ways, then there would be no future generations to stand up to the Shekel's will. What better way to ward off any possibility of battle with heroic, God-fearing warriors, than to eliminate the very ideals that impassioned them to fight to their death.

Lastly, in 1981 AD, the digital Internet, with its foundation built on manmade hardware and software platforms, started to come into its own. It began small, slowly morphing and weaving its web of deceitful connections into the homes of every person. By the twenty-first century, its secularized, distorted information made it hard to tell what was true and what was not. Social networking had mankind thinking that these billions of numerous connections with people all over the world were bringing the world closer together. However, it was the lies and trickery of the coin driving a wedge deep into the heart of humanity. These short-lived relationships were nothing more than instant gratification that held no substance, no morality, and no commitment to the people behind the wire. There wasn't a strong need to see others succeed in their spiritual, physical, and emotional growth. These contacts became disposable as there were a million others waiting to be found and tried. The wicked and foul Shekel was winning the battles on all fronts. It now only needed to outflank the last of the believers and crush any resistance to its power with fear and destruction. A vile enemy was coming into power over Earth, and Man was not even aware of its existence.

The Shekel had now set up the board perfectly. All its pieces were in place and it only had to wait for humanity to move in predictably selfish patterns before the wicked coin could declare checkmate. The 1980s, riding on the coattails of the rebellious 1960s and 1970s, were wrought with individualism and egotism. They sought out power and wealth by building a framework for a false digital world that would become the escape of a struggling society. The false sense of accomplishment had intensified further in this generation by easily creating self-gratifying and individualistic environments. Whole economies were created and products were consumed that didn't exist in the physical world. Man came to believe that he was the Creator. He wielded that power with arrogance, pride, and greed. There was no love or forgiveness, nor was there mercy or compassion. There was only intolerance and greed. What did it matter? It was just a computer.

The next forty years through 2020 AD saw this behavior continue and the power of creation was bequest to these next generations from their parents. Having grown up in a digital world, they inherently consumed this technological power and took it for granted, becoming increasingly intoxicated with its promise of fame and fortune. These secondary Internet worlds allowed their virtual selves to become much more powerful than their physical counterparts. They eliminated the imperfections of their true physical forms, which made them believe they were of an immortal nature. So self-absorbed were these modern creators that they took more portraits of themselves than they did of others or their natural environments. With no real existing relationships and all of their connections being of a virtual nature, society became mistrustful and self-indulgent. Online journalism turned into sensationalism with no need to check facts or report complete truths, but rather only a need to entice advertising traffic from their articles. Embellishment of the truth was considered merely a marketing gimmick to give an edge to competing journalists.

Soon, there became further separation of the classes as the elite and rich became more educated and self-serving. The poor became poorer and the middle class was divided. The top fifteen percent of the middle class became part of the upper class, and the remaining middle class were driven to the poor; with no current skills needed in this ever evolving, sophisticated, and high-priced digital culture, they were discarded as yesterday's hardware. Poverty covered these communities like an ever-growing fungus that sought to extinguish the light of hope for these people. Darkness blotted out the American dream and the winds scattered their minds and hearts across the barren floors of a crumbling technological revolution. Soon, starvation seeped into the crevices of their homes and divided their families.

As the family unit broke down due to poverty and fear, society fell into panic and despair. Mistrust and hunger guided their actions, as they sought to survive in a world that didn't have the experience of working together for the common good. Fights continued to break out, as men and women tried to secure food and resources. Local law enforcement was pitted against communities. Armed hate groups formed and vigilantes seized neighborhoods, as they took the law into their own hands. People were killed in the streets and in their homes by law enforcement fearful of their lives. Police officers were assassinated in their vehicles while parked or on patrol. Entire police departments were attacked and disintegrated with stolen military explosives. So many law enforcement personnel were killed in the line of duty that they stopped patrolling the cities and towns on foot or in their vehicles. Instead, unmanned aerial vehicles (UAVs) and unmanned patrol vehicles (UPVs) were equipped with weaponry, including lasers and rail guns that were remotely controlled from police bunkers. These vehicles maimed or even killed at the slightest resistance to orders belted out by the officers controlling the robots.

In 2033 AD, rebel citizen groups started to make and fly their own UAVs to patrol their own properties. Entire homes and businesses were leveled; men, women, and children were killed in the line of fire when the UAV wars began. Fear and mistrust flooded the cities and towns. No one could stop the disintegration of humanity and fear spiraled out of control. People were fleeing from populated areas to find refuge in the country near heavily wooded lands. Some even took to underground bunkers and caverns. Society was crumbling, and people sought a leader to take charge and restore some type of order. The darkest days were just over the horizon as the Shekel moved in to play his rook. This chariot of destruction was about to descend on the capital, bringing the final blow to society; a society, so filled with naivety, is a most willing participant.

~ Paul ~

The old gent pauses and after lowering his head, he moves his hand along the knotted rope that was tied around his waist. I pour water into a cup from the canteen and go to him. I wait patiently for him to find his place in the knots of history. He would do this during his teachings; take a few moments of silence to find his way through the story and meditate or pray on just how he was going to proceed. Sometimes, it seemed like he was also contemplating the effect of the story on the crowd. He would then emphasize different aspects of it to address the needs of his flock.

While waiting for the Doctore, my mind wanders to a little girl who was subjected to the throes of these evil forces....

Chapter 2

Citizen's Air Defense

~ Paul ~

I met Li'Quari not as a child, but as a young woman during my journey with Domingo and Sevita. She was quite poor and had lived a hard life. The unfortunate girl never seemed to catch a break. Somehow, Papa knew her story. To this day I have no idea how he does it, but he can read people as if their lives were playing out across their irises. He opens their hearts and reads their minds. Thinking back upon the story Papa had told me, it still saddens me how much pain that poor child had to endure right from the very beginning....

In an older part of St. Louis, a city displaced of its history, hid a building nearly falling down around its innards. It stood, barely, at the corner of Lewis and Dickson Street, wavering in strong winds that came from the Northlands. The stone-red building seemed to have more bricks missing than it did holding the structure together. Nearly all the windows had been shattered and the roof leaked rain water in various places throughout many of the interior rooms. However, there were still parts of the roof that were intact and held steadfastly, allowing a few dry areas to remain inside the industrial edifice. It had been these places that the self-proclaimed equalizers, better known as the rebel forces, commandeered their headquarters. The three round windows at the back of the building were port holes facing the sludgy, mud river, in which the rebels could test fly their homemade unmanned aerial vehicles (UAVs). In the darkness of night, it gave the rebels some protection from being spotted while they maneuvered their crafts over the black water.

The Citizen's Air Defense, or CAD, headquarters was right at the edge of the Mississippi River in St. Louis, which was considered part of the central United States. Of some importance, just across the river from this building, was Bloody Island, the infamous spot where duels were acted out when men could not resolve their differences in peace and instead chose to resolve them in death. Many men came to this island to prove their muster or defend themselves against the slanderous words of another. Mostly, men came to die, but there have been times when men survived their wounds and would get a second chance at life. In one instance, that same lucky pair of duelers came back a second time, too arrogant and proud to realize the gift they had been given. They tossed life to the wind and shot once more. This

13

thomas e

time, however, fate did not look so kindly on their decision amidst the rising gun smoke. In another incident, there had been a pair of foolish men who heralded that the duel was to be held five feet from one another. Both men shot and killed one another in a senseless act that resulted in two dead participants. Such seems to be the landscape of Man; mistrust and hot tempers encourage foolish and senseless acts of violence. History has proven time and again that violence only brings more mistrust and worse acts of violence.

At the dawn of 2033 AD, in a rarely found dry room, stood what served as a long table—a sheet of plywood lying across two large garbage cans. Upon the surface were strewn small tools, electronic components, wires, and several dried silver-solder splashes that resembled some type of deformed butterflies. To the right of those stood two electronic test units, a digital multi-meter, and an oscilloscope all which were in easy grabbing distance of Trevor, who diligently worked with the tools and the tiny parts despite the stoutness of his fingers. His eyes, though somewhat awkwardly placed close together, strained to see the electronic components through his thick glasses, which in the most annoying manner would slide continuously down his Roman nose. This was due in part to the humidity in the room and in part to the perspiration that accumulated excessively on his face.

Barnus was busily performing his own surgery at another table. Without taking his focus off of a tiny integrated circuit (IC) chip, he plucked a small pair of needle-nose pliers from the tabletop and carefully maneuvered the IC into place. His tall stool rocked slightly as he leaned forward, but he braced himself, one foot on the stool's footrest and the other stretched out on the floor directly in front of it, and continued to concentrate intently on lining up the pins of the chip. As Barnus lowered it with steady hands into the socket, he was startled and jerked the chip away from its desired position.

"Barnus, we're out of AD9-9383 drivers again!" Trevor swiveled around and rolled out several feet from the bench to glare at Barnus.

Annoyed that Trevor couldn't have waited ten more seconds, Barnus leaned his six-foot frame back from the dilapidated countertop, he gnawed at the side of his left index finger while puzzling over the distance between the antennae trace and the five volt power trace before responding without looking up. "There are a couple of bags of parts in my desk that I lifted from the junkyard. Most of those old cars used the Northstar system, which had similar drivers. They're old and not very efficient, but they get the job done. They're just a little slower in processing time." With his left thumbnail, he scraped at the loose skin from a callous on the outside of his index finger, a casualty from constantly gripping small hand tools a little too tightly, but it seemed to help steady his hands while placing the smaller components into position. "Use a couple of CAC-213 iso-caps in parallel to level out the voltage."

14

"Right, yeah, I can do that." Trevor forced himself up from the comforts of his castered chair and marched across the floor with the sound of a team of driven oxen pulling their cart up a steep hill. Pausing at the desk, he pushed several strands of his thinning bronze hair away from his eyes as his mouth struggled to form a question.

Barnus sensed the question floating between them. "Yes, you should ground yourself on the static discharge mat so as not to short them out," he said, and continued with his task. With his right hand working the pliers, he held the processor chip tightly and lowered it into the socket. Lining up the pins of the chip with the holes in the socket, he extended his left index finger and eased it into place. He then relaxed his grip and removed the pliers. "Ah, there she is, all tucked in nice and secure."

As Barnus admired his work, Trevor searched the desk for the treasured parts. He tugged open the swollen drawer on the top left, shuffled a few papers and cartons around, and shoved it closed again, and then searched the three drawers below, but to no avail. In the last one, six-inches deep in well-labeled bags, he found the components. The drawer, however, seemed to have been booby trapped. It slid out too far and crashed to the floor. The bag in question had opened during the incident and parts spewed across the floor. Trevor, annoyed at having to get down on one knee, called out in pain as he knelt on a component. It cracked under the weight. He began picking up the parts and setting them on top of the desk. After gathering up his supplies, including the cracked part, he stood up again and hovered over the top of the desk. Spreading out the various bits, he started picking out the needed drivers. There were ten of them altogether from both bags. Well, actually there had been eleven counting the one he destroyed by kneeling on it. He put them into a separate pile on the desk and gathered the remaining spare parts into bags that he stuffed back into the drawer.

At his workbench, Trevor began to solder the drivers into the printed circuit boards.

Barnus was just giving his work a last speculative examination. "Find what you need?"

"Yeah, I got ten of 'em. I can put ten more weapon boards together. That'll be enough for these units, and we can test flight them tonight."

"Ten? I thought we had eleven drivers left?"

"I, uh, dropped the bag of parts and accidently knelt on one of the drivers. The pins broke through the casing."

Barnus looked at him with great contempt. He shook his head in disbelief. "Trevor, you know how hard these parts are to come by and what danger I put myself in just searching for them. How could you...it's not like I can steal the GIT's conductive polymer resin and start feeding it into the 3d printer to make my own boards you know!" He screamed out waving his arm towards the corner of the room where the 3D printer stood covered in dust and cobwebs.

Trevor lowered his head. Standing slightly slumped over and in his docile way stared at the cracks in the concrete floor as he took the admonishment being dealt out to him.

Barnus felt bad for him and pulled back his anger. "All right, what's done is done. Don't worry about it. We'll find some more on our next excursion. How many do we have left?"

"I can put ten more weapon boards together. That'll be enough for these units, and we can flight test them tonight."

"Okay, remember no more than eight minutes. We can't afford to lose any more flyers to patrols. Especially these units. It's getting harder to find weapon parts that are still functioning. Fly one at a time let's not get careless. Soon we'll make history as we can stop playing defense and start playing a little offense. I'm tired of getting our butts kicked all over the city by those arrogant thugs."

"Yeah, we got it. Why don't you take off and go home. I'm sure Isabella is wondering where you are by now."

"All right, Trev. Stay under cover."

Barnus made his way to the backdoor of the factory carefully avoiding the puddles of standing water. Looking up at the surveillance monitor that took in video feeds from around the outside of the building, he checked for any movement or patrols. After seeing that all was clear, he cracked the door just enough to sneak through and then quickly shut it behind him.

He travelled along a grayish-white serpent of concrete blockades that had once been a breaker against the Mississippi River. The large, broken wall had taken quite the beating from its rival, but in the end neither of them emerged the victor. The mighty majestic waterway had been reduced to barely a small creek for quite some time. The massive concrete structure had been withered and broken down piece by piece via the harsh elements brought down from the northern territory.

Using the break as camouflage, Barnus made his way through the darkness until he reached his neighborgate; a small enclosed housing community where he and Isabella lived.

In these turbulent times, as most of the metropolitan areas became increasingly violent, many of the communities had taken it upon themselves to provide their own security measures. Gated communities became more and more prevalent in the most affluent areas of the city. These lavish green botanical gardens had twelve foot concrete walls built around them to discourage outsiders from entering unannounced. If that alone didn't ward off trespassers, the top of the wall had been furnished with embedded explosive caps. Anything that brushed across these caps would set off the small charges, which became an effective deterrent for not only the criminal element, but also for any squirrels, birds, or various other creatures that belonged to nature's ignorant habitat. In addition to the community's physical structure being reinforced, sophisticated alarm systems were put into place, hired guards performed twenty-four hour armed patrols, and no one was allowed entry unless proper identification was presented.

While these city fortresses appeared quite intimidating to the outside world, the inside of these gardens were quite beautiful. The perimeter concrete wall was painted green with Parthenocissus Tricuspidata, known to commoners as Boston Ivy. Various maple, oak, willow, and evergreen trees dotted the inside of the neighborhood. Fountains were fed by small manmade creeks and whatever wildlife managed to breech the security wall found a haven worth the risky effort. The beautiful park also featured paths for walking and park benches where the residents could sit in the sun and watch their children play. Though these secured and luxurious environments were available for the upper class families that could afford them, the middle class communities often were not so blessed. However, they too saw the need for providing a more secure neighborhood for their families.

The not-so-well-to-do people of the lower and middle class also began to build their own version of a secured community. With a strong iron fence dug in around the perimeter of these neighborhoods, a whole new level of segregation began to culminate in the city. The tops of these iron monstrosities were sharpened to a razor's edge, thus discouraging anyone from attempting to climb over them. The gates were fitted with electronic entry systems that allowed only the local residents access. While they were not as secure as their more affluent counterparts, they did provide a level of protection that discouraged most of the amateur thugs and thieves. As more and more citizens became fearful of their fellow man, these neighborgates became more common throughout the city. The once great societies of old that had been a melting pot of all people where different cultures and knowledge blended together for the betterment of mankind now became an environment of suspicion and locked gates.

Moving his digital key across the lighted scan beam, Barnus unlocked the security gate; the only thing he actually liked about living in this neighborhood. He hated the three-story bungalow-style flats that were typical of the buildings in the area. Each with a basement, first floor, and second floor apartment, the ugly and impulsive reddish-brown brick made up most of the nearly one-hundred-seventy year old structure, except near its foundation, where wide, white river stone was used for fortification. After ensuring the gate closed, he darted up the wooden steps to his flat, taking them two at a time.

"It's nearly ten-thirty. Must you always be so late?" Isabella asked as he came in through the back door.

"We were getting the last of the flyers together." He dropped his knapsack on the floor by the coat hooks and went into the kitchen.

She followed him, still dressed in the light-blue polka dot sundress she'd favored. Though it was somewhat out of style, he didn't mind. Clothing options were not a priority, and if anyone could make outmoded fashion dazzle, it was her. Even barefoot as she was, she held herself with the grace of royalty. It was a trait that first attracted him to her. He never ceased to wonder how she'd fallen for a techie lunk like him.

"There's stew on a plate ready. You just need to regenerate it."

"Great. I'm starving." He pushed the plate into the regenerator and selected the reheat option.

"I thought you were going to be home early tonight?"

"I'm sorry, Bella. I finally got the weapon's boards together. We're testing them tonight."

"I don't like it, Barnus. It's not right. Two wrongs never make a right. You shouldn't do it." She turned away as if she didn't even want to know him.

"Look, it's not like we're using them on people. We're just going to use them to defend our UAVs against the thug units. We need to keep our neighborgates safe. If we can't defend it, then how are we going to stay living here?"

Isabella turned back around and looked frightfully at him. "Let's just leave. Let's go to the country. I don't feel safe here anymore."

"There are no jobs in the country. All the money is here in the city. Unfortunately, that's also why all the crime and cop attacks are here too. The police can't tell who is good and who is bad anymore, so they shoot at anything that moves from their safety zones. We have to defend this place. There's no one else to do it."

"Violence will just breed more violence. History tells us this is true. Someone has to stop it."

"And who would that be? Who is going to stop it, Bella? His fists were clenched and his knuckles turned white. "You can't stop it by pretending it doesn't exist. We need to fight for our homes and neighborgates; otherwise, they'll eventually just kill us all."

"I can't talk to you when you're like this. As I said before, history has shown us that violence will just get you more violence. I'm going to bed."

She kissed him on the cheek and walked off towards the bedroom. Barnus finished his dinner and tossed his plate into the sink. Leaning over the basin with his hands on the counter, he shook his head in dismay over his quarrel with Bella. She had a point to be sure, but a man has got to make a stand at some point in his life. *What is the point in continuing to run?* Lifting his head up, he stared out the kitchen window across the city. He could see the small moving lights in the night sky. The Police UAVs were patrolling the bad neighborhoods and high criminal activity areas.

"It's just a matter of time before they get here, too," he said aloud. After rinsing his plate, he left the kitchen, but not before turning out the lights.

Three years had gone by since the Citizen's Air Defense upgraded its AOV machines to become more of an attack device that had differed from its predecessor model, which strictly operated in a monitor and defend mode. With a weapon's grade AOV in the hands of the citizen's rebellion, the AOV wars escalated. The police had lost a great deal of units and money to the rebellious forces. The city became an even more dangerous place, especially in the evenings, when most of the attacks took place. Missilets, or gas-propelled projectiles, as well as bullets, and lasers flew through the air lighting up the skies. They often missed their targets and hit buildings, homes, and various vehicles. There was an incredible amount of damage to personal and business property as a direct result of these combat missions.

Later in that same year, 2036 AD, Isabella was at the medical clinic delivering their first child. Barnus was sitting beside the bed holding her hand as she was going through the pains of labor. She had dilated to ten centimeters and she was ready to deliver, so the digital nurse notified the doctor.

"Oh, my heavenly stars. I've never felt so much pain in my life!" she called out.

"Just grip my hand tight; you're almost there," Barnus said.

"I've changed my mind. I want the drugs."

"You know that's not possible. They would do more harm than good. The baby's heart rate is already fast and the drugs would just exacerbate that condition."

"I know, I know. A girl can wish can't she?" She stuck her tongue out at him before her face contorted in pain and she clenched Barnus's hand tightly.

A few minutes later, the young, halved-buzz cut doctor came into the room staring at the m-pad on his forearm. After momentarily looking up at Isabella, he went back to his m-pad to view all the statistics from the room's monitoring devices and cleared his throat several times, as if he were about to break out in an Italian operetta.

"So, we're ready to go, yes? The contractions are every couple of minutes, yes?"

"I don't know if I'm ready, but this kid sure is ready to make an entrance. She's been pounding her fists at the curtains for the past three weeks! And doctor, if ooooohhhhh owwwwwwww!"

"Good, good. I think we're ready right now. I will just put on these gloves and be ready to catch 'em."

"Her! It's a her, doctor," Isabella called out.

"Yes, yes. That's what I said, 'em."

Isabella turned her head and looked directly at Barnus with a somewhat angered and disgusted expression. Her face was flushed red, her lips chapped with dryness, and her bangs that normally swayed to and fro stuck to the perspiration on her forehead. She gripped his hand hard.

"It'll be all right. Are you having another contraction?"

"No, but there's a neck here I'd like to squeeze in a very harsh way," she said glaring at the doctor out of the corner of her eye.

Barnus' eyes wrinkled at the edges and he pressed his lips together as he tried not to break out in laughter.

"Okay, okay. I can see the head. Give me a push. Remember to breathe. Push, push."

Isabella bore down and pushed hard.

"Yes, yes, that's it. I have the head. Okay. No pushing. Wait, wait."

"Is there a shrapping echo in here?" Isabella asked Barnus.

Barnus grinned broadly and kissed the outside of her hand.

"Yes, yes, now push. Push hard. And breathe, breathe," the doctor called out.

A few moments later a baby girl was born. The doctor raised her up to the digital nurse who suctioned out her mouth and nose and cleaned her up. After fitting a little pink cap on her head and wrapping her in a warm cloth, she was given back to Isabella, who placed the child on her chest.

"Oh, look at her! She's beautiful and so very adorable," Isabella said, as she caressed the side of her baby's face with her index finger.

"She is beautiful, Bella, just like her mother," Barnus added and leaned over Isabella, kissing her on the forehead.

"Well, hello little one. Hello, my little Li'Quari." Isabella gazed at her daughter and wondered how someone who had caused her so much pain could instantly take her heart. She snuggled in close to her and pressed her cheek against Li'Quari's cheek. "We are so blessed to have her, Barnus," she said and closed her eyes.

"She should rest now," the doctor said. "I'll be back in a little while to check on her."

"Okay, thank you," Barnus replied. He turned back and stared at the two of them; so beautiful and innocent they both were just lying there together happily, safe in the hospital room. Turning towards the windows, he stared out into the city. He saw the UAVs flying over the city streets patrolling the neighborhoods, ready to pounce on anything that looked suspicious. How could he possibly keep his family safe from all of the danger out in the world today? How could he protect them? What about his own involvement in the underground Citizen's Air Defense group? Surely, he could only keep that a secret for so long before they eventually found him out. He had absolutely no problem putting his own life in danger. He had the resolve to do so for the betterment of the neighborgates. However, putting these two beautiful people in danger was a risk he was unwilling to take. He didn't know how else he could protect them either. There were no simple answers. Perhaps Bella was right and they should just move out of the city and away from the threats. They could move into the country where there weren't countless UAVs dotting the skies.

His mind raced with thoughts and he struggled to come up with a solution that would keep his family safe in a world that was run by indifference and remote control. The human heart had been removed from the decision-making process. Society had turned life into some kind of digital game where the players often confused gaming concepts with real life and real people. If the game wasn't going well, they simply hit the reset button.

Eventually, the UAV worries and Barnus' thoughts on the inhumane world blurred away as their lives had been reset since welcoming their new daughter. His focus had now shifted to something much more precious to him. They brought Li'Quari home to their flat in the city where they loved her and tended to her every need. As the months passed, Barnus softened. He became less concerned with the estranged world outside of his life and more involved with his inside world. Their new daughter melted his heart whenever she looked at him with her soft eyes. He spent less time at the CAD building and didn't seem to have the need to go out quite as often on his late night scavenger hunts for electronic parts. Staying at home with Isabella and Li'Quari was increasingly more satisfying to him than skiving around for parts in old General Motors vehicles.

It wasn't until she turned five years old in the year 2041 AD that the question of moving out of the city came up again. Li'Quari was coming of age, and they refused to subject her to the treacherous city schools. They could use the online schools, but that lacked social interaction. There were no children in their small neighborgate, which would mean that they would have to visit other communities to have her play and interact with others. With the UAV wars getting worse in the city, it was an unacceptable risk commuting from neighborgate to neighborgate in search of friends for little Li'.

Barnus could only see one option. "We will move out in the fall, right before Li'Quari starts school. We need to save a little more money before we quit our jobs. The savings will have to last us a long time, Bella."

"Let's just leave now, Barnus. We have enough. We can live modestly. I don't have a good feeling about staying here any longer than we already have. Let's just go," Isabella pleaded.

Barnus couldn't resist her entrancing stare from behind her dark brown eyes nor the humbleness of her slightly tousled hair. Li'Quari, clung to her mother's skirt with one hand and onto her small blanket with the other hand, and looked up at him with large, innocent eyes. Barnus sighed. "Okay, we'll leave tomorrow. I'll tell the guys tonight is my last night."

Isabella threw her arms around him and hugged him tightly. Li'Quari, seeing her mother so happy, did the same and hugged his leg so hard he nearly lost his balance.

"Thank you! We'll be fine, you'll see. It's all going to work out just fine," she sung out.

When evening came, Barnus went to the small, red brick building that sat just alongside the river, to turn his leadership role over to Trevor Marcois. Trevor had been with him since the beginning and knew how to scavenge for parts, how to put the UAVs together, and was a good electronics engineer. Barnus knew he could trust Trevor to carry on the cause and make good decisions.

Trevor paled at Barnus's announcement. "Are you sure? I mean I totally understand especially with Li'Quari now and everything. But are you sure about this?"

"Yeah, I'm sure. Every night that I come here it frightens me to death that I'm going to be found out and put my family in harm's way. I couldn't live with myself if anything happened to them. I've done all I can do here and it's up to you to take it wherever you decide to go with it."

"It's not going to be the same around here without you. Who's going to have that sixth sense for finding those scarce AD9-9383 drivers?" Trevor smirked.

Barnus grinned. "It's not really that hard. You just have to follow the oil trails from those old Cadillacs." Barnus moved closer and held out his hand. "Be careful, man. Keep your head up."

Trevor shook his hand and hugged him. "Take care of that family, Barnus. Good luck."

Back at the flat, Isabella was tucking Li'Quari into bed. "Okay, little one, it's time for you to go to bed. We're going to be leaving tomorrow for the country. It will be a real adventure."

"Really? We're leaving home?"

"Yes, really."

"But I don't want to leave our home. Where will we go?" asked Li'Quari.

"We will find a place that is much safer and more beautiful than here in the city."

With watery eyes and a worn baby blanket clenched in hand, Li'Quari sat up instantly. "But it's not safe leaving the house. You told me it wasn't safe and not to go outside."

"I know I did, but it's time for us to leave here now. And I have a little present for you." Isabella took a card out of her sundress pocket and handed it to Li'Quari. "I believe you are old enough now to keep a secret. This will keep you safe no matter where you go."

Li'Quari's face lit up and she took the card from her mother and looked at it. "Mommy, who are they in the picture?"

"It's God, sweetheart, and his son Jesus. He will always be there to keep you safe. He has great power and can do many things. I waited to show you until you were old enough to understand. The world outside doesn't like God. We must keep this our secret."

"Why don't they like him?"

"People have a hard time believing what they cannot see or explain. And they don't want to give up their bad ways." Isabella lifted Li'Quari's legs and pulled back the cover from underneath them. "Okay now, get under the blanket and get some sleep. We'll be up early tomorrow." Isabella bent down and kissed her.

"Good night, Mommy."

"Good night, honey. I love you." Isabella left her room and turned on the small light in the hallway.

Barnus was on his way home following the concrete wall along the river when he suddenly stopped in his tracks. *Did I check the monitors before I left?* He looked around the night sky to see if there were any UAVs around. He saw nothing and continued to walk home, however he took a different route and walked a few blocks out of the way just to be sure. *I can't believe I forgot to check the monitors before I left the building. It's a good thing I'm getting out of this business. I'm getting careless.* He was relieved to see his neighborgate community and was excited about leaving the city and getting a fresh start with Isabella and Li'Quari in the country. Spending far too long at the CAD, his nerves were shot and he felt as though he hadn't slept in five years. It would be a great relief to just be a normal family.

After entering the gate, he bounded up the stairs and into his flat. Isabella was waiting for him in the living room, her face bright with anticipation.

He went directly to her, wrapped his arms around her, and kissed her. "Well, that's it. We're free! Tomorrow, we leave for the country."

"I'm so happy! I'm not going to sleep a wink all night. I'm too excited. It will be so good for us to get out of this city."

"I can't believe how relieved I feel just not having to be so tense all the time. It was really taking a toll on me. I think I'm just as excited as you are, Bella! What if we go into the...." He stopped suddenly and directed Isabella to his side as he shifted a couple of steps towards the front door.

"What is it? What's wrong?" she cried out.

Barnus stared at the doorway of the flat and saw a shadow move across the crack underneath the door. He went to the kitchen window and threw open the curtains. Four UAVs were right outside the window. "No!" he cried out.

He started back towards the living room when a loud explosion came from the entryway. He flew into the room and saw that the front door was off its hinges and lay beside the sofa.

Two unmanned patrol vehicles rolled through the doorway belting out orders, "Stay where you are. Don't move!" These vehicles were somewhat small in size. Weighing about forty pounds, they stood about eight inches from the ground so they could easily maneuver under things. They were nearly fourteen inches wide by twenty-two inches in length. Equipped with a caterpillar track, like on a military tank, they could move over any surface. They were fully armed and completely remote controlled. It was death by radio signals.

"Isabella, no!" Barnus called out through the smoke.

She had already turned and was heading towards Li'Quari's bedroom when shots rang out from the UPVs. They hit her in the back and legs and she tumbled to the ground motionless. Barnus ran to her and dropped to the ground beside her. He turned her over and held her in his arms. Her eyes were open and motionless. Blood ran over his hands from where he held her around the back and neck.

"Bella! No! I'm so sorry, Bella!" he screamed out.

"Stay where you are and don't move," called out the UPV.

Barnus' eyes turned wild with hate and anger. His irises grew large and the black pupils shrank to a fraction of their normal size. Every muscle in his body tensed and contracted with emotional rage. The blood boiled inside his veins with such force that he became desensitized to all that was around him. His hardened heart stalled and darkened with blackness. He became the "machine", the very same machine he had despised and fought against. Barnus had now joined their ranks. The device had just one single purpose: to destroy. Time had ended for him, and sound no longer traveled. There was only a deadened silence in a thick fog of smoke and flame. His vision became so narrowly focused that it was as if he had only a pinhole allowing in what little light remained in the world. With one motion he let go of Isabella, the only conduit that had recharged his field of benevolent capacitance, and kicked out his left foot to strike the UPV, turning it on its side. Then reaching out, he picked it up and held it away from his body. It was spraying bullets at the ceiling and walls when he ran to the window and thrust it out into the night where it struck one of the flying UAVs. They both blew up in a fiery cloud of orange, red, and yellow. He felt the shock of the sound wave, but he heard nothing except the dull hum of violence. He felt neither pain nor pleasure in his actions. He was completely numb and didn't stay to watch his small victory as it fell from the sky, hitting another UAV flying just below it. It, too, burst into a fireball.

The second UPV rushed in from the living room and showered the area with bullets and missilets. Barnus dove into the kitchen, tucked his head under, and rounded his shoulders as he hit the floor. He pushed himself into a somersault, rolled out of it, and came back to his feet all in one motion. After grabbing the iron pipe from behind the pantry door, he exited the kitchen from the other doorway. The UPV turned left into the kitchen and started a second attack with a stream of bullets and missilets that exploded through cabinets, tore through appliances, shattered glass, and left the entire room in smoke and fire. Dishes fell to the ground. Pipes had burst and water was spraying from the sink. So many rounds of ammunition were fired into the walls that they tore away from the ceiling and fell to the ground. The UPV stopped to survey the damage while waiting for the smoke to dissipate. A bright beam of light came on and scanned the area. However, the light was merely reflected back as it tried unsuccessfully to penetrate the thick, dark smoke. By this time, Barnus had come in from behind with the pipe raised above his head. He came down hard on the UPV and took out the video and communication devices. He then picked up the disabled vehicle with his left hand and heaved it out the kitchen window right through the glass. With the electronics smashed, it fell to the ground helplessly and blew up upon striking the pavement below.

After turning away from the broken glass, he started for Li'Quari's bedroom, determined to get her out of harm's way. A UAV crashed through the alley-facing window spraying rounds of bullets into the apartment from behind him. The hot metal slugs pierced his body entering through his back and head. Silence engulfed him as a red darkness dripped across his eyes. He had no thoughts or feelings. Everything seemed to just stand still in some dark fold of an empty void. He took several more steps before dropping to the ground in a pool of blood just a few feet from Isabella.

"Secure the flat. Foot patrol is en route. Suspects are down. Repeat, suspects are down."

~ Paul ~

When Papa told me about Li'Quari, my heart just sank and my legs felt weak as if they would give out. I know what it means to lose a parent at a young age. The pain is something I have always carried with me; the devastating experience defined me in ways I couldn't even comprehend until much later in life. I don't know how the Doctore reads a person's history, as he wasn't there when any of this happened, but somehow he knows and can recall it in great detail. After waking up on a thin mattress in the corner of a dirty state ward, little Li'Quari was forever damaged as well. However, she did have a thread of hope – a single remnant from her mother that she would always treasure and that would eventually come to save her. She kept her holy card close to her heart.

Chapter 3

And Justice for All

~ Paul ~

I'm startled somewhat from my reverie when I see the Doctore gazing upon me as he had given me a gentle nudge. I think he noticed, and quite frankly appreciated, the tears in my eyes as I give him a cup of water. I'm quite certain he knew where I had been and equally felt the pain of Li'Quari. After quenching his thirst, he thanks me for thoughtfully recognizing his need.

"It is always my pleasure, Il mio Papa."

With a slight nod he repositions himself on the cathedra and then continues the account of the world's wretchedness.

~ Doctore ~

In the year 2038 AD, an important legal case was being heard inside the Chicago Court building on LaSalle Street. Above the entrance hung a free-form metal art structure, its forged, twisted shape suggested that of engulfing flames that seemed to consume the very freedom of mankind as they entered a judicial system long vacant of the ideals and principles they had once been sworn to uphold. The thirst for truth had been quenched by the gluttony of greed. The judicial system of the government's courts that had started in the pursuit of truth while recognizing their humility in the shadow of a higher power, no longer existed. All signs of their Creator had long been vanquished from the halls of justice; no longer were the oaths taken and sworn before their God. Instead they had been replaced with secular words of consequence. There had been such a preoccupation with the separation of Church and state that society missed the entire understanding that it was impossible to separate the Creator from life because it is in life that the Creator lives. The only thing that this defiant people had accomplished was to push away the love that the Creator had for them. And this was the great tragedy.

Venge Piloti was a young and handsome upcoming lawyer who had just won his first major case. It was a long drawn-out battle and his brilliantly orchestrated defense won him the day. The case was that of the People of Grafton versus Zinc Construct. A large chemical manufacturer, whose plant was at the outskirts of the town of Grafton in Illinois, had been lax in its handling of waste from its products. The underground storage tanks filled with these deadly bi-products had been made of cheap, low grade materials, which eventually cracked, spilling the hazardous material into the ground. It poisoned many of the water sources of the surrounding neighborhoods, causing many children and elderly to become ill. Those who were exposed to the chemicals and were already in a weakened state died from the toxins.

The young and strong Piloti, dressed in his navy blue, tailor made, single-breasted suit, stood before the bench with his thick black hair slicked back. With his left hand placed casually on the bench before the judge, his eyes slowly traversed the courtroom until they fell on the mesmerized jurors who awaited his next words. Piloti, taking in the pause and the silence of the moment, maximized the build-up of the drama and seized the stage for his moment in the spotlight.

"Ladies and gentlemen of the jury, I tell you that this tragic and undeniable senseless event that destroyed so many honest families and persons is to simply be abhorred with all of our minds and hearts. The deaths of these fine people of Grafton are indeed heartbreaking; those elderly, the children, the sick and the weak who were victims of these circumstances—all of them are gone forever. But their memories linger on and ...."

Piloti slammed his fist down on top of the bench and then removed it just as quickly. He walked to the center of the courtroom, between the bench and the jury, and stood motionless. With his head bowed, he closed his eyes as if in a moment of silent reflection. However, he was setting the stage to achieve the maximum effect of his calculated defense, and like a well-seasoned actor, played to the drama of the moment. His head shot up quickly along with his right arm. He pointed his finger to the ceiling while a portion of his slicked-back hair came forward and dropped across his left temple. His voice sounded out in a sonic boom as if coming from a jet just breaking the sound barrier. The jurors jumped in their seats and the judge brought up his folded hands directly in front of his chest, as if he were protecting himself from a surprise attack. The entire courtroom gasped as they tried to recapture the beat that their hearts had just lost.

"Justice! Where is the justice? However, justice is not so easily served. It is a complicated process in which all of the facts must be separated from all of the opinion. Justice demands truth. And the truth of this disaster is that there was no single event that caused this tragedy. I say to you here and now that it was not just the single mistake of a company who had failed to provide adequate safety features for the storing of chemical waste. Nor was it the mistake of the company's agent in purchasing cheaply made storage containers. Nor was it the single mistake of the county's regulators who failed to monitor properly the grounds and water supply near the plant. Nor was it the mistake of the Grafton Water Authority who had failed to communicate to the townspeople about the unsafe levels of toxins they found

28

in their water samples. Nor was it the mistake of the Grafton residents who drank from their own wells instead of the county's premium water supply that is properly filtered and treated. Yes, it comes at a premium price, but isn't it worth your life? How, I ask you ladies and gentlemen of the jury, with so many causes and so many events over such a long period of time—years in fact—can you find only one entity that is responsible for this tragedy?"

Piloti again lowered his head and closed his eyes. Reflecting in the silence, there stood the monument to justice. He captured his breath and reacquired his strength for the grand finale. He opened his eyes and moved slowly to the jury. Putting both his hands on the railing before the first row of jurors, he looked over each and every one of them.

"No, my fellow demanders of justice, it was all of these compounded failures of humanity that caused this tragic end. We are and will always be subject to our own human weakness, frailty, and the imperfections that we all share. We are human. We are imperfect. We are all held captive by our failures and the failures of our fellow citizens. This is what we have come to accept. Fate has taken the lives of these fine people and we can learn by their sacrifice to fix the errors of our past. Justice will be done if we indeed correct the imperfections that led to this tragic day. Only then, will the lives of the victims not have been given in vain."

Constructing his defense argument carefully, he redirected blame across many individuals and organizations, casting responsibility for the tragedy against many, even at the victims themselves. His well architected closing comments could only result in one conclusion: since so many were guilty of sinful actions, then all were equally responsible. Therefore, reparation for the harm would be owed by all. The surrounding population and various companies would all contribute to the cleanup of the toxins and Zinc Construct would see to it that better containers were used in the future. The problem has been resolved and life's lessons have been learned.

Although the truth had been destroyed, it was a brilliant defense and everyone had been left satisfied with the outcome; everyone except the victims. For the parents, the families, and the friends of the people who had died at the hands of the chemical firm, justice had not been served. However, there was not anger in the hearts of these poor folks because they had been conditioned to not expect any true justice or reform. They had been accustomed not to speak too loudly or too negatively about anyone or anything in a position of power or authority. There was only sadness and deep anguish as they shuffled from the courtroom amid the congratulatory comments being made to the company's defense attorney. The people of the local community were so used to being mentally and physically flogged, trampled upon, and sacrificed for the common good that they could no longer see any hope in their lives. The light of promise and faith had gone out some time ago. They simply went back home, packed up the belongings of their lost loved ones, and went about their business. In the new age, it was no longer glorious or commendable to sacrifice for your neighbor, but rather to sacrifice your neighbor for the good of all. There is a great difference between these two concepts, and that difference is freedom of will. The first comes from the heart; the second comes from ignorance and privilege.

Mr. Caspon, president of Zinc Construct, rushed to shake the hand of his lawyer. "Well done, Venge!"

"Thank you, sir. It was a straightforward and simple case to win once the facts were brought into the open," remarked Piloti.

"Oh, on the contrary, my young litigator. It was your magnificent manipulation of those facts that won us the case and saved our company millions upon millions in cleanup costs. You are going to go far, Venge, and I want to make sure you know that you will always have supporters at Zinc Construct."

"Thank you, sir. It is pleasing to hear that I have your support."

It took nearly forty-five minutes to clear everyone out of the packed courtroom. After pressing the palms of many people, the young attorney got his papers into proper order and stuffed them into his brown, Monserrate-styled briefcase. After pushing the nickel-plated hinge lock through the opening, he picked it up and turned, only to bump into an elderly man who leaned on a very old cane hand-carved from ash wood with etchings of various creatures and ancient script running the length of the stick. The old man moved his hand around a brass figure on the top of the cane as if caressing it with some sort of fancy. An angry pit bull—that's what the brass figure was—quite a fierce looking figure, its reputation well reflected in the polished bronzed image of the beast. The man's face was hardened with a similarly cold expression. Deeply etched lines and blue veins ran across his skin. Venge looked into his coal-colored, lifeless eyes and felt the warmth and life drain from his own body.

"Excuse me, sir. I'm late in getting back. Good day," Venge said, and quickly stepped to the side to move around the beastly intrusion. He made his way toward the courtroom exit, relieved to be leaving the chilly air and the thick, dust-ridden room when an eerily scratchy sound echoed through the chamber walls and snatched away his moment of joy.

"You did well today. Your father would have been pleased to see that his litigation skills have been passed on to his son."

Piloti stopped abruptly. Intrigued, Venge turned and walked back to the strange man. "I don't believe we know each other. How did you know my father?"

"I've been in these halls for many, many years." He gasped and struggled to take in another breath. His mouth scrunched into a sourful expression as if he had just swallowed the most bitter lemon peel in the entire city. "I knew your father from the Stackhill versus Sagesy case. Quite a case in its time, wouldn't you say?" The last of his words trailed off into a breathless gasp that sounded like wind blowing across the jagged rocks of a canyon.

"Yes, it was my father's most publicized case. It put him on the map as one of the great litigators and equalizers for the defenseless poor."

"Yes, that's right. It's too bad about his tragic death," the old man mumbled as he shook his head. "Tragedy," his ghostly voice strained at the word. He then proceeded into a miserable, emphatic choking episode where he coughed and hacked while holding a gray, monogrammed handkerchief over his face. Afterwards, he bartered for another round of lemon-soured air. "I thought that you might want to have this memento. I was going to give it to your father after that case, but circumstances prevented me from doing so. I wish to give it to you now."

"Thank you. What meaning does it carry?" Venge asked as he took the coin from him.

The old man looked up and wore a devious grin in which the corners of his mouth turned upward. "Ah, the Shekel goes back a great many, many generations, in fact, hundreds and hundreds of years to ancient Rome." Gasp! And then, he breathed in while contorting his face struggling with the air entering his lungs. "It is said to have brought great...," he started to cough and gasp for the air to continue, "...fortune and power to those who held it."

"You don't say?" Young Piloti smirked. "Well, thank you for the gift. I must be getting back now."

"Ah, yes. Yes, you have much to do. Good day, young Piloti." The scratchy words dropped off and fell fast to the courtroom floor like heavy ingots of lead.

"Good day, Mister, um. What did you say your name was?"

"A.D. Graves, son," he replied in his raspy, shaken voice. Then turning, he started for the side door.

Venge recognized the name as that being of the famous elder statesman who, though never in the public eye, always managed to be in the midst of political hot spots festering with huge debates of utmost consequence and change. Wherever there was a major liberal fight against the old conservative ways, Graves was there to punch it through by winning over public opinion. Venge flipped the ancient Roman coin over in his palm, and then dropping it into his breast pocket, he left the courtroom.

As Piloti's cravings for success, power, and wealth grew, opportunities came to him from every corner. Doors were thrown open, elders anxiously put their arms around the shoulder of their favorite 'son,' and beautiful, influential women waited for him after dramatic courtroom or political victories. Anyone holding a position that he was destined to obtain would meet with a horrible accident or would suddenly resign over personal reasons. The Shekel encircled him with elite coteries willing to aid him in whatever was needed. Working his way through political circles, his youth and debonair personality assured him many positions in state government, bringing about quick success and adulation. As he climbed the rungs of the political ladder, his passion for control and leadership led him to a seat in the United States Senate. It was here he introduced his first bill in an attempt to stop the UAV wars. In the year 2049 AD, the same year when all of Europe was at the height of battle in the religious wars between extremist groups and Muslim, Judeo, and Christian groups; Piloti got the anti-locator bill passed. This bill disallowed all Global Positioning Satellites from being made commercially. It also allowed the military to destroy all GPS satellites that were orbiting the Earth. The only satellites allowed were military units with navigational systems that the public could not access, which grounded all non-military flights across the entire world until they could be reconfigured with older navigational devices. It also shut down all UAV type devices that relied on the GPS system for positioning and eliminated all vehicles equipped with this GPS technology. Cars, boats, planes, lawn mowers, farm equipment—anything with a GPS locator ceased to work, and society was sent back decades with regard to global positioning and mapping.

In 2052 AD, Piloti was elected President of the United States. However, it wasn't until after he had settled into the Oval Office that the Shekel intensified its influential power. The very office that symbolized freedom and democracy now had an ancient curse set upon it. Many astute men had led the American people from this curved sanctuary through history, changing events that had left either an enriching or worsening effect on humanity. The Shekel could invoke complete madness from this auspicious room.

Soon after Piloti's election, in the very chambers of freedom's humbled beginnings, a treacherous and scandalous event transpired. Inside the Capital building, which long had housed learned and cultured statesmen, slithered the evil trickery born of the Shekel. Together, President Piloti and Speaker of the House Stev Draqen restructured the government. They began to undo all that had been once good and just. Congress was modified to have only one chamber, as there was no longer the need for a Senate and a House that had historically taken far too long to make decisions and quite often debated more with each other over power than over the public's issues. The House of Representatives and the Senate were simply combined into one unified Congress with fewer representatives than ever before. Nearly one-third of Congressmen had been contacted and relieved of their service. The evil of Piloti invaded the ancient parchments and ate at the independence Thomas Jefferson had penned so eloquently. Politicians either did not notice or looked the other way as the Shekel drained the lifeblood from American democracy. With no defenders of truth inside the capital, the iron clad words of Madison's Constitution were pillaged and violated, and then replaced with superficial forms of indulgence.

There were two vacant seats on the Supreme Court bench that had yet to be filled. Piloti thought that instead of going through the long drawn out process of finding replacements and then having to go through Senate confirmation hearings, the judicial branch could just be relieved of its services. Having a balanced bench of debating justices was too antiquated an ideal, one that was no longer of any relevance in this highly technical and intelligent society. The nation's laws would be set by a computer algorithm called the Inferred Constitutional Law application or ICLAW. This program had been used in the past to guide the decisions of judges. The digital application could consider all the input from field polls and Internet bots trolling for public opinion on current issues and social behavior. In addition, it considered historical references and past cases of judicial review producing virtual models of predicted outcomes. Using this sophisticated technology, the laws would be better tailored for the best possible outcome; eliminating human weakness, biased views, and error. Congress then approved or rejected the laws. Approved laws went to the President for signature or veto. This new system would be able to govern far more efficiently than the old system of too many checks and balances. This unfettered power and control was thought to be of great progress in a sophisticated and intelligent society who could wield it to focus on the problems of the country.

The Shekel, in the hands of Piloti, had now unleashed its madness from inside the most powerful and influential place on Earth. Man was totally unaware of the significance of the freedoms they had so willingly given up. They meekly followed the herd as they were led to their slaughter.

Chapter 4

The Defeat of the Carroll Zealots

~ Paul ~

How we must despise the Shekel and the plague it spreads from person to person. I hate how it weakens people and turns them against their own hearts. I hate what evil had done to me and how I let it consume my life. If it wasn't for the incredible love and determination of the One giving me chance after chance to make amends – I shudder to think of where I would be right now. The worst of it isn't so much my past arrogance and ignorance, which I am deeply regretful, but how if I'm not careful every step of the way; evil is right there to suck me back into its grasp. Pay close attention to the Doctore and make sure his message is rooted deep in the heart and soul.

After enlightening people of their treacherous opponent, the Doctore begins the next part of the story. Here he proudly conveys the courage of the few who had set out against the Shekel hoping to clear a path for the many who hadn't yet been imprisoned.

~ Doctore ~

The Shekel, though busy changing the very nature of Democracy, also had its eye on the south side of Washington, D.C., in the Anacostia area where the bulldozers had not yet leveled the older neighborhoods. Located in a forgotten part of the city was an old, dilapidated, abandoned hotel that the religious zealots used for meetings and shelter. Standing in one of the lesser damaged rooms and wearing just his trousers, Peter, the impassioned leader of the last religious group, was contemplating his life's journey while dressing for what was most likely to be his final battle. Peter had joined the Carroll fighters with his brother in 2039 AD, shortly after their father had been killed in battle at the very beginning stages of what eventually became known as the European Holy Wars. He gazed at a cloudy mirror left from decades earlier and thought about his father and the wars. *Has it really been fourteen years?*

He barely recognized himself in the mirror. The loss of weight in his body and face, and the graying of his hair and beard had disfigured him beyond recognition. No one would suspect him to be the former muscular and athletic tunnel foreman of years gone by. His youth had long disappeared and in its place were the marks of battle that took their shape across his chest

thomas e

and back. Various scars from run-ins with tree branches while running, or the battle scars from knives, swords, bullets, and missilets had all mapped themselves across his torso like an ancient island treasure map. He couldn't fathom how he had made it this far.

"Master, have I served you well?" he asked looking upwards.

He ran his hand over the finely woven white cloth of his most precious possession—a wool tunic adorned with the Sacred Heart of Jesus on the front and a red cross, not unlike the image the Crusaders had worn, on the back. The tunic looked somewhat worse for wear in its many years use, but its meaning and symbolism had neither faded nor lost its fidelity. He pulled it over his head and smoothed it over his brown and somewhat bloodstained trousers. The pants had been torn at the left knee and a shredded cuff hung unevenly about the tops of his boots.

Moving his head closer to the mirror, he saw that worry etched their tracks across his tanned face while facial hair grew around and over a long horizontal scar on his right cheek. Peter received that "badge of honor" from a heat-seeking, gas-propelled missilet on one of their crusades. He had always faced death head on, as his most driving concern was not for his life, but for the lives of his friends. He feared every decision he made in command because the outcome impacted so many beyond himself. As the leader of the last Christian-American regiment, he was especially concerned for his brother. There is no feeling or words that can describe pain's sharpened blade as it cuts deep and slow through a man's heart at the thought of losing his family. *I can sacrifice myself to the enemy easily enough in order to save my family, but to be held accountable and responsible for leading my own kin to torture and death is altogether different. It can only be justified when the fight for the ultimate truth is worth more than all else imaginable and even unimaginable.*

He reached for his dark brown Franciscan armor, a cloth robe, and held it outstretched in front of himself for a moment. He brushed across the shoulders and the front of it, and then pushed his arms through the sleeves and brought it up over his shoulders. After adjusting it squarely, he tied the rope tightly around his waist. Taking his leather fingerless glove from the table, he pulled it onto his right hand, and then finished tying the knot by holding one end of the strap with his teeth and pulling it tight with his left hand. He was about to reach for his sword when the wooden door slowly creaked open. He took two steps backward, closer to the table, within reach of his weapon.

"Peter, we're ready," Mark, the Kenyan native, called out from the doorway. Mark was shorter than Peter by about two or three inches, but he more than made up the difference in strength and muscle. His large arms and legs could barely be contained in his Dominican clothing. He always wore a brown leather beanie cap that he pulled down just above his ears. Underneath

36

the cap, he kept three holy cards from the funeral of his wife and two children who were killed in the Washington demonstrations of '38.

The demonstrations had started when people had become fearful of losing their freedom to practice their religious beliefs. They didn't want their rights taken away. The groups were well organized and peacefully demonstrated their concerns in the streets before Congress when a small gang of renegades started pushing through the crowds, firing their weapons randomly. The police force and guard units, believing the demonstrators to be attacking them, open fired into the crowd, killing hundreds of people. Panicked with fear, the mob began to run over one another, trampling to death the people who had been pushed to the ground or who had fallen from gunfire. Mark's family had been trying to get to their apartment after visiting a relative and had gotten caught in the fleeing crowd. They were trampled to death. Underneath the stack of cards Mark kept under his cap was a single picture of his entire family so he would never forget that day and do honor for their lives.

Peter reached for his sword and held it with both hands. Since the ban of the Second Amendment, it was the only weapon they had access to and the last method of defense. The brightly polished silver blade was three inches across and over twenty-nine inches in length. The hilt was eight inches and the guard width was nearly seven inches across. The grip was wrapped tightly with black leather, and a red cross was etched into the bronzed, rounded-square pommel. He touched the central ridge, the top part of the blade, to his forehead and said a prayer softly in Latin. "Audacia in bello; et miserere nobis Dominus omnipotens." (Boldness in battle; and the Lord Almighty have mercy on us.) Then reaching over his head, he slid the sword into the sheath that was strapped to his back.

"You look good, Mark. You look ready to fight for Christ."

"We are all behind you." Mark's expression of loyalty and love for his leader seemed even more pronounced in his face by the black gnarled beard that grew unevenly in a swirly type fashion. He was a person of great depth and heart. "I'm ready to go with you to whatever end."

"My brother, that means a great deal to me."

"How can we be the..." Mark paused for a moment. "We're the last defending arm of God. Why do you suppose they still sleep?"

"They've lost their faith. Their hope has been shattered. They cling now only to the wickedness of this life. They have no idea what they have given up." Peter paused and put his hand on Mark's shoulder. "But tonight we'll remind them to fight for all that is holy. And if the battle seeks out our end, we will see the face of our Master. There are others who will take over our plight. The way to the golden city is complete; we have seen to that end."

Mark placed his hand on Peter's shoulder and gripped his forearm with his free hand. "It has been an honor to serve with you, Peter. I would follow you into any battle at any odds."

"As would I," Peter replied, holding onto Mark's forearm and touching his forehead to Mark's before heading down through the hotel to a conference room where the other zealots waited in silent prayer.

~ Paul ~

I watch as the Doctore slides to the edge of his stool and leans toward the crowd as he continues to recall the last moments of the spirited and faithful few who made possible The Way – the route to the Golden City. He loves the zealots and admires the sacrifice they had given for the sake of others. Il Papa, what an extraordinary person. How he loves....

~ Doctore ~

The Carroll Zealots were men and women of incredible faith. Their namesake was taken from Charles Carroll, the only Roman Catholic statesman to sign the Declaration of Independence. Mark and Peter were daring leaders who stayed true in spite of seeing a path of anguish for themselves and for their friends. Did they have to drag themselves to the fight? Did they show signs of depression, fear and despair? No, instead they burst right through those closed conference room doors with expressions of courage and joy to be fighting for their king. The other zealots twisted in their seats at the commotion, then rose to greet them.

Young John was the first to reach Peter, followed by James and Matthew. Peter favored John because he had been the youngest of the religious fighters. He came to them when he was just seventeen years old, nearly four years ago, and had grown up tremendously since then. Battle had changed him. He had seen members of his unit killed in action after eating meals with them the previous day. The agony had changed the way he thought and erased any sense of long term plans. All of the soldiers of the One King lived in the present and thought in smaller units of time: a day, three days, maybe a week. War had forced them to appreciate the little things, the everyday things, and the fidelity of their small group of faith fighters.

Peter extended his arm and greeted John, Matthew, and James. When John took his forearm first he commented on how Peter's face seemed to reflect their Lord's light. Peter hugged him and reminded John that God was in all of their hearts.

James, who was the older brother of John, approached Peter, his feet thudding heavily on the floor until he loomed over him. He wasn't a fast warrior, but he made up for it in strength and might. He could turn a mid-sized car over on its side for cover when in battle, or take down a running deer for dinner. He once ripped out a maple tree by the roots to use as a bridge to get across a chasm. Anything that was needed that required brute strength; James was the one to get it done. He was a man of few words. "Let's finish it," he said as he hugged Peter lifting him off the ground. Joining Peter's group of fighters just one year before young John, James remained with the Zealots to fight alongside his brother who joined him after their mother had passed away.

"Are you sure Sadju is giving us up tonight?" asked Matthew, the most recent recruit was concerned over how the night's events might transpire. Though he was smaller and somewhat weak in comparison to the other men, he had tremendous courage in the field and never left the side of his partner.

"It doesn't matter, Matthew. Sadju has chosen his own path. Whether it is tonight or some other night, we will stand together until it is done. There was a reason you came to us Matthew – to hold firm the twelve." Matthew gazed in awe at Peter and Mark. Their total commitment to the faith and every member of the zealots was astonishing and even somewhat envious. Matthew bowed his head while placing his closed right hand up to his heart.

"The women should stay here. There is no sense in them facing this destiny," Thomas chimed in and pushed his lean frame between John and Matthew to reach Peter and stared at him from beneath a thick mop of uncombed hair that belied his wisdom and cunningness. Despite his brashness, he was well respected by the others for putting himself in harm's way, leading their pursuers on alternate paths to allow the others to escape by a different route. After his enemies tired and could run no more, he exited the area without leaving a trail and met up with the other Zealots at a chapel, underneath a bridge, or some other prearranged location.

He looked with saddened eyes at Salome, his twin sister. Her hair was pulled up and held into place at the back of her head. She wore the Franciscan styled robe with a hood that she had used often to conceal her face in the darkness of night. The two of them had been close ever since they were born. His eyes darted back to Peter with hopefulness and desire to have him change his decision and leave them behind.

"Thomas, it was decided last night. Let it be, brother."

"We have the right to serve our Master just as you do, Thomas," called out Martha.

Salome spoke up. "Thomas, it's all right. We're not afraid. We, too, have love far beyond this wretched life. We'll stand with you." She hugged him, and he held onto her tightly and kissed her forehead.

Peter, putting his arms around the two of them, said cheerfully, "You have always made me very proud. Both of you and Martha have been our strength and hope." He continued over to the remaining zealots. "Really, all of you – I'm so proud of each of you. I'm honored to have fought side by side with you."

"Side by side indeed, Peter. The honor was ours." Phillip responded.

Peter clutched their forearms and patted them on their backs, humbly thanking them for their dedication and loyalty before looking up to see Andrew looming in the doorway, with his brown cloak flung off of one shoulder to expose his full armor, and the etched image of the Archangel Michael glinting in the candle lit room.

Tears formed in Peter's eyes as he embraced him. "Little brother!"

Andrew was young and full of life; there was no room on his frame for anything but muscle and raw courage. His blonde hair and shortened beard had carefully adorned his striking looks. With his exceptional fighting skills and strength, he was unmatched in combat and there had never been so much as a scratch put on him in battle. Andrew had become the perfect soldier of Christ.

"You have made me so proud. If I had not been the elder, I would have followed you to the ends of the Earth. You have the heart of a lion and the faith of a Bishop."

"You always did speak too kindly of me, Peter. If it wasn't for you I'd have been a skag scraping the cupboards for drink," he replied. "You have been an inspiration to all of us."

Andrew hugged him one last time and then pulled him to the side and put his arm around his shoulders. He drew his sword, raised it to the ceiling, and yelled out, "With my brother Peter and for the glory of God! Knowledge…" and the others called out in unison "Understanding! Wisdom! Counsel! Fear of the Lord! Piety! Fortitude!"

"Let God fill us with His good grace and have mercy on our souls, and on the souls of our enemies. Father, forgive them," Peter added.

"Amen!" they called out.

"Let's finish the mission that God has set before us!" Peter exclaimed and led the way out of the building. The fourteen of them moved swiftly through the darkened streets like silent clouds across a night sky. Their shadowy movements blended into the boulevards as they dashed from building to alleyway and back to building, making their way across a sleeping city. The brave Zealots were the last hope for America. They represented the old ways, reminding their fellow citizens why the Founding Fathers had constructed a country in which the very foundation of it was built on religious freedom and God inspired pursuit of perfection. America was always an unfinished project with a constant drive toward the good of all people through the belief that all are equal and free under God.

The Zealots stopped before crossing over Rhode Island Avenue to gaze upon the beautiful brick-red Cathedral of Saint Matthew. Its dome stretched toward the Heavens, waiting for the morning light that would spread its warmth and brilliance throughout the church and the surrounding neighborhood. The grand cathedral had once been a strong and integral part of that community. Mark, Andrew, and Peter looked on as shadows started to move in the streets of the city. Homeland forces were positioning themselves across the rooftops of the buildings surrounding the church.

Alphas and Thad approached Peter from behind. "Peter, the Cathedral is surrounded by forces. There are twenty to thirty snipers on the rooftops. There are another two hundred or so ground forces moving in. There's an exit path to the Northwest. If we turn now we might have a chance to head toward the Potomac Parkway. We might lose them in the gardens," Thad said.

"Alphas, do you agree?" Peter asked.

"It's a small chance, but it is the best one, I believe, for an escape."

Andrew looked directly at his brother. "Peter," he said, "what is God's will?"

Peter turned to face his small battalion of religious fighters: Andrew, his brother, the bold warrior; Thomas, his cunning friend; and his sister Salome, a modern-day Joan of Arc; Mark, his giant and loyal friend; the fiery brothers, James and John; the young and reliable Matthew; the caring Martha. He loved them with all of his heart. Looking each of them in the eye, his warm affectionate gaze showed his admiration for their courage and loyalty. *You are my brothers and sisters; forever will you have my heart.* Then reaching over his head, he withdrew his sword from its sheath. As it met with the open air of battle, its color changed from that of cold steel to a warm glow of dark blue.

"For God, for our people, and forever stand the golden city of Penury!" Peter called out, and then spinning back toward the street, he marched forward with his sword outstretched in front of him. They moved quickly toward the Cathedral entrance. The magnificent steel blades glowed even brighter with a white-bluish light that blinded the snipers trying to take aim from the rooftops. They randomly shot at whatever shadows they could make out through the brilliant rays of light dancing from the sword's edge. Bullets and missilets streamed passed the Zealot soldiers as they made way to the entrance. Andrew deflected bullet after bullet, whirling his sword from side to side in a circular motion so fast and furious that it almost seemed humanly impossible. The metal slugs didn't make a mark on the blade. A team of Homeland ground forces moved in to cut off their path to the entrance, but they were met with the tip of blades from Mark and Peter. The Zealots diamond-shaped formation held firm as they redirected shot after shot from snipers and ground forces emptying their magazines into the small, slowly moving target.

Reaching the Cathedral door, the diamond formation reversed positions; the back became the front and the front became the back. While Thomas worked to open the digital locks on the Cathedral doors, Mark, Andrew, and Peter protected the group from the street-side attacks. The lighted swift sword movements of the Zealots were so impressively hypnotic that the security forces seemed to be entranced by their display and could not resist staring at the traces of light. The Spirit guided the Zealots precision movements with strength and accuracy never before seen in the field of battle.

Within minutes, Thomas pushed open the two large wooden doors. The Zealots rushed into the vestibule and barricaded the entrance.

"Is everyone all right? Anyone hit?" Peter asked as he sheathed his sword.

"Mark stomped on my foot with his humongous size-fifteen boots, and I think he broke my little toe," John said.

Mark grunted. "If you didn't have feet like my sister you'd never have noticed."

"I broke a nail," Salome said holding up her left hand as she walked passed them. Her eyes were fixed toward the altar that lay beyond the church entryway. "O my Lord and my God," she said softly and genuflected while making the sign of the Cross. "Look at that! The sanctuary here is absolutely beautiful!"

Phillip pushes his sword into its sheath and looks as if he is puzzling over something. "Peter, why the Cathedral of Saint Matthew? The Way doesn't come anywhere near this part of DC."

"Exactly," Andrew replied, speaking for his older brother. "We needed to make sure The Way was preserved and undetected." He followed Salome down the center aisle towards the altar. "Wow, she's right. It is magnificent – breathtaking!"

Phillip lowered his head and stared at the inlaid designs in the marbled flooring. "I just wanted to know, so I can one day be as great a leader as is Peter."

"I admire your optimism, Phillip," Peter said as he placed a hand on Phillip's shoulder. "It is a decoy. Saint Matthew was always to be the last stand."

"Well, it's not over until it's over," Simon chimed in.

The Zealots moved one by one towards the holy water vessel on the inner wall, made the sign of the Cross, and passed into the nave of the church, up the main aisle toward God's holy place. They stood before the white marble altar inlaid with precious stones in floral designs. Peter's heart pounded as he gazed beyond the altar at the magnificent mosaic on the back sanctuary wall depicting an angel standing behind Saint Matthew as he held the Gospel. He had often thought of that same imagery in battle, envisioning angels hovering around him and his brethren. The Crucifix suspended just in front of the altar where God's soldiers genuflected in unison before their Lord and Master. Taking a moment in silence, they made their final act of contrition and penance.

~ Paul ~

Papa paused and looks visibly shaken by what he is to reveal next. With his fingers interlocked across his chest, his head is lowered and his eyes are closed as if in deep contemplation. I wish to go to him and ease his sorrow, but I know better. Sorrow is part of his life as is suffering and pain. He seems to welcome it with open arms and is very much satisfied after his meditation. The Doctore has said to me time and again that he doesn't understand people who fear pain and suffering. It is in our acceptance of these sorrows that great power is delivered either to ourselves or to others who are dear to us. Why would we resist the power of the One King?

Il papa looks up to the crowd who waits in anticipation for him to continue. Unlocking his fingers, he places his hands on his knees and embarks on the Zealot's final stand.

~ Doctore ~

So, on that Friday morning June 20, 2053 AD, as had been foretold, it happened: just before dawn, before the warmth of light broke through the cold and dark horizon, the last of the religious rebels succumbed to the military might of American forces. The twelve men and two women were dressed as soldiers that night. The Carroll Zealots were armored in tattered bibles, crucifixes, and worn rosary beads. Outnumbered twenty to one, they held firm, gallantly on their knees in front of the altar while cyanide gas-filled flashpoints crashed through the stained glass windows of the Cathedral. These were followed by dozens of grenades. The small brigade of religious fighters circled round the altar with their arms around each other's shoulders saying the Lord's Prayer. Wearing the Franciscan and Dominican robes, a white wool tunic with a red Cross and the Sacred Heart were worn underneath. The robes were tied tight by homemade fashioned rope made from palms. A brown Scapular and sword finished off their garments.

An intense, bright white light, like that of a lightning strike, lit up the entire church as the flashpoints touched the stone floor and exploded. Shrapnel sliced through flesh and bone in seconds while toxic gas filled the sanctuary, charring the lungs of its victims. Whatever was left of Christ's soldiers was then eliminated by the grenades exploding all through God's holy house. There were no hymns to be sung that night, nor were there any Masses to be said. Priests had long scattered to Europe in search of religious freedom. There was only the splintering and disintegration of pews, the stench of burning religious artwork, and the fragmenting of stained glass windows. However, the wooden Cross would not burn and stayed suspended. So it had ended, thought the victors of secular democracy, but what they hadn't realized was that history was only beginning to clear its throat. Harsher battle cries were still to come and the monster that had been awakened had yet to show its face. The nightmares would follow, and people would no longer be able to tell when it was night and when it was day; for soon, neither would be safe from the sins of man and the evil that would follow.

The secularists, well they began their day by celebrating their victory with cheers and cheap alcohol, while dancing to the beat of digital *Gri'mθtal*. The blood of the last martyrs flowed from the streets of the city that had created the very documents that had once protected them. They thought the Declaration of Independence and the Constitution were antiquated ideals that no longer held relevance. Washington DC's long fought battle against the last remaining Christian right was finally won. "Those superstitious, religious fanatics, who had desperately tried to salvage their lost way of life, were slaughtered while barricaded in the Cathedral of Saint Matthew." Apparently, there had been an insider in the Zealot's camp who had given their position to Homeland Security forces that quickly moved in and brought down the entire church. Sadju received a traitor's reward for turning in the last of the American Christians. A parade to the White House was held in his honor where he received the President's Medal of Freedom. It was rumored that only a few short weeks after that event, he was found dead outside an abandoned church with his wrists cut. The past held true to its course and continued along the path it had taken once before. It had become quite familiar with it even though overgrowth, landslides, and rocks may have hidden the ancient trail from sight. History knew the way that was thought to have been forgotten.

Chapter 5

A New Democracy

~ Paul ~

"Papa?" I said, easing the restroom door open to peek inside. The Doctore is standing at the sink pushing water into his face. Still hunched over, he raises his head and looks at me in the small, oval mirror that hung crookedly on the wall.

"Papa, I'm sorry to interrupt, but there's a small boy who needs to use the – I kept him outside as long as I could."

The Doctore turns giving me the "stare", then says, "Let him in. Let him in. Do not keep the children from me."

I swing open the door and the little boy, still dancing from one foot to the other, runs right into the stall, not bothering to close the door behind himself. Papa just looks at me as if he was trying to comprehend how I could possibly have such little compassion for a small boy. He would do that from time to time. Papa never said an unkind word, and issuing some disappointing gesture was not his way, but nevertheless, he still found some method of communicating displeasure in my more selfish actions or thoughts.

Afterwards, the three of us, the Doctore, the young boy, and myself move through the small store where Papa insists on getting the boy some appled-dough treats; an entire bagful for the young lad and his friends. I give the two coins to Dom and torment over how little money we had left for the return journey. I try not to make a spectacle of my anguish, otherwise I would be given the faith and travel speech. It is the one where Papa says, "If you had just a smidgen of faith you would not worry over what money you had in order to make the journey. Do you think that the One doesn't know where you are going? He will provide the reservations for us. All that is required of you is to simply move your feet. And complain less. Pray more."

The Doctore settles onto his cathedra and asks his audience where he left off. A little game he likes to play to see if they were truly paying attention. I think he enjoys being an old man. He appreciates all of his ailments as if they were awarded for long life. Also, I believe he likes to make out that his mind is fogging up and his hearing is going, so people feel more at ease and are open to him. Of course, he has better hearing and facilities than I do, so he isn't fooling me one bit. I lean against the wall and

thomas e

let my legs take me down to a sitting position where I enjoy my own appled-dough treat while Papa discusses Democracy.

~ Doctore ~

The Shekel, still reveling in its victory over the Zealots, looked to set ICLAW (the Inferred Constitutional Law software application) into action with a new law titled IC Resolution 173E, which called for the immediate dismissal of all political parties. Most of the Republican or conservative Democratic Congressmen and Senators, the so-called "displaced representatives," were removed from office, stripped of their financial status, and sent into the wretchedly poor southern states. The new power had no need for a conservative view point nor did they have any need for the poor citizens in Washington. They, too, were gathered up and sent to the south. There no longer was any room in America's Capital for the tired, the poor, huddled, undereducated, and underprivileged masses.

A few days later, on July 4, 2053, President Piloti signed into law the Washington Act, a doctrine that defined the new social order of equality through the FED-Care health plan, the FED-Work jobs program, the FED-Safe domestic justice program, and finally the FED-Dream education program. The charismatic President vocalized his promises to ensure the American way of life and that all Americans would have commonly shared jobs, healthcare, education, and safe neighborhoods. All of these wonderful amenities would be provided by the largest American government in history, which swore to uphold its new charter for the people, just no longer by the people. The blinded citizenry took the bait; hook, line, and sinker. Unfortunately, "common" didn't necessarily mean desired or needed; it meant equally distributed. What does it matter if everyone equally shared filth, poverty, starvation, pollution, and fear? It was the "New Era" bringing about the "Last Deal," the law that gave every citizen the same hand to play. American passion and justice, that unique formula the Founding Fathers thought would last forever, suffered blow after blow, as freedom and rights were replaced with a new socially equal society. The definition of marriage was abolished. The government redefined it as cohabitation between any citizen of any age, color, race, or affiliation, who wanted to partner together for a period of time equal to or longer than one fiscal tax year. Anyone who was partnered was afforded the same rights of cohabitation.

After reshaping the Constitution, the Washington Act redrew state borders into larger districts or zones: a military controlled Federal Zone and four Domestic Zones that were under a combination of military and civilian authorities. The Federal Zone extended through the original thirteen colonies as far north as Maine and as far south as Florida. The Domestic Zones were divided into four unequal territories.

46

The western most region was named Domestic Pacific, which consisted of upper class society who kept Hollywood and Silicon Valley just as it had been—full of pop culture and high society elitists looking for the next big thing to feed the world's desire for excitement and differentiality. Domestic Central housed the working middle class who were educated just enough to maintain somewhat adequate jobs. These working communities supported the main function of the new America. Domestic North would continue to supply the bulk of the food and fresh water through virtual agriculture and hydro-farming facilities. Sustained climate change through the greenhouse effect had eliminated the harsh winters making the northern states perfect for the large hydroponics facilities. While the north and central zones maintained the country's infrastructure, the south was home to the impoverished and the unhealthy. The land of the free could no longer afford to keep all of its citizenry in the lifestyle they had been accustomed.

The Government-controlled Federal Zone, which consumed the entire eastern seaboard, was officially referred to as the Red Zone because of the prominent red armbands worn by military guards, but civilians in other districts cynically called it 'the Red Zone' because the new American government more closely resembled the Communist Party of the 1960s than a true Democratic society. In this restricted area, everyone worked for the Government. Civilians could obtain passes allowing them access to the territory and conduct government business, but for the most part Red Zone inhabitants either worked for the FED or were shoved out a gate, usually head first. There was no longer any respect for the dignity of Man.

~ Paul ~

Hearing the Doctore speak reminds me how I had seen this brutality firsthand on more than one occasion. I remember visiting the Red Zone for the first time when having to be clinic-certified after my internship. There was a Staff Sergeant Kayop that showed me around not long after President Piloti was sworn in as the last elected official. After IC Resolution 173E, all government officials had to be elected from within the Federal Zone. Representatives from the Domestic Zones were chosen to sit on the Electoral College, which then voted on Federal Zone employees to hold offices. Every Red Zone individual was known as a "Government issued and tagged" resident or GIT. Each GIT had a unique chip that was implanted at birth. There were no unauthorized births in the Red Zone. Any thermal scans that showed moving heat sources that wasn't a GIT or wasn't accompanied by a GIT could be eliminated without question.

Sergeant Kayop escorted me and gave a tour of his beat.

"Yeah, this city has changed, Civ (civilian). It used to be split into four quadrants. Now, they're all bashed together into just two areas—the

47

affluent Northern Pod communities and the larger Southern Anacostia area. That's where us poor GITs hang. This area we're in now, by the Maryland border, is what used to be known as the "Gold Coast" where some of the real gold mongers had lived. It is now home to CPR (Community Pod Row) for the well-to-do GITs. Ever see one of these units, Civ?"

"Can't say that I have, Sergeant,"

"Come on, hang nine and take a gape. There's an empty unit from last week when one of the 'Gaming Dead' bit it." The Sergeant led the way into the building and opened the Pod apartment.

I stepped in behind him and looked over the elaborate pod, which was three to four times the size of other accommodations that housed the more average GITs. With a minimum of fourteen hundred to over two thousand square feet of living space, the wealthier GITs lived a plusher life style.

"Check this out," called out the Sergeant as he pushed a selector to operate the virtual windows. The screens displayed actual views of the city outside, and then could be switched to display a different city, beach, or other location on Earth or in outer space. A GIT only had to choose their preference from the mode selector. The virtual windows could also be turned into a reflective mirror for looking at their latest GIT fashion or bring in live video feeds to watch the latest in Hollywood entertainment.

"What is a 'Gaming Dead'?" I asked.

The Sergeant looked up from the mode selector switch and then grunted. Turning back to the screens, he switched it to the virtual gaming feeds. From all over the world, games could be processed through these digital portals. War games, robotic sporting events, and killing games could all be enacted through these virtual devices. "The Gaming Dead are those that play this virtualized fantasy beyond any nightmare dreamt in the sickest of minds. The InterReaper Company created games so dark in their sadistic pleasure zones that anyone playing them too long would eventually go whack. They virtualize brutal torture chambers where players enact out their most evil and gruesome fantasies. The thirst for blood and their cravings for screams as flesh is shaved from bone become so addictive they butcher themselves during their game playing time. Once they enter this twisted land they never escape it."

"All right, you can turn it off," I said looking away from the screens.

The Sergeant turned off the feeds and headed to the food preparation area. "This is the mess. It comes with a chef-styled food prep area complete with fusion-stove tops and particle-replacement generators."

Continuing the tour, I noticed a horizontal door in the hall. "Look at that, he even had a MediDock. He died having a MediDock?"

"I told you, Civ – once they are InterReaped, they're dead. They don't ever leave their game, not even for medical attention."

This was a fabulous invention that came about during the Holy Land Wars when Israel was attacked by radical Eastern terrorist forces. The virtual hospital bed was connected to top medical staff that could perform surgeries on the fields of battle from thousands of miles away. It allowed more doctors to supply medical aid to the countless military victims of the war. Equipped with the particle-replacement generator, it could reproduce drugs, casts, splints, or other medical necessities including human organs, tissue, or bone. I always thought that this was the game changer of the modern world.

"Foolish GIT. He had all this technology in his home, which could have extended his life to one hundred-ten or hundred-twenty-five years, but instead he couldn't shake his sick fantasy," the Sergeant commented.

I was forced from my daydreaming when I heard the faint talk of 'GITs' coming from the Doctore. I immediately snapped out of it and, after brushing the crumbs from the appled-dough treat from my trousers, I stand and listen to where Papa is in the narrative. I feel somewhat guilty drifting off like that into my own reflection. After all, this is Scientia and we are supposed to be gaining knowledge of The Way, not daydreaming about the past.

~ Doctore ~

However, even though it would seem a Gold Coast GIT had all they could ever need or want, they remained equal to their lower class GITs in that they were prisoners of a city that could never be free. The suppressed aching in their hearts was starting to rot their minds with a cynical and distrustful approach to all of life. They watched all of their possessions as if at any moment a thief would come and steal them away. The fear and mistrust felt among these individuals isolated them further from one another. Using the virtual feeds for social stimulation, they became hostages in their homes, which saddened and sickened them even more from lack of true relationships. Many of these individuals had not been outside their units for many years, as their fear and paranoia isolated them from the world. Those that were weak went mad with the isolation and no amount of time spent in the MediDock could save them from themselves.

This was the new America. The government controlled nearly all aspects of life, including forced population reductions and population control mechanisms to keep costs down. Genetic testing determined the likelihood of couples producing adequate offspring. If there was any indication that the genetic profile was not within the high standards of the GIT protocol, the couple remained without children. These regulations were formed to keep the community running smoothly and to maximize benefits to all citizens with minimal resources. It would appear that the Shekel had thrown a shiny penny down into the sewer and the naïve public chased after it, entering the rat infested ranks of social debauchery. Freedom was more or less metaphorical now, and the ancient passion of discovery was limited to the privileged few. The Earth tilted further on its axis as changes to the fundamental laws of nature were shaking the very foundation of its core.

Chapter 6

Bottom Rack

~ Paul ~

At the end of the first leg of the journey, the various paths people had taken came together. It was where I met Domingo, Sevita, and Li'Quari. In addition, I also met a couple of renegade GITs, which really was quite unexpected. Who would have thought that even the GITs were looking to escape? However, pondering on this more now it makes perfect sense to me. They were just as trapped in their lives as the rest of us, and perhaps had taken even more risk in trying to flee in order to pursue freedom. They taught me a great deal about what it was like living in the Red Zone and to hear them describe it was quite illuminating.

Stealing the words from Papa, there were arrays of forbidding buildings lined up straight and tall in the Capital city. The structures wore uniforms of dark grayed steel and followed the city streets of DC-Red Zone. The faceless cloaked giants stood side by side, dotting the nation's capital, pilfering the morning light. This monstrous labyrinth, formed from cold metal and concrete, created unpredictable wind tunnels throughout sections of the city. It was rumored that certain areas were so turbulent with funneled air that if a GIT was in the proper place at the right moment, they could be lifted from the ground and tossed into one of the metal structures, their face planted against the sunburnt panel, only to be dropped to the ground after the gusts moved on to prank another unsuspecting bottom dweller. I always thought that would have been something amusing to witness firsthand. Of course, il mio Papa is telling the story now.

~ Doctore ~

A colorless city brings about an emotionless people who walk its streets in a lethargic sleep. There was an air of hopelessness and no one could be startled enough from their stupor to recognize the absence of color in their home of martial law. There was no anger as they gazed upon the reddened arm bands of the Military GITs, which boldly stood out like stained gauze used to catch the blood drained from the Declaration of Independence. This indifference was the final curtain call to the mockery of Jefferson's comedy. No one had thought to fight for the ideals which had been etched on parchment not so long ago. The age of the antiquity became more valued

51

than its ideologies. As for righteousness and freedom, minds were clouded and hearts drained of their passion.

So many tall buildings blotted out the sky that daylight dripped through various cracks and seams that eventually accumulated at the street level. The limited precious light formed shadowy pathways for the metro-rats. The dark gray paint, which contained photonisomeric silicon, was sprayed onto buildings to consume solar light. This energy fed into a sophisticated capacitance network pattern that resembled the tetrameric biotin-binding protein, avidin. This algorithmic symmetry orchestrated and increased the charged particles one-thousand fold, which generated enough voltage to supply the entire structure. Though this method was a very efficient use of solar energy, the city had lost its need for color and aesthetics; removing all beauty from a once flourishing artistic metropolis. Man had done what Man does best: continuously tweaked nature by imposing his arrogant will upon her until she either suffocated or revolted violently, destroying all in her path. When respected and treated proper, she responded with love, but if provoked or molested, became a powerfully vengeful and scornful entity who would not hesitate to defend her reputation and honor. Mother Earth had shown divine patience with humanity; however, she too, was preparing her armory to join forces against the corruption and brutality of Man.

Dubbed "Bottom Rack" by the military GITs, the Southern Anacostia location housed the standard-issue living quarters for the average GIT who took residence in run-of-the-mill pods. A single "rack" usually had one or two virtual windows that could be used for interactive entertainment or to splash the latest in foul-promoting digital "street" art. Although small and somewhat lacking in the features of their higher class pod companions, they were far superior to any of the civilian living quarters. The dwellings boasted a six to eight hundred square foot residence large enough to contain a food preparation area, sleeping quarters, and a living space. Most of the single family homes of the past had been bulldozed over to make room for the barrack-style housing and apartment buildings. All along Martin Luther King Jr. Avenue, the old style neighborhoods were lost to more efficient use of energy, space, and land. The residents had to relinquish their homes and were driven out of the Federal Zones into District Central; or for the more reluctant and unlucky souls: District South.

In the Red Zone, paired patrols moved about their gridded beat while other non-military GITs slugged along, moving from building to building carrying out various orders. First Lieutenant George Lyndon set off towards the security gate while trying to shake off the reality of the day around him. It was late September in 2053 AD and already the air felt different. Though here, at an open intersection without buildings casting shadows, the sun felt hot on his back, the wind was cold as it ricocheted through the shadowy alleyways, and that cold air blasted him full in the face as he rounded the corner.

Once or twice, in the course of a week or two, or maybe even four, there occurred an outburst at one of the security gates. Today it had been Gate Nine, which stood at the northwest side of Bottom Rack. It separated the core Red Zone from the Bottom Rack residency. George had no idea what the disturbance was this time, but hoped it was something easy to resolve.

Behind him, a voice rang out. "First Lieutenant!"

Private First Class Baker caught up to him trembling with excitement. He removed his cap to run his left hand over the stubble of his crew cut. With his muscular build, his guard uniform was too tight, his buckles too polished, and his boots laced too perfectly. George could almost smell the boy's ambition. Everything this private did was aimed towards his goal of corporal stripes. No doubt he wouldn't hesitate to do whatever it took to get them just a little bit faster.

"Yes, what is it, Private?" George called over his shoulder as he continued to walk down Nineteenth Street just past G Street.

"Sir, yes sir!" Baker stopped and saluted his commanding officer, bringing up his four digits and tucked in thumb with the precision and accuracy of an ancient Swiss watchmaker. His quickness of movement caught the lieutenant's attention. He stopped and turned to acknowledge the private with a salute, and then continued towards his destination with Baker scrambling along beside him.

"Sir," Baker squeaked out, "we detained a DC-four at Gate Nine."

Lieutenant Lyndon stopped again, and looking downward at an array of darkened splotches in the walkway, shook his head in disbelief. *Of course, why not? The whole universe has already conspired to dig its heels into his already frustrating day; might as well tack on yet another problem.* Staring at those splotchy patterns of gray and black in the concrete, he imagined it resembling a large fattened duck, complete with webbed feet and a long beak. If that were not enough, a short distance away, behind the overweight fowl, were four smaller daubs of oil drops that, though they didn't look so much like ducklings as they did some kind of defective moth with wings spread for flight, followed their overweight mother just the same. The First Lieutenant darted his gaze from spot to spot trying to make out where the father might have positioned himself in this Shakespearean fantasy theatre, but he couldn't seem to locate his well camouflaged form.

"Awaiting your order sir," PFC Baker reiterated smirking slightly.

"What's the DP?" George stretched his neck and looked towards the sky.

After flipping open the m-pad attached to his left forearm, Baker tapped quickly on its crystalline face like a first-time concert pianist rushing through a piece of music to get to the beautiful climax of a magnificent symphony. He began to read off the details of the DC-4 in her domestic profile. "Janis Keal, originated from Domestic Central Iowa. No previous arrests, no warrants, no outstanding security THREATCONS. Works at DC Robotics as a digi-geek. Partnered to William Mann. Twenty-five, brown hair, brown eyes, five-foot seven, one hundred fifteen pounds. Huh, not too bad looking either. She crashed Gate Nine demanding to speak to the SJR."

"Is she bumped?" George asked, meaning he wanted to know if she was pregnant.

"Sir! No, sir. I believe she wants to be, though." Baker laughed sarcastically.

"Do you have brain damage, First Class?" George belted out at him angrily.

"Sir! No, sir!"

"Then I suggest you backwipe that fubar grin off your face, take your ugly jackside back to your post, and try not to be the embarrassment, that clearly you are, to your unit!"

"Sir! Yes, sir! And the DC-4, sir?" Baker straightened himself out and stood at attention.

The military had three ways of keeping law and order when its citizenry became indignant or pushed for more freedom than the government was willing to tolerate. The first method, Red Warning One, involved scare tactics that ranged from loud verbal abuse to one or two punches to the body, and then they were tossed out of the Red Zone on their backsides. Red Warning Two, the second and more severe approach, included a good working over by two or more soldiers. The criminal element would typically be in need of medical attention after this disciplinary action. Lastly, the rarely used Red Warning Three would be applied. This was simply an execution. However, it was usually preceded by a Red Warning Two before the final enactment of the firing squad.

"Give her Red Warning One and toss her out." The Lieutenant positioned himself in close and leaned into the face of Baker. "If I hear she even came close to being given a RW-2, I'll find you, First Class. I'll find you and drop you off in some hole in DS. You got that, First Class?"

"Sir! Yes, sir! Clear as a click, sir!" Baker saluted and about-faced, making his way back to his post in double-time.

The Lieutenant smirked for a moment. He had no use at all for brass kissers or making idle threats. He had trained in the deadly martial art form of Krav Kun Do, which was a lethal combination of the Israeli Krav Maga and twentieth century Jeet Kun Do, the quickest way to eliminate a threat by imposing a series of blows causing immediate death. He showed no mercy for the enemy. He took off his cap, pushed his fingers over his short hair from front to back, and then jammed his cap back onto his head. "Idiotic fool," he mumbled under his breath.

The streets of DC were humming with activity as uniformed GITs moved from building to building. There were forty thousand troops in DC alone that maintained order as peacemakers. There was no longer any need for a police force since the military assumed the role of law and order. There were military personnel stationed all along the Federal Zone border from the northern most post in the areas that used to be known as Maine through New York, Pennsylvania, Virginia, the Carolinas, Georgia, and Florida. There were now some three hundred thousand troops in the Red Zone. The capital city had been turned into one large military base complete with barracks, training facilities, headquarters, and countless other military structures.

George tugged at the cuff of his shirt. His uniform, though well-tailored to his likeness, always seemed to pinch at him despite being in top physical form which made him more aware of the responsibility attached to it.

Today was one of those days when he wished he'd followed a different path, but after training at West Point, his destiny was carved out for him. During his graduation ceremony he met Jackieo, whose father had been the Gunny at boot camp. Within four years, he was made First Lieutenant, after which he had partnered with Jackieo. From that point on, his life's plan was set for him directly by P.O.T.U.S., Commander in Chief of the American forces. So, here he was, stuck in the Red Zone dealing with interminably unjust regulatory issues day in and day out.

He had been walking along Nineteenth Street when he stopped to watch an um-neer (utilities maintenance engineer) working on coating a set of new stairs with polycarbonyasonate. Since its discovery, polycarbonyasonate had been sprayed everywhere there was concrete. Its unique ability to instantly form a strong bond to materials combined with its strength and temperature resistant/retainment properties makes it an incredibly durable surface. The material stays cool in the summer and warm in the winter, so there is less trouble with snow and ice on concrete surfaces. It can also stand up to the harshest of weather or the brutal wear and tear of the military vehicles driving in the city. The um-neer, dressed in the typical gray-on-gray urban camouflage, looked up from his work.

"Anything I can do for you, First Lieutenant?"

George tried to recall a time when he hadn't seen urban camouflage in DC. When he was a boy, his father would come home from work wearing the military uniform; however George didn't recollect that it was something he himself had wanted to do. He had always remembered wanting to do something with his hands. Fixing things, taking apart gadgets, or just making something from a good piece of lumber was more the type of work he had imagined himself doing. He was bound now just as his father had been bound. He was one in a long line of Government issueds who had been tagged, branded, and stuck in a hole. There wasn't any way out of it. The only freedom he would ever see was when they finally draped the red flag over his body.

"No, carry on, Private."

After turning left onto F Street, he made his way toward the 9th District Office. The modern building, painted in military-gray, looked exactly like so many others in the Federal Zone that George spent the first several weeks using the coordinate locator on his m-pad just to find the place. Eventually, he had gotten to know his way around and the subconscious counting of steps ensured that he would always be able to find its locale.

Whisking through security, he took the elevator up to the fifth floor and made his way to his isopod, an isosceles triangular cubicle that had been an engineering answer to space shortage in the city. These pods floated on a track system that gave them the ability to be moved from floor to floor or within the area of the same floor. They could be put onto aircraft carriers or rail floats or flown to other divisions of the city or even transported to Domestic zones.

Upon settling into his unit, the lieutenant picked up the biD or biological-interfacing device from his tabletop, closed his eyes and laid his fingertips across the white oval-shaped, plastic form. The smooth and slick surface of the device had small raised bumps on the exterior that allowed for interaction with the centralized control system. As his fingers seemed to nervously twitch across the biD, his eyes darted mischievously back and forth from under their lids. With a head shake or mouthed obscenity, he diligently worked through the messages of the day. He had just started his report on the morning patrol when his thoughts were interrupted.

"Do impart, LT, I'm going across the street for a J-Cup – you on deck?" Chief Warrant Officer Kayop asked.

"Always on deck for a J-Cup, Chief. I can work on this chit after a little Joe's been taken down. And it's your turn to flog 'em."

"I flogged last week," Officer Kayop replied, looking somewhat puzzled.

"No, you were supposed to flog last week, but someone left their f-card at the button chopper," George replied getting up from behind his table.

"Oh yeah, that's right. Rah that, LT. I'll tell you what, let me get these J-Cs this time around," Kayop grinned.

"You cheap dap, step back before I hurt you," George said, and pushed him into the wall and out of the way. He then walked through the doorway of his isopod and started down the hall.

"Hey, foul down. Did you get whacked by MPs this morning?" the Chief called after him somewhat confused as to why his friend was in such a bad mood.

It was a short hike to the Met Café where the GITs met up for coffee. It was a place where the GITs were more likely to be military than not. The Met had served the city dwellers since the early 1990s, but had recently catered more to military personnel since the downsizing of Congress and civilian aides who had once dominated the city streets. Change had always been a part of the city and either merchants transitioned to the new era or closed up shop. It was survival of the flexible and the quick.

Inside the café, the décor presented framed digital screens hanging on the wall displaying pictures of military heroes of past and present skirmishes. It pleased George immensely that there weren't any photos of personnel above a certain rank; somehow it made them more real. However there was a large, poster-sized picture of President Piloti on the back wall just to remind him who was in command of his fate. The modern furniture was made from PVC that was reinforced with Kevlar. It was designed in simple, odd-looking patterns with structures so thin he often wondered how it could possibly hold the weight of a large man. The color resembled the same dark gray paint of the buildings outside. The urban camouflaged-colored floor was decorated with the names of soldiers who frequented the shop. Along with their signature and the date they upped or had been drafted into service (whichever term a GIT might prefer), there was an outline of the bottom of their boot drawn with a black marking pen. Sometimes a secondary date in red was also displayed. This was their KIA or killed in action date. George had a couple of mates that he etched their KIA into the floor. Sometimes, gifts were left on the squares by friends or family. There were some weeks when far too much of the floor was covered with these sentimental trinkets, especially during the anniversary of the holy battles. GITs were careful to never walk on a tile of a fallen comrade during these days.

The room was noisy with conversation and the clatter of plates and spoons blended into the din like an unconducted symphony of frazzled commotion. George and the Chief lined up behind two other military GITs and waited for them to grab their drinks. The Chief went first and typed a two-count into the control panel with his left hand while also flogging his f-card across its scanner with his right hand. The digi-vendor displayed the sixteen credits that were deducted from his account. After getting their twenty ounce J-Cups, they took their coffee and sat down in the back, away from the crowd.

Moments later, George focused on the center table where a pair of GITs were razzing their comrade. The J-Cups were fashioned with a short straw-like invention called the "tipper" that had tiny pin-sized holes that brought in air to cool the coffee on its way through the cup. As happened once in a while, the device had worn out and sent hot liquid jetting out at his chest, staining his uniform. They started to get wild and somewhat loud when a pushing match was invoked, but it was quickly broken up and tempers calmed when the owner came by with a free round of j-cups to the entire table along with brand new tippers. George recalled an incident when it had happened to him. It definitely can change the mood of the day. It appeared to George that when those everyday things stop working that's when he was most annoyed. The random major crisis was fine and he dealt with it, but those little disturbances that occurred seemed to bring out his anger the most.

"So, what's going down with you today? You're acting like someone stuck a bow knife in your backside," Kayop asked.

"I don't know, Chief. I had a DC-4 today. She wanted to crash the SJR about a bump," George replied.

"Yeah, so we get 'tem crazy bump addicts now and again. Just give 'em an RW-2 and move them on out."

George was silent for a moment. "Jackieo keeps at me about it. We got our second SJR denial," George said looking up from his J-Cup.

"I'm sorry man, really I am, but you know it's like a one in a hundred-thousand chance of winning that lottery gig. You just have to tell J to get that thought right out of her mind. It's nice not having to worry after a little GIT running around anyway. And all that chit they make you do until the kid is in GIT boot camp. Slap me, LT, it's too much work I tell ya. Just tell J-O to sit back, enjoy the quiet and play the digifeed."

"Yeah, well she ain't going to let that to rack now is she?" George said somewhat loudly. He paused and his facial expression changed from anger to concern. Fiddling with the tipper of his J-cup, he contemplated whether or not he should continue the conversation or how much he should tell his partner. He then pushed the cup to the side. "Dink it," he mumbled quietly while closing his eyes and moving his head from side to side. He leaned over toward the middle of the table and lowered his voice. "She's talking crazy talk, Chief. She's talking about looking for the city."

The Chief scanned the room quickly and then leaned in, "What the flip, LT? Don't say that kind of thing in here. You have to set that right. You'll be a brigrat for sure if you pull fubar like that. Besides, man, bump city ain't nothing but a myth. It's just something the bumps made up for hope. A woman with a bump just ain't thinking right."

"We have one more chance with the SJR to arrange a bump. Then it's over man, you know? Nothing I can do about it. That's that." George said matter-of-factly. He removed the cap from his head, then after driving his hand through his hair from front to back, he smashed the cap back down on his head. Leaning back in his seat, he tipped back his J-cup.

The Chief stared at him and shook his head from side to side. He recognized all too well the familiar and defiant pattern of his frustrated friend. George had a rebellious nature and a determined understanding of righteousness in the natural code. "You're one crazed dink. Don't you be going Article Ninety-Two on me now."

The Chief knew that George was frustrated beyond his normal tolerance for military law. But in actuality, this wasn't even a military regulation; this was civilian law. However, as GITs in the Military, they signed up to defend civilian law and the country against all enemies; foreign or domestic. Looking down at his J-cup, he thought about that for a moment in the context of his appreciation for his buddy's dilemma. What he didn't know was what his response would be if his longtime friend did do something stupid. *Could I actually turn him in?* He looked back at George who was still stewing over the entire matter and clutched his coffee so tightly, his knuckles were turning white. *Ah, this is George. He would never do anything against the code. What am I worried about?* The Chief took up his cup and finished off the last of his coffee.

"Listen Chief, I'm gonna take off," George said as he stood up. "I'm going to make sure First Class followed the orders I gave him."

Before the Chief could ask, 'what for', George was pulling open the exit door and on his way.

~ Paul ~

George is a great soldier that is for certain. I never knew anyone as courageous or devoted as he had been during that journey into the unknown. In fact, he saved my life a few times. I owe him a great debt. In addition, never would I have imagined that I could learn so much from a Red Zone GIT, but I soon found that he too had much to teach. One of the first lessons shown to me was how to give of myself for a cause greater than my own. I learned how to trust my unit. "This unit is your family. We have to have each other's backs and are bound to each other. We live as one unit and we die as one unit," he had said. Amazing, isn't it? Here is a man who could snap your windpipe in two seconds while fending off two or three enemies with his sword, yet he had such a loyal soft spot in his heart. George was all right in my BiD.

"Papa, it's time," I said and went to help him up from his cathedra.

"No, it cannot be eleven o'clock already. The people are so beautiful here in Scientia."

"I'm sorry, Papa. If we are to make the Intellectus canton by midday, we must leave now."

The Doctore stands reluctantly and gives his blessing to the crowd. "Good Domusi (People of my house), I have thoroughly enjoyed your company this morning. May our Lord bless you and keep you."

I pick up the Doctore's stool and then begin the incredible task of leading him past the crowd. With the traveling pack over my shoulder, I hook the stool to it and then position it comfortably on my back. I keep my right hand on the back of Papa to move him through the handshakes and good byes as we make our way toward the road that led out of Scientia.

Once on the main road about a mile out of town, we leave the people of the town to walk alone. We head east towards Intellectus.

"You were very good today, Papa."

"I feel good today. I especially like the story of Saul. He is a complicated man, but I have great hope in his change of heart. Have you meditated yet?"

"No, not yet. It's difficult with all the noise and distractions while in town."

"That will come in time and you will learn to drive those things from your mind's eye. You need to seek out the One in the center of your heart. He does not hide from you; you hide from him."

"I do not hide. I just have a hard time with navigation, that's all."

Papa's eyes wrinkle in that distinct pattern which indicates he finds my childlike excuses amusing. He then begins to move his fingers across the knots of his robe-tie. I suppose this is a good time for me to begin my navigation to seek inside myself. I must admit however, if I do find the One, I'll most likely be scared to death of what he might think of me.

Chapter 7

Central Bumps

~ Paul ~

The sun has been beating down upon our white traveling hats for some time as we near the canton of Intellectus (Understanding). I could give a description of the area, but all I can say is that it looks pretty much like Scientia: old, dusty and poor. There seems to be something along the side of the road near the marker at the canton border. It is black in color and seems to blow with the wind like a tarp or bag of some sort. Papa and I continue to trot along slowly making our way through the midday heat.

"It was thoughtful of Saz to meet us," Papa says breaking the silence.

"What? Where? I don't see Saz."

As we came closer to that black tarp, it rose up to greet us. Saz had been squatting low to the ground, which is why I had mistaken her for roadside litter. I don't believe Papa has eyesight that good. *How does he do that?*

Saz is a young woman I met on the second leg of our journey. She is an interesting character to say the least. Living the life of a military GIT, she like George, had been given an opportunity to fight for freedom and something greater than any government could ever provide. She is quite amazing in her own right. Having been a sniper in the military, she has the ability of camouflaging herself in unique ways. The enemy never saw her as they marched on by, and once they were alerted to her presence, it was too late. Quite frankly, the woman scares the socks off of me.

"Papa, it is good to see you," Saz says as she lowers the hood of her cloak to reveal her short black hair. She hugs him.

"How's my knightly girl?"

"I'm good. All of Intellectus is awaiting your return. I am to bring you straight to the square after you've had a moment to freshen up." Saz turns to me. "You look a little thinner, Paul. Travelling with the Doctore has done your body good."

"I have been getting a lot of exercise and my diet has been... interesting."

She smirks as if to say that my reduced diet was just what the doctor ordered. "Well, come along. I'll take you to freshen up after your journey."

After a quick stop at Saz's place, we bring our replenished water bottles and snacks with us and immediately enter the large town square where the entire canton is waiting. Papa receives a warm welcome. As he sits on his cathedra, I thought to practice my meditation and take out the medallion. Feeling a little tired, I sit down and lean back against a building that provides just enough shade to protect me from the glaring hot sun. The rise and fall of Papa's voice is relaxing as he begins the story from exactly where he had left off weeks before on his previous visit.

~ Doctore ~

Beyond the military borders of DC-Red Zone, past the security gates and checkpoints, and some distance away from the red arm-banded GITs, lay Domestic Central. The recognized capital of the American Midwest was the magnificent city of Chicago, known as the proud queen of the Great Lakes and home to the working class. Chicago had once boasted of quality American workmanship and had been home to one of the most recognizable skylines in the world. However, all powerful dynasties eventually come to an end, and there was no king to rescue her majesty from her fate.

Deep in the heart of her kingdom was the nerve center of the city. The Loop was nestled between the Chicago River and the great Lake Michigan. Here had sat the Supreme Court that kept order and ensured righteousness. It was the throne of justice. In addition, it was home to the Mercantile Exchange where countless transactions had taken place, but had been closed down after the DC Federal takeover. It was in this part of the city that her two iconic, sophisticated, and distinguished knights, who once had dressed in dark, protective attire, welcomed her loyal subjects to the city's core and guarded her treasures. As these honored and dignified gents grew old, they were discarded and the city degraded to a mere reflection of what the great metropolis had once known. Sir John Hancock and Sir Willis Tower saw with weary eyes what most of the nation's trademarked and historic figures had seen: a slow and agonizing death through the desecration and neglect of their world. The new citizenry had no respect for the elderly or the history from which they came. No one stood up to the corrupt politicians of the city's trust, who were chosen to uphold her dignity and honor, but instead embezzled her treasures and secrets, escaping with them to the enemy's lair in DC. After their vicious thievery, Chicago was left naked and exposed to the elements. In her weakened and vulnerable state, wretched takers moved in on her and she became the very victim of the prostitution she once kept hidden in her darkest corners. Along the Magnificent Mile, the once fantastic skyscrapers of steel crumbled from pilfering and neglect, while beautiful Lake Shore Drive eroded into the polluted and toxic waters of Lake Michigan. The City of Big Shoulders stood weakened, and though she tried to hold the country together with sheer will, the might of her arms grew feeble and the heaviness of her heart brought her to her knees. Why is it that it takes so long to create something beautiful and magnificent and in just a few short moments evil treachery can turn it to dust? Is the vileness of Man so bent on self-destruction that his vigor to destroy silences his muse to create?

Doctor Saul Kriesh trudged down the sidewalk along Madison Avenue, pausing only to pull the collar of his favorite black wool coat closer around his neck. Trying to keep out the chilling February, stench-filled breeze that was blowing in from the polluted shores of Lake Michigan, he buried his face deep into the fabric to keep from gagging. The thickened air was more reflective of cod liver oil shoved down the gullet of a boy as punishment for crimes of disobedience. Both were similarly revolting. The gray haze had a hint of black and orange that morning. Saul, a somewhat stout man who breathed more heavily due to the exertion of trying to walk quickly to his office, figured they were burning bodies at the prison again. He felt neither regret nor vindication, but had rather become indifferent to their outcome. They simply received swift punishment for their crimes. After rounding the corner at Michigan Avenue, he placed the palm of his hand on the entry pad to open the security gate to the Social Responsibility Care Office where he practiced. Just as he was about to step through, two dressed GITs got out of their military vehicle. They were large and bulky men with etched faces of calculated precision, typical of those who worked in the new military. The vicious repetitive training disciplined them into calculating machines of meticulous movements and unidirectional thought. Decisions were based on comparative training exercises with no room for marginal error or indecisiveness. Circumstances fell through the machine like varied sized coins falling through an ancient, mechanical coin separator.

One of the soldiers strode towards Saul while the other stood firm at the side of the vehicle toward the back door with one hand resting firmly on his holstered weapon as he surveyed his surroundings with a trained mechanical exactness.

"Morn-up, Doc. We have another one for you," the corporal said. He towered over the stout, flabby doctor who stood in the space of the half-opened gate.

"Morn-up, Corporal. All right, give me fifteen minutes to get prepared and then bring her up," Saul replied. With a slight shake of his head, he let out a sigh and continued through the gate and into the building.

Saul hurried up the flight of stairs that led to the second floor. By the time he reached the landing, he was breathing heavily and beads of perspiration dotted his forehead. He wondered how long he'd have to wait before the lift was back in order. It had been broken for more than a week now. Moving his hand across the security reader, the latch released and he pushed open the door to his practice.

"Cassie: lights, messages, first appointments…and coffee," Saul called out in a loud, clear voice as he continued towards his private office.

The office lights came on slowly as the bluish Bio-illuminating LEDs glowed from low power to full power filling the somewhat cold and antiseptic waiting room with a hospital-like atmosphere as Cassie called out the messages one by one in her familiar, mechanical voice. "Morn-up, Dr. Kriesh. Here are your important messages. First message: Doctor Saul, this is Linda. Sorry, but I have to cancel my appointment for tomorrow. I'll reschedule with your assistant for next week. Bye. Second message: Saul, I got the notice from the office of the SJR. It was denied, again. I can't do this anymore. I'll talk to you when you get home. Third message—"

"Stop!" called out Saul. He took off his trench coat and threw it across the office. It landed on the floor just in front of the lounge by the back windows. He stood for a moment in front of his desk with both palms on the walnut top. Leaning over it with his head down, he tried to rationalize the decision handed down. Saul wondered how he could comfort his partner whom he knew was devastated. She had wanted a baby for so long and their time was running out. In another year, they would not be able to have a child as they would have exceeded the age limit of twenty-six.

Saul straightened up and started toward the door, grabbing his white lab coat from the coat rack on his way by. While scrubbing up in the surgical area, he couldn't help but feel resentment and bitterness towards the Office of Social Justice and Responsibility. *Who are they to decide who has a family?* He lifted up his arms and let the water drip from his elbows. *Ah, who are we kidding anyway? What could our messed up genes possibly offer this wretched society?*

With gritted teeth, he addressed his mechanical assistant. "Dana – gloves."

A mechanism came out from the wall and he inserted his hands into the awaiting surgical gloves, then he promptly filled a syringe with a combination of droperidol and midazolam in preparation of a hysterical patient. A few minutes later, the screams and cries of a woman in distress sounded out the arrival of his guests. The two GITs dragged the woman from the elevator by the arms, kicking and yelling through the waiting room. Her legs were bent at the knees, but her feet barely touched the ground as she flung wildly about to get free.

"Just bring her right on back," Saul called out and waved his left hand motioning to them.

The two military gents walked her straight back to the operating area and stood her up directly in front of Saul. It was the first time her feet touched the ground since leaving the vehicle.

"No, doctor, please no! Please, don't hurt my baby," she desperately pleaded.

"Roll up her left sleeve," he said quietly to the corporal. "Don't worry, now. This is just a little something to help you relax and then we can have a calm conversation."

"Doctor, please no! I want my baby!"

The corporal lifted her sleeve past her shoulder, allowing Saul to move in and inject her with the sedative. The woman's knees buckled and the guard picked her up and carried her into the surgical room, tossing her on the table.

"How far is she?" the GIT asked.

Saul was watching the medical monitor as Dana populated the pulse rate, blood pressure, and respiration values of the woman. "Uh, I'd say nearly four months," Saul replied after glancing at her abdomen.

"They never learn. I wonder how she hid it for so long. Are you good to go, doc?"

"Yes, thank you. I got her."

After the two GITs left; Saul removed the woman's clothing with the aid of the digital nurse Dana, and covered the woman with a surgical blanket.

"Dana, secure hands and feet, twenty-five degree pelvic tilt, Class B surgical tray, and get the vid-ray feed going. I need to see what I'm dealing with here."

"Yes, Doctor. Station two tilting in five, four, three, two, one...."

Saul reached for the oxygen mask and was about to place it over the woman's mouth and nose when she began to plead with him.

"No. Please? Please, my baby. My baby," she cried out.

"I'm sorry. Really I am, but you know the law. Why didn't you ask for permission through the SJR?"

Tears poured down her face and fell onto the surgical form making small salt water puddles. "It was denied. We were denied!" She burst out. "Just let me go, doctor. No one will know. I won't tell. I swear on everything that is holy. No one will know. Oh God, save my baby!" she screamed.

Saul covered her mouth with the mask and looking toward the ceiling away from her eyes, he called out, "Administer anesthetic, Dana. Now, please."

The last of the blood curdling screams he heard right before the anesthetic was administered were the worst for Saul. For some reason unknown to him, his memory registered, categorized, and logged each one of them into a neuro network, which would be accessed at some point later in time. These flashes of recollection usually were at the most inconvenient moments. Sometimes, when having an intimate moment with his partner, the screams of a previous patient would penetrate through his mind and consume his thoughts, driving him out of the moment. But the worst of it was during the night, after an especially long day at the office, when he would drag himself home and retire early after dinner. His dreams took him through every abortion with ear-piercing screams echoing through his head. Sometimes, it was the unborn babies who cried out in pain. Regardless of the dreams, Saul woke up drenched in sweat and fear as he made his way to the podbath in search of his benzodiazepine tabs, the only thing that could get him through the worst nights.

After completing his miserable day at the clinic, he walked up to his apartment building and waved his hand in front of the scanner to open the security gate. He hurried up to his community pod on the third floor, worried about Janess.

Janess was sitting on the sofabay.

"How are you doing?" he asked, taking off his coat and draping it over the chair.

"I'm all right, Saul. I've been thinking and pondering about this for a long time; long before I heard back from the Social Justice office today," she said calmly.

Saul sat next to her and put his arm around her.

"You know the SJR isn't going to give us clearance. I mean, look at the two of us. We're short, we're over the BMI index, and let's face it neither of us are the 'pretty people' or the 'brainy people' that they are looking for in the next generation. There's not a chance on Earth that we would ever win the lottery."

"You don't know that. I can't believe that."

"Saul, be honest. You know that's how it works. Above all else, at least we can be truthful about ourselves and our situation."

"So, that's it then? We give up?" he asked looking for some type of rebellious expression in her face to contradict the eerie calm that had taken over her. Something was not quite right, but he couldn't put his finger on it.

"I can't go through another humiliating round of questioning and probing, not to mention the surprised looks we get because we don't measure up to the model features and body types they look for in candidates. I just can't go through that embarrassment again. I hate the way I have to stand naked in front of that awful panel while they scrutinize my body type and compare my structure to those images. The smirks and sneers. And some of the panelists are men! I can't do that again, ever." Janess paused for a moment and then looked at Saul. "Maria said she…"

"Ugh, Maria! We're not going there again are we?" Saul got up from the sofabay and paced around the living quarters. "Geez, Janess. The woman's clearly missing some neuron matter. You can't possibly believe that religious stuff?"

"I believe her, Saul. She's my friend, and she can get us there."

"You believe her," Saul repeated. "You believe in God now? You've gone religion all of a sudden? There's no such thing, Janess. Geez, you'd think we were back in the Middle Ages. In case you haven't heard, religion is dead. There's no God, there's no religion, and there's certainly no magical city where everyone lives their dreams and lives happily ever after. Janess! Wake up! I thought you were more intelligent than that."

"Saul, sometimes you can be such a cold-hearted jasp," Janess said as tears formed in her eyes.

"Do you know what will happen to us if we leave here? You do realize that we will lose everything that we have worked for, don't you? If they found out that we even thought about looking for some crazy religious city, we would be sent to the Southern sewer. And that's if they didn't just shoot us first. We could never come back here."

"There's nothing here to come back to. I'm going, Saul. You can stay here and keep performing those wretched abortions on those poor women, while having nightmares each night if you want, but I need more. I don't care if it is a myth. At least the fantasy of a dream is better than this dingy reality; this useless existence we call a life." She stood up and walked towards the sleeping quarters not even looking at Saul. After entering the back room, she closed the door behind her.

Saul paced the floor for several more minutes, back and forth across the wood-tiled squares while he mulled over the conversation. After a while, he sat on the edge of the sofabay and rested his elbows on his knees, and buried his face in his hands. His knees trembled and his hands started to shake. "I'm not going. She's just not mentally stable right now. I won't turn her in, but I'm not leaving here to pursue death, or worse yet, get shoved into District South," he mumbled to himself. He stood up and went into the kitchen to pour a drink. After whisking down a couple shots of bourbon, he thought for a moment. *I could turn in Maria. She's the trouble; she's the one who planted the seed of this whole idea in Janess's head. Yea, this is the fault of that lunatic, religious fanatic Maria.*

Saul poured himself another glassful of bourbon, throwing in some ice this time. He left the kitchen to lie down on the sofabay. With the glass on his forehead, he thought about his plan of attack and when the best moment would be to have Maria arrested. It would have to be when Janess wasn't anywhere near her. Saul finished his drink and rested the glass on his chest while he closed his eyes and fell asleep.

Almost a week had passed since Saul and Janess discussed the SJR. Saul was in the operating room performing surgery on a woman who had just been brought up. He was about to leave for the day, and though hungry and tired, he thought to get this one last patient done and then send her into auto-recovery until morning. She was twenty-seven years old and was almost four months along. As in so many of these cases he had seen, this one was no different. The SJR denied her and her partner a child, so she stopped using the Medi-Dock unit and thus did not receive the hormone control procedure and got pregnant. He had just removed the fetus and was about to inject it with sodium pentobarbital, when something about this particular infant seemed different. It had a sort of radiance about it; he was perfect in every way. The infant was just under four months, but all his features and form were developed. Fingers, toes, arms, legs, the facial features and beginnings of blondish hair were all present. It was truly remarkable how fully developed the young fetus was, as though he was just a very tiny person. Saul could see the heart dancing inside its chest cavity as it moved with each rhythmic beat. The child's eyes opened and looked directly at him. They were brightly colored blue-green, a color that he had never witnessed before in any person. They were a magnificent cross between a brilliant sea-green and a deepened sky blue that had such depth of color, not even the imagination could have envisioned it. And then, shockingly, without any movement of its mouth, a whispering sound was made that absolutely terrified the doctor.

"Saul."

Saul, momentarily paralyzed and trembling with fear, dropped the injection needle and then fell backwards into the surgical cart; staring at the fetus in disbelief. As he flung his hand backwards on the cart to stabilize himself, it was cut on the surgical instruments scattered about the top and he started to bleed. The contents of the tray crashed to the floor as he held his hand.

"Saul, why do you persecute me?" the infant struggled as if in agony and pain. "Atone in Penury, Saul."

Saul spun around, tripping over the surgical tray that had fallen to the floor, as he ran from the operating room. He stood outside the doors; his breathing was hard and labored, while his heart raced and beat hard inside his chest. Perspiration poured from his forehead like a burst water pipe. He went to the sink, turned on the water, and rinsed the blood coming from the shallow flesh wound in his hand. Cupping his other hand, he filled it with cold water and pushed it into his face several times. After grabbing a towel, he dried his face and hands. He pulled open a gauze bandage and wrapped it around his hand several times before taping it off. After turning around, he stared at the operating room doors. Slowly, after working up enough courage, he went to the operating room and cracked the door open to peer inside. The fetus lay motionless on the table. He pushed the door open further and went inside, moving ever so cautiously to the operating table. The mother was still under anesthetic.

Opening his mouth to speak, nothing came out. Saul cleared his throat and tried again. "Dana, vitals," he managed to get out, never taking his eyes from the still infant; lying lifeless on the cold, stainless steel table.

Saul jumped nervously, like a boy in a graveyard as Dana's voice began to call out the information. "Blood pressure, one hundred thirty over ninety. Pulse sixty. Respiratory is seventeen, Doctor Kriesh." There was a slight pause while Dana evaluated the heart signal over a one minute time window. "EKG showing normal sinus rhythm. Shall I bring her out of anesthesia?"

"And the infant?"

"The infant is absent of any vital signs."

Saul moved closer and looked intently at the infant. He lay motionless on the table, eyes closed, and his small hands were together with his fingers slightly interlaced over his chest as if in prayer. Saul could feel his own heart pounding and felt the pulse in his neck pushing in and out as though it would break through the skin at any moment. He felt as though he had a large lump in his throat and there was a deep fear in the pit of his stomach.

"Okay, okay. Um, yes, yes, bring her up slowly, keep the IV drip going, and put her in section b for overnight monitoring. And Dana, please clean the table."

"Yes, Doctor. Are you all right, Doctor? Your breathing is labored and your heart rate is elevated."

"I'm fine. I'm fine. I just need some rest. Night down."

"Night down, Doctor Kriesh."

Dana worked the mechanical surgical bed and the patient was lifted up and guided along the track. She was directed into the recovery room where she would be monitored during the night. As Saul left the room, he heard the suction engage from the large vacuum tube that Dana used to clean up after surgical procedures. He felt a cold chill move up his spine.

Saul could not remember a more terrible or disturbing day as the one he had just been through. He decided to vindicate himself by believing he had been overworked; that, along with the stress of Janess's talk of Maria, was wreaking havoc with the sanity of his mind.

After dinner, since he and Janess had really still not been talking with one another, he sat down in the living quarters and dozed off with an empty whiskey glass in his hand. He began to dream of his mother who had died during childbirth when he was just six years old. She had always been a very happy, positive, and hopeful woman. There wasn't anything that could put a damper on her loving spirit. Always wearing a smile, she and Saul had done everything together. He remembered going shopping with her, or working in their garden that was against the house in the backyard, or simply just helping her in the kitchen to make a meal.

He could hear her voice as if she were there in the room with him. "Baby, bring the plate over for me so I can put it onto the rack."

Saul finished scraping the chocolate frosting from the plate as he polished off the last remaining remnants of his mother's double chocolate cake. She patiently waited for him to finish. His plate was as clean as a whistle. Then getting up from the table with the spoon still in his mouth, he walked the dish over to his mother, placing it in her outstretched hand. She put it into the dishwasher, then reached for the spoon still in his mouth. She had to wiggle it loose from a giggling Saul, but with her sweet smile she charmed it away from him. After closing the dishwasher, she finished rinsing the sink and wiped off the counter.

"You must have ate a lot of cake, Mommy!"

"Why's that, baby?"

"Your tummy is getting big," he said pointing to her abdomen.

She smiled broadly. "Oh no, Saul, that isn't from cake. I'm going to have a baby in about six months. You are going to be a big brother."

"I'm going to be a brother?" he asked with a look of complete surprise.

"Yes, Saul. You're going to have a little baby brother. You can help me take care of him, and when he gets a little older, you'll have someone to play with. Don't you think it would be wonderful to have a little brother to play with?"

Saul shrugged his shoulders. He wasn't quite sure what this baby brother thing was all about, but he was sure he didn't understand how his mother could have eaten him and he ended up in her stomach. "So, how does he get out of there?" He asked pointing to her belly.

"We'll talk about that some other time. Go and wash up, now, Saul. It's your bedtime."

His mother came into his room to kiss him goodnight and tuck him in underneath the blanket. It was his favorite moment with his mother. She would sing to him *Goodnight sweetheart* as he held onto his stuffed animal or played with her long brown hair.

"Goodnight sweetheart; now it's time to sleep. It's time to dream of all the lovely things. One day you'll have a child and you'll sing to them, then I'll be right there in your heart so proud."

Saul squirmed uneasily on the sofabay as his dream turned from the pleasant memory of his mother to a life-changing conversation he had with his father.

"She's dead, son. She didn't make it while delivering the baby." His father said angrily with tears in his eyes.

"I want to see Mommy!" Saul cried and started to run towards the delivery room. "Mommy!" he screamed out. "Where are you?"

His father chased after him and picked him up. He carried him into a smaller waiting room and closed the door. The room had several small chairs and brown carpet. It was painted completely white and there was a yellowish, pale light running along the ceiling's edge. There was a stench of day's old burnt coffee. The brown carpet was worn thin in various spots and the tan crisscrossing strands broke through. There had been stains of coffee scattered throughout the area, especially closest to the entrance.

"Saul, stop it now. She's gone. Your mother is gone. She's never coming back. That's what happens when you die."

"Why did she die? Where did she go?" Saul sobbed.

"The baby caused her to bleed and they couldn't stop it. You don't go anywhere when you die. You just die. Sometimes, that's what happens in childbirth."

"I want to die, too, and go with her."

"It doesn't work that way, Saul."

"Did the little brother die?"

"Yes, the baby died, too."

"Good. He took Mommy!"

"Saul, he was just a baby. He didn't do anything. Sometimes, bad things happen; that's all." His father took his hand and then opened the door. "Let's get out of here."

Saul continued to look back at the room his mother had gone into and never came out, as his father pulled at his hand leading him out of the hospital. "Mommy!" he cried. "Come back! Come back!"

Saul woke himself from his nightmare. He thought he heard someone saying, "Come back." He didn't realize it was he who had called it out in his sleep. His mouth felt like the inside of a vacbot bag and his head hurt from front to back. Stumbling into the food prep area, he drank the rest of the juice from the container and went back to bed. He would decide what to do about Maria in the morning.

Chapter 8

Southern Tompato

~ Paul ~

With blurry vision, I come out of my meditation and look up to see how Papa is doing. He looks in dire need of a break. Before he starts to unveil the happenings of our southern friends, I bring a fresh cup of water to him. "Papa, I'm so sorry. Here drink this. You look parched."

"Thank you, Paolo. How was your talk with the lady?" The Doctore took a drink while keeping an inquisitive eye on me.

"I must be doing something wrong. I find it very strange to be talking to a medallion; stranger, still, to be meditating on one."

"It is because you are holding on to your pride."

"Pride? How can I be proud? I'm talking to a medallion."

"It is your pride in believing you know as much about this world as its Creator. It is difficult for the educated man to admit his weakness in knowledge. He holds on to the belief that he understands everything that is in his world. However, the truth of it all is that he knows very little. It is the great myth that man tells himself. Let go of the pride and empty yourself out to the mother of the One. And remember, the medallion is a physical symbol that helps us to relate to the spiritual phenomena. The symbols are there for us because of our weakness in understanding. They are not in any way actual representations of the spiritual world."

"I will try, Papa."

The Doctore lays his hand atop of mine and bowing his head, silently says a prayer for me. Then handing back to me the empty cup, he continues the story.

~ Doctore ~

Following the Chicago River, where Saul was left tormenting over Janess and Maria, we take a turn west to the Illinois River. Though the pollution in these rivers killed off all marine life, the moving waters kept the city's sludge flowing southward away from the populous. The slow moving Illinois River dumped into the Mississippi River in the town of Grafton, one of the oldest towns in Illinois, long abandoned since the soil and water supplies had become toxic. This was the same town in which Piloti's infamous case was won for Zinc Construct and where the Shekel claimed its newest recruit. The farmers had been hit first, then the families with children, and finally everyone else either moved away or suffered illnesses of toxicity and eventually died. Government promises of cleanup were always delayed due to insufficient funding and Congress's version of the "red tape two-step". The communities abandoned the area and it has since become home to prairie weed and wild dogs.

The Mississippi river starts out clear in the upper northern territory, and then becomes clouded as it runs through the central zone, until finally trickling into the south as a nasty, infectious, and foul-brown stream with a stench that is nearly unbearable. Moving past the city of St. Louis, where the lowest kinds of human degradation covers more square acreage than that of the river, the waters move through Missouri. After passing Memphis, where the famous have long been forgotten, it turns wildly; groaning like a drunk in the street trying to negotiate the bends of the road. Finding its creviced path through centuries of churning up Man's sentiment, it stumbles across the rock. Once known as the last town on the great river's end, La Balize, Louisiana, had been swallowed up by toxic red algal blooms called Redalge. In fact, the sinister red weed consumed the territory all the way up to Baton Rouge, which is where the Mississippi River now meets the cankerous mouth of the Gulf of Mexico and where this story continues.

Domestic South was home to the poorest of the poor. It was incredibly hot and the air stagnant. The once beautiful Gulf of Mexico was littered with the Redalge blooms that had killed or drove off most, if not all, marine life. The inland rivers and creeks were dried up swamps and marsh land that brought insects and disease. The Redalge had taken control over the southern borders eating its way into the land mass until the properties became worthless and were abandoned. The blistering heat in the summers also added to the migration of the southern states into the cooler Northern areas by those who were able to escape the southern borders before the district zones were divided among the elite that still had wealth.

The mischievous red color, however, was consuming more than mere land mass. It was also consuming minds, hearts, and the very soul of a nation with a bleak and hopeless end. The only work to be found in the south was what was left of the oil refineries. Men worked for fifteen percent of wages running machinery that still remained in working order. Crime and violence were rampant throughout the south as Government forces no longer patrolled the cities, but instead paid southern mercenaries to keep order. These men were given weapons and enough ammunition to keep the impoverished from crossing into Federal and other Domestic Zones. These men were evil and unforgiving monsters that used their positions to terrorize an already devastated community.

Just outside Baton Rouge, was an old Christian town with an equally old church. The town of St. Gabriel grew from the community that had erected its first Catholic church back in 1768, before the United States had signed its Constitution. In recent times, the community had been rundown and devastated by poverty and sickness.

Jackson Duprix, the last Republican Senator, arose before dawn just as he always had done since being driven from his government position. Living in the cottage that his great-grandfather Pappy Grant had built eons ago, Jackson reflected back to his early childhood as he removed the large piece of wood that covered the front window. When he was a child there was no need for such protection against both nature's elements and the evil Southern Guard. The cottages that had once dotted the shores of the Mississippi River were open and friendly. Pappy Grant would row out on the river and they would fish together and enjoy the once picturesque view of the Mississippi valley. Now, the river narrowed to a sludge-ridden stream just beyond the edge of a flat stretch of dead brown field, the result of many years of pollution pouring down from large cities of the north.

Pappy's cottage was a short distance from the river. The small twelve-hundred square foot house was just about the only thing that was still standing around this particular area of the town. Most of the buildings had long crumbled due to abandonment or were pulled down forcibly by the Southern Guard.

He turned from the window and moved through the living room, still fitted with the antique furniture chosen by his great-grandmother. Before passing a small bookcase that housed what were now his most prized possessions, he pushed in the hard cover book by Charles Dickens, Hard Times. Others in his collection were books by Mark Twain, and the little blue book containing The Constitution of the United States, and of course the Bible.

The cottage came with its own drinking well and septic system. It had a few modest acres of land where the ground still produced vegetables and citrus trees, partly due to the fact that Jackson had put in a cross-sectional barrier about two to three feet deep and then brought in soil that wasn't polluted from the river. The back quarter had Valencia oranges and thornless key lime trees that, after some care and tending to, kept the aging senator fed.

It was just past seven o'clock in the evening when the senator headed out to his orchard to tend the lime trees. Standing on a small crate, he hadn't been picking off the ripened fruit for long when he heard an unusual noise. With his beige straw hat tipped slightly back, he placed the limes in a worn wicker basket and focused his senses on branches and leaves being scrunched underfoot. He peered into his dense tree line, squinting to see in the darkness of the longleaf pine and cypress trees.

"Who's there?" he called out. There was no answer, but he could feel someone was there looking back at him, waiting for him to make the next move.

"What do you want? I don't have anything. I'm just an old man picking some limes."

The branches moved and he could see the silhouette of a woman coming toward him. She was wearing dark blue, dirt stained jeans that were torn at the knee and the left hip. The bottoms were frayed and looked as though she was walking through mud-filled streets. A loosely fitted beige top with a short collar was buttoned up half way and underneath was a burgundy t-shirt. She was pregnant, not showing tremendously, but one could definitely tell she was a couple of months along. Her face had dirt streaks that started from her hairline and made their way toward her jawline. However, even under the dirt and grime, her triangular shaped face and slender build revealed that she was a pretty girl.

She bit her chapped and swollen lip and looked down and to the right to avoid his gaze. "The DSG was after me last night and I ran. I was able to hide under the cover of the trees. I just kept running along the tree line all night. I just need something to eat," she replied. "I'm so hungry." She leaned against a pine tree and laid one hand on her swollen stomach.

"I have some cornmeal bread in the cottage, but you can have these for now," he said holding up the basket with the freshly picked fruit. "Valencia is good for the immune system." Jackson winked and held out the basket to her.

She reached in and grabbed one of the ripened oranges. "Thanks," she said. After quickly peeling away the skin, she bit into the fruit. The juice ran down her chin as she took another large bite. "Have you been here long?" she asked wiping her mouth and chin with her shirt sleeve.

"My family has been here for generations, but I just recently came back to the place."

She finished off her orange and reached in to take another. As she straightened up, she looked at Jackson more closely. "You look familiar."

"I was a senator for this state for eighteen years. I just lost my job not that long ago."

"You're Senator Duprix! I'm sorry Senator; you got a raw deal."

"Do you think so? I'm thinking I got off fairly easy for not being able to stop these atrocities from happening. This country has lost its purpose – its soul. Our Founding Fathers would not be very proud of us right now."

The woman just shrugged as if she knew nothing of what he was referring to or just didn't care to debate the principles of old when she had been fighting for years just to stay alive. She peeled away the skin of the second orange and then took a large bite.

"What's your name?"

"Li'Quari. People just call me Li' though."

"It's nice to meet you, Li'Quari. I'm Jackson," he said. "So, is the father around?" he asked motioning to her belly.

"Nah, not really sure what happened to him. The DSG probably got him. You said you had bread?"

Jackson looked at her curiously out of the corner of his eye. He started to turn when the sound of tires spitting up gravel and dirt could be heard just down the road and it was getting louder.

"Guards!" Li'Quari said and ducked back into the trees. "Hide!"

"Keep still and don't make a sound. No matter what happens just stay down!" Jackson ordered and picked up the basket with the left over fruit. He tossed the Valencias into the woods for her and turned away as he walked slowly toward the cottage.

The Domestic Southern Guard emblem was displayed prominently on the side door of the vehicle as it drove up on Jackson's land and tore up his grounds. The logo included a blood red "S" that snaked around the jet black angles that made the "G". Those same angled lines seemed to knife through the body of the snake in a pattern that was all too familiar to communities of the south. The vehicle ran over bushes and toppled small trees coming to a stop just in front of Jackson as he stood in the middle of his garden still holding the basket of limes. Three men climbed out of the three-wheel jank, a hybrid version of a jeep, a three-wheeled motorbike, and a tank.

"Come here old man," one of the men called out.

Jackson walked slowly over to them and kept his eyes lowered.

"What are you doing out here?" asked a grungy looking character with a scraggly, uneven goatee. The man trudged across the uneven earth and stopped in front of Jackson. With his bowlegged stance and hunched over posture, he resembled something out of a Victor Hugo novel. He had long black hair that looked like it hadn't seen water or soap for decades. It was half-braided on the right side of his head and the left side was completely sheared off. A red-dyed dragon tattoo invaded the entire left side of his face, extending into the shaved area of his skull. His clothes were dirty and full of holes and blood stains, which he seemed to wear as badges of victory. The stench of his presence was enough to choke the breath from a small animal.

Jackson swallowed the pride he felt burning in his mouth and answered as mildly as possible. "Just picking limes, that's all."

"Limes?" Dragonhead grabbed the basket with his left hand while pushing Jackson backwards with his right. "Let me see them limes," he barked out with a sarcastic and evil tone.

He had a lazy left eye that seemed to stare at you no matter where you had been positioned. It seemed to be alive and moved of its own accord. Blurry and bloodshot looking, it was almost colorless except for a slight grayish tint to it. It was like looking into a bottomless pit; you knew there was nothing behind it but pain and fear.

"Hey boys look at this! We done got our fruit for the week." He reached into the basket, and grabbing two limes with one hand, threw them at the other two men. The first lime bounced off the man's chest, as he was surprised to see an object being hurled towards him. The fruit fell to the ground and he bent over to pick it up. Dragonhead then took another lime, placed it in the pit of his arm, and squished down on it hard. He pulled Jackson into his chest and pushed his head toward his armpit. Jackson's straw hat fell off his head and blew a few feet away.

"Now, don't that smell fresh? You old cackdirt!"

He swung Jackson around and threw him to the ground.

"We're looking for a tartwod. Have you seen her? There's a reward for her hide," called out the second guard. He was a fat, red-faced, bearded man who smelled worse than the dead marshes.

The third guard, the one who had dropped the lime, was a tall, thin man who didn't say anything, but he smirked and giggled whenever one of the others shelled out a sarcastic remark. His albino skin was so light that he looked like walking death with long blond hair that draped over his eyes like a curtain. With his head lowered toward the ground, he peered upwards through his dirty blonde hair at Jackson. He moved back and forth, shifting his weight from the left foot to the right and back again in a sort of unrehearsed dance, like that of those desert lizards that continuously keep one foot off the ground so as not to get burned.

Jackson thought that he had worn shoes with more intelligence than this dimwitted twig. "I haven't seen anyone walk this way in over a month," Jackson replied, still lying on the ground from when Dragonhead pushed him.

"Filthy lying cackdirt!" called out Dragonhead. He went up to Jackson and kicked him in the ribs. Jackson rolled across the ground from the impact and crawled up on his hands and knees trying to get back his wind.

"Honest, I've not seen anyone for a while now. There's no cause for anyone to come this way – there's nothing here but the dead river."

"You're here old man," Dragonhead walked up to him and kicked him in the head. Jackson spun backwards and lay on the ground looking toward the sky. It appeared to be spinning. There was a metal taste in his mouth and his teeth and jaw throbbed.

"Why don't you go and get me another lime. My other pit could use some freshnin'."

"If you see the tartwod, stick a red flag by the road. We'll see it and get you the reward," the fat man called out as he started back towards the jank.

"Ya got that old cackdirt?" He pulled up Jackson's head by his hair. "If you see her, stick a flag up your snash and hang it by the road. You listening, cackdirt?" He kicked Jackson in the ribs again and spat on him. "Ratz right you're listening."

Dragonhead got in the jank with the others and they drove across the property. After spinning around several times, tearing up the grounds, they started toward the cottage. The jank drove right up on the porch and took out one of the posts holding up the porch roof. The right side of the porch fell to the ground and they sped off down the road.

Jackson got up slowly, first kneeling on one knee. He put the back of his right hand up to his mouth and after taking it away he looked at it. It was covered in blood. He spat it on the ground and stood up. Grabbing hold of his basket, he started toward the cottage. On his way there, he bent down to pick up his straw hat and placed it back on his head. The remains of the porch roof just hung over the entryway. He pulled it down and then kicked it to the side, clearing a path to go inside. After getting a cloth, he ran it under the water for a while and got it cold. He cupped his hand to catch the cold well water and rinsed his mouth out several times spitting the red liquid back into the sink. He then sat at the table with the cloth on his jaw and mouth.

Holding his jaw with his right hand, he moved it back and forth wondering if it had been broken. He hadn't been sitting long at the table when a shadow loomed in the doorway.

Li'Quari stepped in and took the cloth from him. She walked over to the sink and rinsed it out and then brought it back to him, placing it on the back of his neck. "I'm sorry I caused you trouble."

Jackson looked at her with furrowed eyebrows and shook his head. "It wasn't you that caused the trouble." He winced in pain as he moved his head from side to side trying to work the kinks out of his neck. "You got a place to stay?"

"I'll just keep moving. I can catch some rest along the river. If I could just hit you up for a few supplies...."

"You can stay here if you want. You can have the back room – there's a cot in it with a blanket. I sleep there," Jackson said pointing to a torn couch in the living room, "where I can keep an eye on the door and the street."

"I caused you enough trouble."

"It isn't any trouble. I've been beat up by the Guard before and I'll be beat up by the Guard again. It's how it is when you're alive and in the south. It's the tax paid to breathe."

Li'Quari nodded. "Thanks."

Jackson put the cloth on the table and started to get up. "It's gonna be dark soon. I'm going to get the place closed up for the night. Make yourself at home."

He walked slowly out the front door, somewhat favoring his right leg, and limped along the side of the cottage. After picking out some ripened tomatoes, he grabbed hold of a dead-looking plant and pulled it out of the ground. He then dug around the base of the plant with an old screwdriver. After pulling out six potatoes, he replaced the ground with the dirt. He walked back into the cottage and pulled up a floor board where he kept a dark box. Opening the container, he pulled out eight potatoes and replaced them with the six he had just pulled from the garden. He replaced the top on the box and after lowering it back into the crawl space, put the floorboards back into place.

"Ever have tompato pie?" He asked.

"One of the Watchers used to make it when I was staying with them. I haven't had tompato pie in a really long time. The only thing I remember about the tompato from the fotin Watchers was that it wasn't that good."

He looked at her and shook his head from side to side indicating his disapproval. "Maybe we can refrain from using that kind of language when speaking." After a quick wink of his right eye, he continued. "Anyway, I make some of the best tompato pie you've ever tasted."

He put the potatoes and tomatoes on the table. After lighting an oil lamp, he walked back into the living room. Standing in front of the main window, he reached down and brought up a three-quarter inch piece of plywood with metal on one side. He fit it into place across the window and brought down metal levers that held it into place. Reaching above his head, he pulled down the iron lever to cover the top of the plywood and did the same on the bottom. He then walked to the front door and closed it. Three twelve-inch by fifty-inch by three-quarter-inch heavy boards were placed across the top, bottom, and middle of the door. They secured tightly against the door jamb.

"What about the windows in the back?" Li'Quari asked.

Jackson looked up at her. "There aren't any. This is the only way in or out of here unless you break through the walls. And that would take more than a jank considering they're filled with eight inches of concrete. Yeah, this place might look like an old run-down, rickety house, but it could survive category six hurricane winds."

It appeared to him that Li'Quari looked more relaxed. She probably hadn't felt safe in quite some time trying to survive here in the south with the Guard running around causing people pain.

Jackson grabbed the potatoes and peeled away the skins. Taking out a skillet, he placed it on the stove and then lit a fire in the burner. He slid the skillet onto the burner and began to fry them in oil. He tossed in salt and some spices he retrieved from a special jar behind several books on the shelf. While that was sizzling, he cut up the tomatoes in squared chunks and tossed them into the pan. After it had all seared fairly well, he placed some flattened dough over the top of the skillet, letting it drape over the sides. Then taking a large metal container, he placed it over the skillet and let it sit. Every so often, he would lift the container and brush oil and a burgundy colored liquid over it, and then quickly set the container down again over the skillet.

Soon, Li'Quari and Jackson were at the table digging into a plateful of food.

"You're right. This is the best tompato I've ever had," she said, swiping the last of the steamed bread dough across her dish.

"It's an old family recipe I got from my mother, who got it from her mother."

"Why isn't it hot in this cottage, especially with it being all closed up? I mean, I actually feel cool," she inquired.

"Come with me," Jackson said. He got up from the chair and went to the front wall of the cottage. "Put your hand on the wall."

Li'Quari leaned in and placed her hand on the wall and then pulled it away. "That's cold!"

"There's water running through the walls from the well. It keeps the place cool at night. It makes it a little more bearable to sleep."

"How is it you know so much? I mean, I have never heard of any of these things."

"I was educated in the North. I just happen to keep my southern manners and religion. Though, that doesn't seem to fit into this world any more now, does it?"

"I suppose not. There's not much God left around here. Do you think He left?"

Jackson put his hand up and pointed to her heart. "He's right there. He'll always be right there. So, you best take care of that little one and raise him right."

"You know the Guard is going to catch up with me some time, and when they do, the bump's dead and so am I."

Jackson looked at her face. It was dirty and sunburned. She had scars on her scalp from her hair being pulled out by the root. She wore the look of a girl who had seen far too much pain and misery in too short a period of time. He couldn't help but wish that he had met up with her many years earlier, so he might have saved her from her past. "When I was in DC, I heard rumors about a place; a place in Europe that a person could go and raise a family with no fear. There's no secularism, hatred, or violence."

"Yeah, right. I've heard the rumors too: a hidden golden city of riches with no poverty or classes; just one big, happy family of people living in peace. It sounds like a lot of fo....rubbish to me."

"Rubbish or not, I'm going. There's nothing left here for me and I want to try to find my daughter. She was in Florence when the airports all shut down in '49 and I haven't heard from her since." Jackson paused and looked down at the floor. He mumbled under his breath as if the guard were right outside his door. "I know how to contact the person who can get us there."

Jackson waited for a reply, but she just stared at him without saying a word. At first, she had a look of doubt and pessimism. Jackson thought that she figured he got kicked in the head once too often by the Guard and was now having bouts of dementia. But then her expression softened. Possibly, she saw in his eyes an absolute look of determination and faith in his belief. There seemed to be a glimmer of hope in his character and it was contagious. It had been far too long since anyone had any reason to think there could be something more to life. If something did exist, it was far beyond the reach of the Domestic Southern borders. Something that promising was certainly unobtainable for people like Li'Quari and Jackson. How could they possibly have access to such freedom? But somehow it seemed possible, as if a flame had been ignited inside of them. She bit her lower lip as she seemed to contemplate what to say.

"Anyway, it's late. We better get some downtime. Take the lamp. I have another by the couch," Jackson said as he started toward the living room. He lit the small lamp and began to make up his sleeping area.

Li'Quari started down the hallway and then stopped and turned before entering her bedroom, "Lucks," she called out.

"Lucks to you," he replied.

Reaching behind the couch, he turned off the valve to the water supply that fed the cooling pipes in the walls. He lay back against the couch, raised his arms and tucked them in behind his head, and then closed his eyes. Thinking about Li'Quari, his smile reached his eyes. Warmth overcame him, a feeling he hadn't experienced in a long time. She reminded him of his daughter, of family, and of caring for another person. It had been quite some time since he had anyone close to him that he could look after and communicate with on a regular basis. He turned slightly and winced in pain. His ribs ached and his jaw throbbed from the encounter with the Guard.

~ Paul ~

Jackson was quite the father figure. I never met him along The Way. Our paths had taken different directions before we would have had the chance to meet, but I heard quite a bit about him from Li'Quari. Yes, she really did adore that displaced senator. He was quite different than anyone she had ever encountered. And with her own father, who died when she was still so young – poor kid never could catch a break.

Now, Sevita, on the other hand, did catch that break in which she always longed for during her youth. As I mentioned earlier, Sevita and Domingo own that little shop in Scientia. However, that small and modest canton is a long way from the Pacific District in which she had grown up. I must say that she is much better off now that she has left that place of corruption and decadence. Like me, for some reason unknown to us, we were chosen to participate in an excursion. It is a pilgrimage full of promise, change and hope. Due to our previous situations we more than welcomed this chance to make our lives meaningful.

I see the Doctore is ready to start again now, so listen closely to how this young girl was given a golden opportunity to start again.

Chapter 9

Pacific Decadence

~ Doctore ~

The great American nation had plummeted into corruption, debauchery, immorality, and self-indulgence. The power, lust, and greed inherited by the third and fourth generations had overtaken all of what was left of humanity. The sex and violence that had filled their digital world in the late twentieth century bled into their real world in the twenty-first century. Pornography burned its way through the digital age of the Internet consuming minds to the point that they could no longer feel their heart's rhythm. Even worse still was the blood thirsty violence that had engaged them as children through digital gaming. It was now as much a part of their lives as it was in their virtual life. It was not enough to act upon these impulses in a digital world; they needed to bring the stench of hatred and intolerance into their physical world. The alternate personas lived via fantasy corroded their minds until they could no longer tell the difference between real and virtual existence. Brother fought brother, sister sold out sister, and family was nonexistent. There was no need or purpose for family. There were no mothers or fathers of children, there were only biologicals. Many offspring had no idea who their siblings were and most didn't care if they did. Society took whatever pleased them. If it no longer pleased them it was simply tossed aside. Conscience had long been imprisoned and thrown into a place so filled with darkness, hate, and mistrust that it had forgotten its purpose. They drank until they fell unconscious and drugged themselves to hide from their fear. But at some point, everyone must eventually face their fear or forever be consumed by it. The ancient Creator had built in safety mechanisms to allow every person one last glimpse of their final despair into misery and death in an attempt to get them to turn from their wickedness.

There had been no absence of signs from the celestial bodies whose stardust patterns made portents, which were made known to Man in the hope he would recognize his downward spiral of selfish greed and lust. However, the inebriated fool does not awaken as easily from his drunken sleep as one might wish. And even if upon opening a weary, bloodshot eye to gaze at the starlit heavens, there would be little possibility of recognizing the ancient language of the talking skies. Instead, Man's passion is driven by the allure of his next swallow from the fermented potion of that unscrupulous vine rather than its antidote. The ancients had passed down such a tonic from the year of the One. The handwritten parchment had contained the prescription for life's eternal elixir, which had been purchased with the blood of the One. However, it had come all too easy for the wretched masses who failed to appreciate the great gift they had been given. Therefore, they needed a more obvious sign of the intolerance of their decadence.

The Pacific District had been given such a sign, but they failed to heed its warning. Over the last half century, the once mesmerizing coastal paradise had undergone many earthly changes. With all of the geological field studies and monitoring of the southern California fault lines, and with breath held for every hiccup and tremor over a period of seventy-five years, it was the one place they had ignored that turned out to be the great coastline changer.

A distant cousin to San Andreas, a massive fault underneath Sultan Sea shook the west coast with the intensity of a falling mountain that never seemed to find its resting place. The largest quake on record measuring 10.2 on the Richter scale started a chain reaction of major quakes along all Pacific fault lines. The explosive series of shattering rock and the pulling apart of large sections of earth shook the western ridge violently and without mercy until the whole land mass tore off. From the region of Cabo San Lucas, Mexico all the way north to Santa Barbara, the powerful energy ripped along Coachella Canal; creating a new coastline. The two great cities of corruption and malice, Los Angeles and San Diego, were cast into the Pacific Ocean. Shaken to pieces and then consumed by the sea, the drowned metropolis was soon a distant memory that faded into a fabled story. Eventually, the cities were forgotten altogether as society, with its shortened attention span, moved on in favor of new, fresher players.

Ensanada and La Paz became the new North and South island points of that auspicious peninsula that was cast adrift. The broken beach front floated atop the Pacific just off the western mainland. Hundreds of thousands perished with nature's massive restructuring of the North American continent. However, before tear drops were able to find softened earth in the towering mounds of displaced rubble, the less elite inlanders moved in to stake their claim on the new ocean front property. The rebuilding of California's prime real estate had begun. There are no words dismal enough to describe mankind's pitiful display of selfishness and opportunistic behavior. People, who were anxious to be new landowners, quickly charted a course to stake their claim to the riches founded on their brothers' shallow grave. It is in the times of humanity's greatest pilfering and lust that their character shows just how eager and willing they are to plunge from grace. It is also in these times that the Creator becomes the most intolerant of their foolish insolence.

Just north of the lost California coastline was the small town of San Luis Obispo or as the locals referred to it, SLO. Once founded as a Spanish

Mission for the Catholic Bishop Saint Louis, this small community thrived under the religious foundation that had been the core of its stability. However, it migrated away from its roots and became secularized by the modern regime. The old Spanish Mission that had been erected in seventeen-hundred seventy-two, and stood for over two hundred fifty years, was demolished. In its place was built a digital distribution server farm for the digifeed gaming and porn system that fed depravity into communities across the district by the byteful. The monstrous black widow spun its vile, haphazard, glass-fibered web across the nation and the world. There seemed to be no lighted corner on earth in which to escape its dark and blood thirsty entanglement. Once captured by the digital network, it was only a matter of time before the Internet's prey was devoured. Drained of their lifeblood, their carcasses were left hanging until the winter winds shifted and gusts carried off their bones dust-particle by dust-particle. There have only been a counted few who have been able to escape its deadly lair.

Sevita Citta was just seventeen when her biologicals cashed her out, along with her older brother, Danni Ratzlen. Danni had a different biological father than Sevita. However, not long after Danni was born, Ratzlen had left their mother, Charletri, for a cosmetic surgeon who lived in the newly developed city of Angeles Nuevos. Sevita's biological father, Jason Citta, had left all of them to partner with his Southern California college buddy, Kenn Drand. Meanwhile, Charletri partnered with a newly introduced porn digiographer, Ralpho. Ralpho had made an indeterminate amount of riches in the digi-porn industry and had settled in the more affluent and temperate climate of San Francisco. After Charletri moved in with him, he had given her a cash incentive to pay off the biologicals and have nothing further to do with them. It was a golden opportunity for her to release herself of the responsibility of children and she didn't hesitate to take it. She split the funds between them, keeping a little bit for herself to use as a safety net tucked away in case things didn't work out. She left for the Gold Coast region in San Francisco without taking any of her once coveted belongings with her, thinking she'd be shopping for better things once in San Francisco. After all, she was moving up in society and better clothing would need to be purchased. Besides, leaving her older things behind for Sevita eased her conscience for skimming money off the top of their cash buy out.

Sevita and Danni stayed in SLO in the two bedroom townhouse left to them by their mother. The townhouse was paid for and they only had to pay the taxes and utilities on it. However, Danni frequently came up short on his share of the responsibilities and Sevita often had to cover for him. Inheriting her beauty from her mother, she often worked as a freelance model for various clothing companies. Her light brown tan and sun bleached long hair made her the perfect stereotypical California beach girl. Danni was a digital musician trying to break his way into a Gri'mθtal band and found

87

himself out of work more often than not. When he was lucky enough to land a paying gig, he usually spent the remuneration on after-concert parties where the drugs, alcohol, sex, and gambling ran for days.

It was two thirty in the afternoon on Thursday when Sevita had finished a modeling shoot at Pismo Beach and pulled her solar-powered bi-craft onto the porch. The bi-craft was an interesting vehicle in that it used an electro-mechanical field to repel against the Earth's natural gravitational forces, making the craft hover just a few inches above the ground. With a sophisticated computer controlled air-intake propulsion system, it was able to maneuver extremely well.

Taking off her sunshades, she walked up to the front door and spoke into the recognition system. "Front Entry, Sevita." The door popped open and she went inside. Typical of her brother who slept the daylight hours away, she came home to a dark house. "Shades" she called out. The blinds mechanically rolled themselves up to the top of the window and let light spill into the darkened room. She let out a long sigh as the living area was illuminated and the filth reflected back the sunlight. There were empty and half-filled bottles of beer and alcohol on the tables, along with various leftover, half-eaten foods scattered about the room. She made a quick and determined path to the back of the house and stepped into Danni's room.

"Danni!" she yelled out. "Shades!"

There was a slight movement in the bed as Danni; who, half naked, had been sprawled out across the width of the bed, showed signs that he was indeed still alive. There wasn't any bedding on or near the bed, as it was bunched up and sitting in a corner, never laundered from the weeks before. Empty bottles of beer littered the tops of whatever furniture was standing upright. There were shoes and articles of clothing scattered everywhere. Some were men's fashions and some were women's fashions from various encounters that had just left without taking all of their testaments to their foray with them. The room had a vile stench that was a combination of a brewery and a toilet. Pills and capsules, little bags of white power, and auto-injectors were strewn about the room. It was the typical twenty-first century sty indicative of a generation who'd rather live like animals than have to spend energy cleaning up after themselves. They would lose track of time in their digital gaming, or digi-sex, or digi-kill raiding. Playing these violent and tasteless so-called entertainment modules would distract them for hours and even days while it stole their youth and life from them, unchecked and unnoticed. They would forget to eat, sleep, or be so involved in their digital media and stimulation that they'd wet themselves.

"Danni, get up! It's the end of the month. Do you have it?"

"Come on Sevita, let me sleep. It's early."

"Do you have the money or don't you? I need to pay the bills or they'll sell us off."

"Give me another hour, sis."

Sevita, frustrated beyond comprehension, walked up to his digi-feed and turned on the Western music feed, then turned up the volume all the way and left the room.

"Hey, turn that off!" screamed out Danni as he rolled off the bed and hit the floor. His head pounded from the night before and the bright streaming rays of light from the window along with the pulsating loud music pushed through the open sockets of his head like speeding locomotives driving through a tunnel too small to accommodate its girth. Swimming across the floor through the deluge of the contents of his room, his hands searched for the control to the digi-feed. Blinded by daylight, he scampered about like a rat in search of haven from his predator.

"Finally," he called out with relief as he located the remote control underneath a turned-over plate near his shoes. He switched off the painful noise and was able to pull himself onto a chair. His color was ghostly. Years of ignoring the sun had turned his skin the color of grayish yellow. His red, bloodshot eyes were sunken ships torpedoed by drug- and alcohol-filled nights, followed by lack of sleep and irregular meals. The GITs called them the "gaming dead." Most of them didn't live past thirty, often too intoxicated or in a coma to even get to the medi-dock. They died without knowing they were ever alive. The addiction to their virtual lives stole away their physical lives and the most saddened, tragic part of the whole thing was that they didn't even realize it was happening.

Sevita went into her room and slammed the door. After grabbing her dark blue shorts and light yellow top, she stripped off her clothes and put them into a basket she kept in the closet. Once in the shower, she started to relax as the sand and remnants of the beach from the morning photo shoot washed away. It seemed she spent more time without clothes than with clothes these days. All the modeling jobs seemed to be done naked no matter what product they were trying to sell. It was a paycheck though, and it kept the lights on in the townhouse, which was more than she could say for that lazy brother of hers. She was rinsing the shampoo out of her hair when the door opened and Danni stepped inside.

"Look, Sevita. I have a gig tonight. I'll have the cash for you then."

"No you won't. You'll party for two or three days and blow it all on drugs and tartwods," she called out from the shower.

"Why don't you come and see me jam? I can give you the funds right afterwards."

Sevita turned off the water and slid open the door. Danni handed her the bath towel, which she opened up and while bending at the waist dried her hair. With all of the images of her body posted throughout digi-feed land, there was really no point any longer in being modest. Plus, she found it just a little pretentious to act like there was a shred of anything left of her that hasn't already been packaged, marketed, and exploited.

"It's at Jazin's place in the Grig," Danni encouraged.

"I'll stay for the concert and take your money before it disappears into the sludge, but I'm not staying for any of the disgusting events afterwards. You shouldn't stay either. One of these times you're not going to come back from those drug-induced comas you put yourself into. I'm not kidding, Danni. Those people…the way they mutilate themselves and others for kicks—it's not right."

"Thanks for caring, sis. Is there anything for breakfast?" he called back over his shoulder as he left the bathroom.

"Clean up that living area! You're such a gutterscum!" she called after him.

"Look at this place. I need to get a better class of grinders to hang out with," Danni mumbled while pushing his way through to the kitchen. "They even trashed the kitchen," he remarked while kicking debris away from the refrigerator door. Taking a container of Joust from the refrigerator, he opened it and guzzled down nearly a quarter of the bottle. He dropped the cap on the floor, but figured he'd get it later. He placed the bottle back on the shelf, and after kicking the debris out of the way, he closed the door. He took a large garbage bag from the cabinet and shook it open, then began picking up the empty bottles and containers from the kitchen before moving on to the living area floor. There, he emptied ashtrays and added a variety of other party materials to the trash bag, including articles of clothing, half-smoked blunts, auto-injectors, pills, and blowstraws that were lying across the coffee table. He tied up the bag and flung it out the door, where it crashed into the five other bags starting to pile up against the side of the house.

Later that evening, Danni popped his head into Sevita's room. She had been lying on the bed reading with her back against the wall. She closed the book and put it down at her side and looked up at Danni.

"I'm taking off. What time are you coming?"

"How many songs are in your set?"

"Just six and one solo. People want to get to the partying."

"I'll come around nine-thirty. You should be finishing up your last couple of songs by then."

"Yeah, right. Okay. Hey, what's ya reading?"

"Just a book I found in some of Dad's old things."

"What's it called?"

"Lord of the Rings."

"What's a lord?"

"I think it is some kind of commander or leader."

"Huh, sounds really boring," Danni laughed. "Commander of a ring, really? I command this ring to be a circle!" he mocked.

Sevita glared at him.

"Afters," he called, and putting up his hand, left the room. As he headed out the front door, he picked up his g-tube, a tubular shaped electronic device that was used to simulate guitar and rhythm sounds. It mostly distorted the samples into an array of keys and blends that the musician would play by running his hands up and down the small bumps on the tubular surface. The tube was in two parts, one fitting into the other and under resistive pressure. By pushing or pulling the individual parts against one another, it would stretch or push that amount of distortion into the device creating the unique sound. It was somewhat comparable to the pressure on violin strings with a bow for pitch.

Sevita was a few hours behind her brother, arriving outside Jazin's large complex where people were scattered about intoxicated or drugged. Sevita paused to look at the chaotic comedy. People were laughing, crying, screaming, and yelling loudly at one another. It was often difficult to tell if they were suffering pain or pleasure. There were men with men, men with women, women with women, and at times, it was hard to tell what was what in the mix of flapping limbs in the numerous piles that spawned on the outer landscape. She left her bi-craft hovering just outside near a group of palm trees and away from the animation. She wanted to be able to get out quickly. She didn't trust any of the people who went to these atrocities and thought most of them to be simply disgusting. She had tried to get her brother out of this abusive environment, but these people had their hooks into him fairly deep.

The rotten stench of combined vomit, alcohol, smoke, and urine rushed past her as she tucked her head down and made way for the area where the band was loudly playing distorted chords. The only reason for her presence there was Danni's money. They had to make their payments. She hadn't worked this month as much as she normally would, so she had been short with their tax payment. One miss on that payment and the Fed would sell off their home, pushing them out into the terror of places just like this one: home to the desolate and hopeless who had nowhere else to go.

Walking toward the side of the stage, she saw Danni wildly handling the g-tube, producing the distorted sounds of Gri'm∂tal. He swung his head violently back and forth and marched to the beat of the entrancing music. Fifteen minutes later, the band took a break. Danni put his g-tube in the stand and grabbed two bottles of Grimenor from the server. He cracked the first one open and tilted back his head and guzzled the alcoholic beverage down without pausing to breathe. Throwing the empty bottle to the side, he then cracked open the second bottle and took a swig. After wiping his mouth with his sleeve, he negotiated the few stage stairs with the grace of a bull on stilts. Sevita went to meet him.

"Danni," she called out.

"Seevit," he belched and then finished, "ta. Yor not supposed meeting to me until—" belch, "after time," he stammered.

Sevita, looking into his eyes, saw they were dilated and bloodshot. He had already done far too many drugs and consumed too much alcohol to be remotely his normal self. "Do you have the money?" she asked.

"Why don't you drink some more and wait for me. I'm down getting with Jazin. He's so fine. He wants meet to with us," Danni said and took another drink.

"No, Danni. Where's the money?"

"Where da money? Where da money? All you money about think is! Jazin said he'd down wit me if you come, too. I want him; yor coming. He sayings it has both to be us, both us. Everwons doin' it!" He said to her. His eyes were like black lifeless coals. The pupils completely covered the iris with the only color coming from the dark red veins standing out in the sclera, pulsating like throbbing neon lights on a cheap motel.

"You're sick. You're casked on drugs, and it's disgusting. I'm gone," Sevita said and turned away.

Danni lunged forward and grabbed her arm. "I said yor comin." He began to drag her back toward the stage. Sevita tried to pull away from his grip, but she hadn't the strength. His strong fingers dug deep into her forearm cutting off the circulation and causing her great discomfort.

"Danni, no! Please, let me go!"

Sevita screamed in terror, but he paid no attention to her and continued to drag her toward the back of the stage. She grabbed at the railing to the stairs and hung on to it. Danni stumbled and the momentum turned him around facing her, but he clutched tight her arm and kept from falling.

"Danni, please," she cried.

He went to pry her fingers from the stage railing when she lifted up her knee with all her might and jammed it between his legs. He fell at her feet in pain. She quickly turned away and hurried toward the exit. Looking at the ground moving faster and faster beneath her feet, she made her way through the court yard.

She could hear Danni yelling from inside above the din calling her foul names. Out of the corner of her eye she saw Jazin standing on the balcony with women and men hanging all around him, touching him and rubbing up against him. As he saw her making her way out, he pushed them aside and yelled out to stop her from leaving. Sevita broke into a run, exited the gates, and rushed into the street. She jumped onto her bi-craft and waved her hand across the control panel in all one motion. It started up and she hit the throttle all the way forward as she sped off into the night. Two large men who had followed her out tried to grab the end of the craft, but missed it. Sevita sped around the corner and vanished out of sight.

"Find me that pfotten, idiotic g-tubist! He'll pay for ruining my evening. Oh yes, he will pay." Jazin grabbed one of the men who was rubbing his backside and kissed him hard on the mouth. He then grabbed him by the groin with his left hand, grabbed his neck with his right hand, and lifting him up above his head, tossed him over the balcony. He fell helplessly and silently. He didn't flail his arms or legs, but simply plummeted through the air, never crying out a sound. After hitting the concrete courtyard, blood spilled out from his head and flowed in the direction of the hideous, iron gothic fountain that stood in the middle of the courtyard. The fountain did not have water flowing from its mouth, but a red liquid that people had believed was some type of powerful elixir. The lifeless body lay there as the fountain seemed to drain and direct his blood into its reservoir.

"Another round of drinks for my loyal subjects!" Jazin called out with his arms raised in the air. The crowds cheered him on and congratulated him on his awesome strength and generosity.

Sevita parked her bi-craft in the back of their townhouse and rushed up the stairs, "Back entry, Sevita," she called. She was out of breath as she waved her shaking hand across the entry pad. The back kitchen door opened. She flew inside and straight back to her room where she grabbed her modeling bag and emptied its contents out on the bed. She threw a bunch of clothes, account books, jewelry, and her father's books she had been reading into the bag and headed to the kitchen where she added a few snacks from the cupboards. She zipped it up, took one last look around for anything she might have forgotten, and then left the house.

Back on her bi-craft, her heart didn't stop racing until she was miles away from home. She headed toward her friend Vivian's apartment. If she had trusted anyone in this world it was Vivian. She was different than most Sevita had met–filled with inner peace and a humbled personality.

Sevita left her bi-craft in a garage a few blocks away and walked to her friend's building. She was so angry with Danni for setting her up like that she could hardly contain herself. "Everyone's doing it?" she repeated his rationale. The horror of it made her skin crawl. She was sure it was all the drugs and alcohol talking, but she had warned him to stay away from that environment. He needed to be responsible for his decisions.

Checking over her shoulder, she jogged quickly across the street and frantically tried to reach Vivian. "Sevita for Vivian Gonxha," she spoke into the auto-door.

"One moment, please."

Sevita nervously awaited the system to respond and checked frequently up and down the street for any signs that she had been spotted or that Jazin's thugs had followed her. The steady hum of the light outside the building was growing louder and brighter, calling attention to her being there. At first, it seemed like a distant low-pitched methodical sound, but now it seemed to race with her heart and echo in the streets calling attention to every fiber of her being. The wind picked up and blew a breath of salty air across the village, pushing garbage and an empty can down the street. The sound of the can crashed against the curb over and over until it came to rest on the sewage grate, just fifty yards away. The sign outside the apartment complex moved back and forth in the wind making a horrendously loud creaking sound. "Oh please, come on, Vivian!" Sevita whispered under her breath.

"Welcome Sevita. Vivian can see you now."

The door opened and Sevita quickly made her way inside with a sigh of relief. She took the elevator up to Vivian's apartment on the seventh floor where the door was opened and Vivian stood in the hallway waiting for her. Vivian had beautiful Asian-arched, blue eyes with high eyebrows. It was the first thing noticed when introduced to her. Long dark brown hair hung shaggily around her diamond shaped face, which was very light in color. However, she had a Spanish-like quality to her features that further accented her unique beauty.

Sevita ran up to her and hugged her tight.

"Sevita! What's the matter? What's happened? Come inside, darly."

After Sevita gave Vivian all of the dreaded details of the evening, she sat back against the lounge, and stared at Vivian with a hopeless gaze. "I was so scared. What am I going to do? I can't go home. I can't go to my biologics. I have nowhere to go."

"You can stay here," Vivian replied.

"No, I have to get out of this city. Jazin and Danni will be after me, and they won't stop. You should have seen Danni's eyes. It wasn't him, Vivian. It wasn't him." Tears ran down her cheeks.

They sat silent for several minutes contemplating what options she might have.

"You should talk with this woman I heard about. She has a way to get people out of hurtful or dangerous situations. I mean, I wasn't really paying attention when I heard Carl talking about it at the shoot, but I remember he said she had some place down by the Break, a soup shack for the people down there. Her name is...oh, what was it? It's an older name. Maria! Yes, that's it. Her name is Maria."

"Can I stay here tonight? I'll go and see her tomorrow. Maybe she can help me."

"Of course. Stay as long as you like."

"Thank you, Vivian. I wouldn't know what to do without you."

Chapter 10

Northern District

~ Paul ~

Sevita's troubles were many and there is no denying her brother is so far in the Shekel's lair that his light of hope was beyond the reach of any mere mortal. However, there was a time when the same could have been said of me. If it wasn't for the love and determination of the One King, I'd have been lost among the countless victims of the Shekel. Why one person is chosen over another I do not know and would not even want to speculate. However, I'm digressing into my own selfishness when it is time to hear of Sevita's future husband Domingo and how his journey had started. Papa has the most astonishing way of telling a story.

~ Doctore ~

The once cold harsh winters of the North, where temperatures had plunged into double digits far below the zero mark, were now giving way to a milder climate. The burning of Earth's natural resources had changed the atmosphere, producing an ever growing effect that steadily warmed the planet. While this allowed the North to produce more vegetables and beef for the masses, it further tipped the scales of the natural balance in which all things had been kept. Fresh water was no longer in abundance and the natural cooling of the planet from the snow and ice was being slowly eliminated by the overindulgence of the world's resources. Oceans were rising, storms producing tornadic activity were becoming more frequent and intensifying, earthquakes were increasing in number and intensity as they shook cities violently, and hurricanes were growing in number and magnitude. However, in spite of all this, the Northern country was still the most beautiful landscape on the continent. It was rich in fertile soil, rolling green hills, and waterways (which were still not affected by the impurities of the large business farms).

This was especially true in the Minnesota territory of the Northern District. There were still many lakes in this area, over seven thousand. Many of the smaller lakes were starting to or had already dried up, but there were still abundant supplies of water in the area due to the glacial activity of the past. Outside the metropolis of Fergus Falls, there was a small rural town called Aurdal, which had a very small lake appropriately called Little Lake. One could almost wonder how it could be called a lake at all. Upon looking at the definition of a lake, it says: a body of water of considerable size surrounded by land. Apparently, "considerable size" is somewhat subjective on these matters. However, a lake it is called, so a lake it shall remain. On the western side of Little Lake is a small farm that grew fruit trees. These luscious and abundant apple trees, grown from enriched soil, stretched toward the sky in their usual uneven form. Dom Perez, a third generation farmer, had been caring for this orchard near Little Lake for more than fifty-five years. It is and has been, for quite some time, his intention to leave the farm to his only grandson, Domingo.

Dom was sixty-eight years old. His once black hair was now completely white and had started thinning near his forehead. He kept it trimmed short and close, which was partly the reason the sun had browned and leathered his skin long ago while he tended to the apple trees in the orchard. All in all, he had been fairly healthy and remained strong during his later years. This served him well as he was able to keep up with his young grandson and mentor him as a father. Both of Domingo's parents had been killed when fighting had broken out in Washington DC during the demonstrations of '38. There were many good people who fell that day for no other reason than they had been in the wrong place at the wrong time. Dom was fifty-four years old when he had to tell his grandson that his parents were not coming back for him.

Has it been almost fifteen years already? Dom thought to himself. Nevertheless, on this day, this cold February day in the year 2054 AD, Dom was not on his tree farm waiting for the signs of spring so that he could tend to his apple trees, but instead was sitting in a small room waiting for news he had already deduced.

The Personal Care Clinic room was just eight feet wide by twelve feet long; however, Dom seemed to have managed to pace off a mile or two in the time it took the doctor to come to the large digital video screen. Back and forth he went, his gaze concentrating on the faded gray tile squares beneath his feet, the only thing of interest in the plain room—although, there was the Medical Diagnostic Machine (MDM) in the far corner. The MDM was a bright white, seven-foot by three-foot by three-inch platform that stuck out from the wall as either an angel of mercy or the shadow of death. Regardless of the outcome, the machine was ninety-nine percent accurate in the diagnosis of the patient. The monitor flickered and an image began to form.

"Mr. Perez, I'm Doctor Gar Ricord."

Dom stopped pacing and stood in front of the digital monitor waiting for his results.

"Yes?"

"The cancer that had originated in your small intestine has now spread to multiple areas including your liver, pancreas, large intestine, and stomach. It has metastasized in the lungs and bones. You have approximately four to six months to live."

Dom lowered his eyes and reached back to find the chair so he could sit down. Thoughts were swirling inside of his head. He had thought that he would have more time to further teach his grandson about the orchard. It's always that way, though. People believe that they will always have enough time. A person makes a plan for their life and assumes, or more accurately and quite frankly, demands from life that they are given the time to carry it out. More often than not however, it doesn't work out that way. Life has its own plan and doesn't give anyone the opportunity to approve it or make adjustments. After gathering his thoughts and realizing his situation, he looked back to Dr. Ricord.

"Do you have family with you, Mr. Perez?"

"My grandson, Domingo. He lives with me on our farm."

"Mr. Perez, with this type of aggressive cancer you will continually worsen. Your internal organs and bones are being eaten away by cancer. The pain is going to be unbearable and you will become bedridden. I would suggest to you to take advantage of the Dying with Dignity Act. It's a very humane way to die with comfort and dignity. You simply go to their office where you are made comfortable, say your last goodbyes to your family and friends, and then receive an injection that doesn't cause any pain. You simply go to sleep and pass on. There is no suffering, there are very few expenses, and your family doesn't have to watch you suffer and dwindle away while feeling powerless to help or drain your life savings in medical costs."

Dom just stared at the doctor with a blankness and disbelief in what he was hearing.

"Mr. Perez, you would leave with dignity and, most importantly, you would not be a burden to your grandson."

Dom stood up and glared at the doctor.

"Burden? I'm a burden now, am I? Was I a burden to my grandson when I took him in and raised him when his parents died in the Demonstrations? Was I a burden to him when I sat with him at night with a cold cloth on his forehead, praying for his fever to go down? Was I a burden when I made him breakfast, lunch, and dinner his entire young life? Was I a burden when I taught him my livelihood and all the wisdom and knowledge of tree farming?"

"Mr. Perez, listen to me," the doctor interrupted.

"No, Doctor Ricord. You listen to me. There is no dying with dignity in this society's rendition of life and death. It is the quick and easy way out for cowards. The only dignity that there is in death is the same as it is in life. You work hard and struggle through adversity, you live an honorable life, you answer to God, and you love your family and friends. And when you do this, and only when you do this, can you say you have truly lived and died

97

with dignity. I am not a coward, sir. I will meet death the same as I met life; with honor, dignity, and courage. This is how I will teach my grandson his last lesson."

"Okay, Mr. Perez," the doctor nodded. "The pain will become excruciating. Let me at least prescribe for you some pain killers that you can use if you need them. You're the last of the great men, Mr. Perez. Good luck."

Dom reached for his wool overcoat and after buttoning it, put on his scarf and hat. Grabbing hold of the handle, he pushed the door open and received a blast of cold air as he stepped out into the Minnesota February cold. He paused for a moment, looking down the sidewalk to the left. In room after room, people walked in and out with either a smile of relief or a look of despair. There was nothing personal, intimate, or caring about the Personal Care Clinic; rooms were stacked eight high, without a single medical person on the premises. Everything was done remotely. Dom wondered how things had gotten so detached. How did humanity become so afraid of personal contact? A doctor used to be able to put their hand on your shoulder when delivering such terrible news. Sometimes, they even used to give a person a hug and a shoulder to cry on. Not anymore.

He stepped off the sidewalk and walked to where his grandson had been waiting for him in their Farmvee.

"Hi Grandpa. How'd everything go?"

"There were no surprises, Domingo. I'm an old man and this aged apple has seen just about everything it's going to see."

"Ah, you'll live to be a hundred, Grandpa," the young lad replied.

"Let's go home. Drive carefully; the winds have been blowing snow across the roads and it's bound to be slick."

Domingo put the vehicle in reverse, backed out of the space, and started off for their farm.

"Hey, look at that Grandpa. The moon is still out in the sky. I always found it strange seeing the moon in the daytime."

"Did I ever tell you the story about the moon?" Dom asked.

"No, I don't think so. What story?"

"Back when God first created the Heavens and the world, the moon was once part of the Earth. It made up a very large section of territory and was called the Garden of Eden. When Adam and Eve disobeyed the Lord by eating from the Tree of Knowledge, he tossed them out of Paradise to the other side of the globe. And then he threw a rock so hard at the Garden that it broke off from Earth and flew into space. There, it was trapped in Earth's gravity. All the vegetation died and the water dried up. It became a wasteland. Meteor after meteor crashed into it with the fury of God's anger. In the Book of Revelations, it is said that on Judgment Day the Mother of God will stand on the moon, crushing the head of the snake, the same snake that was in the Garden of Eden and tempted Eve with the fruit of the Tree of Knowledge."

"That's some story Grandpa. Where did you hear it?"

Dom's expression changed to one of a pleasing nature as he recalled the story. "My grandmother told it to me when I was a young boy. It's funny how you just think of things out of the blue."

Domingo was nineteen years old, and with the help of his grandfather, he was becoming quite the impressive young man. He worked hard with his grandfather on the apple farm while going to school and maintaining good grades. Working with his hands and being close to nature was exactly the type of vocation he enjoyed and had hoped to do for the rest of his life. He had brought the concept of hydroponics into his grandfather's business by producing a miniature hydro-farm as a school project. Dom had promised him that he would help him build an even larger farm in one of the old, rundown greenhouses that were no longer being used. They had planned to start the project that summer. Domingo was looking forward to working alongside his grandfather and blending the more modern technology with his grandfather's old-fashioned know-how.

Dom waited almost three months before telling his grandson about the visit at the clinic. The cancer was definitely spreading very quickly now, and he was feeling those effects. He was tired and in pain. All that had been left of the Perez family was now sitting on the front porch, drinking iced apple-tea. Dom couldn't recall a better day: the clear blue sky, the setting sun, and a phenomenal warm breeze coming from the direction of Little Lake. The robins and finches were already leaving their nests and started to fly from branch to branch. With a white wicker table between them, Dom reached over and set his glass on top of it, then began life's final lesson for his grandson.

After talking with Domingo for quite some time, he felt relieved. Finally, he revealed his situation. He had never lied or kept anything from Domingo and it had felt wrong to do so for these past few months.

"Is there anything I can do for you, Grandpa? Are you in a lot of pain?" he asked.

"I won't deny that this is some of the worst pain I have ever felt. There will be plenty for you to do for me later as I worsen. But for right now, I want to give you something." Dom reached into the inside pocket of his vest and took out a small leather pouch with a small stem protruding from it. On the single branch was a single green leaf. Dom stared at the worn, tan pouch for several moments, rubbing his thumb over the embossed image on the outside of the leather case, and then handed it to his grandson.

"What's this?" asked Domingo, reaching for it from across the table.

"This is the newest scion from the apple tree that I have been using. It dates back to the original tree I planted here so many years ago. I grafted it with the local rootstock. If you can get this scion to grow in your hydro-farm, you will have apple yields greater than anything you have ever seen. I thought you might be able to try your hand at growing it using your hydroponics technique. I believe you can accomplish great things. You have the Perez thumb, my boy."

Domingo looked at the outside of the pouch where there was an engraved image of an apple seed and the initials "D.P." The leather case was soft to the touch and the single leaf rising from the stem was bright green. It was so full of life and yet very fragile, like a newborn infant.

"Thank you, Grandpa." With tears in his eyes, he got up from the chair and hugged Dom tightly.

Dom embraced him for some time; he didn't want to let go. "You will be fine, Domingo. Remember our talks and what you have learned here. Remember where you came from and who you are; don't ever let anyone take that away from you."

The noble apple farmer passed away the following month, near mid-June. He went peacefully in the Eastern morning light, his favorite time of day; how Dom loved to watch a good morning-red sunrise. Domingo had been at his side, holding his hand, and telling him of his plans for the hydro-farm. Afterwards, Domingo took Dom's ashes to Little Lake where there was a small peninsula to the north. He planted them next to a large willow tree that swayed in an easterly breeze that came from out across the waters. It was the perfect peaceful resting place for his grandfather, where he could watch the beautiful sunrises. After saying goodbye, Domingo walked slowly back to the farm feeling lonely and grief-stricken. He had lost his parents at a young age and now his grandfather. Without siblings, cousins, or really any family to speak of whatsoever, he wondered how he was to carry on and what was to become of him.

Just a few weeks after the passing of his grandfather, Domingo received a notice from the bank. Apparently, there had been a problem with the transferring of the deed for the farm and land. What he had thought was just a formality of transferring the title from his grandfather's name to his own name turned out to be one of the worst days he could ever have imagined.

"But my grandfather wanted me to have the farm. It was his farm! How can you just take it?" he cried out.

"You must understand that we don't want to take your farm from you, but the law requires that in order for a deed to transfer ownership, you must be at least twenty-one years old. A minor cannot own property."

"I'll be twenty-one in eighteen months. Can't you just wait until then?" Domingo pleaded.

"I'm sorry, Domingo. The law is very precise in these matters. The property has been relinquished to the state and sold to the Northern Plains

Hydroponics Company. The Chairman of the company said you may stay on the farm and work the orchard for minimum wages if you like. However, the farmhouse is going to be torn down to make room for more hydro facilities."

"You're going to tear down the house? My grandfather built that house from the ground up!"

"Domingo, the Chairman has offered you a pretty good deal. You can rent a small apartment in town," the bank manager replied. "You just need to sign this release if you want to take the position of employment with Northern Plains Hydroponics. It says you don't have any further rights to the farm, the land, or any of the existing structures."

Domingo pushed the paper aside and hurriedly left the bank. Once outside, he began to run. With the wind streaming by him, he ran past the bank, past the hardware store, and past the general grocer. He kept on running right through the town and straight out to Sophus Anderson Road, where he continued to sprint towards his grandfather's farm. Turning left onto the long gravel road that led home, he slowed down to a walk and tried to catch his breath. Continuing on past the house, he walked straight back to the orchard where he had always felt safe among the apple trees and where there was peacefulness in the silence of nature. Thoughts and images were swirling through his head. Struggling to contain them was of no use. He began to feel anxious. His heart pounded inside his chest and his stomach wrenched as if it were in a tightly bound knot.

"I'm sorry Grandpa. I can't keep the farm," he said rubbing the engraved apple seed of the leather casing Dom had given him. "Oh, God, what am I going to do?" he cried out at the sky.

"You shall go to the church of Our Lady of the Lake," a voice said.

Domingo quickly spun around and saw the most beautiful lady standing in the orchard. She was wearing a long flowing white garment with a blue colored overlay that draped over her head and continued towards the ground. There were no shoes on her feet. Instead she seemed to be standing on a bed of flower petals.

"Who are you?" he asked.

"Maria," she replied.

"Why should I go to the church? How's that going to help me?"

"There is a hidden passage underneath the church in Battle Lake that leads to a Golden City quite some distance from here. This is where you must go. Take nothing with you but the seedling that your grandfather has given you."

"Did you know my grandfather? How do you know about the seedling? Wait, what about supplies? You said it was a long journey to this city."

"I know your grandfather," she said. "Everything you require will be provided for you once you reach the church and The Way. Do not fear the unknown. Once you get to Our Lady of the Lake, look for the staff and shield of the Archangel Raphael. It will lead you to the Golden City where everything is as it should be and you will plant your grandfather's seedling. It will flourish there in the richness of the city's tenderness and beauty."

Domingo felt this woman's warmth and sincerity, and without any reservation whatsoever, trusted in her words. "What about my farm? It was my grandfather's home. He gave it to me to tend to and look after."

"You cannot change what has already been set into motion. Here, the corruption of men's hearts will turn the soil bitter. The fruit moth and apple maggot will run rampant through this orchard and no fruit will escape unscathed. The lake will become like venom and will poison this land. This is the reason your grandfather gave you the seedling, to carry on your way of life."

He looked at all the fruit-bearing apple trees and the rich earth beneath his feet. This land, this beautiful sanctuary, was always cared for by his family and it had rewarded them for doing so with a livelihood that lasted generations. He could never see it owned by anyone else or degraded in a fashion that wasn't how his grandfather had taught. The Perez family had always respected nature's ways and adhered to her law.

"I'll go and look for your Golden City. I couldn't stomach staying here and watching all that my grandfather built turn into an infested, thistle-laden piece of land."

"Leave at once, Domingo. They already have plans to take this land, by force if needed. They have wanted it for some time. Their hearts have rotted and are hardened with greed. Take the seedling and travel to Our Lady of the Lake."

Chapter 11

Hidden Paths of Legend

~ Paul ~

My duties as the Doctore's assistant are to care for his physical needs and help him stay healthy and well. With Papa, this can often be quite the challenge, as he is a stubborn man who often does not listen to the sound advice of his servant. It is in these circumstances that I have to be more forceful in my approach and in doing so it often means that I need to also become an entertainer of sorts. It's a complicated business being a Doctore's assistant. I love the job and I'm not complaining; I'm just trying to give a little insight into the more difficult assignments of the position.

Nearby, children sit cross-legged at the curb looking out across the square. Two of the boys I recognize, Razzi and Carton, picked up small pieces of rounded rock and rolled them back and forth. They've been playing at it for some time throughout the sermon, though I feel sure they were still soaking up Papa's words into their being. Twice, when their giggling and laughing became too loud, mothers cast them a kind smile and a slight nudge, but no one seemed to mind; they are good boys.

Women wearing light cotton dresses stood with their babies safely tucked in against their bodies, swaying slowly they move to the rhythm of the words. Every so often, they lift the cloth that had kept the sun off of their babies' precious faces and ensure the children were breathing easily.

Not far away, some men were leaning against a store wall while others stretch out on a piece of cardboard with their arms above their heads and their hands locked underneath. With their eyes closed, they wait for the next words to come from their teacher. Normally, they would be working a field, on a construction site, or bartering for services along the various shops and offices. But today is too hot for work, and besides, it isn't every day that Papa comes to the city to teach.

Turning my gaze back to the old gent, I see on his face a look of parchedness. His lips are dry and cracked while his voice is raspy and equally dry from blowing street dust. Once he immerses himself into the depths of the story, he forgets about food, water, and rest (often to his own peril). This is my cue to get the attentive crowd out of their captivated state. I will attempt to get the blood to flow into their legs again while at the same time, give the teacher a bit of rest and nourishment.

"Papa," I whisper to him as I place my hand on his shoulder. "I think the people could use a morning stretch to lift their souls."

"Ah, my ever-watchful guardian – you are a good man." He takes my hand in both of his and gently shakes it. This is an opportunity for me to monitor his temperature and pulse.

"Papa, here, take this pear – and here is some bread to eat. Please, nourish yourself while I get the people's blood flowing again."

"Grazie, Paolo, mia guardia. Grazie."

"Prego, Papa." I turn back to the shop owner to ask him how much it would cost for a whole bushel of apples.

"A whole bushel?" the owner asks with surprise. He lifts his hand to the back of his head and gives it some thought. "Uh, for the Doctore…you can have it for twelve rinos."

"Twelve rinos? The sign says four for three rinos."

"Yes, but it's the Doctore. Go ahead, take it. I have more." The merchant smiles broadly.

Laying my hand on his shoulder, I thank him and hand over the coins. After lifting the bushel, I move out in front of the resting teacher where he says a prayer over the basket. Upon completion of the blessing, I begin my part of the lecture; or perhaps more appropriately termed: "the diversion."

"Brothers! Sisters! Our good Doctore has given us remarkable insight into the past. Wouldn't you agree?"

The crowd cheers while waving their hands. Some of the people held pieces of cloth which they flap wildly in the air.

"We've been sitting for a good spell now, haven't we? I think it's time for us to stand up and stretch our legs a little. Let's get that blood moving through our veins again. Come on, everyone! Stand my good citizens of the golden city!"

Looking out over the crowd, it appears that my wonderfully engaging and exciting voice is having the opposite effect that was intended. I see a few yawns taking place and several blank stares rise with the heat, as if I escaped from some Red Zone smack-tank. *Well, I guess it's time for Plan B,* I thought. Taking an apple from the basket, I throw it high into the crowd across the street. Then, I reach in with both hands grabbing four more apples that also quickly went sailing through the air to find the hands of young boys and girls, fathers, mothers, and grandparents. The audience leaps up to share in the afternoon's delight of fresh apples and the rewarding game of trying to catch them before they touch the ground. "Don't forget to share with your neighbors! Break them in half and share in the rewards of this generous merchant!"

After emptying all of the apples from the basket, I hand it back to our merchant friend and thank him for his kindness and generosity. Moving back to Papa to see how he has been coming along with his small meal and cup of water, I am disappointed. He has only eaten the pear and was still holding on to the bread. The cup of water did not appear to be touched at all. Paleness seems to have come over him as he stares blindly at the cup in his right hand.

"Papa, you must finish. You cannot go on without nourishment. What is it? Do you not feel well?"

"There is evil brewing in the world. I can feel enormous rage coming from the west. The shekel is angry with the zealots for keeping their mission concealed from him. It knows now about The Way and will seek to destroy it."

My stomach turns on end and a lump in my throat chokes off my words. A feeling deep within weeps for others who would not have access to The Way. Memories of my own journey through the mysterious passages flood my mind with fondness. Tears fill my eyes. After a few minutes, I'm able to get out the words that so desperately sought an answer. "But how will others come to the city?"

The wise one looks to heaven and then turns back to me with serenity settling over his face. "He will send us the answer in His own time. We needn't worry of such things. Now, we must attend to these fine people." The color returns to his cheeks, and after placing his palms on his knees, he rises from his stool.

"Um, not so fast Papa. Please, you still need to finish your bread and water. The One might take care of The Way, but I need to take care of you. Come on now, drink."

Papa nods and after saying a prayer over his meal, he finishes the bread, then tilts back the cup and drains the contents from it. He hands the cup back to me. "You are a good man, Paul. I'm blessed to have you with me as my guardian."

Feeling such a tremendous warmth of love and hope from his few words of encouragement, I nearly floated across the broken sidewalk. Strutting back to the merchant owner, I give him the cup and thank him.

After taking it from me, he looks at the bottom of the cup, and then grabs my arm as I was turning away. "The cup! Look! It has wine in it. I had only filled it with water." He smells the empty cup again and then tips it upside down where a drop of red liquid falls onto his fingers. "Look! It is wine," he says breathing in the aroma of the droplet before it evaporated into the warm air.

"Yes, my brother and merchant friend. It is indeed wine. Why do you look so puzzled? Is he not the Doctore? Has he not taught the Good News of the One? Has he not shown all The Way? Where is your faith my brother?" I reach out to hug the stunned fellow and pat him on the back. As I head back to Papa, I see that he was moving about the inner circle of the gathering. I see him give a familiar nod to the men or a kindly gaze to the children; I

encourage him to return to his small stool. With his Jesuit robes shaken out
and settled around him again, he makes himself comfortable on his cathedra.
The crowd hush themselves into silence waiting for the story to continue.

~ Doctore ~

"Good people of faith, though Man's journey has always been
spotted with darkness, and his insolence has sometimes led humanity off
onto crooked paths, there has always been the light and hope. Hope fuels the
light and makes visible the true path. Wherever there is light and hope, there
is truth. And where there is truth, our true destiny is laid out before us. The
One is always there for us to reach out and grab hold of him. At times, he
seems hidden, but it is only our own mistrust and weak faith. There are times
when wretched circumstances pull us down to the ground. We are trampled
upon, kicked, and humiliated. But we must always remain hopeful. We must
always search out the light that is in each and every one of us. We must use
that light and unite with others who hold it in their hearts. Then together we
shall see The Way and follow it home. It is through this example that others
will follow and we shall all be united with the One who gave us The Way
and the truth.
My dear brothers and sisters, do not worry over the evil in the world.
Its corruptness can never overtake the light. Evil tries to frighten and
intimidate those into believing there is no hope and tries to extinguish their
hope by surrounding them with darkness. The light, with hope and love, has
been given to each and every one of us by the One. However, it is always our
freedom of choice to either keep this gift fueled or to let it be smothered by
choking off its breath. Never allow this beautiful gift, which has been
entrusted to you, to fall to despair. If your heart and soul are consumed with
love and hope, there will be no room for fear. However, you must fight with
every fiber of your being until your last breath has been spent. Only then will
you truly be free, and you will forever be able to make your home in the
heart of the light."

Part 2: The Guide

Chapter 12

Praevian I

~ Paul ~

Papa has, for the most part, introduced the people who were part of that initial leg of the journey. We had all come from lives that were built on ignorance and selfishness, fear and intolerance. I often reflect on that past life and think, "Was I really that incredibly foolish and stupid? Or was I just a victim of a society that had lost its way?" Papa calls this period of time "the Great Myth" and has tried to teach me not to dwell in the past, but to learn from it and use it as fuel to keep the flame burning brightly in the present. "There is no point in crying over your past sins by playing out the *if only* possibilities. This is energy wasted. Instead, use that energy and determination to do today the things you ought to do. We must always ask, 'How can I make use of my blessings to help my fellow man today?'"

As I contemplate on this, I am startled by the realization that Saz has instantly appeared and is standing next to me with her hood over her head. I nearly jump out of my skin and my heart starts thumping like a mad dog.

"Really, Saz? I hate when you do that! Why must you freak everyone out?" I admonish.

"I don't freak everyone out; just you," she replies sarcastically.

"Oh, well that makes me feel much better. Thank you."

"What's wrong with Papa?"

"What do you mean?"

"He's not himself. He looks stressed and seems to be worrying over something. It's hard to tell, but there's definitely something going on today. There seems to be an air of fear in the wind today."

"How do you GITs know this kind of stuff? Do they teach you these skills in GIT college or were they injected at birth?"

Saz moves directly in front of me, and while staring at me with cold, dark eyes, pushes her index finger into me, piercing my abdomen in the most uncomfortable way.

"Ow! What's wrong with you?"

Saz begins her interrogation. "Tell me what you know, or I'm going to carve my initials in the wall behind you."

"I don't think – ow!"

Saz pushes her finger further into my stomach. "Talk, assistant. Carving the first letter 'S' is the most painful."

"All right, all right, already! Ease up."

Saz pulls back her hand and gives me relief.

"Papa said that the Shekel knows about The Way. He believes it will take action to try to destroy it."

"No," Saz whispers and takes a step back.

I look down only for a moment and try to come up with the right words. "I know, but…" and when I look up again she's gone. *I hate it when she does that, too. GITs are the strangest people I have ever encountered.*

With all that seems to be going on right now, Papa has no trouble moving into the next chapter of this amazing story. He is a resilient old gent. I'd say that I didn't know from where he finds his strength, but that isn't quite true. I do know.

~ Doctore ~

In April of 2054, First Lieutenant Lyndon had taken a two week leave in which he and Jackieo had made arrangements to go to Fort Sumter and Charleston for a little rest and relaxation. Having the opportunity to take time off and head to the Eastern coast would be just what a couple of GITs needed to deal with the current stress of work and bump talk. However, fate stepped in that afternoon before they left for the South Carolina territory. While Jackieo was walking back from the food preparation area into the living quarters, a Federal Notice came in on the Digifeed from the Office of Social Justice and Responsibility. She stared motionless at the crystal panel.

"George," she called out from the living quarters. Her voice sounded somewhat strained and in a panic.

"Yeah? I didn't forget your BiD it's already packed," George replied as he reached for a stack of shirts lying in a pile of things to still pack with their gear.

"We just got a SJR notice on the feed."

George immediately dropped the shirts back into the pile and quickly left the room. Jackieo stood, seemingly frozen in time, directly in front of the digifeed staring at the blinking red messagecon. She pressed her hand up against her mouth and nervously fidgeted with her lower lip. George moved in close and put his arm around her, holding onto her shoulder.

"Are you ready for this?" she asked.

"Yes, I'm ready; let's do it." He paused for a moment. "Play messages," he called out.

"Notice one-two-eight-four, April tenth, two-thousand fifty-four. Sender: Office of Social Justice and Responsibility. Start Message: After a complete reanalysis of the DNA of First Lieutenant George Lyndon and social partner Jackieo Elizabeth Fannin, it is the decision of this office to deny procreation."

110

Jackieo's heart dropped and she put her head down. Tears formed in her eyes and dripped from her cheek bones. The digifeed continued. "The number of genetic markers for diabetes, heart disease, asthma, hypertension –"

"Stop message," Jackieo called out in a strained and sobbing voice. Tears continued to roll down her cheeks. The digifeed stopped the message and the room went silent. She turned to George and buried her face into his chest and wept.

He pulled her closer to him and held her tight. He desperately tried to think of something to say, anything that could be reassuring or comforting at that moment, but nothing came to mind. There were no words he could muster that would have eased their pain. All he could do was hold her and feel the same frustration, pain, and agony that she had felt during these last several years. She had been the only person he had ever let get that close to his true self. With Jackieo, he had no defenses. They could nearly read each other's minds and finish each other's thoughts. On this sad day, her pain had been every bit his pain as well. The only thing that she had ever wanted was a family. She had talked about having a bump for as long as he could remember. Dreams of how she would redecorate their pod, how she would organize their room, and what kinds of things she would get to make up the nursery were always on her mind. She would talk with George in detail about them. She had picked out the color schemes and furniture; there was nothing that she hadn't thought of for their child. But now it was all gone; there was nothing left but mere fantasy.

Nearly three weeks passed after hearing of their life-altering news. They had postponed their trip for a later date since neither one of them was much in the mood for a holiday. Jackieo fell into a state of depression and despair. Until one day something changed. When George came home after his shift, she could barely contain her excitement. She had met with the woman named Maria who had made quite the impact on her. Jackieo, who was thoroughly convinced that Maria had all the right answers to their current situation, began to tell George the story of her encounter. When she first saw Maria, she was mesmerized by her kindness and gentleness. Their time together, though somewhat short, had been the most beautiful and heartfelt moments that Jackieo could ever recall. George listened carefully, but suspiciously, not quite believing everything he was being told. Jackieo had spent nearly two days talking with George about what a wonderful experience it had been and how she knew in her heart it was the right thing to do. After much debate and pleading, Jackieo was able to convince George to also go and see Maria. Jackieo arranged everything and now it was time for George to choose for himself. Maria insisted on each person making their own decision and it was absolutely imperative for that person to meet with her personally.

"I don't know exactly why each person has to meet with her. She said something about freely choosing one's own path. She's really a wonderful person, George. I've never met anyone like her," Jackieo said as she handed George his battle-dress uniform (bdu) jacket.

"Why did we have to meet by the old shrine? It's been torn down for years. If I get stopped, what excuse am I to give for being that far north?"

"I don't know why she picked that location. She just said to have you meet her by the National Shrine ruins, near the woods behind where the Basilica used to be located. If someone stops you, just say you were headed to the Gold Coast to look at the affluent pods that are located up there."

George stared at her out of the corner of his eye. "When did you get so calculatingly devious?"

"You're not the only one who's on a mission you know," she winked.

"I do like your style, Chief." George replied, and after moving in close and taking her in his arms, he kissed her.

She hugged him tight, and with her head resting on his shoulder, she whispered, "Watch your six, LT."

George placed his cap on his head and left the pod.

It was about eight forty-five in the evening and the sun had already set, yet there was still a faint orange glow on the horizon. George took the hover shuttle up to Michigan Avenue and then got off with the other academic GITs. This part of the city had been torn down and turned into the FED training grounds, which was used primarily by the newer GITs and GITs who were being primed for promotions.

He took his time getting off the shuttle, letting the other GITs move on ahead of him. After lagging back and seeing that the shuttle moved on, he continued north onto Harewood Road to the spot where the Basilica of the National Shrine of the Immaculate Conception once stood. The buildings had all been demolished and new gray isopod towers were erected in their place. In the gray dusk, the buildings stood like shadows of the night. Their darkened gray color, gave them a stealth-like stance.

A rush of air blew across the road in the opposite direction of the towers, and George followed after it. Walking across the street, he passed an old brick structure that was once part of the Basilica. Cautiously negotiating the small path that led back into the wooded area, he continued about one-fourth a klick inward and headed towards a small light he saw in the distance. As he came closer, he could see the shape of a woman standing alone. She wore a simple long white dress with a rich blue-colored overlay. Covering her head was a white shawl that draped loosely around her face. She appeared to be a younger woman, possibly in her early twenties; however, her mannerisms and her expression of anguish and concern made her appear to be much older than her facial features would have otherwise indicated.

The light seemed to come from behind her, though George couldn't make out its source.

"Maria?"

"It is a beautiful evening, so peaceful," she said while staring into the night sky. She turned her head toward George and motioned with her hand at the ground directly in front of him. "This is still holy ground because Mass was once held here; remove your boots."

"What? My boots?" he looked down at his feet and over the immediate area, half expecting to find an indication that something special was there. After seeing nothing, he looked back to Maria. "Listen, Maria, my name is—"

"George. Yes, I know. Take off your boots, George, and walk with me for a bit."

Maria had a way about her that was difficult to describe. Her demeanor had been both humbling and commanding at the same time, yet with the utmost humility. She seemed to speak, not just to you, but through you. There was something in her voice that resonated deep within you.

George felt the need to do what she asked, but couldn't understand exactly why. However, he reached down and undid his boots and then slipped them off. After tucking his socks inside the boots, he picked them up and carried them. Maria turned slowly and started to walk in the opposite direction of the street. George stayed alongside her and for the most part was silent. He felt very comfortable just being near Maria. There was a calmness that came over him and he felt at peace with no anxiety or inquisitiveness about what she was doing there in the dark woods at night.

"What is it you wish to ask of me?" Maria said after a few minutes.

"The city…is it real?"

"It is."

"Where is its location exactly?" George asked intently as he toddled after her on the pathway.

"What do you hope to find there?"

"We want to have a bum….uh, a baby," he caught himself from using the typical GIT jargon.

"You can have a child here in this city. I can arrange it."

George looked at her oddly. He scanned her arms; particularly her forearms and noticed she didn't have a GIT tattoo. She didn't dress like a GIT, she didn't look like a GIT, and she wasn't tagged like a GIT. She screamed out civilian in every way, yet she seemed to go undetected by the security systems, which typically only took two or three minutes to detect heat sources that were non-tagged personnel.

"How is it that the GITs haven't found you? You're not tagged. You should have been detected by now and quite possibly eliminated."

"I do not answer to your law. I cannot be detected nor eliminated." Maria's expression seemed to indicate that she was somewhat amused by George's comment. "What do you hope to find in the city?" Maria asked again.

George stopped and looked down at his bare feet. There was a bluish light that followed Maria, and he could see his toes against the dark path, but he didn't feel any discomfort from walking barefooted on the gravel and stone walkway. In fact, he found it hard to feel the gravel at all. It was almost as if he had been cushioned from it. The oddness of it gave him the security to speak his mind. "Freedom. I hope to find freedom. I would fight to the death for freedom and for truth. I just don't feel I belong here. There's nothing here I would die for; well, nothing except for Jackieo. I would give anything for her."

"If I tell you the way to the city, you can never come back to this place. The journey is dangerous and you might even get caught. You may die. Once you have chosen, you must stay committed to The Way, no matter what happens. Are you willing to give up everything for it? Even if Jackieo turns back, you must not follow. You must continue on The Way."

George didn't hesitate or even blink. "Yes, I am committed to the city."

Maria looked deep into his eyes for several moments. She seemed to search straight through to his very core for the truth in which he spoke in his words. George was not uncomfortable in her penetrating stare and looked directly back at her. He felt there was kindness and warmth in her face, along with honesty in her eyes. There was a deep sense of peace and protection being close to her, as though somehow protected from any earthly circumstances of harm. Standing next to Maria, he was enveloped in her arms of blue light. Jackieo was right; this woman was unlike anyone he had ever met.

"Offer to me your hand." Maria reached out to him with her left hand.

George extended his right arm and placed his hand in hers. Maria pulled back the sleeve of his uniform jacket exposing the GIT tattoo. She placed her right hand over it and whispered something in a language he did not recognize or understand. A strange bluish-white light emanated from her fingers. The soft glow lingered over her hand in a sort of pulsing fashion. In a minute or so, his tattoo was gone.

"You are no longer a GIT, George. Your tracking element has been removed. You must leave in three days. If you stay longer than three days, the GITs will notice you are not one of them and they will eliminate you. Do you understand?"

"Yes. What of Jackieo? Is she ready, too?" George asked.

"Jackieo is more than ready. She is waiting for you, so you can go together. I removed her tattoo almost two days ago." Maria looked with concern at him.

"I understand; three days. We will leave right away. We will not wait," he said with determinedness.

"The journey begins for you at Saint Peter's church on Capitol Hill. Do you know it?"

"I know it. We can leave tomorrow."

"Look for the mark of Archangel Raphael's staff and shield at St. Peter. Follow it. It will lead you all along The Way. And George, there is one more warning. There is an ancient story of Saint George killing a dragon. Along your way, you too, will come across a red dragon with which you will have to do battle. It's an evil, one-eyed dragon with no honor. He has slaughtered many people for his own wicked enjoyment. Show him no mercy; for he will not show any to you."

George tilted his head in confusion, not quite understanding the warning, but acknowledged it just the same.

"Your faith will grow along The Way. Trust in it. Believe in the messages you receive along your passage. They are there for you; to guide you to truth. God bless your journey." Maria raised her arm and pointed down the path from which they had come, motioning for him that it was time to part.

"Thank you, Maria. Thank you for all of your help."

Maria closed her eyes and lowered her head slightly. George started back toward the street. After he had walked about thirty feet or so, he stepped on something hard. It was a rock.

"Ow," he said and lifted his foot. He turned to look back towards Maria, but she was gone. Looking around the area, there was no trace of her at all. The wooded landscape was darkened once again to where he could not make out anything beyond the dark tree line. He sat down next to the gravel trail and put his boots back on. After standing up again, he quickly made his way to the station where the next hover shuttle took him back home to Bottom Rack.

Chapter 13

Praevian II

~ Paul ~

And so the lady Maria was helping the travelers discover The Way dug twenty years earlier by the late Carroll Zealots. However, it would appear that the method of escape may be threatened as the evil Shekel is closing in on their secret, bent on destroying what it thought was already destroyed. I don't know where Saz was off to in her somewhat disturbing exit, but I suppose that is a worry for another day. Taking a cue from the Doctore, I will tend to the present day's tasks. "We must do what good we can with today, for tomorrow's worries will take care of themselves. There is plenty of trouble in this day to have concern over." Papa does have a point.

I can see the Doctore is ready to give us another dose of Saul, a man with such a selfish and arrogant nature that it will take a great deal of faith to cut through his pride. However, if there is any person who might help him, it would be Maria.

~ Doctore ~

It had been two months since Saul had the frightening encounter with the blue-eyed fetus, and yet its voice still haunted him. He and Janess had barely spoken to one another since their argument. They each simply went through the motions of their duties towards one another, but there was coldness and isolation between them. Saul had taken to sleeping on the sofabay and his nightmares were getting worse with each passing day. He wasn't sleeping well, he wasn't feeling well, their relationship was drifting further than it had ever been before, and he felt as though his entire life was unraveling before his eyes. On one particular trying day at work, Saul came home and had every intention of making amends with Janess. After putting down his bag, he went to look for her in the back room. However, she wasn't there. As he went to leave, he noticed a folded note on the table by his side of the sleeping bay. He sat down on the edge of the bay, picked up the note, and read it aloud. "*Saul, I can no longer live like this. We barely speak and you don't respect my feelings or my opinion on this matter at all. I know you don't believe, but I do. I made arrangements to go to the city. I can't live here, and I certainly can't live like this. You have my love always, Janess.*"

117

Saul drooped with despair. Anguish settled in the pit of his stomach and he looked around the room. The walls were all bare; painted with a bland off-white color. There were only the essentials of day-to-day living scattered across the furniture tops and in niches. Janess had her workspace with the BiD lying to one side. There wasn't anything here that he would miss. His home had been built on nothing but Janess, and with her gone, he was left only with emptiness. His practice made him sick to his stomach, and his nerves had been shot to pieces. He had to do something different. It was time for a change. Any change would be better than what he had been living through these past years. The infant had told him to atone in Penury. He wasn't sure what that meant exactly, but he was sure that this emptiness wasn't going to work for him. With a last glance around, he walked out.

He needed to find Maria. She was the key to this whole thing and his only hope in finding Janess so that he could make amends. He had remembered hearing about an unusual woman who handed out food to the poor near Lower Wacker Drive. *It had to be her. It must be Maria*, he thought. So, with great urgency, he hopped on the L-Shuttle and soon found himself walking through one of the poorest areas of the city late in the evening. Descending a stone staircase near Lasalle Street, Saul inched down into the cold and dingy lit tunnels of Chicago's sublevel. The lower street level was gritty and gothic looking. It was the dark area of the city where most of the displaced people were found leaning against walls or curled up in small crevices. It was a place where people didn't ask questions and where after searching for food all day, they came to rest in the small niches along the darkened street. The lighting gave off a yellowish-green color, making the atmosphere eerily frightening, as if at any moment something was going to jump out and take him.

Saul walked quickly along the street, his eyes cast downward but constantly scanning for any sign of danger. A stench rose from the warm air of the sewers, which mixed with the foul air of the sublevel—urine and vomit, and clothes that had been slept in far longer than intended. As he walked through the lit up circles showing the oil-covered pavement, moans and whimpers escaped from the cracks in the walls. Someone or something was weeping just a short distance ahead. Saul sped up his pace; his footfalls were attracting more attention than he had anticipated.

"Hey coat. Spare credits?"

"No, no credits," Saul stammered and kept moving.

"What'd ya' doin' down here, boy?" A shadow called out to him.

Saul kept moving faster and faster. His heart was pounding and sweat beaded on his forehead. The tunnel seemed to get darker and the foul stench in the air thicker. The moans and groans became the din of the night, broken only by a sudden scream or a loud cry. The entire experience was like that of hospital wards where the terminal patients were in so much pain and agony that they had wished for death to come quickly in the night, so they might have peace and reprieve. He felt as though he was moving through a kind of cemetery where the people didn't know they were dead. A loud crash came from behind him and he turned quickly to look, but didn't see anything. He spun back around and rushed away, but ran into a cart and was jolted backwards.

The burly man behind the cart growled at him. "Watch yourself, crack!"

"I'm sorry. Do you know where I can find Maria?"

"I'm Maria!" he said laughing loudly and waving his hand in the air. "Out of my way!" He pushed the cart into Saul again and mumbled to himself about voltage and current across a diode.

Saul stepped out of the way to let him pass, then continued down Wacker through the moans, whimpering, stares, and mumbled criticisms. He drove on deeper into the bowels of the city in anguish. He wasn't sure where this courage had come from, since for the most part he had more or less been a coward in such things. He had always planned everything and kept himself safely out of harm's way. Analyzing his actions and his frail state of mind, he assumed it was an act of sheer panic and desperation to find Janess, who was the only person who had given his life purpose. As he neared a curve in the street, he heard someone call out to him from a dark niche in the crevice of a wall filled with graffiti.

"You're looking for Madre Maria, eh?"

Saul stopped suddenly and strained to see in the darkness, but he couldn't see anything, not even a shadow was revealed to him. Feeling his heart pound inside his chest, he searched out the darkened corner from where the voice had called out. Every fiber of his being was frightened and his body became a pulsating and quivering sponge. The fear made him sick to his stomach, which caused perspiration to form over his face and hands, which also went cold. His knees became weakened to where he didn't know how much longer they would keep him upright. He felt a cold, damp chill run up through his entire body. However, with the minute strength he had left, he took a step forward into the darkness.

"Yes, I'm looking for Maria," he stammered.

There was silence. Saul moved closer to the place where the voice called out. "Do you know where I can find her?"

"Si, I know," a raspy voice called out in an almost whispering tone that cracked into pieces as it hit the dense air of the sublevel.

Saul walked further into the darkened corner and strained his eyes to catch a glimpse of anything; a shadow, a silhouette, a movement. As he neared the tunnel wall, he tripped over something and fell to the ground. His face was planted against the cold, wet pavement and he felt his left knee throb in pain. Someone placed their shoe onto his back and pushed him down hard into the street as he tried to get up. His worst fears were now realized as he lay helpless on the ground at the mercy of the street people. There wasn't anything he could do. His strength had long deserted him. All that remained now was fear.

"Que quieres con Maria?" The raspy voice asked.

"I just want to talk to her; that's it. Just to talk."

"That's a nice overcoat you've got perro; lot better than mine."

"Let me up and we can talk about a trade," Saul replied turning his head slightly to try to catch a glimpse of the man who was talking to him.

"Try anything and I'll carve you a new smile from ear to ear. Or maybe I'll just lift out your spleen. Comprende?"

"I don't want any trouble."

There was silence for several moments. Saul felt the pressure lift off his back and he slowly got to his feet. He started to turn around to face the voice.

"Don't turn around! Tu abrigo, perro!"

"What about Maria?"

"Coat first, then habla."

Saul removed his coat and handed it to the man behind him without looking back.

"Si, a very nice abrigo. Here's the trade; stay here," the man threw his coat over the head of Saul.

Saul, startled at first with something being over his head, quickly ripped the tattered coat off his head and spun around. There was no one there. He turned and looked up and down the street, but no one was moving about. He looked at the coat that had been tossed over him. It was full of holes and smelled awful. He slowly walked over to a trash container and tossed the man's coat inside. Something fell out of it and struck the pavement making the tinny sound of metal hitting, "Clank, clink, clink." The sound echoed off the walls, but then faded quietly into the street. Saul bent down to pick it up. It was a small, round silver metal object that had an inscription written on it. The darkness of the corner was too great to read it, so Saul moved under one of the few lit street lights. With the yellowish light he was able to make out the letters A, V, E on the silver metal.

"Ave," Saul said aloud. The instant he said it there was a soft blue light coming from just behind him and he quickly turned to see a woman dressed in a white dress with a blue overlay. She wore a shawl on her head that fell around her face and neck.

"It is pronounced Ave, Saul."

"You are Maria?" he asked.

"I am."

"I want to go to the city to find my Janess."

"And should you find her, what then?"

"I want to talk with her. I want to apologize for my behavior."

"I can give her your message. There is no need for you to go," Maria said and started to turn away.

"No, please wait! Please!"

Maria turned back around and looked directly into Saul's eyes. He felt her penetrating stare deep inside of his body, almost as if it were cutting into his very heart.

"You ask something more of me? What could someone who has thought so little of infant life possibly have to say to the mother of Man?"

Saul had never felt so uncomfortable in all his life. It was a feeling of fear, of deep sorrow, and utter embarrassment in which all of his insides were going to implode upon themselves and he would simply cease to exist. Everything appeared to him as dark as night and there was a cold emptiness in his heart. However, upon searching through all of this shadow and fear, he found there was still a shimmer of light. And with that very small portion of hope came a shred of courage.

"Can you tell me what 'atone in Penury' means?" he asked softly.

"Where did you hear this? Only those who have been to the city know this name."

Saul paused and looked downward at the street, his mind drifted to that day at the clinic. Again, he felt deep despair and humiliation flow over him as the shame choked off the air to his lungs. Sinking steadily like a lead ingot, he was drowning in his own sea of painful memory. Reliving the miserable acts of uncaring cruelty, he struggled desperately, flailing about to find his way back to the surface. An entire ocean of innocent infant blood came crashing down upon him, as the tiny faces flashed before his eyes over and over again while he sank further into the darkness. He was not sure how long he had stared at the stains in the asphalt, but he could feel Maria's penetrating eyes peeling away at the layers of his conscience, like a child unraveling a ball of string only to find there was no substance or core. The conquering darkness was heading directly for his life's flickering light; striving to steal away his last hope. The shadow was winning and it was just a matter of time before it captured him. There was no strength left within his heart to stay them off. He could see it surrounding and closing in on the faint candle, fortifying its position, and readying itself for the final battle to extinguish it once and for all. But then, he felt a touch on his arm and the flickering flame brightened. It stood up straight with a renewed energy and reached for the sky. The darkness retreated and the memories softened. Saul was given another breath, and gasping for air, he quickly took hold of it and inhaled deeply. He found his courage again.

"An unborn child told me to atone in Penury," Saul replied and raised his eyes to Maria.

Her penetrating eyes softened and her face seemed to glow at the mere mention of the child. She nodded her head slightly and the signs of relief and tranquility seemed to come over her as if one of her children had just escaped a dreadful incident.

"You are a blessed man, Saul. This holy child has interceded for you; imploring for an opportunity to show recompense for your life." Maria then became quite serious and a look of utmost concern came over her. "Do not waste it by imposing your own foolish will, but give in to your remaining faint light. Fuel it with love and charity for your fellow man and save it from the darkness of your own selfish pride, or you will suffocate in that ocean of despair you have created." Maria paused as Saul reflected on those words. "Your way to the city starts at the Assumption Church on Illinois Street; it is a short walk from the L-Shuttle. You shall follow the staff and shield of the Archangel Raphael." Maria paused again for a moment. "You will not remember the name of the city. Farewell, Saul."

Maria turned and started to walk away, but Saul reached out and grabbed her shoulder and pulled her back around to face him. "No, wait!" He cried. But as he removed his hand from her shoulder he realized he had grabbed the man who had traded him for his overcoat.

"There's no take-backs perro! Once a trade is done, it's done!" the man yelled at Saul.

Surprised and startled, Saul replied. "I just wanted to say thank you."

The man nodded his head slightly and continued back to the street. Saul had never felt so unsure and uncertain in his entire life. He had always been a man of science and reason, and what he had just witnessed defied all logic. He felt as though he was in a dream or some sort of stupor from which he would wake at any moment. However, it wasn't a dream or a nervous breakdown. He had lived and been a witness to every moment of it.

He reached a staircase leading to the street level and quickly climbed out of Lower Wacker Drive.

Chapter 14

Praevian III

~ Paul ~

While Saul contemplated his unnerving experience into the bowels of Chicago's streets, I'm getting a similar feeling about the uncertainty of the day. The Shekel's knowledge of The Way is disturbing and Saz's disappearance is also sitting somewhat uneasily in the pit of my stomach. Taking a cup of water and a peeled orange to Papa, I inquire upon his thoughts of the whole situation.

"These are the concerns of men who have shallow faith, Paolo. It is natural to worry after our friends, as we sometimes have trouble seeing the plan of the One. However, in the end we must not spend too much time on it. The Shekel can never overtake the One King. The One has power over all things."

"Yes, Papa, but what I don't understand is why the One just doesn't eliminate the evil altogether. Why let it live?"

"Evil is a byproduct of freedom. Without the ability to choose, you could not have freedom. There are those who choose good and truth with love. Of course, there are those who choose evil, hate, and deceit. Evil has to exist just as good has to exist. However, there *will* come a time when the two will no longer be thrust together. They will be separated like the wheat from the chaff. The wheat will be gathered to the One, and the chaff will be tossed into the flame."

Papa works on finishing his small snack before starting the next segment of the story, which if I'm not mistaken is about Barnus and Isabella's daughter, Li'Quari. She has been getting on quite well with Jackson as she was in need of a strong father figure. At the same time, he was in need of a loving daughter.

~ Doctore ~

Li'Quari woke with a start and sat up, caught between a disturbing dream and reality. She tensed and listened. Footsteps. She pulled the covers up to her chest and stared at the faint light coming into the room from beneath the door, remembering the terror of shadows moving across the floor when she lived in a Southern District care facility. There, the Watchers, bound by the Southern Government to look after wards of the District, came in the night, to take advantage of the young dwellers. She used to cower in her bed, her heart racing and her stomach wrenching at the turning of the door handle, knowing the sinking feeling in the pit of her stomach would turn to absolute horror when the door swung open.

She had run away from the complex when she was twelve years old, but the screams and the weeping of the residents there left indelible stains on her heart.

She reached into her pocket and felt for the safeguard that had sustained her throughout the brutality—a holy card she had received from her mother when she was five years old that depicted a long-haired, bearded man in a white robe. He stood against the backdrop of blue sky and fluffy white clouds embracing another man who, with his back turned from view, looked like a younger brother. Above the two of them was a beautiful white dove with its wings spread wide. Surrounding the entire picture was a large pair of hands holding them up in the sky. This imagery became Li'Quari's lifeline. It was a promise from her mother and she clung to it whenever she had to escape from her reality.

Wiping the sleep and the remnants of her nightmare from her eyes, she calmed herself down as reality replaced the fading nightmare and horrid memories. For the first time in a long time, she had nothing to fear. She was safe here in this cottage by the orchard, guarded by Jackson. She lumbered across the room in her sandals and swung open the door to the aroma of freshly baked doughbread and oranges. With a contented sigh, she headed down the hall to see what Jackson was up to in the main part of the house.

"Breaks," Li'Quari said, as she shuffled into the kitchen. The lit candle flickered on the neatly set table casting a wandering dim light over the stove where Jackson had been hard at work cooking breakfast.

"Mornin' breaks. Sleep all right?" Jackson asked.

"Yeah, I slept just fine. Unusually fine. I'm starving!"

Jackson tapped the back of a ladder back chair. "Here, sit. I have some doughbread and orange jam." He laid a plate in front of her and joined her at the table. Li'Quari settled into the seat with one foot tucked underneath her, reached for the doughbread and covered it with a thick layer of jam. After taking several large bites, she picked up the water glass and drained half of the cold, refreshing well-water.

"Your water here is clear; it doesn't stink of rotted fish. I don't understand it. You're so close to the river, I can't believe you get this from a well."

"The well here goes down nearly a thousand feet. It taps into a small spring that flows beneath the river. It's not polluted, so it's very clear and doesn't smell, although it does have a very high mineral content." He paused for a moment to look over the table and noticed that something had been missing. "I forgot the browns," he announced as he got up and went towards the shelves near the sink. After lifting up a bowl containing sliced potato wedges, he brought it over to the table and set it in front of Li'Quari. Getting comfortable again, he asked Li'Quari about her family and if they were still in the south.

"I don't remember much about my biologics. They were killed when I was very young. Sometimes, I think I remember hearing voices and conversations about a trip we had taken or maybe were going to take. I don't know. I recall that we had lived in a city, and I wasn't allowed to go outside. I remember my mother giving me a card and telling me that it would keep me safe. Mostly, I remember this one night where I had a nightmare and hid under my bed holding that card. There was a really bright light and smoke. Then something pinched my leg and everything went black. After that I was in different places with different people. I'm not sure how I ended up in the Southern District except that me and a bunch of other kids were bussed around a lot." She shrugged her shoulders at her indifference to the whole topic. "I was sent to different Watchers over the years. Some were okay, some not so okay." She took another bite of doughbread.

"I remember my mother having long brown hair and she wore brightly colored dresses. I don't recall my father very much. I guess maybe he wasn't around or worked or something. There's not much to tell really. I don't think I had any other family. The last set of Watchers I stayed with were evil janks; that's when I decided to leave and go on my own. They left the back door open one day when they were bringing in a bunch of supplies, so I snuck out the door. I just kept running. I think the guard's been after me ever since."

Jackson knew all too well of the pain and misery that was going on in the south; especially the atrocities that were being done to children. While holding his office as Senator, he saw firsthand the reports of violence, crime, and filth that had overrun the southern states mostly due to poverty and the lack of interest from his peers in government office. State after state went bankrupt. Most if not all of the civil authorities left their posts in the south for paying work in the north. With the broken communities left to fend for themselves, the takers moved in and took advantage of an already defeated people. The crime lords took and took and kept on taking until there was nothing left. And then, after the land was pillaged, they turned the people, who were still left breathing, into slaves, setting up a tyrannical rule. Out of this new order of law was born the Southern Guard, which Washington did nothing to stop. The new president was delighted to let it run its course so that he didn't have to spend much on resources. He simply paid the new land-supers a management salary for keeping peace and order. It had all made Jackson sick and angry, but at the time, his priority had been protecting his own family. However, dealing with the abstract reports was much easier than seeing firsthand the damage that was being done to these people.

"I'm so very sorry, Li'Quari, that you had such a rough time of it." Jackson picked up his doughbread and was about to take a bite when he stopped. He lowered it back to the plate, but still held onto the end of it, which made it appear to just hover there like a suspension bridge hanging in a night's fog.

Li'Quari could tell from his furrowed expression that something was weighing on his mind. The deepened lines and marks in his forehead and around his eyes seemed to have been etched more prominently from life's concerns than from life's years in the sun.

After a few moments, he finally spoke. "I'm to go today and talk to a woman about the golden city. I'm told that she knows the way, and I want to leave as soon as possible. I'd like for you to come with me – that is if you would want to go, also," Jackson said.

"You would?" she asked with a look of pure bewilderment. No one had ever taken much of an interest in her or to think to include her in anything. In the past, she had always been, more or less, ordered around or left on her own to fend for herself. There were never any negotiations or time to think, there was only forced decisions or reactionary behavior based on survival.

"You're not safe here by yourself and the guard *will* come back," Jackson said. "What do you say? Would you like to travel with me to look for the city?"

His eyes were wide with hope, warmth, and friendliness, but it was his wiry, gray hair standing on end on the left side of his head and his large, aged brown hands resting on either side of his meal that endeared him to Li'Quari. She couldn't keep the smile out of her reply. "Yes!"

"Good. That's good," Jackson said relieved. He picked up his doughbread and began to eat it while still nodding his head approvingly over her decision.

After finishing their meal, Jackson removed the barricades on the front door and pulled it open. The daylight, with its already rising heat, flooded into the dark room with a roaring effect. It hit the floorboards first and marched across them like an army infiltrating behind enemy lines. After consuming the floor, it continued its fury across the walls, illuminating every crevice, knot, and bump along the way. Li'Quari shielded her eyes against the brilliance.

"Wait here until I've had a look," Jackson said. "If anything should happen, run back into your room. Underneath the chair there is a trap door. You are to hide there until the danger passes." After slipping his backpack over his shoulders, he grabbed his beige straw hat and the walking stick from the corner and went out onto the porch. Li'Quari stayed back just inside the doorway where she could still see him, but remained hidden from view. Jackson, squinting from the brightness of the morning light, scoped out the area surrounding his home. He walked off the porch and looked down the road as he listened intently to any indication the Southern Guard may have been in the area. There was only the gentle sound of a breeze blowing across the lime and orange trees and the singing of a few birds coming from the orchard.

"Okay," he said and turned toward the door. "We meet Maria just down the highway, about two miles down the river; across from the old Cana factory."

"Isn't that where the doughbread lady lives?" She asked as she stepped off the porch.

"Yes, that's Maria. She is the one who passes out doughbread to those who don't have any way of getting food for themselves."

"I didn't know her name was Maria. I like her. She's the nicest person, and so beautiful."

Jackson smiled and nodded in agreement. He lifted his walking stick momentarily to point in the direction of the factory, and then began their hike. The sun had still not risen above the tree line. He figured it to be somewhere around six-thirty, and that they should be able to make it to the old factory just after seven o'clock if they didn't dally.

"Let's pick up the pace a little bit," he said and quickened his stride. He wasn't sure exactly why, but he felt the need to hurry along. There was an uneasy feeling that had come over him as if danger were just behind them and would soon be coming upon them.

About twenty-five minutes later, Li'Quari could see the old factory buildings. The concrete had cracked and crumbled, and the various buildings were in terrible condition. All of the oil containers were rusted and had giant holes in them from where the takers had helped themselves to the stored fuel. Windows were smashed and the structures were on the brink of collapsing. Bricks, rock, dirt, garbage, pipe, and metal objects littered the grounds. Everything was colored in green, rust-orange, or grayish-brown hues. There was standing water in various sections that contained mold and algae where the stench drifted with the passing winds.

Jackson continued to lead the way. They hastily crossed over the gray highway that paralleled the river to get to the cover of the trees and shrubbery that grew between the river's edge and the road. Somehow, nature seemed to find a way to resist the corruption of Man. There were still a few places along the river where the foliage grew in spite of the polluted waters. When they had entered into the greenery, he slowed the pace and began to look for signs of Maria. They found a trodden path and followed it into the center of the foliage. The morning sun flickered in and out of the branches overhead as a summer breeze blew in from the north. It didn't take long before Li'Quari called out with joy and pointed to the east. Jackson followed her gaze and saw Maria. How beautiful she had appeared to him as she stood

127

in a small open area of the woods, her back to them, with the sunlight streaming in all around her. Birds were flying in circular patterns near her; diving, soaring, and hovering as if they were in some type of joyous dance. She laughed and played with the winged creatures.

As Li'Quari and Jackson approached, she turned to them with a radiant smile as if she had known they were there all along.

"I do so enjoy the morning. A new day brings so much joy, love, and hope."

"Morning breaks, Maria," Jackson said as he removed his straw hat. "You were absolutely right about the timing we spoke of the last time we met. It had been too soon for me to leave. I don't know how you knew, but I'm grateful to you for having me exercise more patience."

Maria tilted her head slightly in acknowledgement, and then she turned to Li'Quari. "What is it you seek my child?"

Li'Quari moved a step closer to Maria. She thought she was the most beautiful woman she had ever seen. Maria had the kindest face, which seemed to light up more brilliantly than the sun rising from the trees behind her. Everything about her seemed to be of something good and generous. Once standing in front of her, Li'Quari felt as if she were standing before royalty. However, she didn't feel as if she was unworthy to be standing there, but more like Maria existed at that moment entirely for her. It seemed Maria's presence was made possible simply to help Li'Quari in her time of need; to give her that much needed advice at just the right time and to ease the pain that had accumulated for far too many years. Li'Quari's gaze moved from Maria to Jackson, back to Maria, and then drifted slowly to the ground.

"I would like very much to go with Jackson to look for the city. I feel safe with him," she said quietly.

"Jackson is a good man, Li'Quari. But what do *you* hope to find in the city?" Li'Quari kept her head lowered and she stared at several twigs lying on the ground in front of her. She tried to think of something that she would want in the city. She didn't know exactly what she hoped to find there, and she didn't want to give a wrong answer. She had no idea what the city had to offer except for what rumors she had heard. She knew she didn't want to stay in the Southern District. She was certain that if she stayed, she and her child would surely die. Her thoughts raced inside her head and her eyes darted between the broken branches in search of an answer when Maria reached out to her with an open hand and gently laid it underneath Li'Quari's chin. She lifted her head up to look into her eyes. Li'Quari, somewhat awkwardly looked up and immediately fell into Maria's soothing eyes. A feeling of tremendous calm came over her and her racing mind settled and became clear. She reached behind her taking a small card from her back pocket. After looking at it, she handed it to Maria.

"My mother gave me this when I was very young. I hope to find this love in the city."

Maria took the card from her hand and looked at it. The light in her face brightened even more as if the stars themselves were emanating from just beneath her skin. She closed her eyes, raised her head toward the sky, and put the card up to her heart while whispering something in a language Li'Quari did not recognize. After a few moments, Maria opened her eyes again and handed the card back to her.

"It is a wonderful vision, and if you are strong and willing, you shall find it." Maria turned to Jackson. "Your journey starts at Saint Gabriel's. Follow the staff and shield of the Archangel Raphael. Remember what I have told you: a young woman cared for, protected, and loved – is a daughter. You will see her soon enough."

"Thank you, Maria. With all my heart, thank you," Jackson replied. After replacing his straw hat atop his head, he guided his walking stick back around and started toward the road.

"Li'Quari, take care of your son while he is within you. He will come hard, but he will come healthy. Listen to Jackson, do what he asks of you."

Li'Quari ran up to Maria and hugged her tightly. Maria's long and flowing garment felt like liquid silk and had the aroma of the most wonderful wild roses. With her eyes closed, Li'Quari felt as though she was suspended weightless in a breath of air. It was the most indescribable feeling she had ever encountered. Only one word came to mind that could possibly express how she felt at that moment: loved. She walked quickly after Jackson to catch up.

Chapter 15

Praevian IV

~ Paul ~

Li'Quari's a great gal. She really has a lot of courage and hope. I admire her "never-give-up" attitude in spite of incredible odds that never seem to go in her favor. It's curious how a group of complete strangers, who were suddenly thrown together in a situation of complete chaos and bewilderment, all came together in such a way that we were almost like family. When we had nothing to rely on and all of what we had once known became useless; the people who shared that wonderful experience with me became my lifeline. I knew many things about the physical person and even the psychological explanations of human frailty, but I had never learned, in any of my studies, how much people can be capable of when they follow their hearts.

Of course, Papa would say that people should think with their hearts because that is where the Creator lives and breathes into us the message of love and hope. Children are the best at it. It seems that once we lose our innocence, we become infatuated with our own sense of self-worth. Only we aren't worth half a rino if our heart is blackened. Well, maybe not exactly like that, but the Doctore would definitely be speaking along those lines.

Papa has time for the last segment, which will complete how our wonderful guide, Maria, led her children to safety. We must then be moving on to Timor Dimini, or we will be getting into the canton long after sunset.

~ Doctore ~

Just east of the old abandoned San Luis Obispo Airport, running along Los Osos Valley Road was the "Giant Break." The Los Osos reverse thrust fault line, running through the city of SLO, had broken open exposing a deep cavern after the major earthquake hit. This crevice's width varied from a mere three inches wide to just over six feet. The fracture in the Earth ran northwest until reaching Morro Bay, where it took a sharp western turn driving all the way to the Pacific Ocean. Standing out from the fault's walls was sharp, jagged-edged rock that could tear a man to shreds should he misstep and fall into the Break.

As with most mysterious and dangerous places on Earth, people seemed to be attracted to this treacherous spot of land and had set up tents and makeshift shelters close to the fissure. Many were poor and homeless. However, there were also the wealthier, younger individuals who showed up at the Break's edge to look upon the great rupture in the Earth and then dared each other to jump across its widest parts. There on the dark rock walls of the breach, the jagged edges were tainted red as they had torn at the victims' clothing and skin, leaving incriminating evidence behind. These unfortunate souls mistimed the jump or slipped on loose gravel before leaping from the edge. When the Pacific winds whistled through the fault line, the sound resembled the screams of victims being pulled apart on the twenty-mile drop.

After her narrow escape from her brother's gang at Jazin's estate, Sevita woke the next morning in Vivian's living room. She was still quite shaken from her terrifying evening the night before, but after having something to eat; she packed up her things and was grateful for the food and water offered by her friend. She thanked Vivian for all of her kindness and help. After leaving the apartment, she began to follow the Break just before eleven o'clock in the morning. Starting at Los Osos Oaks Park, she walked parallel to the large fracture, but still kept some distance between her and the people who seemed to be mesmerized by the limitless depth of it. Walking east, Sevita searched for Maria along the Break, but didn't see her at all. She asked people along the way if they knew Maria or where she might be and always she received the same answer, "Ah, Maria? Yes, I saw her here yesterday or perhaps last week, but not today."

Sevita continued to walk as the sun moved across the eastern sky. The path along the Break was mostly dirt and rock with patches of green foliage, nothing like it had been when it belonged to farmers producing strawberries, wine grapes, lettuce, cabbage, and broccoli. Now it was mostly barren of such crops; the farms had long since been abandoned. Many in the Pacific District were wealthy and had their own food generators, and the not so wealthy ate the food imported from the Hydro farmers located in the northern district, which left very little need for California's once booming agricultural industry.

After walking for nearly five and one half hours without finding Maria, Sevita stopped just in front of the abandoned airport to rest under a palm tree. She eased her backpack to the ground, unzipped it, and took out a container of water. The temperature had been rising all day. The further away her mission took her from the ocean breezes, the warmer the air seemed to become. Pressing the water container to her lips, she drank nearly a quarter of the container, and then ate a vitamin snack bar while she contemplated why she had not seen Maria along the Break. *Perhaps she showed up after I was already there and I missed her.* She took another bite of the snack bar. *Maybe I should stay here the night and wait for her. She's bound to show up at some point.* She finished her bar and thought how tired she had felt all of a sudden. She hadn't had any sleep the previous night, and with all the walking she had done, she was starting to feel drained and alone. Her biologics abandoned her. Her brother, Danni, betrayed her. The only friend she had was Vivian, and she didn't want to involve her in the situation.

"I have no one," Sevita said aloud.

"You always have someone, Sevita," a soft voice spoke from behind her. It almost sounded like a song being carried by the wind from far off in the distance.

Sevita spun around. A beautiful woman in a simple white dress with a rich, blue overlay stood just behind a palm tree. Covering her head was a white shawl that draped loosely around her exquisite face. Her eyes seemed to dance with a light.

"Maria?"

"I am."

"Maria, I'm in trouble. I have nowhere to go and my brother has gotten mixed up with some bad people who I believe are after me. I'm very scared of what they would do to me if they found me." Tears rolled down her cheek and dropped to the ground.

"There is much evil here. It consumes everything it touches. There are few who will escape it. I can help you to get away from this place, but you can never come back here."

"I do not ever want to see this place again, honest."

"You must also look deep inside of yourself and into your own ways. You must respect yourself and the body that you have been given. It is not a thing to be used to promote goods. It is a sanctuary that holds the very spirit of your existence."

Sevita, feeling embarrassed and ashamed, looked down at the ground as she realized how much she had given in to the contemptible social pressure of the world in order to survive in it. The more she gave into that pressure the more it demanded until there was nothing left to give. But to her credit, she did not give herself to the evil of her brother's cult. Knowing that she still had integrity deep within her gave her the courage to face Maria. "I know I can do better with a fresh start."

"You will have your chance, Sevita. There is a beautiful city very far from here. It is a city full of good people doing good things in this world. There are many hidden paths in this country that were created to lead people like you to this golden city. These paths were carved by the bravest of men who died for their fellow man for the sole purpose of giving others the opportunity to live. Your way lies in Santa Barbara at the church of Our Lady of Sorrows. It is more than a three-day walk from here, but the journey is safe along the 101 Highway. Rest here the night and leave at dawn's light. When you get to the church, follow the Archangel Raphael's staff and shield."

"Thank you, Maria! I will remember everything you have said."

Maria bowed her head slightly. "I will see you again along your journey. Until then, you will be provided what you will need. Trust in your inner voice and listen to its warnings. Have a blessed journey, Sevita."

Maria turned and went on her way. She walked slowly, effortlessly, passing in and out of view as she moved from tree to tree as if she was floating across the ground, until after passing behind one particularly large palm tree, she disappeared from sight.

Sevita moved from place to place trying to get a glimpse of her from different perspectives, but Maria was nowhere to be seen. She had vanished completely from sight.

Sevita returned to her palm tree and discovered two loaves of bread wrapped in cloth, a large jug of water, and a type of overcoat with a hood. The coat was very soft and the silvery color seemed to blend in with the surroundings. It reflected the color and imagery of whatever was close to it.

That was so thoughtful of her to leave me supplies, she thought. She sat down with her back against the tree and reached for one of the loaves. After breaking off an end, the most pleasant aroma rose to her senses. Sevita savored the flavor and chewed it slowly. Reaching into her backpack, she took out the book left by her father and continued to read it as she ate. In between pages, she would take another bite of bread or a swallow of water from the jug. Soon she struggled to see the print on the pages as the sun had long set upon the day. It seemed that time had drifted by so very quickly that day. She closed the book and placed it and the extra loaf of bread into her backpack. There was very little left of the first loaf, but she placed that into the pack as well.

There was thickened foliage growing near one of the other trees. She placed the jug of water there to keep cool and made up a bed beside her special palm tree. Using the backpack as a pillow and covering herself with the overcoat left by Maria, she nestled in for the night. The air was starting to get cool and she pulled the hood over her head and tucked her arms in close to her body. While staring at the stars in the sky, her eyelids became heavy and she dozed off.

The next morning, Sevita was awakened by seagulls' cries as they flew across the empty airport in search of food in the dawning light. After quickly gathering her things into her backpack and retrieving the jug of water, she began her journey south along Edna Road towards Arroyo Grande. It was here that the path took her away from the Break, as it moved east towards Newsom Ridge. It was six-thirty and the morning's citrus-colored orb seemed to obligingly guide her way. She found herself reveling in how beautiful the heavens looked that morning. With the orangish-red glow just starting to rise out of the eastern horizon, a retreating dark backdrop crept across the western sky where the pale twinkles of light were lagging behind their night's matriarch. Sevita hadn't noticed such things before even with all of her time spent at the beach. She had never taken the time to just admire the beauty and wonder of it all.

It was ten o'clock by the time she had reached Highway 101 where she stopped to take a rest. Just a few yards northeast of the overpass were large trees and overgrowth in which she shielded herself from the rising sun. She took out the container that Maria had given her and took a few large gulps of water. Trying to ration her food and water, she was surprised to see that not much water was missing from the jug. *I must not have drank as much as I thought.* Her legs were sore from walking and at times she wished she had gone back to get her bi-craft. However, it was too risky to be riding it. She would not have blended in with the others who did not have the means to own one. She unwrapped the loaf of bread from Maria and broke off the end. After taking a bite, it still seemed as warm and fresh as the night before. Leaning back against the tree, she took out her novel and read through the rest of the chapter while nibbling at the bread.

By eleven o'clock, she was back on Highway 101. She wanted to make it to Nipomo before two o'clock. Nipomo was the town in which the Break met back up with the Highway and once again they paralleled each other through the hills and ridges. The hours seemed to go by quickly while she mulled over various topics from her father's book that she had been reading to Maria and what the city might look like, to her troubled brother, and then back again to the story. In her past, she had never remembered having the time to contemplate such things, but was always so preoccupied with day-to-day events that she'd had little time to just let her mind wander.

She reached Nipomo on schedule and continued right on past the small town. She walked and walked along the highway. Every once in a while she glanced up to look at the Break running alongside the neglected, broken concrete path. Her face felt warm from sunburn, her legs were sore, her feet hurt, and the small of her back was starting to ache. Nevertheless, she continued on her journey and didn't stop again until she entered Santa Maria at almost six-thirty in the evening, completely exhausted.

Finding a dense patch of sycamore trees between the highway and the Break, Sevita collapsed on a patch of long, pale-green grass. She removed her shoes and massaged her sore feet. There were the beginnings of blisters on the sides of her feet near her big toe and on the back of her feet above her heels. Leaning back against the trunk of the tree, she closed her eyes and let the Pacific breeze blow across her sun- and wind-burned cheeks. After a quick dinner of Maria's bread and the last of her snack bars, Sevita turned in for the night. The stars had already begun their march across the sky, punching small holes in heaven's floor. The wind had picked up and she felt chilled from the air, mostly due to her overexposure to the elements while walking. Pulling the hood to Maria's covering over her head, she also tucked her legs in underneath it, and nestled close to the trunk of the tree. She soon was dreaming of a magnificent city of white and gold where children ran through the streets and parents looked on with gratifying expressions. Walking along the dreamy streets of gold, she ate an apple and watched the families huddle their children together. She heard her name being called out as she turned away from the children and walked towards the city's gate.

"Sevita!" the voice called out.

She went to the gate and as she got closer she saw the shadowy figure of Danni with both hands on the bars of the gate and his face pressed up against them.

"Sevita! Let me in!" Danni yelled. His face had a long bloody scar on his right cheek and his right eye was blackened. It looked as if his nose had been broken and there were many cuts and marks on his arms.

"What are you doing here?" she asked. "What happened to you?"

"I was tortured because you left. Why couldn't you just meet with him and do this one thing for your own brother? Now, let me in!"

Sevita started to back away from the gate. "No, Danni. You don't belong here."

"Sevita! Open this gate!" he screamed at her. His eyes turned angry and the veins stood out in his neck and forehead. "I'll find a way inside and I'll drag you back!"

"I feel sorry for you – you have nothing, but pain and anger. You have no one. Goodbye Danni," she replied, and then turned away from the gate and walked back towards the city.

"Sevita!" Danni shouted out and pounded on the gate, rattling it inside its frame, but it would not give. "Sevita!"

Sevita awoke from her dream, startled. It was still dark, but by the light of the crescent moon in the night's sky she saw two figures walking along the Break.

"Sevita!" one of the figures called out.

Oh no, it's Danni! She thought to herself. *How did he find me? Oh please don't let him see me.* She pulled the covering tighter around herself and lowered her head against the ground.

Danni and the other person continued to walk along the Break coming nearer and nearer to her position. She should have chosen a place that was further away from the Break. She should not have stopped here in Santa Maria. Many thoughts and second guesses shot through her mind at the speed of light as she trembled with fear. They were only twenty-five feet away from her now as they stopped and looked around.

"Check over that way and I'll look around over there by those trees," Danni said.

The two split up, each taking an opposite direction. Danni walked up the slight hill away from the Break and toward Sevita's sanctuary of sycamores. The shadows of the trees made the ground dark; the light from the crescent moon did not break through the large branches. She could hear the sounds of his footsteps coming nearer and nearer as her heart began to race faster. What would she do if he found her? She'd rather die than go back to that wretched and disgusting house. *Oh Maria, please help me.* She dared not move. She took shallow breaths. Danni was so close she could have reached out and touched his boots.

"Where is that pfotten natwotch? If I find her she's gonna get the same thing I got. I'll never forgive her for getting me into trouble with Jazin."

Danni looked at the jug by the base of the tree and went over to pick it up.

"What's this?" he asked aloud.

Oh no, Sevita thought. She had left the jug of water by the tree in between the two large roots growing up from the ground. *Now, he'll know someone has been here. Maybe they will stay here the night. Maybe they will see me when daybreak comes.* Terrible thoughts of horror ran through her mind as she tried very hard to not scream out, to not run. She was so scared she just froze, completely motionless.

Danni uncapped the container, turned it over and put his hand underneath the spout. Nothing came out of it. Putting it up to his nose, he breathed in, but didn't smell anything. Frustrated that he couldn't find one clue of where Sevita may have gone, he tossed it to the ground.

"Did you find anything?" called out his counterpart.

"No, let's keep moving along the Break. She couldn't have gone too much further. The skant is here somewhere."

Sevita, from underneath her covering, watched the back of Danni's boots as they went back down the hill to meet up with the other man near the Break. The two of them continued along the large crack in the Earth until they were finally out of sight. It wasn't until then that Sevita began to breathe easier. She couldn't believe how lucky she had been that Danni hadn't seen her. In fact, she was incredibly mystified. Sitting up, she looked more closely at the overcoat that Maria had left her. It was barely visible to her. She took it off and laid it on the ground. It disappeared in the darkness, camouflaged with the long grass and rocks around it. It seemed to reflect whatever was near it like a cloth mirror. Picking it back up, she put it around herself. She was so thankful to Maria for helping her. She stood up and went to reach for the jug of water that Danni had thrown. The cap was on it and the container was nearly half full of water.

"Oh Maria, I adore you. You are heaven sent!" she cried.

Sevita rested until sunrise and then quickly gathered her items and started south. Almost three and one half hours later, she came to a crossing at Foxen Canyon Road and Santa Maria Mesa Road. She turned onto Foxen Canyon Road and followed the winding path with great patience, but wished it had been more of a straight line. It had been only thirty minutes since she had taken the turn when she spotted Maria by a small pond. Sevita felt such gratitude that she sprinted towards her and after reaching Maria, she threw her arms around her with thankfulness. "Oh Maria, I was so afraid when I saw Danni. But he never saw me under the covering you left for me. And the bread was constantly warm, and fresh, and delicious. And the water, oh my, the water it's though it is alive. It seems to know when it needs filling and has a life all of its own! Thank you, Maria!" she said, as she still held onto Maria.

Maria hugged her close and smiled. Her eyes sparkled with light. She stood in front of Sevita and looked at her with kind, loving eyes. "You are welcome, Sevita. There is much courage and strength in you. Do not underestimate yourself." Maria clasped Sevita's face softly between her hands. "You have a touch of the sun on your face."

But Sevita didn't even notice the pain anymore as she stood in front of Maria. All she could think of was how grateful she was and how much she loved her. All of her pain and fears seemed to just fall from her body like an old gown that was in need of laundering.

"Go and wash your feet in the pond. Completely wash each foot three times and then come back here," Maria said and lowered her hands from Sevita's face.

Sevita went to the pond. Brown hills rose just behind it. Reddish-brown clay surrounded the entire perimeter of the pond. There wasn't a blade of grass or patch of green anywhere near it. Off in the distance, littering the ground between the pond and the hillside, lay rusted farm implements: tractors, tractor parts, and old tires. The water was somewhat shallow and murky. Patches of moss and algae floated atop of it along with the occasional dead insect.

At the edge of the water, she winced as she removed her shoes. The blisters on the sides and backs of her feet had broken and the raw skin was exposed. She put her right foot into the cool water and began to move her hands over the top and underneath. She cried out in agony as her hand rubbed over the raw, exposed skin, but she did as Maria asked and washed her entire foot, and then did the same thing with her left foot, which was even worse than her right. She screamed out in pain as she cleaned over the areas that were raw and bloody. The blisters burned immensely and she felt as though she would die if she touched the open sores again. Putting her right foot back into the pond water, she washed it again, only this time it didn't seem to be as painful as before. By the third time, there wasn't any blistering or rawness on her skin. Her feet were completely healed. She stared at her reflection in the water. Her sunburn had vanished as well. She put on her shoes and jumped up to run back to Maria, only there was no one there. Maria was gone. Sevita was saddened that she hadn't the chance to talk with her again.

She walked to where Maria had been waiting. The water jug was full and there was a sack of fresh bread. She gathered her supplies in her pack and started off towards Los Olivos. Feeling refreshed from her encounter with Maria, Sevita was much lighter in her step despite having over five hours of walking before she reached her next resting place. She wanted to get there before sunset as she was anxious to reach her final destination, Santa Barbara, which was still more than a day's walk. She hoped she would not run into Danni again along the way.

~ Paul ~

I step up to Papa's perch and lay a hand on his shoulder. "Papa, we must go. Our friends are awaiting our arrival in Timor Dimini. We are very late now."

The Doctore shakes a few more hands and blesses a few more children before we head out of the canton. After walking backwards for nearly fifty yards still waving to his flock, Papa finally turns around and we leave Intellectus.

"They are such good people. I do love every one of them."

"Yes, Papa," I reply rather shortly.

"Do you have something you want to say?"

It's a trick. He's just testing me and trying my patience. I must stay quiet. "No, Papa."

We walk along the side of the road on to the next canton. It is after dinner and the sun has long ago set. As I thought about the dreaded walk, I start to get annoyed at having to get into town so late in the evening. I start to stew in my anger and impatience. The more I think of it, the more it angers me. I could just feel the boiling of my temper inside, cooking away at my patience.

"Actually, yes, I do have something to say."

"Ah, what is it Paolo? What has you troubled?"

"Why can't you ever stick to our planned schedule? I make every effort to plan our allotment of time, carefully allowing us enough leeway to go from canton to canton and make sure we are there before nightfall. Yet, you insist on never adhering to that plan. Why? Why, oh why, do I painstakingly go through that tedious task of building a schedule if you so willingly toss it to the wind?"

"Why indeed, my dear Paolo. Life's journey is not something to be planned and arranged in incremental allotments of time. The Creator has already done that for you. All we must do is let ourselves be open to that plan."

"Well, exactly how does that work, Papa? I mean, without arranging any kind of predetermined plans, just how will we know when to meet with others? Where will we stay? How will we get along?"

"Paolo, have you ever seen a bird make plans? And yet, the birds eat every day. They nest every night. Does not God take care of them? If such care is made by our Master to see to the smallest detail of a bird then wouldn't you think that you are far more important?"

"The birds make their nest."

"Yes, from the twigs and leaves that have been shaken from the tree for them."

"You are so...."

"Yes, I am so fully trustful of God. I have no need to worry if my heart remains open to His word. You must work on letting go of your incessant obsession with control. Control is an illusion. You really are not in control at all. This is your lesson for tonight. You must meditate and pray on this."

"Yes, Papa," I replied. Of course, my anger vanished, however the guilt returned. Half of the time I felt the need to hug this man for all of his love and insight he shares with me. And the other half of the time I felt the need to push him down a hill for all the love and insight he shares with me. It's a complicated relationship.

Part III – The Way

Chapter 16

The Way to Penury I

~ Paul ~

Leaving late from Intellectus, Papa and I arrived in Timor Dimini last night. I had made arrangements for us to stay with Markus, however he had gone to pick up his son who was staying with his friend in Intellectus, which we just left. I'm surprised we did not see him along the way. However, in his absence, his wife Denora made sure we felt welcome and looked after us from our long journey.

After a deliciously prepared meal of fowl and taters, we went to bed and slept quite soundly. Of course, Papa was up early with the sunrise this morning. With our prayers complete and an egg breakfast under our belts, we were in the canton's square before nine o'clock.

Speaking of cantons, Timor Dimini means "fear of the Lord." I often wondered about this and why we should fear our Creator who is so loving and merciful. The Doctore has this to say on the matter: "The Father created everything, has power over everything, and needs nothing. It is out of his mercy and love that we are allowed to exist. It is important that Man know his place in the universe. If we do not fear the Creator, or we take for granted His love and mercy, then woe unto us when His judgment is thrust upon us. This is the reason why it is so important to cultivate humility in our lives."

I get Papa settled onto his cathedra while the crowd finds their seats. This morning's teaching begins to the sound of birds singing the opening hymn.

~ Doctore ~

In the early morning hours of May fourteenth, before the sun had yet to kiss the horizon, First Lieutenant George Lyndon slipped on his field pack. He moved quickly through the GIT pod picking up various items including extra clips of ammunition. Slipping the twelve-inch survival knife into its sheath, he secured it to his right calf by tightening the nylon belts. He left behind all of the digital communication devices so the FED could not track them. His left forearm felt naked without having the m-Pad attached, however he couldn't risk taking it. Accessing the GIT system would only give away their position and he needed their expedition to remain covert.

Jackieo was in the food preparation area gathering supplies when George entered.

"We need to go. St. Peter's is over two klicks and it's a forty-minute hump. We need to cross the MLK Bridge before sun-up at o'six-hundred," George said as he placed his cap over his head.

"I'm set. Here are the rations, and I filled all four canteens." Jackieo grinned mischievously. "I brought your favorite dark chocolate bars too."

"Rah that, J-O. You're looking mighty fine in that GIT-wear." Grabbing her bottom he pushed her towards the back entrance. "Let's move it out!"

Jackieo tucked her hair under the GIT cap, and then they proceeded out the back entrance. Once out on 16th Street, they quickly made their way under the cover of darkness towards GH Road, or what had once been known as Good Hope Road. From underneath the Anacostia Highway, they could clearly see the MLK Bridge and the two military GIT figures that marched across it in the opposite direction with their backs turned towards them. Jackieo did not like the fact that the patrols were moving right along their path and looked to George to see if he would propose an alternate route.

"Let's give them four minutes, and then we'll make for the bridge. If they spot us, remember what I told you," George said as he looked up from his field watch.

"Got it," she replied somewhat nervously.

The two military GITs crossed the bridge and turned north continuing their patrol. George and Jackieo came out from the cover of the Anacostia overpass and started crossing over the MLK Bridge. Once on the other side, they made their way to Virginia Avenue. It looked as though they may have a clear shot all the way to Third Street until two military GITs turned onto Virginia Avenue at Fourth Street. As soon as George saw them, he started to jog towards them and Jackieo followed. Once they came close to the patrol, George stopped directly in front of them.

"Morn-up Private First Class," George called out, pretending to breathe somewhat heavily.

"Morn-up First Lieutenant," the two GITs saluted.

The smaller of the two men stood down first from the salute and looked at George inquisitively. "What has you up at this hour in full gear, First Lieutenant?"

"Ah, well, you see, Household 6 and I are doing R-A-R in a week and we've been doing a bit of PT to get ourselves primed up for diving at Fort Sumter."

"Roger that, LT." PFC looked at George's uniform tag and typed the number into his m-pad. "And you are Jackieo Elizabeth?"

"Yes, that's right, Private First Class."

"What kind of weight are you carrying?"

144

"About twenty-five pounds," Jackieo replied.

"A scuba tank weighs forty – you are a little light aren't you?"

"It doesn't weigh forty in the water. And I won't be jogging with it either," she grinned.

The GIT nodded in agreement and turned back to George.

"Enjoy your R-A-R, First Lieutenant; North C is mighty fine this time of year," he said and saluted George.

George and Jackieo resumed their jog and turned north at Third Street where they stopped underneath the Southeast Freeway to catch their breath.

"I was so nervous," Jackieo said to George.

"You did fine. Remember, they don't know anything. We're just a couple of GITs up early." George looked at his watch and then looked out at the eastern sky. "Come on. Sun up is in about five minutes and we still have an eight-minute hump to the church. It's double-time here on out."

"I got your six," Jackieo replied.

George turned and looked curiously at her out of the corner of his eye.

"Go!" she said pointing in the forward direction.

They jogged all the way to Second Street where they slowed to a casual walk. They could see St. Peter's steeple rising in the distance just as the morning sun broke the horizon and a soft orange glow gently touched the front of the church. George passed the front entrance on Second Street and continued around the corner to C Street where there was a locked metal gate that led to a basement entrance. George scanned the area for any sign of GIT patrols, and satisfied that they were in the clear, he hopped the gate and helped Jackieo over it. They both quickly descended the stairs and came across a wooded door. He pushed against it and the heavy oak door opened easily, but as it closed behind them, it also shut out the only light coming into the room. Feeling in the darkness, he undid the Velcro flap of an interior chest pocket, took out his military lamplight, and turned it on to illuminate the stone hallway. It smelled of mildew and mold. The floor had many cracks and there were broken pieces of stone and mortar scattered about the area. Earth and moss grew from the cracks and in the areas missing stone. The growth was steadily thicker the deeper they went. George held the lamplight up to the walls and began to scan the faded drawings and etched markings on the stone and brick walls.

"Look for the staff and shield of an angel, the Archangel Raphael; that's what Maria said," George instructed and set the lamplight down in the middle of the floor facing the wall.

They both searched the wall starting from opposite ends and working their way towards the center. Running their fingers over the rough stones and bricks, they scanned for anything that resembled a staff and shield. By the dim light of George's military lamp, they combed every square inch of the stone structure. After scraping their fingers over the entire wall and coming together in the center of it, George stopped and took a step back.

"I don't see it. Did you find anything?" he asked.

"No, nothing. Maybe it's not here in the entryway. Maybe it's somewhere else."

"Let's move on and see what else is down here."

George held the light out in front of himself and moved to the only other exit from the small hallway. It led into a dark area with a staircase against the far wall. From the middle of the floor and looking straight up, George could see light coming down from very high up.

"We must be under the tower. I think that's daylight up there."

"Hey, shine the light over here. I think…." Jackieo stared at a figure carved into the wooden rail of the staircase.

George brought the lamplight over to her and looked at the image. It had been carved into the wood staircase. There was a circle in the center of the image with a vertical line starting from outside the top of the circle, cutting straight through the center of it, and ending just outside of the circle. Near the top, the line was drawn heavier, like a type of a handle that stayed outside the circle but was connected to the vertical line. There was another line inside the circle that went horizontally from west to east, but did not touch either side of the circle and cut across the vertical line. Seemingly, behind the circle was a sort of half-finished, upside-down triangle in which the tip was left open. The open end of the triangle seemed to point in the direction of the stairs, going upward.

"I think this is it! The circle is the shield, this line is the staff, and this open-ended triangle could be angel wings. It's the sign of Raphael!" Jackieo said excitedly.

"I think you're right. Way to go, J-O! Well, start climbing; looks like we're going up."

After ascending four flights of stairs while continuously looking for further signs, they came to a landing. There was still one more flight of stairs to go, but they hadn't found any more markings. The light from the top of the tower was streaming into the stairwell, and it was getting easier to see the walls and staircase. There were beautiful oil paintings and faded photographs of Holy figures hanging on the walls that had not been damaged. Jackieo had been staring at one of them for several moments.

"Jackieo. Hey J-O. I think I found it." George waited a moment, but Jackieo didn't respond. "What's wrong?" he asked.

"This picture—it looks just like Maria. But it can't be, look how old it is and…never mind. You found it?"

"Yeah, but I don't know. It appears to be pointing inward towards the wall. Here; hold the light for me. I'm going to try something." He handed

146

the light to Jackieo, took a couple of steps back, and then lowered his shoulder and rushed at the brick wall.

It didn't move.

"Ow, fackers! That was stupid," he said rubbing his shoulder.

"No, it moved. I think you're right. When you hit the wall, I saw a crack appear that runs all the way down to the floor. There must be a lever or a lock or something that's holding it in place."

"Hand me the light," he said. He held it close to the image and noticed that there was cracking around the brick that held the image. He pushed it inward with his thumb. There was the sound of brick rubbing against brick, and the piece moved inside its space. The wall shifted slightly and showed the full length of the crack in the brick and mortar. Pushing once more against the wall, it opened into a hidden and dark interior room. George shined the light around the inside and then turned to Jackieo, "Come on, there's another entryway."

"Just so there aren't any spiders in there. You know how much I hate spiders," she said and followed him in holding her hands and arms up to her chest and close to her body.

The passageway, lit only by George's lamplight, was very narrow with only enough room for a single person to walk through it. George lowered his head as he pushed through the tight path. His shoulders rubbed the wooden-planked walls, which were carved with stars, kings on camels, mangers, men sitting at large tables, crucifixes, a tomb with a large stone to one side, and many a bearded men seemingly leaping or floating into the sky. There were pictures of men and women dressed in robes of brown or black usually kneeling before a cross.

Jackieo and George continued until they came to the end of the path, which held what looked like a type of elevator shaft with ropes to work it. There was a small wooden platform in which a person could stand and use the ropes to lower the platform downwards. George inspected the shaft, first putting one foot on the platform and pushing his weight against it to check for its sturdiness. After grabbing hold of the ropes, he looked up at them and pulled against them testing their strength.

"It seems sturdy enough. But there's only enough room for one person on this platform. We'll have to take turns. Do you want me to go first?"

"No, we can fit together. I'm not going down by myself and I'm not staying here, either. We can fit," she replied looking over the platform.

"I don't know. There's really not that much room in here."

Jackieo pushed him into the space with his back against the wall and then pressed herself against him with her arms around his back. "See? Plenty of room. Let's go LT," she said with a smile and then buried her head inside his chest.

"All right, here goes nothing." George pulled the two latches holding the elevator to the sides of the shaft. It made a loud thud and moved downward slightly. After grabbing the ropes, he pulled on them from the top to the bottom moving the platform downwards. "Why would they have us climb all those stairs to the top of the east tower only to reach an elevator that goes back to the basement?" George asked while getting quite the exercise working the elevator ropes.

"I guess they wanted to hide the entrance. Judging by how far we walked through that path from the east tower, we must be clear over on the other side of the church. This shaft has to be close to the west tower, if not inside the west tower. I wonder how long this has all been here."

"I don't know. I imagine a long time judging by the antiquated technology they used to build it," George replied.

After nearly ten minutes, a light appeared from the bottom of the shaft, and the platform hit bottom. They stepped out of the small elevator and into a large tunnel system that seemed to be well below the church. There were bio-effervescence light emitting diodes (beleds) that drew their energy from the rock and soil. Producing a very soft bluish-white glow, the entire tunnel was well lit. George and Jackieo stood for several minutes outside the shaft and stared in amazement at the sight of the tunnel.

"Wow, it appears that people have updated the tunnel since it was built. Those are beleds on the sides of the tunnel."

George could not believe his eyes as he took in the entirety of the underground cavern. Just the sheer size of the inside of the carved out passageway amazed him. He tried to calculate what it must have taken to excavate out all of the earth and rock from the tunnel. *What kind of machinery did they use? How did they get the earth out without being detected? How could anyone have created something this large without someone realizing it was right below them?*

~ Paul ~

I am pleasantly interrupted from listening to Papa's story as Markus came to stand beside me. He looks as strong and military-like as he had the first time I saw him. We hadn't been on the second leg of the journey very long when we first met. Oh, and what a meeting it had been. I must say that it wasn't under the friendliest of circumstances. Of course, I'm getting too far ahead of myself again, so let me just say that since that time Markus and I have become good friends.

"Markus, you look good. How are you?"

"I'm doing well. How are you and the Doctore? Did you have all that was needed during your stay last night?"

"Oh, absolutely. Denora was a very generous hostess. She tirelessly made sure we had everything we needed and made us feel right at home."

"Good, I'm glad you enjoyed your stay. I apologize for not being there, but Carton wanted to play with Razzi. You know how close those two have become."

"I saw them in Intellectus while we were in the square. I was surprised we didn't see you also."

"I saw you, Paolo. Saz and I were talking–"

"You met with Saz?"

"Yea, we talked for quite some time."

"I wondered where she had gone off to in her stealth-like manner."

Markus chuckles. "She does have a way of popping in and out, doesn't she?"

"She seems to take more pleasure in doing it to me."

"Ah, well, it's just her way." Markus shrugs. "I'm going to head on back and sit with the family. I just wanted to say hello. Give my regards to Papa, will you?"

"Of course, it will be my pleasure."

After slapping me on the shoulder, Markus walks back to where his family was sitting and listens to Papa. I, too, turn my attention back to our speaker.

~ Doctore ~

George's scientific contemplation of the logistics in the making of the tunnel was interrupted when Jackieo walked up to the right side of the cavern and moved her hand over a large carving, tracing its figure with her fingertips.

"Look," she said. "Raphael is pointing down the tunnel. We're going the right way."

George took out his compass and looked at the needle. "The tunnel is heading straight east. I wonder where it leads." He closed the cover to the compass and put it in his jacket pocket. After taking off his pack, he removed the canteen and offered Jackieo a drink.

"You better take some water. It looks like we have a long walk ahead of us," he said.

She tipped back the canteen and after taking a few sips handed it back to George, who also took a large gulp. Tightening the cap and replacing the canteen, he swung the pack over his back and they started their journey down the tunnel.

The tunnel floor was hardened clay and brown rock that continued up the walls and across the cave's ceiling. The passageway was large enough to drive a couple of medium-sized, military K-trucks side by side through it.

George wondered how many years it must have taken to dig out the massive burrow. The walls and roof were reinforced with timber and metal beams. There seemed to be a constant flow of air that drifted past them and just when George decided that it was coming from behind them, the direction seemed to switch and the breeze hit them from the front. The bluish colored beleds were spaced evenly throughout the tunnel and lit the path every fifteen yards or so, except it seemed every so often there was a very well lit up area with ten to twenty beleds that illuminated a small shrine. The first shrine was coming up on the right hand side of the tunnel and Jackeio stopped in front of it.

"Look at this little memorial inside the wall. All of these pictures of two boys growing up," Jackieo said staring at the images.

George looked through all of the images too. Underneath some of the photographs was text that had been etched into the clayish-rock wall, 'Brothers Andrew and Peter.' George stared at the images one after the other. Andrew and Peter at age eight and twelve, and again at eighteen and twenty-two. He saw the two brothers practicing their sword skills with one another from young ages. There was a picture of Andrew sitting at a long wooden table with his arm stretched across it holding a bottle of whiskey. His head was down on the table and his long gnarled hair lay across his other arm.

As George stared at the picture, the scene came to life in his mind's eye: Peter put a blanket over Andrew and patted him on the back.

"Leave me alone! Get away from here," Andrew bellowed in anger.

"You're drunk again. Have you no honor?"

Andrew pushed back from the table hard and the chair flew to the side and crashed to the floor. He stood uneasy and unbalanced from the whiskey, but he stood and stared with angry bloodshot eyes at his older brother. Peter, who had always maintained a calm and patient demeanor, looked back at him with disappointment.

"Don't talk to me about honor. What honor was there in our father's death? What honor was there in his life being cut down, leaving his young sons and their mother with nothing?"

"He fought for his beliefs. He fought for doing right by God. Andrew, where is your belief?"

"Don't you dare. Don't give me your lecture, brother. I've heard it enough. They're your beliefs, not mine." Andrew turned to the table and picked up the bottle and held it up to Peter's face. "Here is my belief. Now, leave me."

Peter swung his left hand and knocked the bottle from his brother's hand. It hit the floor and shattered, spilling the dreadful liquid onto the pine boards. Angry, Andrew stared at Peter with penetrating eyes that could kill a viper. He grabbed two broom sticks and threw one to his brother.

"Defend yourself – if you lose, you go and get me another bottle!"

Peter caught the broomstick, spun it several times, and held it out in front of himself. The sound of wood cracked loudly and could be heard echoing in the room as they circled one another, slamming stick against stick. Andrew avoided a blow swung just left of his head from Peter and spun to his right; coming out of the spin he slammed his stick against his brother's back. Peter lunged forward in pain. Andrew charged at him and pushed against him with his fists while still holding the stick. Peter backpedaled off balance and hit so hard against the outside door that it flung open and he stumbled into the back yard. He turned to face him.

"Why don't you avoid receiving even more pain and go get that bottle," Andrew said.

"Why don't you use your skill for something more than your thirst and fear," Peter retorted.

"Fear? It seems to me you're the only one afraid." Andrew lunged out and took three quick strikes that were met with blocks from Peter. Peter returned a quick blow to Andrew's ribs and he winced in pain from the hit. Crack after crack the sticks came together sounding out like firewood burning in an open-pit bonfire. Peter moved in and went to try to lift Andrew's leg out from underneath him, only Andrew stepped back and punched Peter in the face. He caught him right across the mouth and chin. Peter's mouth began to bleed.

"Give it up, you are no match. Run and get the bottle of Johnny."

"I got your Johnny. Right here." Peter swung eagerly and their sticks clashed. Andrew was becoming winded and he swung wildly at him again. Peter stepped out of the way and stuck his broom handle in between Andrew's legs. He tripped and fell to the ground. Jumping on top of him, Peter seized the opportunity and held his stick across Andrew's neck and shoulders.

"If you weren't so drunk you'd have had me ten minutes ago. There was a time when you were the best. You are by far the better warrior than me. You have more of our father than I do. Why do you dishonor him inside a bottle?"

"Let me up! Get off of me!" Andrew tried to push Peter off, but Peter would not budge.

"I'll let you up when you answer. I will not give up on you; I will not leave you to your own misery. Answer me! Why do you find honor at the bottom of a drink?"

"Peter, get off! I swear I'll hurt you! I hate you and all your self-righteous ways. Your faith is that of a fool. Get off me!"

Peter's eyes began to tear, but he would not move and he only pushed down harder across Andrew's chest.

Andrew saw the hurt he had put in his brother's eyes, but he saw something else as well. There seemed to be a reflected light. It was an odd light that took the shape of their father. It was then, at that moment that something broke inside of him. He stopped struggling and put his hand on Peter's heart.

"I miss him. You're exactly like him, Peter. I don't want to lose you, too."

Peter pulled back and tossed the stick to the side. He sat next to his brother and looked at the ground.

"I miss him, too. Don't you think that I relive it every single day? Time after time I play it over and over in my head. I think that if I had been there I might have saved him. Andrew, he died fighting for what he believed in; he died so that we might have the same religious freedoms that he had growing up. I only hope that I might have that same courage one day. I pray that nothing ever happens to you. My heart could never take anything happening to you, little brother."

Peter stood up and held out his hand. Andrew grabbed it and Peter pulled him up.

"Come on, I'm hungry. Let's see what's to eat around here." Peter winked.

Andrew hugged him, and his ever-watchful brother pulled him close. He grabbed the back of Andrew's head and neck and he touched his forehead against Andrew's. "You are my only brother—all that I have left. I love you."

"I'm sorry, Peter. You gotta keep helping me."

"I'll always be there for you. You're already halfway there. I'm proud to have you as my brother. And you're a much better fighter than I am when you're not drunk."

Andrew chuckled through the tears in his eyes. "You are a bit slow-witted with the hands."

"George? Hey, LT!" Jackieo yelled out.

"What? Yeah?" George blinked his eyes several times while still staring at the photos; he then looked over to Jackieo.

"Where were you just then?" Jackieo asked. "You were really out of it."

"I...I don't really know. I just had the weirdest experience looking at these old photographs. It's like I was there listening to them. The two brothers were talking about their father; how he was killed in the religious wars."

"Your father died in those wars, too, right? It probably just brought back painful memories."

"Yeah, but my father was fighting for the Fed. These guys were fighting for the Zealots. It's like I was right there with them. I heard and saw them. I felt their presence. They were arguing with one another and physically fighting with each other. And then, they just stopped. The two of them joined together to fight with other religious fighters. It was strange, but it was so real. I was ready to go with them."

"We'd better get going. Come on, LT. You can fight with them another day." Jackieo moved away from the wall and pulled at his jacket.

George took one last look at Andrew and Peter, and then followed her back to the center of the trail.

After they had been walking for some time, George looked over to Jackieo. Sensing him staring at her, she turned and asked him what was wrong.

"I should teach you about hand-to-hand combat."

"What? Why?"

"You never know when you might be in a jam and it would be helpful if you knew a few moves. You're in good shape. It's just a matter of using your body and muscle in controlled movements. Here, wait...."

George stopped and took off his backpack. Setting it on the ground, but still holding it with his left hand, he removed two escrima sticks from the side of it. "Take this," he said after handing her one of them.

Jackieo took the black stick and held it out straight in front of her.

"Are you ready?" George asked.

"Yes."

George hit her stick hard and it flipped out of her hand. "Oww!" Jackieo called out. "What did you do that for? That hurt!"

"Never leave your weapon in a horizontal position where it can be taken from you so easily. Keep it more vertical to your body, not horizontal. Okay, try again. I'll go slowly. Watch my eyes and try to predict where I'm going to attack."

Jackieo steadied herself and held her stick more vertical this time. She and George circled one another and she watched his eyes. He moved his escrima stick from side to side and she blocked his moves. Striking faster and faster, he increased the speed and direction of his attempts.

"Good, that's it. Follow my eyes; predict the moves." Their sticks struck once, twice, three times, and then George spun around dropping low to the ground where, with his legs, took out Jackieo's feet from underneath her and she fell to the ground. George knelt over her and pinned her down.

"You can't just watch my eyes the whole time. You have to be ready for anything," he said.

She gazed at him for a moment, her eyes and lips visibly softening. "Come here LT; I want to kiss you."

George moved in close to her face and with closed eyes went to kiss her. Jackieo took her right hand, closed her fingers tight making a fist, and punched him in the abdomen with all her might, then bringing up her right leg she pushed against him throwing him off to the side. She scrambled to her feet.

thomas e

"You have to be ready for anything, soldier," she grinned.

Realizing his only weakness was Jackieo, he smirked. "Pick up your stick. We're not done yet."

After several more lessons in fighting technique, George put the sticks away and they continued down the tunnel. Along their journey they stopped, rested, and snacked on some dried packaged food they had brought with them along with the water in their canteens. Afterwards, they continued to move through the tunnel, which wasn't quite as wide as it had been when they first started out. George wasn't sure exactly how many miles they had walked, but keeping track of their time and calculating the average time to walk a mile he had guessed they had gone about thirty miles when they reached a very well-lit portion of the tunnel with a stone fountain that had been carved into the cavern walls. The exquisite bluish, marble-like fluorspar reflected the beled lighting with such softness that it appeared more like a wondrous work of art. The rich, charcoaled blue mineral had streaks of dark majestic purple containing unique patterns of white and black lines that cut across the fountain with unrestricted precision and strength. This magnificent rock contained flats, ridges, and valleys, which were independent from one another, yet had all blended together into a single glorious design. The kingly blue emanated from the crystalline structure, mirroring the beled light into the pools of water, which recast the shimmering reflections across the cavern roof and walls.

"Wow, look at this place. It's beautiful!" Jackieo remarked, approaching the fountain.

George put his hand into the water and brought it up to his lips tasting it carefully.

"This is the purest water I've ever tasted. Dump your canteens and fill up with this water. It's also a few minutes after nine o'clock, so we might as well camp here for the night. We've been going since before sun-up this morning. We need to rest."

"I'm all for that, LT. My feet are killing me. I'm not used to trekking these kinds of distances. I always exercised in short strenuous bursts."

George took off his pack and laid it against the wall. Pushing up his sleeves, he cupped his hands, filled them with water from the fountain, and pushed his face into them. He did this several times and pushed the water over his face and head, then ran his hands across his hair pushing it back.

"Hey, look at this. There are blankets and bread here in this cubbyhole," Jackieo said. She lifted out the bread and smelled it. "It smells delicious like it was just baked, and it is warm!"

George watched her as she broke a piece off and popped it into her mouth. "Well?" he asked.

"Oh my, this is amazing! It's the best bread I've ever had in my life!"

154

"Let me have some," George said holding out his hand.

"No way, this bread is mine. You can eat your k-rations," she said grinning and moved the bread behind her back.

George went after her and she started to run around the cavern teasing him with the bread. She broke off another piece and put it into her mouth. "Oh, this is so good. Wouldn't you just love to have a piece? It's so good, LT. You don't know what you're missing," she said and started laughing.

"Jackieo, don't start. Give me a piece of bread!" George chased her around the area by the fountain again. He caught up to her and grabbed her from behind, pulling her backward into his chest. Reaching around her, he tried to grab the bread, but she held it out further in front of herself trying to keep it away from him and laughed mischievously.

"You're such a child, I swear!" George said. "Hey, I have an idea...." His hands started to roam up her shirt. He had gotten two buttons undone when Jackieo quickly turned around and faced him. "If I can't have any bread I'll just have to have something else," he said grinning.

Jackieo tore off a piece of bread and shoved it into his mouth, and then kissed him.

George kissed her back and then started to chew his bread. "I'm still going to want the something else," he said with warm, dancing eyes. And then, he furrowed his eyebrows and his expression changed to that of wonder. "This bread is amazingly good. I wonder how it got here?"

They walked back to the fountain where George took out the blankets. He laid one on the ground and placed the other on top of it, pulling back one of the corners. The beled lights seemed to be losing their brightness and the cavern was getting dark. George looked at his field watch and then up at Jackieo.

"Come on, J-O. It's time for rack. We'll get an early start tomorrow."

They got comfortable on the blanket, and George pulled the top blanket over them even though it wasn't really that cold in the tunnel. He seemed to have done so more out of habit than anything else.

George didn't know how long he had been sleeping when something disturbed him. Whispers? Remaining perfectly still, he looked around the cavern. The beleds were barely lit and just provided enough light to make out the fountain and the walls. Jackieo was resting peacefully. He got up to look around the area. *Maybe I was just dreaming.* He continued walking further down the tunnel. Seeing nothing and hearing no other sounds, he started back towards Jackieo and the fountain when something caught his attention behind him. Something had lit up on the tunnel wall. He turned around, and there against the cavern wall was another picture of the two brothers Andrew and Peter. They were older and seemed to be somewhat worse for wear as they stood side by side with their arms around each other's shoulders. Peter had a bloodied scar on the right side of his face as if something had scraped him – a knife or sword possibly. George looked intently at the two brothers who, even though they looked a little worn out, still were grinning widely and seemed to be quite happy in each other's company.

A second light now appeared near his feet. He looked down expecting to find another picture but instead discovered a sheathed sword. He picked up the sword and slid it out of the sheath. It glowed a pale, dark blue. By the light emanating from the picture of the brothers, he saw writing on the handle of the blade. He squinted and looked closer to make out the letters: *Andrew*. George looked at the picture again and said, "Andrew? Is this your sword? It's a good weapon; it looks solid." George took a few steps back and swung the blade from side to side, cutting through the air several times. The steel made its high-pitched mark on the severed air that echoed in the tunnel's chambers. The weapon was well balanced and spun easily in the palm of his hand. Bringing the tip back to center, he touched the flat part of the blade to his forehead and brought it forward towards the picture. With a slight bow of his head, he saluted the brothers.

A firm voice whispered into the silence of the tunnel, "Take it and lead like my brother Peter."

George quickly dropped the sheath to the ground, clasped the sword with both hands, and he spun around with the sword in attack position. Scanning the area for threats or movement, he moved cautiously around the tunnel. Seeing and hearing nothing, he went back to the wall and picked up the sheath. The picture was no longer lit. The entire wall was dark and he couldn't make out any of the pictures or drawings. He looked down at the sword again. It still glowed a faint bluish color. He shook his head. He didn't understand any of this or what he was doing down in these tunnels. Nothing made sense. He slid the sword back into the sheath and carried it with him back to the fountain. Though there was no logical reason to any of what he had witnessed since meeting Maria, he knew there was no other place he'd rather be right now. He also felt deep inside of himself that this journey; this mission, given to him by Maria, was something he was supposed to do.

Jackieo was still asleep when he got back to their basecamp. He laid the sword above his head and got back underneath the blanket. Putting his folded arms underneath his head, he closed his eyes. Jackieo rolled from her right side to her left side and put her head on his chest, and then put her hand around his side and pulled herself closer to him. After draping his left arm over her, they fell back asleep.

George awoke the next morning to the sound of Jackieo humming by the fountain while cleaning up. He quickly reached for the sword above his head to make sure it was real and not a dream. It was exactly how he left it last night. Getting up, he placed it by his pack and went over to Jackieo.

"Morn-up, J-O," he said. He reached into the fountain and splashed water on his face, then slicked his hair back. After brushing his teeth, he replaced the brush in one of the many pockets of his fatigues.

"Morn-up, LT. Sleep well?"

"No, not really. You?"

"Yeah, I slept like a rock. It must have been all that walking."

"Yeah, it was a lot of walking to be sure. I could sure use a j-cup. You don't suppose that there's a coffee bar down here do you?"

"Let me know if you find one. Here, have a piece of dark chocolate. It's got caffeine in it, too."

"Thanks." George took the piece of candy and ate it. He shook out and folded the blankets and stuffed them back into the cubbyhole. Then after slipping the backpack over his arms, he slid the sword through one of the open bands on the pack so it lay against his back.

"You don't want to take the blankets?"

"No, we can't risk the extra weight and bulk. Let's just keep it simple."

"What's with the sword?"

"It's a long story, I'll tell you about it on the way. Let's get moving."

They continued hiking down the tunnel at a steady pace as George revealed to Jackieo what had happened to him the night before with the sword. He told her everything as it happened and didn't leave anything out. That was how it was with the two of them. They were always honest and open with one another whether it was good or bad news.

"That's unbelievable. Everything that has been happening since we met Maria is just all so – unbelievable. I can't even put it into words."

"I know. I thought the same thing. This is far beyond my comprehension. I'm just taking orders now and moving forward. I figure it's just like the military – you stay strong, get your orders, maintain your courage, and keep moving."

"Rah that, LT." Jackieo looked to her left and smiled at him.

"You wouldn't happen to have any of the bread left, would ya?"

"Yeah, I think there is some left." Jackieo spun her pack around and unzipped it. "Well, that's strange."

"What up?"

"The bread – it's a full loaf," she said and held it up to show him.

He stared at it for several moments in disbelief and then just shook his head. "Some things, J-O, you don't even want to question. Just be thankful and break off a big piece for me," he said and held out his hand.

After several hours of walking through the tunnel, George stopped suddenly and pulled Jackieo to a stop beside him.

"What is it?" she whispered.

"Do you hear that?" he asked.

Jackieo tilted her head and listened closely. She heard running water. "Another fountain?"

"I don't think so. Come on!" George said and started to jog towards the sound farther ahead in the tunnel.

As they picked up their pace, they jogged around a bend in the tunnel and were amazed at what came into view. On the right side of the cavern, the wall angled inward and a fast moving river rose up out of nowhere. The entire tunnel wall seemed to have been cut out like a window in which to gain access to the river. The river itself was only about eight or ten feet across and it didn't look very deep. One really couldn't tell; not because it was muddy or dirty, but because the water was moving so fast that all that could be seen were the white rapids. The ceiling over the river wasn't very high either, maybe four or five feet above the water's surface. At the very far left of the tunnel window was tied a type of tube-like boat that seemed to hover at the water's surface. Jackieo knelt down at the river's edge while George went to check out the tube-boat. It was nearly seven foot in length and just a couple of feet wide. There was a back to it that one could lean against and the seat was just several inches off the floor. There was also a small shield on the front of the vessel that was slightly lower than the back.

Jackieo put her fingers into the water and quickly withdrew them. "Ow!"

"What's the matter?"

"The water actually hurts! It's driving so hard that it feels like needles against my skin."

"Yeah, well I think we are supposed to take this tube-boat wherever it is supposed to go," George said and motioned her over.

"What makes you say that?"

"Archangel Raphael is right there," George said pointing at the image of the staff and shield.

"Do you know what I hate more than ugly spiders?"

"Fast moving boats?"

"You guessed it," Jackieo said with a frown. "Do you think there is room for both of us in there?"

"I don't know; let's see. I'll get in first, and then you sit in front of me between my legs." George stepped into the tube-boat and slid his legs underneath the hull. His feet found two pedals of equal size that could be pushed down and released. They didn't appear to do anything when he moved them up and down. "Okay, J-O, step on in. I think there's plenty of room for you. Take off your pack first."

"Oh, right." She eased into the boat and slid her legs underneath the hull. With her pack in her lap, she leaned back against George.

"Are you set?"

"I guess so, why?"

"Do you see that lever right there? Once I pull that I think we're going to drop into the river and take off like a UT-3 out of Dover."

"Oh, no. Um, hold on." Jackie pushed her pack further under the hull and then put her hands up to her face. "Okay, I'm ready."

"All right, here we go! Three, two, one, liftoff!" George pulled the lever, but nothing happened.

"What's wrong?"

"I don't know. I didn't build the thing, you know." George looked around the inside of the craft for another lever or something, but didn't find anything. He pulled the lever back to its original position and then pulled it down again. Nothing happened.

"I don't know, maybe it's broken. Wait a minute; I have an idea." He pushed the lever back to the original position once more. This time he also pushed down on the pedals and then released the lever again. The craft dropped into the water and took off down the river like a rocket.

"Whoooooooweeeeeee!" George said. "This is some ride, huh J-O?"

"Oh no, it isn't! I want a refund!" she screamed. "Awwwwwww! I'm too young to die. I'm too young to die. And I'm too cute to have my face splattered all over a cave wall!"

George worked the pedals that were now fully functioning. Like the rudder on a fighter plasma-thruster jet, they guided the tube-boat through the river. By making very small corrections, the craft could be steered to keep the tube-boat in the center of the river, which comes in very handy. Bouncing off the sides of the river bank at high speeds proved to be somewhat uncomfortable, as George found out when he miscalculated the pedal movements and they crashed off the river bank and then hit the other side. They bounced off the sides several times until he got control of the craft again. The hard impact of that error could really be felt in their backs and buttocks.

"Ow, George! Keep it straight!"

"I'm trying! Hang on!" George replied, as the tube-boat went screaming down the river at a record setting pace.

Chapter 17

The Way to Penury II

~ Paul ~

I am sitting on a bench here in Timor Dimini with my legs outstretched as Papa continues his storytelling of our fantastic journey. The sun feels warm, but there is a nice breeze blowing from the north. I haven't been meditating for very long; however, I was really making an effort to focus.

Okay, remember, the medallion is a physical symbol that helps to understand the spiritual; a physical symbol to understand the spiritual. I say this to myself over and over. Closing my eyes with the medallion in my hand, I concentrate on the lady who I had met. I don't know how long I was in deep thought, but something happened.

"You have such difficulty letting go of the physical world."

"Maria!" I said. "I cannot see you."

"You cannot see because you are like a blind man. You have seen what very few have been blessed to see. Yet you analyze with your head instead of your heart. You are throwing away the most precious of gifts."

"Maria, help me to understand."

"It is not within your grasp to understand; you must accept it on faith. Only through faith will you be able to obtain the wisdom you seek. However, first you need to be more pious and learn right judgment."

"I will keep trying Maria. Please, help me to see The Way."

"You have the prayers of many. They will give you the strength you need to leave your pride and fear. Paolo, be the servant. There is only one Master. Farewell."

"Thank you Maria."

I felt myself jerk awkwardly sideways as I clench the medallion in my hand. *Was I dreaming? Stop it. These are just the kinds of thoughts that I don't need right now. Only through faith can I obtain wisdom. Let go of the physical world.* I reiterate these thoughts to myself as I look to Papa.

~ Doctore ~

Saul crossed over New Orleans Street and then continued on to Illinois Street. He shuffled his feet against the strong wind that blew along the polluted shores and through the deserted city boulevards. Paper scraps, large particles of dirt, and small pieces of garbage were caught in the breeze and carried along the curbside, until they collected at the back wall of a perilous alleyway. He glanced at the dark sky. Another two hours must pass before the break of day would glean across the waters of Lake Michigan.

There was something unfriendly about a Chicago night's walk in the downtown area. It was best to tiptoe silently so as not to disturb the sovereign host's rest. He was not a gracious host or one who would tend after the needs of his household. It had been some time since he had any reason to see joy in throwing open the gates of the inner loop. His city had been pillaged, his lady ravaged, and his children murdered. If one was to awaken him there would most certainly be a spirited confrontation in which the nervous guest would soon wish he had left for home well before dusk settled across the western skies.

Looking from side to side, Saul scanned the surrounding areas until he had convinced himself that there were no other life forms in viewing distance. Making a right turn, he followed a broken sidewalk toward a side door of an abandoned Catholic Church where large and small grayish pieces of broken concrete were scattered about in a random display of abstract art. The ancient, arched door with faded, red peeling paint swung open easily as if well lubricated on its rusty metal hinges. He stepped inside and was immediately hit by a musty, damp odor. In complete darkness, he stayed close to the wall rather than risk turning on his handheld beled lamp. Slowly, he crept along the wall feeling his way forward. After moving just a few feet, he stopped. Maria had warned him to follow the staff and shield of the Archangel Raphael. He needed to wait for the light of day so that he could see the signs rather than crawling around in the dark. He was also afraid of falling down stairs or cracking his head in the darkness. With his back against the wall, he slid down and sat on the cold stone floor and waited for the eastern star to light his path.

He didn't know how long he dozed off, but he was awakened by a light coming through the stained glass window. He had to force his tired eyes to open. Slowly getting to his feet, he rubbed his eyes and the back of his neck, which had become quite stiff from leaning up against the stone wall. The dry, chalky taste in his mouth felt as though he had been chewing on a piece of nineteenth century plaster all night. Puffs of dust and dirt rose around him, floating up from the ground as he moved his feet. Coughing slightly to clear his throat, he opened his bag, took out one of two water bottles, and took a small sip. After swooshing the liquid around in his mouth, he tilted his head back and gargled with it for a few seconds, then spit it on the floor. He took another, larger sip and swallowed. It felt refreshingly cool and tasteful across his tongue and the back of his throat. Tossing the bottle back into the bag, he slipped the leather strap of the bag over his shoulder.

Judging by the beams and peak of the roof, he was directly under the steeple of the church. He began to look for the image as Maria had instructed.

After searching the walls, he tripped on a loose piece of concrete and found the sign etched into a large broken tile in the floor. He knelt down and looked closely at the direction in which it seemed to point. The open end of the shield and staff seemed to direct him toward the south wall of the steeple. There was very little room in this eight-foot by eight-foot area, but Saul maneuvered his large frame and found a second archangel image on the wall amongst thirty or forty other images near the base where the stone wall met the floor. The image appeared to point inwards towards the wall itself.

"Okay, so what does this mean? Am I to go through the wall?" Saul said aloud.

He pushed on the wall, but it didn't budge. Running his fingers along the sides and front of the wall, he searched for a crack or opening in the stone, but found nothing. Squatting again on the floor, he looked at the image with intensity and strain. Using his thumb, he wiped over the stone and pushed on it. It seemed to give. Encouraged by this event, he pushed hard on the image inward with his thumb. The whole stone moved with a scraping sound followed by a much louder echoing thud, then a section of wall cracked open from within, leaving a five-inch space running vertical from the floor to the ceiling. Saul stood up and pushed against it, allowing himself to squeeze through. The room had a slight glow of light emanating from deeper inside the hidden area. After pushing the stone wall back into place, he continued on through the newly exposed room. Though, upon a more thorough inspection it could hardly be considered a room at all, but a long narrow pathway that was made from old planks of pine wood.

Saul continued his journey following the signs of Raphael that led him to an elevator shaft. He squeezed himself into the small box and lowered it using the rope pulley system. It appeared to be some distance below the church's crumbling foundation. At first, the air was quite thick and seemingly full of particles making it hard for him to breathe. With the exertion he was expending working the ropes, he felt as if someone had been standing on his chest and his breathing became quite heavy and labored. However, after descending quite far beneath the church, the air became cleaner again as if it was being fed into the shaft from an outside source. There was no light in the elevator itself, nor was there any light coming from outside the shaft. Saul found himself in complete darkness, which gave him an uneasy feeling in the pit of his stomach. The only thing that was keeping him from having an anxiety attack was the fact that he concentrated on working the ropes of the pulley. Counting out a pace in his head helped him to keep a steady rhythm.

"One, two, pull, rest. One, two, pull, rest. One, two, pull, rest."

Saul was surprised and hopeful to see light emanating from beneath him in the darkness. He picked up the pace of his counting as this new discovery was a welcome promise of something more inviting. The elevator neared closer to the bottom of the shaft until it came to a halt and settled on the ground. After wiping his forehead with his sleeve, he stepped out. It took a moment for his eyes to become adjusted to the light; however once they did he saw a long and well-lit tunnel that curved around to the left. After taking another sip of water from his bottle, he continued on through the tunnel following the mark of Raphael. He had only been walking ten minutes or so when he started to hear an unfamiliar noise. Somewhat frightened, he stopped in his tracks and listened more closely. Straining to hear, it sounded like a child's voice. Slowly, he moved forward and walked closely along the tunnel's wall. Every now and again he would stop and listen. The sweet voice was becoming more prominent and was definitely a small child talking quietly, but asking many questions. Saul moved to the center of the tunnel and called out.

"Hello?"

"Children, come here quickly!" a whispering, panicked voice called out.

There was a small commotion and scampering of little feet could be heard from a short distance.

"Hello. My name is Saul."

"What do you want here?"

"I was given The Way by Maria. How is it that you are down here?"

A woman dressed in a long blue religious habit stepped forward with two small children hanging on to her garment just behind her. The children peered out from the woman's pleats and stared at him with large, saucer-like eyes.

"I am Sister Guinevere of the Franciscan Sisters of the Immaculate. We had a small orphanage in the church. Everyone perished in the attacks. We just narrowly escaped from the wickedness. You are Saul?"

"Yes, Saul Kriesh. How is it you have come to know this place?"

Sister Guinevere smiled politely, but said nothing.

"Well, it's good to have met you Sister Guinevere. I must continue on my way," he said and motioned down the tunnel.

"We will go with you. Come along children. Gather your things."

"What? No, wait – I'm travelling alone."

"Why travel alone when you can have us to accompany you?"

Saul looked at the sister's face. The light from the tunnel's belds reflected in her large eyes and brightened her cheeks making her entire face appear to glow from within. His gaze quickly moved from child to child and then back again to the sister. How could he take on such a weakened lot? They would surely slow him down, which quite possibly could lead to them all being captured. He looked back to the children hiding in the ruffles of her tunic. The girl clutched a tattered, blonde haired doll. However, there was a large area of the head that had hair missing from it. The doll wore no pretty dress, but instead had a hand-sewn poncho that hardly covered it. The boy, barely more than a toddler, held tightly onto a small piece of cloth. It could not have been larger than a child's book. The way the small boy wrapped his fingers around the cloth so tightly; Saul thought that it was probably the only thing left that he owned. His heart sank and for a moment he forgot about his own troubles.

"All right, come along then if you must. I shall not be delayed though. If you fall behind you will stay behind."

He marched on down the tunnel while Sister gathered her small hatchlings, the few belongings they had, and sauntered after him. The dark-haired boy was so tiny for his age that she carried him with little effort. He never made a sound. Quite the opposite, the little girl, possibly five or six, tagged along at his side, her blond curls bobbing around her face as she chattered away about nonsense, voraciously curious about everything she saw along the way.

After some time walking through the tunnel, they came upon a stone fountain that had been carved into the cavern walls. The fluorspar, which is a mineral made from calcium and fluoride, reflected the beled lighting all throughout the cavern with a richness of blue from the pools of water. It was a small piece of paradise. Saul stopped in front of it, cupped his hands together, and drank the pristine water flowing from the fluorspar. The water was cold and refreshing. It tasted like a virgin spring that had never been touched or corrupted by man. "I have never tasted anything so pure and refreshing. Fill whatever containers you have and take them with you." Saul said as he emptied his bottles onto the tunnel floor, then refilled them with the fountain's elixir.

Sister Guinevere helped the children get water from the fountain, and only after she had been convinced that their thirst was satisfied, did she pull her veil to the side and drink. After reaching her right hand to her lips and gently brushing the droplets away, she looked up to see Saul adjusting the bag on his shoulder, ready to continue moving down the tunnel.

"The children must rest. They haven't had anything to eat yet today."

"What have you to give them, Guinevere?"

"It is Sister Guinevere, if you please, sir." She lowered her gaze to the ground.

"I apologize, Sister Guinevere. Do you have a breakfast buffet hidden in that religious garb?"

"I do. I have the blessed bread given to me by our mother."

Reaching inside her tunic, she removed a white cloth bundle and began to unwrap it very carefully. There were two loaves of white bread. She broke off a small piece and gave it to the boy who had been standing close to her, still clinging to her dress. She then broke off a larger piece and handed it to the girl.

"Eat slowly, Mia."

Mia stared at Saul as she took a bite of the bread and slowly chewed.

"Not yet, Mia. You must be patient." Sister Guinevere broke off another piece and offered it to Saul.

"You better save it for the children. It's a long journey."

"There is plenty to share," she replied.

He took the bread from her hand and thanked her.

She then broke another small piece off the loaf for herself, tightly wrapped the bread up in the cloth, and tucked it away inside her tunic. She then knelt down on the ground and made the sign of the cross. With her head bowed, she moved her lips and silently prayed. Then after making the sign of the cross, she sat on the ground with the children and they ate. Saul sat down with them.

"This bread is amazingly fresh and warm. For such a small piece it was quite satisfying," Saul said. "What did you pray for, Sister? Long life? Safety through the tunnels?"

Sister Guinevere looked at him intently and responded softly. "If you are not a believer, why are you here? What is it you hope to find?" She paused a moment before continuing, "I thanked our Lord for his blessings, for giving us this food and the fountain of water. I do not ask after my own needs, but patiently await the Lord to grant me what is necessary."

The small boy began to cough. Saul looked down at him and realized that this was the first time he had heard any sound from the boy since he had met them.

"Slowly, Razzi. Eat slowly. We are not in such a rush that we cannot enjoy our meal." Sister pulled the small boy closer to her. Draping her arm around him, she snuggled him, comforting him against this unfamiliar environment. As he ate, she hummed a melody and gently rocked him.

Mia was staring intently at Saul's bag. "Why does your bag have two snakes wrapped around a pole trying to eat a bird?" Mia asked.

Saul was taken aback by the girl's direct line of questioning. "What?"

Mia pointed to the image on his black bag.

"Oh, that. That is the Greek symbol *caduceus*. It means medicine."

"Actually," Sister interjected, "the doctor is not quite correct. The Rod of Asclepius is an image of a staff with one snake, which is the Greek pagan symbol for medicine. The *caduceus* is the symbol of Hermes, a fake god of pagan mythology. I have often found it confusing to see the use of the caduceus as the meaning of medicine in this country."

"Are you a Greek scholar, Sister?" Saul asked somewhat perturbed, partly at the fact that she had corrected him in his inaccurate definition, and partly because at the same time, she implied that the whole medical profession was somewhat dimwitted. Or perhaps it was even that the whole symbol of his lifetime work was based on a mythical pagan god. Regardless the reason, he had been used to being the smartest person in the room and this fanatical religious nut was correcting him on matters of academia and mythical beliefs. *She has some nerve matching wits against me. I highly doubt she finished her remedial coursework much less pursued a doctorate of science.* He felt his face flush with both embarrassment and anger, so he looked down and pretended to draw on the dirt floor with his shoe.

"I have studied Greek and Latin, Doctor."

"What makes you think I am a doctor?" Saul asked and looked up at her from his floor etchings. "I could have stolen this bag."

"You have quite clean hands for that of a thief. Your movements are somewhat of precision. And I saw you wash at the fountain, letting the water drain down from your forearms. You are a surgeon?"

Saul stood up. "I think we've been here quite long enough. It's time to gather your flock, Sister." After adjusting his strap on the shoulder bag, he started down the tunnel.

"Come along, children. Mr. Kriesh is right. We must be going, now."

"He's not very nice," Mia whispered. "Why is he mad at us, Sister?"

Sister Guinevere picked up Razzi and they followed Saul deeper into the tunnel. "He's not mad, Mia. He's just afraid."

"Afraid of what?"

"He's afraid he will find what he does not believe," Sister said.

"You know, it's really not polite to talk about a person when that person can hear you," Saul called back over his shoulder. "And it's Doctor Kriesh."

"The talk was intended for you, Doctor Kriesh," Sister replied with a slight grin.

"Of all the people in the world, how is it possible that I'm stuck with the know-it-all religious nun?" Saul mumbled under his breath and kicked at the cavern's dirt floor.

They plodded along the seemingly endless tunnel in silence, their interest piqued for brief moments when they came across the colorful carvings, written names of people and families, and old photographs that were scattered at random intervals along the tunnel walls. They would step up close to them to look at the faces of the past, and even though they didn't know the particular story of the people pictured, they somehow knew they too had come to escape various dangers with the hope that they would make their way safely to freedom. Even Saul, in his cynicism, could not help but stop to look at them. The entire tunnel was like an underground museum. He found himself daydreaming at the outcomes of the cave dwellers until he was startled by Mia's voice.

"Sister?"

"Yes, Mia?"

"Can you carry me, too? I can't walk anymore." She had been making a gallant effort to stay close to the sister since they started, but her short legs had to move at thrice the rate of her adult companions. Her feet had been dragging against the dirt for the last several minutes as she struggled to keep up.

"Saul, we must rest. They are just children."

Saul turned around and looked at Mia. He then looked at his watch and shook his head.

"We've only been walking for an hour and five minutes. We'll never get there if we keep stopping. I can carry her."

Mia looked up at Sister Guinevere with her mouth and eyes equally wide with horror and fear. She slid closer to Sister. "It's okay, Mia. It will be all right. He's not a bad man. Go on now; I cannot carry the two of you."

Saul drew up close to them, and although Mia turned and hid in Sister's skirts, Saul bent down and scooped her up. It was the oddest thing he had ever done. It seemed so foreign and awkward to him, yet at the same time it felt so natural to have the child in his arms. His motions were simple and mechanically precise as if he had done this small task one thousand times. Mia put both her arms around his neck and laid her head on his shoulder. In no time at all, she fell asleep. As Saul continued to hike through the tunnel, their breathing seemed to fall into sync with one another.

"She is a wonderful child with an equally wonderful heart," Sister said. "Her parents were killed for their beliefs and she was left an orphan. That is how she came to us. With the clothes on her back and her blonde curls, everything she owned was in her blessed, contagious smile."

"What about the boy? Where are his parents?"

"We never found out about Razzi's parents. He was left beside a garbage dumpster. Can you imagine? A child just left beside a heap of trash. God forgive them."

Saul felt such a weakness and sense of despair that he could barely move his legs. It was a struggle just to continue walking. He didn't know what was causing this emotion, nor did he understand the impetus for it, but whatever it was that seemed to radiate from deep inside of him, he decided to keep it suppressed and thought of other more pleasant things. Though, he struggled even to find such pleasantries in the caverns of his mind, he had but one source in which to draw from a drying well; he focused his energy on Janess. How happy he would be when he saw her again. Playing and replaying that first meeting with her, he rehearsed how he would start the conversation, and how he would ask for her forgiveness.

They continued on in silence until Sister heard the sound of running water. Quickening her pace, she held tightly onto Razzi as she passed Saul and rounded a turn in the tunnel. After several more yards, another miracle came into view for the faithful Sister Guinevere.

"Look! It's another fountain. How absolutely beautiful are these carved fountains. They remind me of the fountains of Rome. And look over there! It's a shrine of Our Lady!" Guinevere sprinted to the shrine and in all one motion, switched Razzi to her left arm, knelt down in front of the shrine, made the sign of the cross with her right hand, lowered her head, and said a prayer in silence. After several minutes, she made the sign of the cross again and stood up.

Saul looked at her with a sense of weariness. "You do seem to pray a lot, Sister. I'll say that for you."

Saul, taking a firm hold of Mia, lowered himself to the ground and then tried to get her to stand up. "Mia. Mia, wake up. We are at a fountain." He eased up on his strength holding her in a standing position, but her knees just buckled and he steadied her again.

"Mia, come on now. Stand up. You must wake up," Saul said more loudly.

Mia reluctantly opened her eyes. They were very glassy looking and she stared at Saul somewhat dumbfounded. Saul could tell she was trying to recollect just who this person was and why she was standing in front of him at the moment. However, when she saw Sister Guinevere praying, she relaxed as if everything hazy had become clear again.

"That's right; it's time to wake up." Saul said happily.

"Where are we?" Mia asked.

"We're by a water fountain. We want to eat something and take a rest. We're getting tired, too."

Saul, looking at Sister Guinevere, said quietly, "I'm going to take a look around. I'll be back in a little bit."

"I'll get the children settled in and fix something to eat. I'll have yours ready for when you return, Doctor Kriesh." Sister replied.

She looked at him directly in the eye as if she were looking for some kind of sign that he was a good man with character and integrity. Saul wondered why she stared at him in such a way and then it occurred to him that she was trying to get some indication of whether or not he would return for them, or if he would leave them alone and desolate like so many others had done.

"Don't worry. I'm coming back, Sister. I just want to have a look around that's all."

Sister Guinevere gave a slight nod, then turned back to the children and gathered them around the fountain to wash up before their meal.

Saul continued along the left side of the tunnel wall. The cavern walls of uneven rock and earth seemed to go on for miles and miles. The dirt-colored hallways carved underground were brought together by wood beams just overhead. The tunnel's bored-out sides were black, dark-brown, and gray in color with a jaggedness from rocks and uneven earth. At times, there were flat spots among the rock-filled walls. At these flattened sections, people had left their heritage and mark. Walking slowly, he stared at the various photos and drawings that had been left behind for future generations to contemplate.

He could no longer hear the sounds of the children since he had now put some distance between them. Looking over the pictures, he wondered about their stories and what might have become of them. The tunnel was starting to narrow at this particular juncture and he was just about to turn around to head back when something caught his eye. It appeared as a beam of light, but upon looking more closely there seemed to be something standing in the corner of the bend reflecting the light of the beleds. He moved towards the object and as it came into view he was astonished to see a sword. Picking it up with his right hand, he held it out in front of himself looking it over in the light. It had a red cross etched into the pommel of the grip and was quite light considering the length and breadth of the blade. He was surprised at how new it appeared. There wasn't a mark on it. It looked as though it had just been manufactured.

His eyes caught sight of a shadow near where the sword had been leaning against the wall. Lying on the ground was a black sheath with a long leather strap. "Funny, I didn't notice that was there before," he said aloud and bent down to pick it up. Sliding the sword into the sheath, he noticed the name 'Paul' had been embossed across it. Carrying the sword with him, he started back to where he had left Sister Guinevere and the children.

As he approached, Sister gave him a slight nod of approval. "Sit, I saved you some bread and fresh water. There are also some dates for dessert."

"Thank you. That is some tunic you have there, Sister. You even had blankets tucked away?" Saul asked noticing the children had snuggled up in a large brown blanket.

"No, of course not. I don't know how they got here, but they seemed to have just appeared out of nowhere. One minute I looked and they were there. There are three, one for the children and one for each of us. The Lord has a way of providing for his children."

"Did He provide this, too, Sister?" Saul asked holding up the sword.

"Yes. Everything that we need is given to us for a purpose. We need not question it, only that we use what is given to us to the best of our ability for the betterment of Man to fulfill God's will."

"I haven't much use for anyone's will but my own."

"Is that why you are alone?"

"It may come as a surprise to you my fanatical naïve friend, but I am partnered to a woman—Janess. She has gone ahead of me to the city."

"I will pray for her wellbeing and her safe journey. Finish your bread and then we will rest."

Saul shook his head in resignation and mumbled under his breath while he arranged his blanket on the opposite side of the fountain, "Keep praying, Sister. That's what you're good at."

Chapter 18

The Way to Penury III

~ Paul ~

Death will find each of us. There is no escape from it. Society can try to outrun it and keep building machines, technology, elixirs, and whatnots to extend our brief time here on Earth. However, it will all end the same way for each of us. We will breathe our last breath, our heart will measure out its last beat, and our mind will think its last thought. This concept once frightened me a great deal; that all would one day go black. However, since being invited to the journey and listening to Papa's teaching I am no longer afraid of the end of my days. No, now I'm frightened of what may come after those days. There is definitely no shortage of fear in my life. What will the One King think of me? How will he receive me? How might I answer for my life?

We lost one of our own along that first leg of the journey. I never met him myself, but I heard many great things about the person afterwards. I am certain that they were able to answer for their life in a way that pleased the King and was received very well. And with that, I'll let Papa finish the story before we must leave for the canton of Pietas. I can hardly wait to see my wonderful friend again.

~ Doctore ~

Li'Quari and Jackson had made it into Saint Gabriel Church. Following the instructions they received from Maria, they soon came upon the marks of freedom. However, what they did not realize was that they had been seen going into the church by Dragonhead and his two foul accomplices.

"I'll take the front. You two go around back and don't let anyone get past you," the evil-eyed one had said. "I'll give you twenty ticks. Go!"

As he counted down the twenty marks, he readied himself at the door. "Five cackdirt, four cackdirt, three cackdirt, two cackdirt ...." He kicked open the door while holding the rifle out ready to fire. Peering over the front sight of the weapon, he panned from left to right. Seeing nothing in his immediate view he lowered the gun. Moving quickly through the church, he searched for his two enemies. He yearned to taste their blood on his lips.

The two other Southern Guards came into the main area of the church and they met near the front pews.

"Did you see anything?" Dragonhead asked.

"No, nothing. Not a sign of 'dem in here."

"Don't give me your scuzes. I saw 'em coming into this place! That old cackdirt didn't just up and diz'pear. Find 'em!" Dragonhead pushed hard at the two guards in opposite directions. "I don't care'n if we have to burn dis building to the ground and sift through'n all the rubble! I want that cackdirt and tartwod. I will see 'em suffer greatly."

The tall albino stumbled from Dragonhead's forceful shove and after regaining his balance, he trotted off to the east side of the church without saying a word.

The other fat, red-faced guard mumbled under his breath, "freak." His fat, hairy belly pushed out from his body like overstuffed luggage and then rolled over his pants two or three times. He had scars from knife wounds and tips of swords. There were dark holes where bullets had entered and never seemed to exit. As he scuffed off to the west end of the church, a haze of his filth and stench followed with him. He walked between pews, looking under and over them for any sign of the traitors. "One-eyed freak. Who does he think he is; the General? I'll tear out his other eye and burn that dragon right off his ugly head!"

Dragonhead's colorless death-eye roamed the church seeking out its prey. He kicked over pews, tore fixtures from the walls, and shot holes into the aging plastered walls. The more time that went by in which he found no trace of his prize, the more frustrated and angry he became. The reddened dragon tattoo carved deep into his skull seemed to deepen to a darker shade of blood red and pulsed as rage and hate ran through its veins. His two other guards had given up and snuck away. He snatched up a broken pew and tossed it out the window into the scattered remains of the other items he'd trashed. He knew the tart and old man were there. The taste of fear was in the air and he would not be cheated out of obtaining his trophy.

As the last light of day trickled over the horizon, another day was put to rest in the horrid District South. Dark clouds pushed their way across the night sky drowning out any light from the stars or the moon. Rain began to fall on Dragonhead's search and the misery of his failure forced him to relinquish the pursuit until morning. Hunkering down near a corner of the narthex, he sat wallowing in his anger and frustration. Sounds of scampering feet could be heard through the rain echoing off the walls of the now emptied church. An unsuspecting and frail rat scurried along the wall looking for crumbs. With a quick hand, Dragonhead grabbed the destitute victim and bit off its head and consumed his meal in the darkness.

Li'Quari and Jackson had taken the manual lift that descended into the tunnels and began their trek. Guided by the mark of Raphael, they made their way slowly in an easterly direction. Jackson had been mostly silent as he led the expedition. Diligently progressing forward, he pushed along the cave floor with his walking stick.

"What is your daughter like?" Li'Quari asked, breaking the silence.

Jackson stopped midstride. The tension in his face faded as joy sparkled in his eyes. "Elicia is a lot like you, I would say: strong willed, smart, and stubborn. She has a very kind heart, which she got from her mother. She would never say no to a person who was in need and was always the first person to give of herself. She's a doctor you know. That's what she was doing in Europe when they shut down all the airports and communication in 'forty-nine. She was there helping as a surgeon for the wounded soldiers. I begged her to get out of there days before the front lines reached them, but there was always one more surgery to do; one more soldier who had come in with burns and gunshot wounds. Yes, she got that good heart from her mother. The stubbornness and sarcastic wit, of course, she got from me," he winked.

"She sounds like a great lady. Did she have dark hair like yours?"

Jackson reached into his pocket and took out two small photographs and handed them to her. Li'Quari carefully took them and looked at the photos.

"Oh, she's beautiful, Jackson."

"Yes, she got those looks from her mother, too."

"She has your eyes and mouth." Li'Quari said. Placing Elicia's photo underneath the second one, she looked at the other picture. "And this is your wife?"

"Yes, that's my Jasmya. She passed away in forty-six. She wouldn't have wanted to be around for all of this hate and violence. She was a church-going woman. And she had some pipes, too. She could sing like no other that I've ever heard. Mm, she was some kind of a woman. She had cancer. She didn't believe in all of that artificial treatment either. She used to say, 'When the good Lord calls me, I won't need to be called a second time.' Yeah, Li'Quari, my Jasmya was a good woman. She'd've liked you."

Li'Quari smiled. "I like her already, too. I don't recall anyone ever singing. I'm not sure I even know what that would sound like exactly. I remember a girl in the home who used to sort of hum quietly at night. I don't know any songs."

"None?"

Li'Quari blushed and shrugged.

"Well, we can't have that now, no ma'am. That, my dear, is what the old scholars used to call a tragedy." Jackson's face lit up and his voice came on stronger and louder. A burst of energy seemed to emanate from his entire body. "Songs are those little things in life that stay with you forever. You associate moments in life, good and bad, with a song. And by remembering and singing the song you remember those moments in your life and always keep them with you, close to your heart. Okay now, pay close attention. You sing these words – It's a joyous day."

"It's a joyous .... day" Li'Quari said in a voice more like talking than singing.

"No, no. Listen. Sing them child. Sing them from here," Jackson said and pushed slightly on her diaphragm. "Like this: It's a joyous day."

"It's a joyous day."

"Yeah, that's it! It's a joyous day," Jackson repeated louder.

"It's a joyous day."

"It's a joyous daaaayay, Li'Quari."

"It's a joyous daaaayay."

"It's a joyous daaaaaaay, louder."

"It's a joyous daaaaaaay."

"Yeah, it's a joyous daaaayay." Jackson started to clap his hands together to form a beat.

"It's a joyous daaaayay."

"Jesus taught the news—keep going." Jackson pointed at Li'Quari.

"It's a joyous daaaaaaay."

"Jesus taught good news." Clap.

"It's a joyous daaaaaaay."

"Jesus taught such good news." Clap

"It's a joyous daaaayay."

"Won't you walk his way." Jackson danced and spun in a circle as he continued to progress down the tunnel while singing louder and louder.

"It's a joyous daaaaaaay."

"It's a joyous daaaaaaay." Li'Quari belted out the notes right behind him and began to dance. She brought her elbows up close to her body, moving her hands up and down, side to side, and clapping in beat with Jackson.

They continued down the tunnel singing and dancing together with brightened faces and large smiles. Jackson took Li'Quari's right hand and lifting it up towards the cave's roof, he guided her into a series of twirls, in which they finished off still holding hands. Jackson wrapped his free arm around Li'Quari's waist, and she followed suit as they continued to dance down the tunnel, singing, "It's a joyous daaaaaaay!"

Their energy began to fade after several rounds, but the mood buoyed them along for a while longer, until their strides got a little shorter and a little slower. Jackson's age caught up with him, and his breathing grew heavier. Just as they were both reaching the point of giving in to their exhaustion, the tunnel lighting ahead changed to a brilliant glow. The wondrous light was emanating from just beyond a curve in the tunnel path. With a quick glance at each other, Jackson and Li'Quari quickened their pace. Winding through the bend, they came upon a stone fountain carved into the cavern walls. The bluish fluorspar reflected the beled lighting with such softness it was absolutely breathtaking. Reflections of the blue crystalline structure coming from the pool of water danced across the cavern roof and walls. Jackson stopped in front of it, cupped his hands together, and drank. The pristine waters were cold and refreshing.

"Oh, this water is magnificent, Li'Quari! Let's rest here for a while." Jackson leaned his walking stick against the wall, then he removed his backpack and flipped open the flap. Reaching in, he took out a metal cup and handed it to her.

Li'Quari dipped it into the waters of the fountain and put it up to her mouth, emptying the cup without pausing for a breath. "You're right this water is so pure." She dipped the cup back into the fountain for a second drink.

Jackson dropped his backpack on the ground, reached inside for a loaf of doughbread and handed a large piece to Li'Quari. She sat on the floor and leaned against the cave wall just beside the fountain with her legs stretched out in front of her. She placed her hand over her belly on her child.

They sat together in silence eating the bread and sipping from their cups. Jackson gazed at the various pictures, drawings, and paintings that were on the cave walls. There had been many of these types of works scattered along the way, but there seemed to be more of a concentration of them here next to the fountain. Many people must have used these areas as resting places. The time spent here was put to good use in decorating the areas with more passion.

"Who is Jesus?" Li'Quari asked.

"Hmm?" Jackson responded somewhat out of sorts. He had been daydreaming, as he stared at the family pictures on the wall.

"The person in the joyous day song, Jesus. *Jesus taught good news.*"

"Oh, yes. You've never heard of Jesus?"

Li'Quari shook her head.

"Well, stand up then and follow me," Jackson said with a friendly smile. He pushed himself to a standing position and walked over to the cave wall where pictures and drawings were either hung or had been carved into the rock. "This person here in the drawings—this is Jesus. He lived some two-thousand years ago. God sent him here as the One. The One who would become like us, human; to teach us how to live and love one another. He also came here to die for us. He was ridiculed, beaten, and was nailed to a piece of wood called a cross, and then was left to die." Jackson pointed to each of the pictures as he told the story.

"If Jesus was the One, why didn't he just take out all the wicked people and save the good people? Why did he have to die?"

"Jesus came not just for the good people, but to save all people. He did this to show the unconditional love God has for each and every one of us; the good and the wicked. If God could still forgive and love us, even after all that we had done to his son; then maybe Man's hearts would be opened. And with an open heart, we might believe in him and love him as well."

Li'Quari stared at the photos and drawings. "He looks like the man on my card."

Jackson looked at her inquisitively. "What card?"

She reached into her pocket and took out the card she had showed to Maria and handed it to him.

Jackson held it with his arm stretched away from his eyes so he could focus on it, then he smiled and nodded. "Yes, that's Jesus. You see the outstretched hands? Those are God's hands welcoming us all into his love and forgiveness. And Jesus is giving each person a hug, welcoming them into His kingdom where there is no suffering, no poverty, and no pain."

"Like the city?"

"In a way, yes, like the city. But the city is only a glimpse of what is yet to come. It has the same limitations of life. It is a place here on Earth. Jesus's city is in Heaven. It lasts forever where people never die and there are no limitations. It is a place of pure love."

Jackson handed Li'Quari her card back. She looked at it again before placing it back into her pocket. "I'm sort of tired. It's hard to tell the time down here in the tunnels."

Jackson looked at his watch. "It's a quarter past eight. We've been walking for quite some time. This is a good place to get some rest." Jackson turned and started back towards the fountain when he noticed blankets near a cavity in the wall.

"And apparently, others had thought so, too. Look!" Jackson pointed.

"Blankets!" she ran over to the small cubbyhole. "And doughbread! It smells so good and it's warm!" She said holding it up to her face.

She broke a piece off the loaf and handed it to Jackson.

"Mm, this is some amazing bread."

"Maria?"

"Oh yes, Maria," Jackson replied cheerfully.

Spreading out the blankets near the fountain, the beleds seemed to glow fainter as if to signal a time for rest. Jackson and Li'Quari made themselves comfortable and turned in for the night. Their bodies were tired from the journey and they were in need of rest. They both were quite ready for a good night's sleep. The cave ceiling danced with the shimmering glow of the water's reflection, but it danced somewhat slower now with the dimmed lighting. It was more of a slow waltz than the earlier jazz rendition of the show.

"Lucks," Li'Quari said turning on her side.

"Lucks to you my little song bird," Jackson replied.

Li'Quari quietly said, "It's a joyous daaaaaaay."

The next morning Li'Quari and Jackson awoke to brightened beleds and the most pleasant aroma of fresh bread. They were feeling well rested despite the aching they felt in their muscles.

"Mornin' breaks," Li'Quari said.

"Mornin' breaks," replied Jackson.

"Did you make doughbread?"

"No, but I smell it, too." Jackson looked around the fountain area and in the cubbyhole where the blankets had been was a cloth bundle wrapped tightly. "Doughbread!"

"How does she do it?" Li'Quari asked.

"I have no idea, but I'm sure glad that she does. I'm hungry."

After replenishing their energy for the day's journey, Jackson and Li'Quari made their way as before through the tunnel. They would stop every so often when a particular picture or drawing on the walls captured their attention. However, they mostly kept on the path and made progress towards whatever destination lies ahead for them. They put their faith in Maria's words and hoped they would reach the city soon.

"How did you get to be a senator? You must be really smart, huh?"

"Oh, no, not really that smart, I don't think. I did have a good education and went to good schools. My father made sure I had opportunities available to me. Actually, as fate would have it, my Great-Great-Great-Grandfather was a slave here in the south. And now, all these years later, I too, have become a slave of the south. My family is once again fleeing for freedom in the underground. Imagine that, huh? Look how far we've come in all these years."

Li'Quari just shrugged her shoulders. She didn't understand Jackson's sarcasm. She wasn't taught of the history of America. In fact, not many people knew of the pain and misery, nor the triumphs and progress of the past. As far as everyone knew, there was only the present. There wasn't anything to learn from the past. According to the new way of thinking in the world, there was no past.

"My father was a history professor. He loved history and learning about the struggles of the past. He loved this country and he understood from studying the events of the past, just what had made America great. Constantly, he talked about the American people and what they had to endure and conquer in order to maintain a free democracy. When I saw how passionate my father was about America, I knew I wanted to do something to help her maintain her greatness. So, I studied hard and became a trial lawyer. Eventually, I ran for Assemblyman and the rest is history as they might say."

179

"Wow that is really amazing. I only understood a little of what you were saying, but it's still so amazing to me."

"You've had such a hard life, Li'Quari. I feel bad that my fellow government leaders and I let so many people down. We could never see past our own agendas. We should have been fighting for people like you who were caught in the crosshairs of the political parties and their meaningless battles. It was all such a failure of leadership and accountability. Such a disappointment," Jackson drifted off.

"It's not your fault Jackson. We are all dealt a hand of cards that we play with; mostly that's just the way it is. I'm quite enjoying this newly dealt hand, though," she said and put her hand on his shoulder.

"Thank you, Li'Quari; that means so much to me in these later years." He placed his hand over hers and squeezed it gently.

Jackson felt a cold chill in the air. Coming from behind them, drifted a foul stench. He stopped and turned to look back down the tunnel from where they had come. The beleds had changed from their normal glow to red. Jackson took a firm hold of the top of his walking stick and he pulled the bottom away, drawing out a long, military saber with a thirty-four inch blade of silver. It had a twenty-four carat gold handle and in the blade was etched *United States Marines*.

"Jackson, what's the matter?" Li'Quari looked at him confusedly.

"Something evil is coming this way. Run Li'Quari! And don't look back. Just run!"

"No, I'm staying here with you!"

"No! Protect that baby, Li'Quari. I will handle this foul creature," Jackson pushed ahead, and then retraced his steps back towards their resting spot.

Li'Quari ran through the tunnel with tears streaming down her face until she was out of breath. She stopped and stood in the middle of the tunnel frozen in a moment of time. The beleds glowed red and seemed to pulse with a violent rage. Wiping the tears from her face, she put her hand on her stomach and said, "I'm sorry little one. He's the only father I've ever known, and I will not leave him here alone." She turned and walked back, staying close to the cavern walls.

Jackson continued to walk down the center of the tunnel when he saw the shadow of something running towards him. As it got closer, it slowed its pace until it finally came into view.

"Filthy, lying Cackdirt! Where are you heading off to in such a hurry? Didn't even say goodbye old fool," Dragonhead slithered along, eyeing Jackson from head to toe with his colorless, lifeless eye. "And where is that tartwod? I would expect you should have turned her into us. Or did you want to keep her for yourself, you old filth!"

"Yeah, that's right you foul-smelling rodent. Keep walking this way and you'll meet a real soldier." Jackson whirled the saber's handle in his right hand, spinning the blade around several times before he brought it up to his head.

"You calling me out, Cackdirt? I'll enjoy tearin' you into strips. I'm hungry for Cackdirt meat." Dragonhead pulled out a large sword with a wide, thick blade. His muscles contracted and bulked up with each wave of the blade through the air as its sheer weight was well pronounced.

Jackson touched the blade of his saber to his forehead and brought it back in front of himself to signal his readiness for battle. Dragonhead spit on the ground and started to move towards him swinging his blade wildly from side to side. As he came within a few feet, Jackson moved to the right of Dragonhead's strike and used his saber to deflect it from hitting his person. The clash of the blades echoed throughout the tunnel. Dragonhead grunted and cursed, holding his sword high he charged at Jackson again and again. Jackson moved each time out of the way and sliced at Dragonhead's arms and legs with his blade. The Marine Corps blade was stained with blood as it sliced through flesh with a razor's edge.

Feeling the pain of the cuts, Dragonhead only got angrier. The dragon tattoo pulsed in his head and turned an evil blood red. His good eye was that of a wild beast and the other was that of wickedness that Jackson had not ever witnessed. Jackson, remembering his training from the Marine Corps, kept his distance and used his skill and cunning to inflict injury after injury to the creature of the guard. As Dragonhead stood looking dumbfounded at Jackson's skill, Jackson decided to move in for the kill. As he lowered his shoulder and went to push his blade through Dragonhead's chest, Dragonhead stepped to the side, and reaching out, grabbed Jackson by the throat. Lifting him up off the ground, it had appeared that the battle had turned.

"Filthy Cackdirt, do you think you could win over me? I'm going to squeeze your windpipe and crush it like a lime. Then, I'm going to roast your flesh for dinner."

Jackson grabbed Dragonhead's hand with his left hand and tried desperately to pry his fingers from his throat. He couldn't breathe and he felt his body's strength weakening. He struggled physically to get free while his judgment and thoughts became clouded.

"No, Jackson!" Li'Quari called out.

Dragonhead looked up and saw Li'Quari standing near the tunnel's walls. An evil grin came over him. Jackson lifted his saber and stuck it into the arm Dragonhead had pressed around his neck. He screamed in pain and dropped Jackson to the ground.

thomas e

Jackson regained his breath and form. Wielding his saber, he sliced Dragonhead several times in the chest and stuck the point of his saber into Dragonhead's hand.

Screaming out obscenities, the beastly Southern Guard dropped his sword and sat bleeding in the center of the tunnel. Jackson held his blade at his throat and stared at him.

"Show mercy. I'm not armed," Dragonhead said.

"How often did you show any mercy to your victims?" Jackson asked.

Dragonhead said nothing.

"Ah, you're not worth it." Jackson lowered his saber and started to walk towards Li'Quari. She bounded out from behind the cavern wall with a huge grin on her face.

"I thought I told you to run," Jackson said, still approaching her.

"I couldn't leave you," Li'Quari said tearfully.

Just then a gunshot echoed in the tunnel and a missilet sped away. Jackson stopped suddenly and stared at Li'Quari. Dropping to his knees with a look of pain, surprise, and concern, he pushed his saber towards Li'Quari.

She screamed out, "No! Jackson!" And ran to him. Sinking to the ground just in front of him, she held him up and close to her with her arms around him. The blood ran over her fingers as it flowed out from his back. Dragonhead, with the gun still in his hand, got up and started walking towards them laughing a sinister laugh.

"Filthy Cackdirt! I told you. You were no match for me. Now, I'm going to finish the job!"

Li'Quari held onto Jackson and buried her head in his chest. She closed her eyes and called out for Maria. Dragonhead came to within a few feet of them. He drew out his sword, and struck out at the two of them. His blade came down and clashed with that of another blade glowing brightly with a blue light.

"I think you might want to reconsider your position," George said calmly to him.

"Ahhhhhggg!" Dragonhead growled out in anger. "And who asked you to interfere with my battle?"

"You don't look much like a warrior to me. You look like a jacksided fubar," George retorted. After swiping Andrew's sword in a circular motion several times, he held it upwards vertically. Then touching the blade to the top of his forehead, he took his stance.

Dragonhead smirked at him and then mockingly imitated him with his own sword showing his disrespect for the military protocol with weaponry. "Cackdirt! Here's my answer to that," he said. Then holding his gun in his left hand, he took aim and shot at George's head.

182

George swung his sword with such quickness he deflected the bullet and it ricocheted off the cavern wall. He then ran at Dragonhead and swung the sword hard, hacking off the enemy's left arm just below the elbow. The forearm and hand with the gun still in it dropped to the ground. Dragonhead cried out in pain and fell to the ground. George swung again and sliced the wicked creature's right arm, which fell to the ground along with Dragonhead's sword. Standing over him with the blood dripping off his sword, George looked into the face of his enemy. Dragonhead looked up at him with his evil eye darting back and forth. He could see the GIT uniform and his GIT weapons attached to his military belt.

"You're a GIT officer. Mercy!"

George, while staring at his lifeless cold eye, saw the red dragon tattoo carved into the right side of his head. He remembered the words of Maria. "I think not, Red Dragon fubar." George swung his weapon and the head of the dragon rolled off to the left while the body fell helplessly to the ground. The lighting of the tunnel turned from the reddish glow back to its normal bluish color. After George pried Dragonhead's gun loose from his hand, he searched him for other weapons and ammunition. Taking what he wanted, he then turned around and went back to the others. Jackieo was kneeling beside Li'Quari trying to comfort her while she sat beside Jackson.

"Jackson, you can't leave me. Maria can help you. Just stay with me," Li'Quari told him as she held his head in her lap. "Maria will come." She then looked up at the cavern ceiling and screamed out, "Maria! Maria, please help us!"

Jackson's breathing was shallow and he winced in pain. George could see him struggling and his eyes were distant. Reaching into his pocket, Jackson took out the pictures of his wife and daughter along with his wife's cross necklace.

"Maria has already helped me, Li'Quari. I can see my daughter and Jasmya. They are calling me home." He handed her the pictures and the necklace. "Put up our pictures by the fountain for the next generations to ponder. And Jasmya's cross...," he winced and moaned in pain as he struggled to take another breath. "I want you to keep her cross. It will serve you well in the city."

"No Jackson. You're coming with me to the city. I can't do it on my own."

"You can do it. I believe in you." Jackson held her hand tightly. "Lucks to you, daughter. I love you," he said, and then closed his eyes, breathing his last breath.

"I love you, Jackson. I love you!" Li'Quari sobbed and rocked back and forth holding onto him. Jackieo hugged her and tried to comfort her.

George was becoming increasingly nervous while time continued to march on. Making matters worse was the fact that Li'Quari didn't appear to

thomas e

be letting go of Jackson anytime soon. "I hate to have to disturb you, but we need to leave. We have to keep moving. The tunnels have been compromised. We don't know how many more of those trolls are down here." He shook Jackieo's shoulder to indicate for her to get up.

"Come on, honey," Jackieo said to Li'Quari. We have to go; it's not safe here. There's nothing more you can do now." Jackieo pulled her away from Jackson and helped her to her feet. They all went down the tunnel together, but not before Li'Quari turned around and took one last look at the one who saved her.

~ Paul ~

"Papa, come, it's time. We must be leaving now."
"Paolo, why do you rush me? Are you in a hurry?"
"Papa…."
"Is there someone waiting for you in the next canton?"
"Papa, I will leave without you. You know, my training is incomplete and there's no telling what I'm capable of doing."
"Well, I suppose we must be off then. We wouldn't want to keep her waiting."

We made our way out of town and headed towards Pietas (Piety). What makes this canton special to me is that my guide is stationed there. I haven't seen her for quite some time as she had gone quite far into the city where I could not follow. I received a note from her not long ago that said she was teaching in Pietas and I should come for a visit. She also mentioned that she was certain I could learn some things in Pietas.

184

Chapter 19

The Way to Penury IV

~ Paul ~

As we enter Pietas, I practically push Papa from behind to move him along faster.

"Paolo, I'm an old man. We will be there soon enough," he says in his gentle voice.

"I'm sorry, Papa. I will go on ahead and make sure someone is there." Before Papa could even answer, I move quickly ahead of him and was soon knocking hard on the door.

Upon the wooden, weathered door opening, Sister Guinevere looks at me and says, "I see your hastiness has not improved."

Her comment really didn't even register. I just stand there for a moment in admiration, grinning broadly. "Hello Sister. It's been a long time since I saw you last."

"Hello Paul. It is good to see you. Are you doing well?"

"Quite well. I've been learning a lot from Papa and just the other day I had an extraordinary encounter with –"

"Where is Papa?" Sister interrupts.

"I am here, Sister," Papa calls out from the street.

"Oh my, you left Papa in the street?" she whispers and pushes past me to hurry out to him. Getting on one knee before the Doctore, she kisses his hand. Papa places his other hand on top of her head and gives her his blessing.

"Sister Guinevere it is always pleasing to see you. I trust our dear fellow is still in your prayers?"

"Oh yes, Papa. He is in my daily devotions just as Maria instructed."

"Good, very good. Well, lead the way, Sister Guinevere."

After a delicious meal cooked by the Franciscan Sisters, Papa politely excuses himself and goes to his room. The other sisters were cleaning up after dinner whilst Sister Guinevere and I sit at the table to talk about old times. It is still so amazing to me that she had so much love for a complete stranger and had made such sacrifices for me. I owed her much more than my life.

"Do you think about that day often?" I ask.

"Yes, of course."

"I can't get it out of my mind. It's always there in the background. I sometimes don't know if it's real, a memory or a dream. How he suffered."

"How he loves you. Remember, his suffering was the gesture that shows his true love for us."

A wave of emotion overcomes me and the tears fill my eyes. "But I was so cruel to him. All of those vicious things I did to him. Why? Why does he still love me?"

"Because you are his child and because he is God."

After wiping my eyes and absorbing Sister Guinevere's words, my final question comes to my lips. "And what about you, Sister? Why did you help me? Why did you suffer for me?"

"You are my brother. Because the One told us to love one another as he has loved us. And lastly, because Maria asked me to look after you. She said her son saw the good in your heart."

"I have so much to atone for my past."

"It's getting late Paul," Sister said as she stands. "Papa will be up early tomorrow."

I stand as well and hug her, thanking her for everything. I tell her again how much I missed her and how it was nice to be able to see her again. She nods and leaves the room.

The next morning came slowly as I could not sleep well. However, it wasn't due to stress or worry, but, on the contrary, it was due to the excitement and renewed commitment I felt towards the journey. Sister Guinevere does have an amazing affect upon me.

So, here we are in Pietas, the canton of piety, with Sister Guinevere. This territory begins to take on a less impoverished look. It is very clean and well thought out as far as the design and layout of the town. The chapel is on the west end of the canton, but faces east to capture the morning sunrise. The purpose of Pietas is to teach devotion, respect and humility. Unlike the other cantons we have visited, this place is very peaceful and serene. The people busily do their chores silently and work in prayer and meditation.

Papa has positioned himself on his stool and is ready to start. This morning he is talking about our dear friend Sevita, who had escaped her evil brother Danni yet again with the aid of Maria. If I'm not mistaken, this is the part where Sevita will meet her future husband Domingo, who together will eventually run that quaint little fruit store in Scientia. Isn't it wondrous how everything seems to fit into a grand plan?

~ Doctore ~

Far to the west at the Pacific edge, where the Break starts in Santa Barbara and continues its quest south towards the border of Mexico, was the church of Our Lady of Sorrows. This once beautiful white stucco structure

186

was the place of worship for many generations. Its Spanish style design had been surrounded by the elegance of sophisticated palm trees that gently shaded the courtyard. Curved in the form of a crescent moon, the piazza had wrapped gently around the side to the back of the church. The large, arched wooden framed windows dotted both the first and second stories, granting access to many a sun-filled California day. Finishing off the glorious building, there stood a squared, white tower. It competed with the rising palm trees for Heaven's real estate. Capturing the rays of dawn's and dusk's light, it created an orange glow in its belfry that reflected through salt water winds.

When Sevita arrived at the church, there was only a hint of what it had once been in its past glory. The arched wooden frames were torn off, the windows were all broken, most of the white stucco had cracked and peeled away, and the courtyard and grounds were all overgrown with weed, burnt brush, and wild thistle. Even the sculpture of the King that had graced the entrance of the church had been taken away; unknown was its fate. Sevita entered through the back where the door lay on the floor several feet from where it had once hung open, welcoming people into the choir area. There was litter and dirt scattered throughout the inside rooms. Vandalized walls, floors, and ceilings accompanied the chilling air that swept through from the El Nino winds. Sevita began to look for the signs that Maria had spoken of in their previous conversation.

In a small area of the tower where the light came through the four open columns at the top of the belfry, she spotted the pattern Maria had described. Reflected in the orange shimmering glow, the Archangel Raphael rose prominently from an unbroken Spanish floor tile. She stared at the image for a few minutes and thought it to be pointing towards the ground. There was a small crack that surrounded the tile, and she used a small, flattened stick to try to pry it upwards. Moving just a tad, the stick broke into two pieces. She looked around the floor for something else that she could use that was sturdier, but saw nothing. Walking outside again, she looked around the grounds and finally spotted the head of a garden rake. Although it was missing the handle, it looked like it would work in prying up the floor tile. She carried it inside, knelt down beside the tile, and wedged the prongs of the rake into the crack. She leaned her weight on it and the tile started to rise up. However, the rake head slipped out of the crack and flew across the floor. The tile fell back into position. She repeated the process, only this time she wedged the broken stick under the tile. When the rake slipped, the stick stopped it from falling back into place. With the stick holding the tile up, it was much easier to push the prongs of the rake further underneath the tile. After grabbing a good hold of the rake head, she pulled it back and lifted the tile up off the floor and pushed it to the side.

There, below the tile, was a wooden door with a metal, hinged handle in the center. Grabbing hold of the handle, she stood and lifted it up, revealing a long, winding staircase that looked like it went on forever into the Earth. It was lit with a strange glowing bluish light. Sevita looked around, took a deep breath, and started down the staircase. After taking several steps downward, she reached up and closed the door above her. She had wondered about the tile being left off of the door, but then thought that Maria would somehow take care of it. Continuing down the spiraling staircase, she carefully placed her foot on the next step and held onto the railing. The walls surrounding the staircase were made of some type of concrete, but they felt very smooth and warm to the touch. She could still not see the bottom nor had there appeared any indication that it would come soon. It seemed that she had already gone at least five or six floors, but she did not turn back. She drew her courage from Maria and the fact that every so often another Archangel image would appear on the wall that directed her to continue descending the staircase. She thought to count the stairs to pass the time, but after losing track several times, she stopped counting.

Sitting down on a stair to take a break, she lifted her pack off of her shoulders and took out the water jug. She opened the container and took several good size gulps. Never had she tasted water such as this where it was always cool and refreshing. After tearing off a piece of bread from the loaf, she finished her snack and took another sip of water. She continued working her way down the winding staircase until finally she spotted a bright, warm glow coming from just beneath her feet. Excited to the see the light, she quickened her pace, but still held on tightly to the handrail as she could not afford to lose her footing. As she rounded the last few steps and finally felt the dirt floor beneath her feet, she breathed a sigh of relief.

She proceeded through a narrow passage and passed through a large oval opening into what appeared to be a large cavern. It was brightly lit with the same bluish lights as in the staircase, only there were many more of them and they were much brighter. Sevita readjusted her backpack, took a breath, and began her journey through the tunnel. She had no idea what time it had been, but she had guessed it was about six or six-thirty. When she had first come to the church, the sun was already starting to set low in the sky and she had figured it then to be about four o'clock. Without having the sun as a guide for time, it would be difficult to know how long she had been walking. Her only guide down in the strange tunnel system was the Archangel Raphael who kept her moving in the right direction.

She pondered how she had spent her entire life as a fashion model with everyone paying close attention to her. She had always been the center of attention. However, this adventure was quite different down in lower Earth. She wished Vivian had come with her; she could have talked with her to break the silence. Alone, as she was, her mind would wander with thoughts of her past and of Danni. She wondered how Vivian was getting along, and if she was still safe.

"I wonder if I will see Maria again?" she whispered to the empty tunnel.

She pressed on, walking at a consistent pace. It seemed to her that after spending some time now in the tunnel that the bluish light was getting duller. Either it was her eyes getting used to the strange glow of light or that indeed the lighting was starting to dim. Off in the distance, she thought that she heard the sound of water. It almost sounded like a small creek or water dripping from a height. She quickened her pace and came upon a widening of the tunnel, more brightly lit than the area that she had been walking through. On the right side was the most beautiful fountain she had ever seen. The crystal oasis seemed to just float out from the cavern wall. Made from dark blue and black crystal-like rock, the waters accumulated in the bowl where she reached in her hand. It felt very cool and smooth. Scooping the liquid into her hand, she brought some up to her lips and tasted it.

"I think now I know where Maria gets her water," she said aloud, enjoying the wondrous spring.

Beside the fountain in a small nook in the wall was a blanket. She wondered how it might have gotten there and then disregarded such an obvious question. She took it out and spread it open on the ground next to the fountain. Then sitting down on the blanket, she leaned against the tunnel wall and took her book from her backpack. After reading just half of a chapter, her eyes ached and she felt extremely tired. The lighting had become quite dim in the fountain area. She placed her book to the side and lay on the blanket. Using the backpack as a pillow, she reached for the end of the blanket, pulled it over herself, and was soon fast asleep.

When Sevita awoke, she felt refreshed and well rested. She was anxious and excited to continue her journey through the tunnel to reach her final destination—the city of which she had heard such wonderful things. There were stories of a mystical place in which people had lived in harmony with one another. They had freedom to start families or to move about within the city as they wished. There was freedom to pursue one's faith and their understanding of their existence without criticism or persecution. It was a city built upon the idea that people were always given a choice. However, that choice was never to be limited by another person or entity. It was a community where people were encouraged to make choices in the spirit of how the One had made choices. In sacrificing one's own selfish needs for the needs of others so that the entire city could flourish with growth and prosperity.

She rolled up the blanket and was about to place it back into the cubbyhole when she noticed a wrapped bundle. She took it out and immediately the rush of fresh bread came to her senses. Undoing the cloth at one corner, she peeked into it and saw two loaves of Maria's bread.

thomas e

"How does she do it?" she asked. "It's a good thing, too, because there is only the small end left of the bread in my pack."

After breaking off a piece and popping it into her mouth, she closed her eyes, savoring the warmth and sweetness of the gift left to her. She rewrapped the bundle, and after gathering her things, started out on her quest to find the city. As she walked alone in silence, she reflected on her life and decided that she had wasted much of her time and energy in just trying to survive in a world that really did not care. She had watched her mother do the same thing. They had used their beautiful triangular faces and pretty features as a method of getting the necessary means to survive in their world, but at a great cost to their inner beauty. Though, surrounded by crowds of onlookers and encircled by people trying to gain from their outward beauty, she often felt isolated, alone, and mistrusting of everyone. She felt ashamed that she had wasted so much of her time trying to live in that world. Why hadn't she sought out Maria several years ago when their father first left? The more she thought of her past the more sorrowful and remorseful she became, until tears started to roll down her cheeks as she walked towards her second chance at life.

Up ahead, she heard the sound of running water in the distance. She reasoned that it was another fountain and wondered if Maria had left anything for her there. The thought then occurred to her that possibly Maria might be there waiting for her like she had before, so she took off in a sprint with hopes of seeing her again. As she came around the end of a bend in the tunnel, she saw a large hole in the cavern wall. It ran the length of the right wall and it appeared to have a stream running through it. Walking up closer to the tunnel window, Sevita noticed a small craft in the water. Inside the craft was a young man, perhaps her own age, lying inside the boat. She cautiously and hesitantly moved a little closer to see if he was alive. Leaning over the tunnel window, she poked him with her finger and quickly moved back. The young man moved slightly and scratched his shoulder where she had prodded him. He had dark disheveled hair with a strong jawline. Sevita thought he was quite the handsome man, and then poked him again.

"Who are you? What are you doing here?"

The young man opened his eyes slowly at first, and then he quickly started to look for something in the tubeboat. After finding what appeared to be a leather pouch, he was more at ease. Hopping out of the craft, he stood up and stretched his arms above his head.

"What are you doing here?" Sevita asked again.

"I imagine the same thing you are doing here. Were you sent by Maria?" he asked.

Sevita seemed to relax and became more at ease. "Yes, Maria sent me." She paused for a moment. "My name is Sevita."

"Domingo," he said nodding to her. "Hey, where are we anyway?"

"What do you mean?"

"Where did you enter the tunnel system?"

"Santa Barbara," she said.

"California?" Domingo looked very surprised.

"Is there another Santa Barbara?"

"I can't believe I've come this far west."

"Why? Where are you from?"

"Little Lake in Aurdal, Minnesota."

"Minnesota? You came all the way from Minnesota in that thing?" she said in an astonished and almost terrified look while pointing to the tubeboat. "How long did it take?"

"Not very long at all. The waters move fast. Unbelievably fast." Domingo bent over the craft and took out a small bag with a strap, which he draped over his right shoulder. "Which way?" he asked.

"That way." Sevita pointed in the direction she had been heading.

"Okay, lead the way then, California," he said with a quirky smile.

Sevita rolled her eyes and started down the tunnel. Domingo held back for a minute and shrugged his shoulders. "What'd I say?" he asked quietly, then hurried after her, and after catching up, walked along side of her.

They walked the tunnel, always pushing forward. Domingo liked to look at the pictures and drawings on the cavern walls. At one particular group of pictures, he had taken considerable more time than usual and when Sevita looked back he was far behind. She stopped walking and turned around.

"Are you coming?" she asked.

"Have you seen these photos and drawings? They're beautiful." Domingo said.

"Yes, I've seen them. They are all over the walls."

"This photo reminds me of my grandfather. I know it's an older picture and hard to see, but it really looks like him. I mean, I know it isn't, but the resemblance is remarkable."

Sevita went to the wall and looked at the picture he had pointed out to her. "Where is your grandfather?"

"He died a little while ago. He was an apple farmer. I'm an apple farmer, too, just like him. I went to college in Minnesota and studied hydroponic techniques."

"Really? I thought most of that was all automated now."

"Most of it is, but my grandfather and I had are our own farm. The Fed took it away from me though after my grandfather died. That's when I met Maria and she told me to come here. So, here I am. How about you? How did you meet Maria?"

Sevita stepped back from the wall and looked towards the ground.

Domingo, noticing that she looked rather uncomfortable with the question tried to retract it.

"We should probably keep moving. We've been here for a while now," he said.

"Yeah," Sevita agreed and turned away from the wall to follow him down the tunnel.

"This tunnel is amazing. I mean, can you imagine how long it must have taken them to dig this entire thing out? They had to reinforce the roof with beams, put in retaining walls, and figure out the airflow system. They also built that magnificent waterway system. I have never seen anything like that before in my life."

"I guess I never thought of it that way. It is pretty amazing. I wonder how long it took them to build it."

"It had to be decades. These tunnels go on forever, and they must be all over North America. I mean I made it from Little Lake, Minnesota to Santa Barbara!"

Sevita nodded.

"My grandfather and I had this great apple farm. He had a real green thumb, my grandfather. He used to call it his Perez thumb. That's our family name, Perez. He called it his Perez thumb because he had come from a long line of tree farmers and he would say it was in our blood. Before he died, we were starting to work on hydro-farming to try the new technologies with some of the old school ways. You know, sort of a blended approach. Hydroponics has some great techniques, but you still can't produce the same kind of fruit like you can with the real soil. There's just something about the natural ways that always seem to produce higher quality fruit. Anyway, we were going to try some different approaches to see if we could get better production, but still keep that same natural taste."

Domingo went on telling Sevita about the apple farm and his grandfather for quite some time. He talked of his dreams and the plans he hoped to carry out when he arrived at the city. Sevita was mostly quiet except for a remark or a question on something he said. After a while, he stopped talking.

"What's the matter?" Sevita asked.

"What do you mean?"

"You just stopped talking."

"I've been going on now for ages and I'm doing all of the talking. I talk a lot. I talk more when I'm nervous," Dom replied, pushing his hair back with his hand.

"Are you nervous about something?"

"I should probably just stop talking now."

"I liked listening to your stories. I haven't had anyone to talk with for a while. I've been on my own now for quite some time, so I like listening to you." Sevita said.

"Thanks. Well, what about you. What stories do you have?" Domingo asked. "How did you meet—"

Sevita held her hand up to silence him. She tilted her head to the side trying to listen more closely. "Do you hear that? It sounds like running water. I wonder if it's another fountain."

"Fountain? Maybe it's the river again." Domingo said.

They continued on, and within one hundred yards or so they came across another fountain.

"Wow! Look at that. It's beautiful, Sevita," Domingo said and ran up to the fountain.

Sevita walked up behind him. "Yes, it is beautiful. This is the second one I've seen down here."

"That's fluorspar," Domingo said pointing to the blue crystal.

"It's what?"

"It's fluorite or fluorspar. It's a calcium fluoride mineral that is usually found in mines and such."

"How do you know this stuff?"

"I studied geology in school as part of my program for soil work."

"Taste the water. It's the best water you'll ever have," Sevita said.

Domingo reached his hand in and brought it up to his mouth. "Hm, that is good. And it's cold." He took a bottle from his pack and emptied it out on the ground and then filled it with water from the fountain. Then carefully taking out his grandfather's pouch, he opened it up, and took out the scion. He reached into the fountain with his other hand and dripped water over the base of the scion. After wrapping the base with the burlap again, he put it back into the pouch.

"What's that?" Sevita asked.

"It's a root for an apple tree. My grandfather has been using this particular root for generations. I am taking it to the city where I can start an apple farm there. I can use this scion to grow more apple trees just like my grandfather had back home."

"That sounds great, Domingo; it really does. Do you want to rest here for a while?"

"Sure, this is a good spot to take a breather."

They sat down by the fountain and leaned against the cavern wall. Sevita handed Domingo a large piece of the bread that she had found by the last fountain. Sitting together, with the sound of the fountain echoing in the cavern, gave Sevita the courage to open up to her new friend.

"I was a model and lived in San Luis Obispo. Modeling was how I made ends meet."

"Of course, I mean how could you miss?" Domingo commented.

"My biologics had left my brother and me when we were in our teen years and we had to make it on our own."

Domingo stopped eating the bread and looked up at her with sympathetic eyes.

"My brother, Danni, he got involved with some terrible people and they corrupted his mind. I just barely escaped from them with my life. That is how I came to know Maria. She helped me to escape and led me to the tunnels. I've been on my own, supporting my brother and myself for a long time, so when he betrayed me…it's just difficult for me, you know?"

"I'm sorry. Really, that's not right. You should be able to count on your family. I know people consider us North District folks somewhat backward and still clinging to old ways, but I could always depend on my grandfather. He was a rock; an immovable, stable rock."

"Thank you for being understanding. Why don't we finish our meal and get going. I don't know how far we have to travel, but we must keep moving onward."

Domingo nodded his head in agreement and quickly finished eating his bread. Tipping back his water bottle, he gulped down several swallows and then refilled it from the fountain. Within a few minutes, they were back on their feet and walking the trail again. Side by side, they hiked down the center of the tunnel path, sometimes talking about what the city might look like and other times walking in silence, at least for as long as Domingo could stand it before starting a new conversation.

It had been almost two hours since their break at the fountain when Domingo felt the hair on the back of his neck stand up. Sevita stopped dead in her tracks as the light in the cavern turned from a soft bluish white to a darkened red color.

"Something's wrong," she said in a shaken voice.

"I feel it, too. There's something coming down the tunnel. Listen…."

Sevita quickly scanned the cavern for a place to hide. There wasn't a lot of deviation in the floors and walls of the cave. There were no corners or holes in which to crawl into. She felt a panic come over her and her eyes searched desperately for something that they could use to hide behind. There at the west wall towards the top of the tunnel entrance, where the cave started to bend there was an indentation just wide enough for the two of them.

"Quick! Over there," she pointed.

Domingo went over to the crack in the wall and then turned to her.

"What? This isn't cover. Whatever is coming will see us!"

"Trust me. Just get in there and get as close to the wall as possible." Sevita took off her pack and reached in pulling out the hooded overcoat that Maria had given to her. As she did, it appeared larger than she had remembered. She put it over herself and moved in closely against Domingo.

Lifting up the cloak's hood, she put it over his face and head. "Don't move a muscle!" she whispered. She put her arms around him and they buried themselves into the cave crevice.

A terrible shrieking, like the sound of a thousand tortured screams, echoed throughout the cave and with it the sound of wings flapping hurriedly like that of a large insect. Domingo drew Sevita close. Through the cloak he could see the vile creatures flying through the air. They looked like a cross between a cave bat and a type of locust. Their ugly head covered with short, brownish fur looked like a city rat. They had large bloody front teeth and dark black beady eyes. Domingo did not see any type of nose on these creatures. With short wide ears, they moved back and forth appearing to search for sounds in the cave. The body size was approximately five to six inches in length and two inches in width. The creatures had four very short legs and two large back legs along with two sets of wings, which overlapped each other just like a locust. They were the foulest looking things Domingo had ever seen. There must have been hundreds of them. The cave blackened as the swarm flew through. The horrendous shrieking and the sounds of the wings sent chills up Domingo's spine. He could feel Sevita shaking, and pulled her close. Her head was buried in his chest and her arms wrapped around the back of him. He continued to watch them through the hood of the coat that was over his face. After several long minutes, they seemed to have vanished just as quickly as they came. The beleds color changed back to a soft bluish light.

"I think they're gone," Domingo whispered.

Sevita stepped back with the cloak still over her to look out across the cave. As she turned around to inspect the area, Domingo was astonished to see her completely vanish into thin air. He reached out and touched the space directly in front of him and hit something.

Sevita turned around to face him. "What is it?" she asked.

"That is some overcoat you're wearing! You completely disappeared into the cave ambiance. How is that possible? Where did you get it?"

Sevita smiled. "Maria. It's saved me twice now from danger." She took the hood down and looked at Domingo. "What were those things?"

"I don't know. I've never seen anything that looked like that before. It was some kind of half-bat and half-locust creature. It had wings and legs like an insect, but its head and body looked more like a bat or a rat. I sure didn't like the looks of it, though, whatever it was."

"It sounded hideous and evil. I'm glad my back was turned to them."

"How do you suppose the lights change to a red warning color? This tunnel system almost seems alive and aware."

"I've learned to not ask questions such as that since I've met Maria. It seems everything is possible where it concerns things related to her. And when you listen to her instructions; well, things seem to just work out."

195

"Maria does have a way about her, doesn't she? I mean, when I was standing in the orchard with her it seemed that I just needed to do whatever she asked of me. It was almost a primal instinct from deep within. Being there was like being in the presence of royalty or something."

Sevita nodded in wholehearted agreement. "Come on, let's keep moving. Hopefully, we won't run into anymore of those things."

It was after three o'clock in the afternoon when they reached the river. They stood just beside the incredibly fast moving waters. Domingo was already in the tubeboat trying to get Sevita to join him.

"Come on, what's the worry? I've done this already and it's really not that bad." Domingo coaxed.

"Maybe we should continue down the tunnel. I mean, how do we know this is the right way for us?"

Domingo pointed to the Archangel Raphael image at the water's edge. "It can't get any clearer than this. I don't understand; what's the problem?"

"I can't swim," Sevita said looking down at the water.

"You grew up in California; how is that possible?"

"Yeah, well it was something I was always going to get to, but never got around to it, okay?"

"It's all right. We're not going to be in the water anyway. We're going to stay in the boat. Trust me; you don't want to be in the water. With how fast these currents move, it would tear you to shreds if you fell into it."

"Oh, well that makes me feel much better now, thank you. I'm continuing down the tunnel. So long." Sevita went to turn away from the tubeboat when Domingo reached out and grabbed her hand.

"Come on, Sevita. Maria will look after us. We need to go wherever the river takes us. It's how this all works. You follow the angel and trust in the wise ones that came before you."

Sevita looked at the fast moving water and then back to the tubeboat. Gazing into Domingo's honest face, she sighed. "Well, make room for me then. And don't let the boat tip or move or anything as I'm getting in!"

"I got 'er," he said and smiled as she climbed into the craft and sat down in front of him. She leaned back against him and her hair brushed across his face.

"This is kind of cozy. How about a kiss for good luck?"

Sevita smirked and pushed her elbow into his side.

"Uhhmmph," he said wincing from the unexpected blow. "Okay, maybe not then. Hold on...." Domingo pushed down on the rudder pedals, released the tubeboat from the dock, and the last thing heard after the craft hit the water and took off down the river was Sevita's screams echoing off the cavern walls.

Chapter 20

Jazin's Pursuit

~ Paul ~

Somehow, it seems when things are going well, that's when evil shows its head to put fear and doubt into Man. There are those who have become the most fearsome weapons in the Shekel's arsenal. They inflict pain and misery for sheer enjoyment. I wouldn't want to be anywhere near these wicked and vile creatures without a topnotch GIT officer standing right beside me.

Once Papa gets through this darkness, I will bring him some nourishment. He is moving his fingers across the knots on his rope-belt, apparently trying to find the place to start. We are nearly through the first leg of The Way.

~ Doctore ~

Through the Break, the Pacific wind carried the tortured screams of a broken society. A mistrustful, greedy, and selfish people who are left to fend for themselves will only become a testament to failure. They are unable to stand as one united force. They, unlike the great societies that flourished in the past, could not dedicate themselves to one another to strive for excellence. They were unable and unwilling to sacrifice for a greater good. The Shekel struggled to keep its house in order, as it had perceived a division in power among his dark leaders. Abandoned of all hope, they struggled to care for one another and they became instinctively paranoid of one another. Since the Shekel had convinced the people to remove the higher power from their culture, society had to settle for a lower power. The lot of them did not have the heart or the passion to drive for the betterment of society. The Pacific District was the worst of all the zones. Its corruption and decadence was so infused into their culture that they even fought amongst themselves, constantly positioning for better status.

This was the plight of Danni looking to move up in the ranks of Jazin's *Gri'mõtal* army. So, in the darkness of night, he stole into Vivian's building and then broke into her apartment. Slithering across the floor, he made his way to the back room where she slept. He had doused a piece of cloth with chemicals for putting her into an unconscious state. Standing directly over her, he put the cloth over her mouth and nose. Her eyes

197

immediately opened in a panicked look of terror. She grabbed the hand that had covered her face and tried to desperately remove it. Holding her breath and struggling against the strong fingers covering her mouth and nose proved to be too much, she ran out of air and inhaled. Her tensed body went lifeless and her eyes closed again as she fell prey to the fumes of the anesthesia.

When she awoke again, she found herself hanging from her arms that were tied with chains fastened to a concrete wall. She pulled against the chains, but they were strong and her strength was no match for them. Looking around at her surroundings, she appeared to be kept hostage in some type of basement. There was dampness and coldness all around her. It was dark and there was a foul stench in the air. The entire place reeked of danger and evil. She bowed her head and called out to Maria.

"Oh Maria, if you can help me, please come for me. And if you cannot, please keep Sevita safe. Don't let me die in vain," she cried out.

It wasn't long before Danni and Jazin came down a concrete staircase. They strutted over to her with smugness on their faces, so proud of their triumph in taking her from her home and bringing her to their place of misery.

"Danni, you did not tell me she was so fine a creature. It will be difficult for me to enjoy my acts of torture. Look at that pretty face." Jazin grabbed her face from underneath her chin with his thumb and fingers stretching across her cheeks. He squeezed them together tightly stopping the blood flow. "It's almost too pretty to cut up…almost." He ripped his fingers from her face leaving large red marks where his fingers had pressed her skin into her cheek bones.

"What do you want from me? I don't even know who you are," Vivian asked.

"You know what I want. Where is that pfotten wretch?"

Vivian looked at Danni, who shook his head from side to side, and then back to Jazin. She tried to act ignorant of the whole affair. "What wretch?"

"Don't be coy with me girl! Do not take me for one of your producer fools that you manipulate with your looks. I can read through your lies like they were written in iron. I have knowledge that you couldn't possibly understand and power you couldn't imagine. Perhaps you need some type of demonstration of this power. Yes, a little motivation might be in order for you to reconsider your position." He smiled at her with a sinister and threating look.

Jazin tore at her gown and ripped into it in several places. Even though her flesh was exposed and in the hands of her enemies, she still had complete control of her thoughts. With the power of free will in her mind, she kept repeating to herself. *I will not give up my friend. Maria, help me to be strong. Do not allow this horror to weaken my spirit.*

Jazin reached into his belt with his right hand and took out a long filet knife. Running his left hand slowly over her shoulder, he looked directly into her eyes. "It would be a shame to carve up such a pretty and innocent girl. There aren't that many of you left you know." He paused and stared at her. "No?" he asked while playing with the handle of the knife.

Vivian just looked at him in denial. Jazin stuck the end of the blade into the side of her shoulder and then slid the knife down carving off a large section of skin from her left arm. Vivian screamed out in pain and grabbed at the chains tightly. Jazin took a step back and looked at her mockingly. Imitating an artist judging his art, he looked first at the left side of Vivian, with the skin gone from her arm and blood running down it, and then the right side.

"Oh, no, no, no – this will not do. We cannot have that – she is uneven. Look Danni, do you see it?"

Danni looked on and smiled. "I see it, Jazin. You are always so right in everything."

"There must be balance in this artwork." Jazin then took his knife and carved an equal section of skin from her right arm.

Vivian again screamed in pain. Her arms, still in the shackles that hung from above her head, dripped blood from their wounds. She kept her head down and stared at the concrete. In her thoughts, she begged Maria for help. She asked her for strength. *I will not give up my friend. Maria, help me to be strong.* Preparing herself for even harsher torture, she gripped the chains that held her captive.

"We have a strong one, Danni. No wonder your sister kept her as a friend. But what kind of friend is Sevita that she could leave you in this perilous way while she runs free to do as she pleases? Tell us what we want to know and you can go free. Right now, a couple of minutes in a MediDock and you're as good as new. However, a couple more minutes with me and not even the MediDock will be able to decipher what species you belonged to."

She knew that Jazin would never let her go regardless of what she did or didn't tell him. Besides, it wouldn't have mattered; it wasn't right in her heart. Vivian remained silent. And even as Jazin tore the flesh from her bones one stroke at a time, it was though she no longer was there. Her mind had gone far from that cold and damp basement. It had drifted to the warm and gentle sand of the beach where she imagined Maria walking across the sand, only not really walking at all, but hovering just above it. Danni could no longer stand to watch the butcherous actions of Jazin. He stared at the floor and kept moving away from the trail of blood that seemed to seek him out.

Vivian grew more and more weak and death was upon her. Jazin stared into her eyes as he brought the knife up to finish her off, but then he saw in her eyes the reflection of Maria. In fear, he dropped the knife to the ground and spun around behind him to see if Maria was there. However, there was only Danni staring at him. Turning back to Vivian, her head had dropped to her chest. He picked it up by her hair and then dropped it again. She was dead. Jazin was incredibly angry at his failure. He turned that anger and aggression at Danni. Grabbing him by the shirt with both of his bloody hands, he flung him against the concrete wall. Danni's head hit the concrete hard and it started to bleed. Jazin, with his left arm, lifted him up off the floor right next to the hanging body of Vivian. Then with his right hand, he grabbed his face digging his long pointed nails into his cheeks.

"G-Tubist! Look at her. She's dead! We didn't get anything from her. How dare you bring me such an innocent lamb to slaughter? You better find that sister of yours or your flesh will be lying with hers!"

Jazin hit him several times in the face and scrapped his head against the rough concrete cutting his cheek and eye. "Look G-Tubist – if you don't bring me the wretch by sundown this Friday next, your blood will run with hers. I will not be made the fool in front of Master Ire. You will do this or you will die."

Jazin hit him hard in the abdomen and then dropped him to the ground. After picking up his knife and wiping it off, he left the basement by way of the concrete steps. Danni struggled to get to his knees and stayed there for a moment trying to regain his breath. After a few moments, he was able to breathe normally. He noticed his right hand was in a pool of Vivian's blood and he quickly lifted it out. He used her gown to wipe off the blood, but the stain remained on his palm. He rubbed the cloth harder against his hand, but to no avail. The red stain remained. He looked up at Vivian in terror and anguish. Then, fearful of being alone with her in the basement, he quickly scampered up the stairs.

Unitas

Chapter 21

Voyage to the City

~ Paul ~

I often hear Papa's words echo in the silence. They seem to come to me when I need to contemplate on something of importance. I remember Papa saying to me, "The One King had said 'A house divided against itself cannot stand.' The Creator's house is unified and unbreakable as it is built on pure love. If only we would open our hearts to it we would never want for anything."

After preparing a small meal, I bring it to Papa before he starts another narrative. "Papa, here is a bowl of brown rice and bread. I have a cup of water, also. Please, take a break and I will attend to these fine people. Once you finish the next section of the story, we can go back to Sister's for you to rest. You are not looking well, Papa."

"I am fine, Paolo. You worry too much."

"Papa, I am under orders. You must rest for a couple of days before we leave for the canton of Consilium. What would happen to your flock if you were to take ill?"

"You are a good man, Paolo. You watch over me like the good Archangel Raphael. I will eat now."

While Papa says the blessing over his food, I take over the stage to begin my theatrics with a bushel of oranges. However, I repeatedly look back to Papa as he really didn't look well. All of the traveling has not done him a bit of good. He gets up too early and stays up too late praying. He pushes his elderly body to the brink of exhaustion. I have to get him back to Sister Guinevere's where we can care for him and get him the rest he so desperately needs. If we can just get through this last segment we should be all right.

~ Doctore ~

George and Jackieo were sitting together near a fountain finishing their daily ration of bread and the water from the fountain. Li'Quari was on the other side of the cave sitting with her back against the wall. With her head hung low, she held the cross necklace and the photos of Jackson in her hands.

"The poor girl, I feel so bad for her. Imagine having to witness that murderous slug killing her father," Jackieo said softly.

thomas e

George looked up at her and finished the last of his doughbread. "She'll be all right. People can be very resilient when they have to be; I've seen some horrendous battles and men doing unheard of and amazing things. She'll be all right, J-O."

Li'Quari stared at the photos that Jackson had given her, particularly the one where he stood with his wife and daughter. They were all nicely dressed and looked like they were at some type of event for his daughter. Jackson looked very happy and proud. His smile stretched clear across his face. She remembered what he had said to her: *Lucks to you, daughter. I love you.* She had never known anyone who had ever loved her like a father. Jackson had been more of a father to her than anyone she had ever known or at least remembered. How fortunate she was to have met him. Reaching up, she wiped the tears from her eyes and slowly got to her feet. She went to place the photos on the cavern walls with the others, but she couldn't see how they were attached. They seemed to be just stuck to the dirt and rock without anything holding them up.

"Strange," she whispered to herself. She placed the photo of Jackson's daughter against the rock to see how it would look. It stayed there, held firmly in place, which made no sense but at the same time it seemed so acceptable. She placed Jackson's second photo of his wife next to the first. And finally, taking another look at Jackson in the last photo, she put it up to her lips and kissed it, then placed it above the other two photos. The clay seemed to wrap around the edges and pulled it inwards toward the wall.

"Thank you, Jackson. I'll always love you, too, my father." She touched the photo one last time. "It is a joyous day."

She turned and walked back towards the fountain where George and Jackieo had been sitting. The lights in the tunnel were becoming dim and everyone was tired from a long day.

"Are you all right, honey?" Jackieo asked.

"I'll be okay."

George stood up and stretched his arms towards the cave's ceiling. "We should get some rack, it's got to be getting late now and we'll be losing the tunnel light soon." He reached for the blankets near the fountain. "Huh, would you look at that."

"What's wrong?" asked Jackieo.

"Three blankets – one for each of us. Last time there were just two."

"It's a strange cavern; it's like it has a mind all of its own," Jackieo replied.

George handed Li'Quari a blanket and then made up the sleeping area for Jackieo and himself. During the night, he could hear sobs from Li'Quari and found himself wishing that he had gotten to Jackson and Dragonhead just a few minutes earlier so he could have saved his life. He

204

turned onto his side and tried to quiet his mind so as to get some much needed rest for tomorrow's trials.

The next morning the newly formed trio was up early, fortified with a grotto breakfast, and well on their way into the next leg of their journey. Li'Quari had been lagging behind George and Jackieo by a good twenty to thirty yards. This began to frustrate George, who wanted to maintain a good pace. He didn't know how many more enemy singletons or forces were in the tunnel, but he sure didn't want to get ambushed from behind. He slowed down to let Li'Quari catch up. When she reached them, she was crying again.

"Listen Li'Quari, I know it's hard to see someone you love die, but we have to keep moving. There must have been some reason Jackson didn't make it and it ended the way it did. I wish I had come just a few minutes earlier, so I might have been able to save him. But I didn't. It didn't happen that way. Maria knew I would meet up with the Red Dragon and she had warned me of him, so she must have known too that Jackson would be killed. There must have been some purpose to his death or he had simply completed all that he was to complete in his life. It was time for him to go on to a better place."

Li'Quari stopped crying and looked at George. "He said he saw his daughter and his wife. His daughter must have died in the European war. He didn't know that until just before he died."

"Yes, you see? He had done everything he had to do here. It was time for him to go to his family just as it is time for you to continue on with your family," George said pointing to her womb.

Jackieo put her arm around her and pulled her close. "We know it's hard, honey, but Jackson wouldn't want to see anything happen to you. He left you in our care now and we want to make sure we get you to the city in one piece."

"He told me he believed in me. He called me his daughter," Li'Quari said through a stream of tears and her voice quivered.

"I know he loved you so much. It's why he died to save you, so you could have more joyful days," Jackieo replied.

Li'Quari looked up at her and rubbed the tears from her eyes. "Joyous days?"

"Yes, joyous days."

Li'Quari hugged her tightly and thanked her. And then, turning she started down the tunnel singing joyfully.

> "It's a joyous daaaaaaay.
> It's a joyous daaaaaaay.
> Jesus taught the news
> Jesus taught good news.

> Jesus taught such good news.
> Won't you walk his way.
> It's a joyous daaaaaaay.
> It's a joyous daaaaaaay."

George looked at Jackieo and whispered, "What did you say to her?"

Jackieo just shrugged her shoulders and smiled, and then she joined in with Li'Quari singing and dancing. "It's a joyous daaaaaaay."

As George led his small unit through the tunnel, heading east along the southern terrain, Saul and his group had been marching southeast from the Chicago metropolis. Sister Guinevere was carrying Razzi on her hip and Saul carried Mia, who had her arms wrapped around his neck. They had been moving through the cavern for over two hours since they awoke. Just when it seemed to Saul that they were making headway, they came to a split in the tunnel. The left path led to the east and the right path led towards the south. Saul put Mia down and searched the walls for Raphael's mark that would indicate which way to go.

"I don't see the mark. It's not here, Sister."

Sister lowered Razzi to the ground and set him next to Mia while she searched the cavern walls for the sign of the archangel. After nearly fifteen minutes of combing over the cavern walls, she looked up to Saul. "It's not here."

He pointed towards the left tunnel. "It must be this tunnel that leads east. We've been heading in an easterly direction the entire trip, so it would only be sensible to continue on in that direction."

Razzi stared into the left tunnel, his body hunched in fear as he began to cry.

"Razzi? What's the matter, my darling boy?" Sister bent down and picked him up.

He pointed at the left tunnel and shook his head with fervor.

"What's the matter with him?" asked Saul.

"I don't know," Sister replied. She then turned to Razzi, "Do you want to go in the right tunnel?" she asked facing him in the direction of the other tunnel.

Razzi nodded.

"I think you're right, Razzi. We should take the right tunnel," Sister agreed.

"Now look here, Sister. I'll carry them, walk slower for them, make more stops for them, break longer for them, but I will not let infants dictate the direction in which we travel. By what logical thinking can you give to follow such nonsense?" Saul bellowed out in a loud voice.

"Children have an innocence and purity we couldn't possibly understand. They follow their true instincts and can determine quite readily when there is danger or evil present. We need to humble ourselves and follow and trust in their judgment at times of uncertainty."

"That is the most ridiculous thing I have ever heard. I'm going to the left; if you want to follow the instincts of an infant, then be my guest. It's been nice knowing you, Sister." With an insidious huff, Saul picked up his pack, swung it over his shoulder, and started down the left side of the tunnel. His footsteps became faint and distant in a short amount of time.

"Come along children. We will go the right way," Sister Guinevere said as she took hold of Mia's hand. Still carrying Razzi, she made her way into the tunnel's entrance on the right.

Not too long after they had split up, Sister came across a small shrine dedicated to the Holy Family. She decided to rest there with the children. After she had gotten them settled with some bread and a small ration of water, she knelt down in front of the shrine and prayed softly.

"Oh Heavenly Mother, I have tried to do your bidding and have prayed numerous rosaries for the doctor's soul and change of heart. He is the most stubborn, selfish, and uncharitable man. Please my dear Lady, please aid me in looking after these dear young souls. And I beg of your patience once again, give Doctor Kriesh another chance to show his honor and willingness to humble himself before God." Sister Guinevere continued to pray deeply as tears filled her eyes and rolled down her cheeks. In time, she made the sign of the cross, wiped her face, and went back to the children.

In the other tunnel, Saul began to slow his pace. He found the tunnel lighting was somewhat darker in this section than it appeared in the other tunnels. He continued to look for any sign of the Archangel Raphael's mark, but came across nothing. There was also a difference in how he felt in this part of the cavern. It was a feeling of isolation as if he were drifting out to sea away from land and civilization. Of course, his practical mind attributed this queer feeling as that being of guilt because he had left the Sister and children who were frail and vulnerable.

"Why should I stay with them? She is obviously a crackpot who has no logical sense about her whatsoever!" he called out in the emptiness of the tunnel. His voice echoed against the rock and came back to him in dark whispers and ghastly sounds. He moved closer to the wall and walked a little further down the path. "She'll probably end up getting me killed," he mumbled.

"Killed," the echo replied in a deep growling murmur.

With each step he took, the light seemed to turn a shade darker. He stopped and turned to look back towards the entrance. There was a bright light far off in the distance that seemed to call to him in a friendly voice. Ahead of him, there was only darkness and a feeling of emptiness that caused the hair on the back of his neck to stand up. Coldness and fear gripped him, and he screamed into the stillness, "I'll never hear the end of it. I despise that woman!" He slowly turned around and headed back in the direction from which he had come.

Sister Guinevere and the children were still sitting near the shrine finishing up their snack when Saul walked up to them with a somewhat sour expression on his face.

"It is kind of you to rejoin us, Doctor. We were just about to get moving again as we've finished our snack," Sister remarked as she stood up and brushed the dirt from her habit.

Razzi lifted up his arms towards Sister and she reached down and picked him up. Likewise, Mia turned to Saul and raised her arms. Saul couldn't help but to give her a little smile as he took her in his arms. He started down the path walking at a leisurely pace as Mia turned her head to the side and rested it on his shoulder. Sister Guinevere bowed before the shrine and said, "Thank you, Lady of the Tunnel."

"Are you coming, Sister? Don't be lagging back there," Saul called over his shoulder.

"I'm coming, Doctor," she replied.

About seventy yards from the shrine Saul stopped and looked at the cavern wall. After shaking his head, he continued on. Sister, being a few paces behind him, glanced at the wall in Razzi's tunnel. She couldn't help but smile when she recognized the mark of Raphael pointing his shield in the forward direction.

After walking steadily for a couple of hours, Saul heard the sound of running water and was pleased to be able to take a break. A fresh drink from the fountain would do them good. "Sister, I can hear another fountain just ahead. It should be a good place to take a breather."

"Good. Razzi could use something to drink and a little snack."

However, as they rounded a slight curve in the cavern, they were surprised to see a running river underneath a sort of cavern within a cavern. It was as if the river carved out a small path in the tunnels. The roof over the river was only five or six feet above the water. It was a very narrow and a very fast moving river. Along the sides of it were two watercraft that just seemed to hover above the waterline.

"This is amazing. I've never seen a manmade river like this," Saul remarked. "That water must be moving at forty or fifty miles per hour. Maybe more!"

Saul put Mia down and moved closer to the tubeboats. He inspected them and pushed down on them with his foot. "They seem solid enough."

"You're not suggesting that we go in those small crafts are you?" Sister asked.

"I'm afraid so," Saul replied.

"No, we couldn't. It's not safe for the children," Sister said with a look of concern.

Saul pointed to the mark of Raphael near the bank of the river and then looked up at Sister with a penetrating stare. Taking off his pack, he set it down on the ground near the edge.

"Let's take our break and give the children their snack. We'll make our way down the river. I'll take the first raft with Mia and you can follow in the second with Razzi. It will be fine. With how fast this river is moving it should take us to where we are going a lot faster than walking."

Sister Guinevere looked again at the river and the tubeboats. She closed her eyes and moved her lips in silent prayer, then gave the children their doughbread and water along with some raisins for a treat.

After their luncheon meal, Saul was eager to get to the watercraft. He went over to the tubeboat and looked over the outside from front to back. He climbed into the craft and maneuvered himself in the small space. He pushed the rudder pedals back and forth to make sure they were in working order. He concluded the strange lever with an arrow pointing downwards at etched symbols of water was intended to release the craft into the river.

He climbed out of the tubeboat, and with Sister and the children watching his every movement, he went to the second craft and began his inspection of that tubeboat as well.

Sister felt her heart begin to race, but outwardly her demeanor never changed; she looked as calm and peaceful as if she were going to Sunday Mass. She gathered up the children and put away the water bottle and the small cups.

"Okay, Sister, are you ready?"

Sister Guinevere nodded her head. "Razzi, we're going on a little boat ride. It will really be fun." She stepped closer to the edge of the river with Razzi hanging onto the folds of her habit.

"Okay, you step into the boat first and then I'll hand Razzi to you," Saul said and took hold of the small boy and helped Sister Guinevere board.

Sister was a little unsteady at first, but slid her feet underneath the front and sat down with her back firmly pressed against the stern, and then held out her arms for Razzi. In one swift movement, she settled him on the seat between her legs and wrapped her arms around him to secure him into place.

"How does this thing work?" she asked.

"There seems to be only two mechanical devices on this boat. There's a lever here," he said pointing to the lever on the right side of the boat. "I believe this will drop the boat into the water. There are two pedals at your feet that probably act like a rudder to steer the boat. Use your feet and push down on them to steer the boat right or left."

"Like this?" Sister moved her feet pushing down on the pedals.

Saul looked over the back of the boat and saw the rudder moving back and forth. "Yes, that's it. It's working fine." Saul looked at Mia and smiled. "Are you ready to go for a boat ride?"

Mia nodded her head.

Saul took her by the hand and they boarded the other craft.

"Are you ready, Sister?"

"We're ready!"

"I'll count to three and then I'll push the lever. After we're off you count to twenty and push the lever. That should give us enough spacing so we don't run into each other."

"Okay, we'll count to twenty." Sister repeated.

After experimenting with the controls and understanding their workings, Saul called out, "Here we go. One! Two! Three!" He pushed in the pedals and pulled the lever down and the tubeboat shot off like a bullet from a gun.

"Oh, sweet Jesus keep us safe!" Sister held Razzi close with her left arm and then held her right hand over the lever. "Here we go, Razzi," she said starting her countdown from twenty. "...five, four, three, two, one!" She pushed hard down on the pedals and pulled the lever down. The tubeboat hit the water and took off down the river. Water sprayed up into their compartment and hit her face, but she didn't blink an eye. Sister maneuvered the tubeboat from side to side using very small corrections like a seasoned fighter pilot. Working extremely hard to keep the craft in the middle of the river, she worked the pedals left and right keeping it very steady and nearly dead center. Razzi had his head down and felt the wind blowing through his curly hair.

Sister didn't know how long they were skimming the river at breakneck speeds, but she had never felt so relieved when the white rapids gave way to calmer waters. The tubeboats slowed and Saul and Sister guided them towards the dock. Saul and Mia climbed out first onto the riverbank. After Saul lifted Mia out of the craft, he reached his leg over to the land and pulled himself out. As the weight was taken out of the tubeboat, it rose up and latched itself to the side of the cavern wall. Saul just stared unbelievingly at the entire mechanism.

"That's just amazing. I wonder how that works?" he said scratching his head. As he turned, he noticed there were two other tubeboats latched to the cavern wall as well. He wondered who may have come over in those crafts and how long they had been there.

"Doctor, would you please help Razzi?" Sister Guinevere called out to him.

Saul quickly turned and went to reach for the young boy. After carrying him ashore, he reached out to lend a hand to the sister. She eagerly climbed out of the tubeboat and came ashore.

"Oh I pray we don't have to do that again," she said softly.

After taking a quick water break, they picked up the children and started walking in the direction Raphael had pointed. In less than an hour, they came to a very bright portion of the cavern. The light's intensity was so strong that it lit up the entire tunnel. Even though he still had Mia holding onto his neck, Saul quickened his pace to reach the entryway. As he came upon it, he stood in the arched doorway in complete amazement.

Standing beneath the large, arched, stone-carved doorway, he peered into the grand room. It was the largest room Saul had ever encountered. It was filled with brightly glowing beleds that illuminated the many beautiful fountains and shrines. The entire area seemed to glow a bluish-white that nearly blinded him from being able to take it all in. The beleds wound along the cavern walls, stretching down both sides of the room, and joined at a large marble statue of winged man in white robes that also glowed. Saul considered it the most beautiful work he had seen. The statue's large, intricately defined wings stretched from just above his shoulders to well below the knees. The tips of the wings came together softly just behind his legs. In one hand, he held a long sounding horn, while the other rested on the top of the horn as if readying himself to call everyone from all ends of the earth to join together in this grand parlor.

As Saul was trying to catch his breath, Sister Guinevere and Razzi came in behind him. She too, was in total awe. She made the sign of the cross and said a prayer in thankfulness for the beautiful statue. "It is the Archangel Gabriel. His spirit lives in the tunnels and has guided us with his brilliant light. This is truly the work of our Lord. Man could never do this of his own power."

"Hello?" A man's voice called out.

Saul's eyes were getting used to the brightness of the room and he could see a man walking towards them.

"Hello," Saul replied.

The man approached Saul and the sister, his taut expression visibly relaxing when he realized they were holding children.

"Are you here because of the lady?" he asked.

"Yes, Maria has led us to The Way," Sister replied.

"I'm George. Over there is Jackieo and Li'Quari. Maria has sent us here as well."

"Where did you start from?" Saul asked.

"We came from the Red Zone near the capital. Li'Quari came from the Southern District."

"You're a GIT?"

"No, I was a GIT." George stretched out his right arm and lifted the sleeve of his shirt. "Maria has conveniently removed the tag."

"We came down from the Central District; Chicago," Saul offered.

"We haven't been in this Grand Terminal very long, but from what I can tell, this must have been used as a sort of main boarding station."

"Boarding station; boarding for what?" Sister inquired.

George pointed to the far end of the room where a large craft stood near a corner of the cave. It was docked by large iron arms that were bolted to the floor holding the immense structure into place. It closely resembled the tubeboats from the river, but was far larger and was completely enclosed. He turned and led the way towards the amazing looking boat or submarine or whatever it had been called.

As they approached the craft, George began his presentation of what he had found out already. "The craft seems to be some sort of water vehicle. Judging by the size of it, it was used to transfer a large amount of people, maybe two or three hundred at a time. I can't find a way in, or a mechanism that would release the latches from the floor. I searched everywhere, and I just can't figure out how we would enter into the craft."

"There isn't an Archangel Raphael sign on it?" Saul inquired.

George shook his head. "Negative, not that I have found."

By this time, Jackieo had walked over to them and George introduced her.

"Dr. Kriesh, the children really must eat and rest now; they have had a long day," Sister said.

George pointed them in the direction of the North wall. "The fountain over there has blankets, water, and fresh doughbread."

"I can take her over there, if you wish to talk with George longer," Jackieo said to Saul.

Mia looked at Jackieo and then tightened her grip around Saul's neck and buried her head into his shoulder.

"Thank you, but I better take her. She is tired and probably isn't ready for a new face just yet. Go ahead, Sister; I'm right behind you." Saul walked along with Sister Guinevere and they made their way toward the fountain.

As the lights started to dim in the Grand Terminal, Domingo and Sevita pulled their watercraft alongside the others that had already been docked at the river's edge. Sevita was relieved to be out of the fast moving rapids. She just sat for a minute in the calmness of the moment.

"Sevita? Uh, we can get out of the boat now," Domingo said softly. As much as he had enjoyed having Sevita that close to him, leaning against his chest all the way down the rapids, his right leg was starting to fall asleep and he needed to get out of the tubeboat before he lost all feeling in it.

212

Sevita, startled for an instant, as she had not quite remembered he had been there, looked over her shoulder and replied in a declarative voice, "I'm never doing that again."

She climbed out of the tubeboat and stood on the bank as Domingo stretched his tired muscles for a moment before standing and leaning most of his weight on his left leg.

"What's wrong with you?" she asked.

"I'm waiting for the blood to flow back into my leg."

"What are you saying? I was too heavy?"

"No, I'm not saying that at all. My leg just fell asleep, that's all."

Sevita rolled her eyes and started off towards the center of the tunnel. Domingo smiled and limped after her. They quickly found Raphael's mark and made their way through the tunnel. Sevita was hoping to reach a fountain area for the night as the beleds were losing their light. After walking for about 45 minutes, the beleds changed color to a dark red. Sevita and Domingo stopped suddenly and looked at each other.

"Not again," Domingo said looking around the tunnel.

Sevita felt a chill go up her spine. Something was definitely wrong. She could feel it. "Run!" she said and took off down the tunnel.

"Wait!" Domingo said and ran after her.

"Sevita you wretch! Don't you run away from me!" Danni called out from a distance.

"Anything you want to tell me?" Domingo asked, as he ran alongside Sevita.

"Just keep running. Please, just run!"

Sevita and Domingo ran through the tunnel as fast as their legs could carry them. They could see a brighter and wider opening coming up just thirty yards away. They heard a loud crack and saw dust and smoke coming from the side of the tunnel. It was a gunshot! Danni fired a warning round into the side of the tunnel wall.

"Faster!" Sevita called out.

They ran to the entrance of the widening of the tunnel, and as they went through, an arm grabbed them and pulled them to the side. George and Saul were standing together with their swords drawn. The swords glowed with a tremendous blue light. They stepped out into the tunnel together side by side.

Danni and the two goons that he had with him came to a stop.

"What's this? A couple of GIT rejects, I presume?" Danni said sarcastically as he waved his gun from side to side. The other two laughed a wicked and taunting laugh.

"Keep laughing rats. I've eaten things almost as ugly as you," George called out.

"Our beef isn't with you, GIT. Just send out my sister and we'll be on our way," Danni said.

"Why don't you turn around and crawl on back from where you came," George replied.

"You piece of …." Danni raised his gun and fired right at George.

George swung the sword and the slug ricocheted off the tunnel wall.

"Dazgles! Did you see that?" One of the goons said to the other.

"Shut up!" Danni bellowed at them. Turning back to George, he stared with red eyes. "I want my sister. I'm not leaving here without her."

"Girl, do you know this rat?" George called over his shoulder.

"Yes, he's my brother," Sevita called back from against the inside wall of the Grand Terminal.

"Do you want to go with him?"

"Never!" Sevita said.

"Sevita you need to come back with me, now. It didn't go well for Vivian. I don't think you want to aggravate Jazin anymore than you have already."

Sevita appeared in the doorway. "What did you do to her?" she screamed out in terror.

"Let's just say that she went to pieces over Jazin." He smirked. "Now, let's go."

"I despise you. You are not my brother. Tell Jazin I hope he meets with the same fate."

"You wretched fool. You're coming!" Danni went to reach for her, but George stepped in the way.

"It looks like she doesn't want to go with you," George replied. "On your way, rat."

Danni growled at him. He started to turn back and as he did, Saul saw him give a look to one of the men who had been standing directly behind him. Danni swung back around and fired another round at George and then dropped to the ground. George's sword quickly dispensed the round, and while holding the sword pointed downward with his right hand, he reached behind his head for a knife with his left. Meanwhile, the man behind Danni lifted his gun and was about to fire when George's hand came to the front with a small throwing knife that he let go instantly. It wisped through the air making a whistling sound until it stuck in the neck of the man with his gun drawn. He grabbed his throat. Blood spilled out over his hand as he fell to the ground before he could take a shot. The other man dropped his gun, turned, and ran down the tunnel, leaving Danni kneeling on the ground.

"Well, are you going to fight or run?" George asked.

Danni glared at George, but he knew he was outmatched by the GIT officer. He threw his gun to the side and stood up. "I'll be seeing you again, and we'll have another go round, GIT. I'm sure there are some Reds interested in having a word with you."

"Yeah, you do that, rat. I look forward to you coming back with some more vermin for me to kill. Run home before I take off your rat head."

Danni sneered at him, but turned around and walked down the tunnel. George and Saul stood there for ten minutes and made sure he kept on walking. Before long, the lights slowly came back to their bluish color. Only then, did George and Saul return to the room with the others.

Sevita started to thank George and Saul for helping them as they entered the Grand Terminal, but all of them were distracted—the entryway began to close. A large boulder from the far side of the opening rolled in front of the arched cave entrance and came to a stop with a loud, thunderous roar.

"We're trapped!" Saul said. He ran to the large boulder and pushed against it.

At the same time, the large watercraft jostled inside the cradle with loud sounds of creaking and moaning. A slim door slid open, exposing an entryway into the craft. A bright bluish-white light streamed from inside the craft with dazzling brilliance.

"Look at that! It's opening," called out Sister Guinevere.

They all rushed to the watercraft to see what, from inside the magnificent structure, had been kept hidden from them. It had the same kind of beled lighting that was in the tunnels. It was completely enclosed except for the recently exposed doorway, and it was still securely bolted to the floor. The inside of the craft was a very soft white that looked almost like a type of polymer material. It had a type of finish that seemed neither reflective nor dull. There was a short ramp that extended about three feet out from the entryway to the ground.

"I'm going in to take a look around," George called out.

"I'll go with you," Saul said and took position right behind him.

George nodded and started up the ramp. The men entered the craft and veered to the left. The inside of the craft was very well lit with a ceiling that was only inches from the top of George's head. It had enough seating for about one hundred and fifty people. George walked to the back of the ship and turned. There were no windows. The entire craft took a very minimalist approach with clean lines and not much in the way of any type of luxury or convenience. He made his way back towards the entrance and met up with Saul.

"Just a lot of seating," George said.

"There's a skinny stairwell off here to the right. And a small galley," Saul said pointing to the small set of stairs.

"We might as well have a look." George ascended the staircase and made it to the top, where he found another level of seating to the left and towards the back of the ship. There was seating for another twenty-five people on the second level. Also, there was a command console with a set of short glass windows that were only six inches in height and eighteen inches in width. They were centered on the ship's front wall facing the bow, but were lower towards the console. Just below the windows were two control sticks with handles that came up from the console's frame. There were also two switches that were set to the off position just to the left of the leftmost control stick.

"Whoever built these boats sure didn't waste a lot of energy with technological functionality," Saul remarked.

George looked at him and nodded. Saul was right. The tubeboats, this large vessel, the tunnel, the tunnel lifts—all of it was composed of primary needs. There was nothing fancy, nothing extravagant, just plain and simple function without any of the distractions of unneeded flash. There was something honest and elementary about it all.

"Let's check on the others," George said. "This ship is secure."

Back down the spiral staircase and to the ramp, they were immediately greeted by the others.

"So, what was in there?" Jackieo asked.

"Not very much. There's seating for a couple hundred people. It has a small control console and a galley. That's really about it," George replied.

"Can we go in?" asked Mia.

"Sure, you can go in and take a look around," Saul answered.

"I'll go with them." Sister Guinevere took Razzi by the hand and they went in together.

"So, what now?" asked Li'Quari. "This can't be the end. This isn't the city."

Everyone was silent. George squatted down and was drawing with his finger in the dirt and sand. As his finger pushed through the loose sand he pushed against a hard substance that rose to the top—a small clamshell. Still squatting, he looked up at the cave entrance that was now blocked by a large boulder. Moving his thumb and forefinger over the smooth seashell, his eyes suddenly became wide and his heart began to race. Quickly, he stood up and went to the fountain and inspected it. Looking underneath it, he found barnacles attached to it. "Oh, this isn't going to be pleasant. I wonder how much time we have." He said softly.

"Whoever has containers for water fill them quickly at the fountain," George yelled out coming back to the group. "Saul, go back into the ship and see if there are any containers we can use to fill with water." Saul didn't hesitate and left instantly for the ship. Then turning to the others, George called out orders like a troop commander. "Check the fountain areas for doughbread and blankets; gather whatever is there. Do it quickly and come back to the ship."

"George, what's wrong? What is it?" Jackieo asked confusedly.

"This cave is about to fill up with the ocean." He said staring at her intently. "Go; help them get the supplies on the craft."

Jackieo went to each fountain and gathered all that she could carry. Doughbread, blankets, and water containers filled her arms and she brought them onto the ship. George inspected the area for anything that they might need to take with them. The beleds in the room were growing dim and the light from the large ship was growing brighter, or perhaps it was an illusion, as the cave was getting dark. George was about to turn when he saw Domingo kneeling down near the cave wall with his hand on the ground. He had dug a small hole in the dirt and it quickly filled with water. Domingo pushed his hand into it, cupped his fingers together, and brought the liquid up to his face to smell it and then he tasted it. He looked up at George.

"Sea water!"

"Come on, Domingo. Get back to the ship!" George called and started for the ship himself.

George ran back to the watercraft calling out to everyone to get onboard. He stood by the entrance helping people carry their supplies on board while at the same time bellowing out to the individuals still running about the Grand Terminal.

"Come on! Whatever is left just leave it! Bring what you have now!"

Sister Guinevere and the children had already boarded. Li'Quari stepped in, followed by Jackieo, Sevita and Domingo. Saul was trudging along carrying four very large containers of water from the fountain. George looked down at his boots. The water was five to seven inches deep and had been flowing over them for several minutes. He could feel the ground getting soft beneath his feet. The beled lighting in the tunnel was very dim and appeared that at any moment would darken completely. He went to Saul and took two of the containers from him. Saul jumped on board the craft; put the water containers to the side and then bent down to take the ones that George was handing up to him. George walked back into the Grand Terminal and took one last look around. The water level was halfway up the calves of his legs. As he turned around to go back to the ship, he thought he saw a man hovering over the craft, but as he strained his eyes in the darkness, he realized nothing was there. He quickly jumped on board and the entrance way slid shut. He inspected the door to ensure it had made a good seal. When he turned around everyone was looking at him with doubt and fear, wanting to know what he had seemed to already know.

"What's going on? Why did the cave seal up and why is it filling with water?"

"Listen everyone; I don't know any more than you all do. I noticed a seashell in the dirt floor and there were barnacles underneath the fountains.

This could only mean that this isn't the first time this cave has filled up with sea water."

"Sea water?" Saul repeated and stepped forward.

"Yeah, sea water. I think the tunnels curved around eastward and I believe we're right at the edge of the Atlantic."

"He's right!" Domingo said. "I saw near the cave entrance that there was a spring bubbling up and I thought it was the fresh water from the fountains, but when I tasted it there was definitely salt in it; sea water."

"I don't know where the city is, but I think the first leg of our journey ends here and the second leg starts. It looks like we're about to head towards Europe by means of the Atlantic Ocean," George said calmly.

People started talking all at once to one another and to George. There was excitement, uncertainty, and a sense of frustration and fear as some were worried about the rumors of the condition of Europe after the Holy Wars. They would be riding directly into a European port without any way of knowing if it was friendly or not.

"I suggest we all go up to the top level. The command console is up there, and there are small windows so that we can see what is going on outside. Secure everything that is loose and store the supplies in the galley. Let's get everyone upstairs." George motioned to Saul to follow him.

They both went up the metal staircase and took their seats at the command console. The beled lighting on the top level was much dimmer than the lower level. It was especially darker at the front of the ship near the console. George sat on the left side while Saul made himself comfortable on the right side. They both peered out the small windows trying to make out what was happening outside of the ship.

"Can you see anything?" Saul asked.

"Negative, not a thing. The beleds are completely off – there's no light coming from the Grand Terminal that I can see."

Sister Guinevere came up the staircase with Razzi in her arms. Mia was right behind her holding onto her tunic. The minute she saw Saul sitting at the console she let go of Sister's clothing and ran over to him. Saul reached over the chair's armrest and picked her up and held her on his lap.

"What is that?" she asked pointing to the control stick.

"It's probably to operate this ship. It's like the pedals on the tubeboat that steered the tubeboat on the river. Well, this stick will steer this ship on the ocean."

"Why are there two of them?" Mia asked.

Saul looked at George and then back to Mia. "It's a big ship."

That seemed to satisfy her for the moment until she had spotted the switches near the control stick where George was sitting. "And what are those?" she asked pointing to the bank of switches.

"I think…," Saul had started.

George interrupted and finished Saul's sentence. "We think they release those large iron buckles that hold the ship in place."

"Oh," Mia said nodding her head with complete confidence that everything made total sense.

Sister Guinevere got Razzi situated with his snack of doughbread, a cup of water, and some raisins. While he was occupied, she went over to Saul and Mia.

"Mia, you should come with me and have your snack now. Dr. Kriesh and this man need to work now."

"Can I come back later?" she asked Saul.

"Yes, you can come back later."

Sister nodded to Saul and he lowered her from the chair. Sister took her hand and led her back to their seats.

Domingo reached into his pack and took out his grandfather's pouch containing the scion. He carefully unwrapped the burlap from the roots and then drizzled the water from his bottle over it, making sure to get it well saturated.

Sevita watched him and thought how patient and carefully methodical he was with the small plant. It was the one thing that his grandfather had given to him that meant everything in the world to him. She thought of her own family and how seemingly uncaring they had been towards one another. She felt terrible that Domingo had been dragged into her mess with Danni. "Domingo, I'm really sorry about what happened with my brother. He wasn't always that way." She turned away and stared at the floor.

Domingo looked at her. "It's not your fault how your brother turned out. We all have free will and it is up to us how we choose to use it. We can learn from our mistakes and choose good, or we can choose evil and let it consume us and all that we love."

"I know; I'm just sorry that I might have put you in a dangerous situation. I wouldn't want anything to happen to you because of me." Sevita eyes were teary and she quickly turned away again.

Domingo put his arm around her shoulder and reassured her. "It's all right. I have free will myself and if I didn't want to, I wouldn't let you put me in dangerous situations. It has been an honor being able to travel with you on this journey, wherever it might take us and whatever danger we may have to fight to get there."

Sevita turned and hugged him. "Thank you."

Saul had been staring out the small glass window. He put his hand over the top of it to block out the reflection of the interior light and gazed out the window towards the cave ceiling. He looked over to George. "Is that the water line?"

George nodded.

"I didn't think it would fill up that fast," Saul said in a low voice. "I guess this isn't a boat."

"No, it's a submarine," George confirmed.

"And when did you come to know this?"

"I had my suspicions when we first inspected the ship. The glass is two inches thick."

"And you didn't find the need to let us in on that knowledge?"

George turned his head and looked back to the women and children. Then, without any emotion, said, "I didn't."

"You didn't. Well, that's just great," Saul retorted.

The Grand Terminal completely filled with water. There was not a dry spot left in the entire place. Outside the watercraft, it was completely dark. Inside the craft, the beleds were softly glowing, keeping everyone calm. However the interior beleds were losing their brightness. The passengers were talking with one another and the children were entertained by the newness of being in a large craft. Everyone seemed relaxed, until a loud, outside noise coincided with a tremor that was felt throughout the ship. There was dead silence as they strained to listen very carefully to any further sounds.

"I'm going to see what's going on out there," Domingo said. He got up and walked to the front of the ship, towards the console.

Jackieo, seeing Domingo's courage, also stood up and followed him to the front.

Domingo approached Saul. "What's going on out there?"

Saul moved back from the window to allow Domingo to have a look.

Jackieo walked up behind George and put her hand on his shoulder.

"There's an exit opening up just in front of us. The tunnel system was all underground and this main room is under the ocean. Once that doorway is opened all the way, I suspect we can release the clamps and slide right into that jet stream," George pointed out the window.

Jackieo peered out of the window and saw a large section of the main room had slid out of the way. The ocean was entirely visible now, and there was a magnificent shimmering light everywhere. She had never seen anything so beautiful in all of her days. A fast moving stream of white water was directly in front of the cave opening and rushed out to sea. The flowing tube of water swayed to and fro ever so slightly, but held very close to its form and direction. "How is that possible?"

"Are you kidding, J-O? How is any of this possible?"

"It's truly amazing. It's a miracle," Domingo said.

By this time, the others had come over to peer out of the portals to see what was happening. They stared in amazement at the beautiful ocean, the stunning jet stream, and the impressive journey that they were all about to embark upon. The blue waters swirled about inside the Grand Terminal, and curious fish had already found their way into the cavern as they swam around the ship. The entryway into the vast deep was fully opened and had stopped moving. It was time for them to set off on their new course.

"Hold on everyone, we're going to release the clamps. We may be in for a bumpy ride," George called out. Then looking at Saul he said, "We need to work together on this one. We each have a rudder control. If we're going too fast we can work them opposite one another and slow the ship down. If we work in unison, we'll go faster. Are you ready?"

"Check. Onward, to the city," Saul called out.

George put his hand over the switches and with one motion flipped them upwards. The ship gave a moan and creaked and crackled, but it lifted upwards. The muffled sounds from outside seemed to be that of the clamps falling into their resting positions on the floor of the terminal. The craft slowly moved towards the exit. As it got closer to the opening, it picked up speed as if the ocean currents were pulling it in the direction of the jet stream.

"I can't believe it. I never thought this day would come. We're on our way to the Golden City!" Li'Quari called out.

End volume one.

CPSIA information can be obtained
at www.ICGtesting.com
Printed in the USA
JSHW021725190621
15914JS00001B/4